Bedazzled

Madison Michael

BEDAZZLED by Madison Michael

Copyright 2016 Madison Michael

.

This book is dedicated to three of the infamous Four Girls - you know who you are - without whom this book wouldn't have made it to print. To the eldest for introducing me to romance novels, and to the middle two for agreeing that trudging to class in winter was a bad idea.

And to Barbara Ann who provided me with inspiration, confidence, gorgeous jewelry and one-liners.

.

A pair of bright eyes with a dozen glances suffice to subdue a man; to enslave him, and enflame him; to make him even forget; they dazzle him so that the past becomes straightway dim to him; and he so prizes them that he would give all his life to possess 'em.

William Makepeace Thackeray

Love, she thought, must come suddenly, with great outbursts and lightnings,--a hurricane of the skies, which falls upon life, revolutionises it, roots up the will like a leaf, and sweeps the whole heart into the abyss.

Gustave Flaubert, Madame Bovary

He stepped down, trying not to look long at her, as if she were the sun, yet he saw her, like the sun, even without looking.

Leo Tolstoy, Anna Karenina.

CHAPTER ONE

"We'll miss you so much Keeli, but I am green with envy."

"I wish I was as brave as you are, Keeli. Your life is going to be so glamorous and exciting. Lucky you."

"Yeah, and no more Weinberg telling you what to sell. You can finally be your own boss, selling your own designs."

"And making some decent money."

The hugs and good wishes from Amelia and Sharon caught Keeli by surprise. So did their confidence in her ability to succeed. She could not remember the last time someone – other than herself – had believed in her talent.

Assuming she had never really fit in, Keeli was surprised by Amelia, Sharon, Keith and Steve's generosity and good wishes. Because Keeli never bothered to share more than a "Hi, how's it going?" with them, she was particularly touched by their kindness now.

It wasn't that she was unfriendly. Keeli just tried to stay focused on her work, head bent low over her workbench or on her feet assisting with clients. She had put in ten-hour days, trying to get ahead and make enough in commissions to stay afloat. She carefully avoided office gossip and water-cooler chitchat but by doing so she forfeited the opportunity to connect with any of her colleagues. At this last minute, she regretted that she never made more of an effort. They might have been wonderful friends.

Too late now, I guess, but learn your lesson here. Yep, I will try to open up and let people in a bit more. It would be very good for me.

The women reached out to give Keeli a farewell hug and after a moment of awkwardness, Keeli slid a battered shoebox onto an uncluttered bit of countertop, freeing her arms to return their affection. The box contained the smattering of personal items that were a sad reflection of her time at Weinberg and Sons. The small box held the precious jewelry tools she had amassed over her brief career and a hastily rinsed coffee mug with a small chip in the handle. The red mug with the saying "I'm a jewelry lady. See me bling" was wrapped in a rumpled scarf she forgot to wear home last Friday, the tools slid safely into that one warm glove; the other she lost weeks ago. She hoped the fabric would protect her few possessions if she were jostled on the train.

She tucked the envelope containing the Target gift card and congratulations card into the box under her tools for safety and replaced the box lid. The small group understood that things might get tough for Keeli, recognized how much more valuable a practical gift card would be than a spa certificate. They had given her the cards during a hastily thrown farewell party – cake and coffee in the break room just a few short minutes ago.

How embarrassing that they are right about the Target card. It will be much more useful. Did they know when they bought it that it might mean the difference between groceries and hunger? Stop that. Think positive. It will not come to that.

After a few minutes of good luck wishes and laughter, Mr. Weinberg joined them, cutting himself a huge slice of cake and dropping bright pink frosting on the dress shirt straining over his bulging belly. His presence quickly altered the mood of the festivities, bringing them to an abrupt end. The awkward silence was a sure sign to Keeli that it was time to hit the road.

"Thanks again for the party, and the gift certificate. It was so generous. You guys are the best. I'll stay in touch and let you know as soon as I know how you can reach me."

Keeli meant it when she said it, although she never stayed in touch with prior colleagues for some reason. She was not a Facebook user, which would have been an easy way to stay connected, but she hated people knowing her business. That would change now that she was starting her own company. She had ordered a new phone line and accompanying Internet address for work, but she knew by the time both were installed she would have moved on with her life, leaving this group behind.

Disentangling from one final, group hug, Keeli found tears gathering behind her eyes and, knowing her voice would reveal her sudden emotion, Keeli settled for nodding farewell to the group. Standing straight and tall, she pasted a determined look on her face, slid her small parcel under her right arm, hoisted her raincoat and oversized purse over her left shoulder and used a hip-bump to push open the heavy glass door.

Heels echoed on the faded, mosaic floor as she strode away from her past and toward the elevators without a backward glance. For a brief moment, Keeli was reminded of "The Devil Wears Prada," when Anne Hathaway's character described 'clackers'. This floor was perfect for amplifying every step. Keeli imagined herself as Anne Hathaway, dressed in Chanel, makeup and hair perfect, and for a moment, she allowed humor to edge out her fear.

As if.

The image faded, allowing Keeli's fear to hit her like a ton of bricks. Her straight back sagged against the cool marble wall as she waited for the elevator. Keeli felt terror wash over her. She just quit her third job in five years. True, each move had allowed her to move up in her profession, but it was still a lot of turmoil.

I should have been content with what I had.

Keeli had been battling herself for days. She had achieved more than enough success for most people with her background and education. She worked in Chicago's prestigious jewelry district, getting pointers from skilled, experienced designers every day. She had been able to interact with the wealthy clientele that were her target market.

But Keeli was who she was. She would never be 'most people'. She could never content herself being a sales clerk; she was a designer. She was eager to show the world her contemporary and unique style, but Mr. Weinberg insisted she push the traditional, more expensive pieces. It was his business. He was certainly allowed to call the shots, but he had promised Keeli an opportunity for growth when she joined his firm and she had waited as long as she could for that opportunity to materialize. At first, he had encouraged her to create her own designs, offering to place them prominently in his display cases. She created beautiful pieces that she placed lovingly onto the velvet only to watch him remove them. Eventually he explained that her aesthetic was not his.

After that, going into work had been harder and harder. It was more than the cold January rain and snow that made Keeli hit the snooze button every morning. One ten-minute snooze last month had grown to two this month. Keeli felt the dread mushrooming until she couldn't breathe. Her commute, which she had previously enjoyed, was suddenly unbearable. Keeli's heart was no longer in it. She had lost her enthusiasm for the job – again.

"Leave, stay, leave, stay." It had been a battling loop in her brain ever since the Christmas rush ended. Two weeks ago, listening to the nagging voice at last, she handed in her notice. Mr. Weinberg made a half-hearted attempt to keep her but they both recognized, despite her talent and hard work, that she was no longer a good fit at Weinberg and Sons.

So here she stood, waiting for the elevator to take her to a solo life running Keeli Larsen Designs. From this moment forward she was financier, designer, manufacturer, sales woman and grunt. No colleagues, no steady paycheck, no safety net.

She had so many doubts and almost no friends or business associates. There was no mentor to dispense advice at this critical juncture, no cheering squad to support her dreams. Her small group of friends and family fell into two camps. Half believed she was making a brave and brilliant move. Half believed she could not hold down a steady job.

Keeli was not naïve. She had enough smarts to know she was undercapitalized, with a weak professional network and no useful connections. From today forward she would have to churn out product and pound the pavement, find time to balance the need to design, create and market, keep books, save for taxes. Assuming she made any money. Keeli believed she could do it. If she hadn't she would have found a way to suck it up and stayed in her job as she had been forced to do many times before. But from now on, no doubt about it, every penny mattered more than it had before.

If she had a good summer working the art fair circuit, that would help. The fairs had been helpful the previous two years with supplementing her income. She had hoped to be noticed, boosted by the venues, but nothing had happened yet and she felt she needed to devote the next four months creating an inventory that might springboard her at last.

She would have to survive at least six months on her small nest egg. That was her estimate of how long her money would last, so that was how long she had to get her business off the ground. If it took any longer, she would be in big trouble.

Speaking of longer, where was the elevator? Even for this old building, it was taking longer than usual. As an artist, Keeli appreciated the craftsmanship of the vintage building. She loved the elegant brass-work surrounding the doors of elevators that had once been operated by young men in livery, but right now, she wished for modern efficiency. Keeli could hear the faint mechanism of the old machinery as the car moved closer, then the ding of the old fashioned bell as the doors eased open.

No wonder it took so long to arrive. The elevator was as full as Macy's on Black Friday. It must have stopped at every floor. Clustered to one side of the large space were Hassidic Jews heading home for their Sabbath. Barely looking at her, they retreated under their black coats and hats, conversing in rapid-fire Hebrew. The newer merchants, who were predominantly Indian, filled the remainder of the space. The two groups clustered tightly, creating an opening in between them. Watching her step, careful not to bump anyone with her parcel, Keeli stepped into the middle and moved toward the back of the car.

The chatter in the elevator lightened her mood immediately, reminding Keeli of all the people who had started with only a few dollars and a dream. In many cases, they had made it without knowing the language or customs of their adopted country. By comparison, she had many advantages and quickly felt better about her choice, more confident about moving forward on her own. Mr. Weinberg had let her take many of her pieces with her when she left his employ. There had been no severance check, of course, but having a ready inventory, even a small one, was a gift. Keeli let the confidence surge through her body, standing straight and looking ahead.

That was the moment she saw HIM. He was the best thing - by far- about working in this building. She was standing face to face with the virile, gorgeous, sexy man she saw in the elevator regularly. Well, almost face-to-face since he was a good 4 or 5 inches taller than her own 5'10". He was what she would miss most about this job - those random opportunities to ride the elevator and watch him, getting to stand close to him, allowing her imagination to run wild with fantasies (all starring him of course).

Most of the time, he hid mysteriously behind a pair of Wayfarers, but the rain today afforded Keeli a chance to admire the intelligence and concentration in his azure eyes. He stood with his shoulders back, head towering over the bent heads of everyone else. Looking up, Keeli locked eyes with his and his mouth lifted in a half smile. Keeli shyly dropped her head as a blush rose to her cheeks and her heart sped up. She knew the smile was just because he was polite. She wanted so much more. She wanted him to notice her the way she noticed him, feel about her as she did about him.

If only he had the same visceral response to her that Keeli had to him, perhaps he would have talked to her by now. She could not overcome her shyness to initiate a conversation, but if he longed for her as she did him, maybe something might have happened. Obviously, he was not interested. Now she would leave this job and never see him again. Her disappointment was way out of proportion for what she should feel for a stranger. But he had this pull on her. Instead of thinking of him as a stranger, she thought of him as hers.

Hers. What a laugh. Wake up Keeli!

Everyone watched him - man and woman alike. She had noticed it in the elevator or when he walked through the lobby. Yes, he was particularly tall, a few inches over six feet. However, it was more than his height that drew the eye. He was compelling, confident, and assured. He was beyond handsome with his chiseled features, thick wavy hair and well-muscled body clad in custom suits. Keeli was drawn to him like a bee to honey. She had seen other women catch his eye, seen them smile and flirt easily. She was overwhelmingly shy around him, preventing her from ever making him 'hers'.

Why, oh why is facing forward considered appropriate elevator etiquette? I just want to stare at him one last time. Today needs to be the day to think of something to say, some witty conversation opener. You are out of time, stupid.

Over the last 16 months, they crossed paths at the coffee kiosk or in the elevator at least once a week. She knew she was projecting her own desires, but sometimes it seemed to her that he was seeking her out. Even so, Keeli never exchanged more than a polite "hello" and he was always polite, but aloof. Although she longed for some reason to speak more than pleasantries, she was unable to move past that invisible barrier she felt between them.

Her brain searched now for a reason to speak, knowing it was her last chance. Instead, she reluctantly turned to face the doors. He was standing so close. She felt the warmth of his breath on the back of her neck, goose bumps travelling up her arms in response to the moist heat. She was rocked by her immediate, erotic reaction.

Reigning in her body's response, Keeli reminded herself that the warm breath was just a result of proximity, not desire. She was a non-entity to him and had been for 16 months. His polished appearance, custom suits and elegant leather briefcase contrasted with her wild red hair, shabby jacket, scuffed shoes and faded Old Navy dress clearly delineated their differences. He epitomized elegance and privilege; she embodied shabby chic. Maybe not even chic - just shabby. She could never bridge the gulf.

Besides, he was Wyatt Lyons Howe IV. Unreachable, untouchable, unavailable to someone like her. He was the sun. She was lucky to feel a tiny touch of his warmth, to orbit occasionally. She was Pluto – far, far away.

Nonetheless, she was drawn to him, so she did her homework. He rode the elevator to the top - the executive floor for Lyons Howe Real Estate - the company that occupied the top four floors of the building. LHRE owned this building as well as at least 100 other buildings around the Loop, more throughout the Midwest and God only knew what else. The first time she saw him hit the button for the top floor she Googled LHRE.

There he was, his handsome face staring at her from the screen of her computer. His picture was at the top of the home page, just below the elegant logo for the prestigious firm and a serious-faced photo of his silver-haired father, Wyatt III, the CEO and President. Wyatt's gorgeous blue eyes stared back at her, so compelling that he could entice her with only a professional headshot. Below his picture, his title indicated he was Chief Information Officer, obviously a top member of the LHRE executive team. He looked like a younger, more handsome, version of his father.

The family resemblance continued with his brother who appeared about ten years his junior, fresh faced and innocent, but already a vice-president. The beautiful woman pictured there was identified as his sister and Chief Financial Officer. She looked just a few years Wyatt's junior, serious and aristocratic. Together they embodied the perfect example of a privileged family and a solid, trustworthy executive team.

Once she knew his name, Keeli devoured every bit of information she could find about Wyatt. She knew she was standing just inches from one of Chicago's most eligible bachelors. Wyatt Lyons Howe was American blueblood, old money, European tours, private clubs and the best schools. Heir to the massive LHRE empire, he oozed success from every pore. He moved like he owned the world, or at least a sizable chunk of it.

Here she was, basking in the warmth of the sun that was Wyatt. Keeli knew if she just inched back she could be touching him. After all, she lusted after him, fantasized about him endlessly, dreaming with him, marrying him, growing old with him. He was everything she was looking for in her perfect man – intelligence, sophistication, a commanding air, sex appeal and those staggering good looks.

Oh yeah, and he had that power thing going too. He radiated power. It was such a turn on.

As she caught a hint of his clean, outdoorsy scent, Keeli pictured him behind her; his gorgeous face, that end-of-day shadowed jaw, the slight tan he sported even during a Chicago winter. Wyatt dominated her dreams, waking and sleeping. She had fallen in love with him the first time she heard him laugh a hearty, full-bodied sound that gave her a sense that he knew how to enjoy life. He was her dream man. He was her "complete package".

So what if we have never exchanged two words? Details, details.

At that very moment, she envisioned him reaching out from behind her, slipping his arms around her and pulling her up against him. She could imagine the rough feel of his wool trousers, scratchy against her thighs, followed by the softer feel of his fingers sliding up her legs. She felt goose bumps rise on her skin as she fantasized about his lips caressing her neck moving from there to her cheekbone as he spun her around so she was pressed against him, his mouth, descending to claim hers in a kiss. She pictured herself dizzy with desire, all feminine softness clasped against the hard power of his thighs, the length of his erection....Oh my god, she was getting damp just standing near him, letting her imagination run wild.

Keeli's heart thumped above the workings of the old elevator, so loud she wondered if Wyatt could hear it too. Was he looking at her with those piercing blue eyes? Was he flashing her his perfect smile, clear evidence of great genes or years of orthodontia? She wanted to turn around and get one last look at this beautiful man to store in her memory but she was so aroused she feared he would notice.

Standing in front of him now, Keeli's head just reached his shoulder despite her own above average height. Her body itched to sway back the scant distance necessary to close the gap between them. She imagined resting her head upon his broad chest, feeling the softness of his fine shirt, leaning her rounded contours against the hard planes of his chest.

I will have to wear heels when we date. As if I would ever have an opportunity to stand beside him in any circumstance other than this one. Who am I kidding? Damn, did I think the elevator was slow? This ride is going way too fast.

They had quickly dropped from the upper levels of the building and the doors opened on the fourth floor. Two more people stepped into the already crowded space and automatically, Keeli backed up to accommodate them.

And it happened. In a split second, without thinking or planning,

Keeli backed into Wyatt, her hand resting solidly against the front of his pants. Thank heavens he couldn't see her face now, flaming every shade of red. He didn't move at first, shocked perhaps, and then his large hand swiftly nudged hers away. Had she felt an erection? Wanting to die of mortification, Keeli feigned ignorance and Wyatt chose to do the same.

It was one thing to imagine it, but to do it, even by mistake. She wanted to crawl in a hole and die. In moments, they were at lobby level. The doors opened, the bell jingled, and Keeli felt the unmistakable feel of his hand on the small of her back, warm, strong and certain. It was solidly placed and it was electric. The sensuous touch heating her skin through her light dress caused Keeli's whole body to vibrate.

Before she even registered the contact in her brain, her senses alerted her to the silky feel of his hand snaking its way over the curve of her hip in an unfaltering caress. The contact was swift but significant. He had her round derriere in the firm grasp of his large palm. He never looked her way, although Keeli would swear he had just quite intentionally grabbed her ass.

Am I wrong? Is this an accident? Could he really have been unaware?

The elevator was emptying as she stepped out, still feeling the erotic heat of his breath on her neck, and his hand moving on her behind. Flustered, she remained mute. He too said nothing, cool and composed as he stepped from the car. Then he was gone, moving from the elevator through the crowd with that long, easy stride, unaware of the overwhelming desire coursing through her.

He must have done it on purpose, right? He must find me desirable. Hang on, Keeli; maybe he thinks you're a piece of meat. Who the hell does he think he is anyway? Dammit, am I supposed to be excited or offended? What a turn-on. I am an idiot; I just let a total stranger grope me. Of course, I did grope him first...

Her heart pounding, her skin tingling, Keeli was hot all over from the combination of her fantasy and the very real feel of his large hand on her ass. She basked in the sensations overwhelming her body, relived the moment until the fog lifted from her brain and allowed it to reengage. She regained her composure, shoved her arms through her coat and checked to make sure it was closed. She secured her box under her arm and headed with the crowd toward the revolving doors.

Rain was falling, cold and unrelenting. Keeli pulled her inadequate coat closer and stepped away from the protection of the building. She felt the warmth of her desire and her chances of seeing Wyatt ever again slip away as if running down the nearest storm drain, replaced by the chilly rain. She walked the short block to the "L" station getting drenched. With each step, the warmth of the unbelievable encounter disappeared to be replaced by the sad reality of cold, wet, and broke.

CHAPTER TWO

Wyatt got all the way to the garage before he turned sharply on his heel and strode back to the elevators. A quick scan of the lobby and he knew the redhead had escaped. Aggravated, he punched the button for the elevator, stabbed at it repeatedly, impatiently. Wyatt entered the vacant elevator and prowled it like a caged panther until the doors opened at the top floor.

Wyatt had just crossed the line with that beautiful woman and he should be mortified. But in the last 16 months he had struggled to keep his hands off of her, stopping just short of smoothing her red-brown curls, staring rudely into her eyes, resisting brushing against her. Once he caught himself just before he leaned in to kiss that spot on the nape of her neck that was exposed when she tossed her head. Today was too much. He was too close. He could not stop himself anymore.

What is wrong with me? I am a grown man. I have a reputation to maintain of the cool, sophisticated dude and man about town. I have been around the block – several times. I always maintain control – always - except around her, damn it. She makes me lose it.

His heart was still racing and his pulse pounded in his ears. He was unashamed he had touched her. She felt amazing; soft and round, strong and sexy. Wyatt was completely turned on even as he imagined his mother scolding him for his behavior.

"You don't grab a strange girl! That is not what my son does. I raised you to be a perfect gentleman, I did not raise you in a barn." She loved to remind her children of their manners, conduct and good breeding by using that remark. As if any of them were unable to recognize that the Howe estate was the antithesis of a barn.

Wyatt wanted to blame her for touching him first, but he

could not. He knew her hand had been an accident, an erotic accident. His grope had been intentional.

Get over her already. She is just a girl, like all the others. In fact, she is likely poorer than most of the women I mess with, so I need this to just stop. I absolutely cannot – will not – tangle with another user who pretends to want me when she wants what I can buy her. Pretty? Oh yeah, she is pretty. Sexy? Yes, unbelievably sexy. OMG, that ass was incredible. Shake it off now, boy. Poor girls only want you to open doors for them and buy them presents. They want one thing and it is not my heart. You already learned that the hard way Wyatt. Smarten up.

Wyatt freely acknowledged that he was drawn to this woman, to her combination of sexpot and girl next door. He loved the way she always said "good morning" or "good afternoon" to total strangers. He found it endearing that she made small talk with the barista at the lobby kiosk and knew all about his family. The eloquent Wyatt Howe IV rarely found himself tongue-tied, but he had been unable to strike up a conversation with her for more than a year. He figured if he just had a simple conversation, he could move past this obsession. However, as soon as he saw her he was aroused - aroused and silent. His hormones ruled his brain just from a smile and a sweet, little hello. Seriously, he found it embarrassing. He found it a problem.

I think I could care about this one. She could do some serious damage when she walks away and they always walk away. Either I won't marry them, or I won't give them access to the money. Or I don't take them to meet the right people. They all have some excuse. She could mess me up I think. I have been there before; got the t-shirt. I am done getting my heart broken.

In his effort to protect his heart and his wallet, Wyatt had been diligent about keeping his responses to a polite but cool "good morning" or "good evening" when she was in a crowd with others. No conversation alone. No smiles, no encouragement. It was not easy for him either. Not when she walked away, hips swaying provocatively, and he could stare at those long, long legs and that heart-shaped ass. He found himself struggling to put her out of his mind and today he decided to do something about it. He touched her. Oh man, did he touch her!

He couldn't help himself. Today had just been one disaster after another and the pressures on him were heading toward a boiling point. Life was closing in, forcing him to make tough choices, squeezing out the ability to make good judgment calls. Wyatt was a little bit saint and a little bit devil and the two started warring the second she stepped on the elevator and he caught a whiff of her light floral perfume.

Don't I deserve just a little treat? I have been working like a dog. Besides, I just did what she did and copped a little feel. I suppose I could have made it look more like an accident. It was beyond my control, if I am honest. The moment she made contact with my crotch, I was a goner.

Wyatt's erection had been inevitable; his body responded so fast that he had no choice but to move her hand away. In one more moment, the effect she had on him would have been obvious. On the other hand, did moving her hand away just draw attention to the growing bulge?

Wracking his brain for an excuse, Wyatt knew that moving her hand did not logically extend to grabbing her ass. He meant nothing by the harmless, light hand he rested on the small of her back to steady her in the crowd. That was a well-meant, innocent gesture. Before he could control what he was doing, the innocent gesture gave way to a serious caress of her luscious behind. In that few inches of contact, done quickly, he managed to get a sense of her curves, of her softness and warmth. After that taste, he hungered for more.

Wyatt, you bad, bad boy. His saintly side chastised him.

Worried now that she might think him a dirty old man, he hoped that she thought his touch was reflexive, unintentional in the jostle of people.

I should have grabbed more. Way more. The devil prevailed.

He had fixated long enough. Today she opened the door and he stepped through it. He had been compelled to touch her and now he was compelled to take things further. This Friday afternoon felt different. Desperation gnawed at him, demanded he finally connect with her. He could not explain it, but suddenly he was forced to act, to move things forward; it felt like time was running out and he could not let her get away.

Stomping out of the elevator, Wyatt bulldozed through the huge glass doors with the large gold LHRE logo on them, barking at his assistant half a corridor away. She looked up through cat-eye glasses, unfazed by his shouting.

"Annette," he bellowed moving across the plush carpeting toward her. "There is a girl getting off on the 12th floor every day, red curls to the middle of her back, green - no blue- no green eyes. About normal height, gorgeous long legs and really bad clothes. She has that sweet, girl-next-door personality. You can't miss it. I need you to find her. I want to know everything about her by end of day Monday. Got it?" Without waiting for a response, he turned on his heel and headed for the door.

"Should I get her shoe size too, Wyatt? Are you planning to buy her a new wardrobe?" Annette quipped as he yanked the door open with force.

"I mean it, Annette. Find her."

Wyatt relied on Annette for everything and she never disappointed. He knew that by this time Monday he would have the necessary info and by the end of week he planned to have that luscious body in his arms, that mane of red hair spread over his pillows. He knew Annette was a bulldog who would find her, and fast. Wyatt had a new confidence, a bounce to his step as he strode back through the double doors.

Yeah, she is probably just someone else to use me, but user or not, I need to see where this leads. I need to see if a date or two cures me of this obsession or intensifies it. Definitely. Annette will find her by Monday and I will ask her out next Wednesday. Don't want to look too anxious.

Wyatt was almost correct. In only two hastily placed phone calls, Annette obtained the name of the showroom that employed Keeli along with the information that she had left with no forwarding email or phone. Wyatt was still striding through the garage when Annette also knew that Wyatt was a few hours too late. She would let him keep that bounce in his step a few days longer. Monday would be soon enough to let him know that the less-than-chic redhead had slipped through his fingers.

CHAPTER THREE

"Do you think he will come over here? I really want him to come over here. I want him to come even if he is brings that woman with him. Oh, I do not really want him to bring that woman. Oh hell, do you think he will remember me at all?"

"Do you think perhaps you could stop bouncing and take a breath, Keeli?" The broad smile on Clarice Washington's face helped take the sting from her words.

Keeli noticed Wyatt immediately, despite the growing crowd at the Wells Street Art Fair, despite the fact that she had been tucked into a corner of the booth pretending to read Shakespeare. Once she spotted him, she could not stay hidden; energy vibrated through her just knowing he was near. She ventured from the safe haven and cool shadows provided by the back of the booth to pester Clarice, her best friend in Chicago.

In Keeli's opinion, Clarice was a brilliant sculptor and a wonderful friend. Clarice was funny and immensely talented and she knew the art market well. They had met over two years ago, when Keeli started making the art show circuit. Since then, whenever possible, they requested placement next each other when registering for art fairs. Today their request had been met.

"It's been almost twenty minutes. I don't even know if I even want him to come over," Keeli chattered, dancing from foot to foot as if she had coiled springs in her shoes, despite the hot sun and humidity. Wiping the sheen of perspiration from her upper lip, she reapplied lip-gloss and fluffed her hair. Obviously, she did want him to come her way.

"Why would he stop here anyway unless he wants to buy that blonde a piece of jewelry? I want him to buy something, something really big and expensive," Keeli says longingly, "but not for her."

"Seriously, are we going to have this conversation every Sunday? You either need to get over him or go talk to him." Clarice moved toward an approaching customer, unable to hide a bit of exasperation. "I do have to agree though," she tossed back over her shoulder, "the man is a hunk of gorgeous."

Keeli was left standing alone, admiring Wyatt's tall form and broad shoulders clad in an unwrinkled linen-shirt. Even from this distance, she was able to see his biceps strain the sleeves. She admired his easy loose-limbed step. She watched him with longing as he maneuvered through the throngs of people with ease, narrowing the gap between them.

"If he keeps showing up every Sunday, I guess we will have the conversation every Sunday." Keeli followed Clarice into her booth, keeping one eye on the small space where she was displaying her jewelry, ready to jump if a customer approached.

"Well, you haven't been with a man for ages so I can see why you live in a dream world. Have you even had a date since Christmas?" Clarice's probe was meant to be gentle, but her blunt ways, while endearing, stung now. "My guess is that if you let go of your superman and set your sights back here on earth you might find a real guy."

"You mean a man like that would never go for a woman like me, and I get that. I do. I don't expect a real relationship with Wyatt, but a girl can dream, right?"

"Yeah, dream all you want, but it won't keep you warm at night."

"That's not fair, Clarice. I have been launching a new business, and I work every weekend."

"Excuses, excuses. You still got an empty bed. I'm just sayin'…" Clarice tossed the words over her shoulder as she moved to stand in front of her tent again. With Wyatt in the world, Keeli struggled with even the idea of settling for another man. He would come up short. They all did.

Business was slow, allowing Keeli the luxury of staring at Wyatt over the tops of the heads of those surrounding him. She admired his hair, pushed back in front and curling along his neck. She wondered how he managed the perfectly trimmed shadow on his square jaw and what it would feel like to run her cheek against the scruff. Everyone around him appeared hot and sticky, while he appeared cool and…well, perfect.

"Do you think he remembers me, Clarice? I bet I never

registered as a blip on his radar. Why would he remember me?" Keeli was starting her usual litany, and Clarice knew from experience that in 30 seconds Keeli would be talking about how Wyatt was so influential, so rich, and too important for her. Even if Clarice agreed, Clarice knew that Keeli's insecurities, once unleashed, would just spiral.

"Don't go there honey. You are just as good as he is. You are probably a much nicer person, too. Rich people are snobs. I read in the New York Times that rich people have less empathy. Look at you. You care so much. Those rich folks have no feelings."

Keeli's mind hovered on the word 'feelings'. It was all about the feeling, the touching. Keeli was certain Wyatt did not know or remember her, although she could not get him out of her head. She remembered his touch. She never for a moment forgot the instantaneous, electric reaction she had to his fingertips. It was a moment etched in her memory and on her body. She craved an opportunity to repeat that touch and so much more.

"He has plenty of feelings, Clarice. Remember, he felt me." With a laugh, Keeli turned to assist two young women looking at her collection, keeping sight of Wyatt out of the corner of her eye.

She longed for him to stop at her booth, wanting an excuse to connect and, in truth, because she needed every penny from every sale right now, even a sale to Wyatt's current girlfriend. With the sluggish economy, plenty of people wandered the art fair but few bought more than small items. Keeli was earning enough to cover her material costs, fees and displays, but there was nothing left over that could be considered a regular salary. It was not reassuring that other artists were also complaining and looking to increased sales at the Gold Coast Art Fair or perhaps Evanston or Milwaukee. Keeli could not afford to wait. She needed at least three significant sales today if she was going to be on time with her June rent payment.

This was the third weekend in a row that Keeli was on her feet at a long, tiring art fair. With the addition of set up and take down, they ate into her creative time. However, Keeli was well aware that if she sold enough it was all worth it. Even better would be to catch the eye of just one boutique owner. It would just take one, if it were the right one. Plenty of people stopped to admire her work, but cash paid the bills, not compliments.

Battling her natural shyness, she resisted returning to the back of the booth and "The Tempest," standing out front, trying to attract more business and racking her brain for an excuse to meet Wyatt. She wanted to meet him for real and progress past that moment in the elevator. After all these months, Keeli was looking for an opening that would allow her to find her voice and connect with him. She felt ensnared by him, his easy confidence, the warmth in his smile and his sexy body. She had never forgotten that elevator encounter and now she needed to seize her chance to rekindle what she felt was an intense and very real chemistry.

At least, I feel it. Would he even remember me?

Doubts always plagued Keeli when she saw him. He had crossed paths with her at almost a dozen art fairs between last summer and this spring. He sauntered past the artwork with a different woman on his arm every week. Each woman looked like a model, long and lanky, dressed in the chicest fashions and totally gorgeous, of course.

Losing sight of Wyatt momentarily, Keeli returned her attention to potential buyers. Wells Street Art Festival, early in the Chicago Art Festival season, tended to be a good forecaster of sales for Keeli's entire season. A slow day did not bode well. The scene was festive with steadily swelling crowds, but she longed to move her merchandise more quickly.

Over four months had passed since that day in the elevator. Four and a half months during which Keeli worked day and night, seven days a week. She focused all her energy on creating her designs and shyly marketing herself at the boutiques she had identified as her best opportunities for success. She had given herself six months to get her business moving at a steady pace, but here she was, still limping along. It was a constant struggle to get her designs accepted at the boutiques where the right clientele shopped. She had the right resume and owners admired her collections, but they stopped short of agreeing to carry her work. The rejections were increasingly difficult to overcome even as Keeli lost sleep watching her bank balance dwindle.

Art fairs, like this one, were barely covering her expenses and tight finances were preventing her from upgrading the quality of materials for her jewelry. Her use of lower quality gems and metals prevented her from breaking into the high-end boutiques business where they wanted to sell unique items made with high-quality metals and precious stones. Her designs were creative and unique, but with low-end materials, Keeli could only charge low-end prices. Moreover, low-end prices meant low-end profits and less cash for new materials. It was a vicious cycle, but just one substantial contract to consign with an elite boutique could break it.

Turning browsers into buyers had been a challenge all weekend, but now Keeli happily boxed a chunky bracelet and matching ring for a mother and daughter who had come by her booth to look earlier, left and later returned to buy. Two more sales like this and she would reach the quota she had set for this fair. Looking around for more opportunities, she spotted Wyatt again, only about 30 yards away.

Wyatt attended almost every fair where Keeli showed. She noticed that he always showed up on Sunday afternoon, the last day of each show. He arrived for the last 2-3 hours, wandering up one side of the street, then down the other, giving her a chance to see him maneuver through the crowds for a while. He stopped often to talk to painters, sculptors and photographers. They all seemed to know him. She enjoyed watching them defer to him and although she never saw him make a purchase, the artists always gave him plenty of time and attention.

Up until now though, he had not stopped at her booth. She resigned herself that today would be no different. Discouraged, she returned to hide behind her book in the dark back corner of the booth. From here, she could avoid the rejection of attendees who failed to stop at her tent and watch Wyatt's every move without being detected.

Keeli watched him, and watched everyone else watch him too. With his height and commanding presence, heads turned when he passed by. He was hard to miss but Keeli suspected many people recognized him from the press while the rest were drawn to his handsome face. He had a movie star quality with his chiseled features and loose-limbed stride. In addition, he had that assuredness that comes from having wealth all his life. He looked like a man who had it all, and knew he had it all. His rich, easy laugh diffused any sense of entitlement that might have been off-putting, drawing people to him. He combined approachable with untouchable perfectly.

Most Sundays Keeli only guessed what he was thinking behind his dark sunglasses, but today he had them tucked into the opening of his shirt. She was able to get a glimpse of his gray-blue eyes and those tiny laugh lines fanning out at their corners. He stood straight and tall and it was almost as if he looked straight at her, blue eyes locking with green. She even imagined a quick look of shocked recognition on his face before remembering she was hidden in the shadows. Besides, he was busy whispering in the ear of his date, their heads touching each other. The cold reality of her insignificance returned to Keeli like an icy shower.

He cannot remember me from the elevator. It has been months and months since I last saw him. While he made an indelible impression on me, face facts Keeli, you have seen for yourself how all these gorgeous women surround him. You will never, ever compete with them.

As if driving home their differences, Wyatt and his date really stood out in the crowd. They looked stunning, cool and well dressed compared to the crowd decked out in cut-offs and flip-flops. His clothes looked expensive - not that Keeli was an expert. The woman looked high fashion, but less fussy than the women he usually brought to these fairs.

Keeli watched the sun kiss the top of Wyatt's head, watched it pick up red and blonde hues as he moved from sun to shade to sun. He had a ready smile and it was mesmerizing. She was intrigued by him and grateful to be sheltered in the corner where she could stare openly. He was a beautiful man full of vitality. He looked about 30 but Keeli knew from Googling him that he was 34. He had an air about him but he also possessed a boyish charm and an easy, athletic grace. Women followed him with their eyes as he walked past in jeans that fit like a glove - first to see his arresting face, then to admire his tight butt.

Keeli kept her eyes on him as he drew closer, stopping to admire Clarice's sculptures. Keeli was holding her breath staring into the sunlight from the shadow of her corner, hearing him exchange polite greetings with Clarice. She had been scrutinizing him for at least six or seven art fairs now and even came close to saying something once or twice when he passed her display. Never once had he made eye contact or noticed her. He certainly had not indicated that he recognized her.

Once or twice he had inspected her stock of earrings, necklaces and whatever was in easy reach of the tent entrance, slowing down but never stopping to venture inside. Now, to her complete dismay, he was finally actually entering her booth but with a gorgeous woman clinging to him. At least she was a different woman than last time. So far, none of the beauties had earned a second invite.

Keeli's heart fluttered while she conjured various tortures to separate Wyatt from this woman. Trying to get her emotions in check, she rehearsed a basic exchange in her mind. She imagined them sharing witty repartee reminiscent of "Sex and the City", just before he purchased her most expensive piece and asked her on a date. She was shaken from her lovely daydream by a smooth, deep voice.

OMG it's him! He is actually standing in my booth talking to me. Get your act together, idiot.

"Excuse me, can you help us please?" She loved the sound of his voice, low and mellow with no evidence of the local, Chicago twang. "We would like to see that ring please." He pointed to one of her favorite pieces.

What is he saying? Wow, he is so damn hot! Calm down Keeli and focus.

"Of course, I would be delighted." She jumped up, patted her frizzing hair into place and cursed the humidity. She turned away briefly to reach for her display keys while she surreptitiously wiped an annoying bead of sweat from her upper lip. She leaped forward to open the case, hoping the crazed look she was feeling didn't translate into a crazed smile. Placing the ring on the black velvet background to show it to best advantage she offered, "This is a new design this season, South Sea pearls in 18 karat yellow gold."

"Ooh babe, it is beautiful, isn't it?" the willowy blonde on his arm batted her eyelashes and looked up at him with a simper.

Did women really do that anymore? I guess this one did.

Wyatt didn't seem to notice, or he didn't care, instead studying the workmanship of the ring, the quality of the gold, the styling of the comfort fit, the size of the three pearls nestled against each other so they appeared to float in their setting.

"Try it on," he commanded her. "How much is it?"

"$985." Keeli made up the amount on the spot, the highest she felt she could charge for the piece, prepared to come down a bit before selling. She hated talking price, never knowing if people would think something was too expensive, or even worse, too cheap. "This is a very good price for a piece of this quality. That is 18 karat gold and two carats of very high quality pearls." She babbled, even though she knew that remaining silent at this point and letting the merchandise sell itself was the more successful tactic. With an effort, she clamped her lips shut tightly, using the moment to stare openly at this virile man.

The price didn't faze either of them. "Of course, it is obviously well made." He was checking out her workmanship carefully when he looked up from the ring to stare right into her eyes. He was standing very close and she was stunned by the proximity and the reality of him. "Are you the artist?"

"That obvious?" she quipped with a just a hint of sass, her heart pounding uncontrollably. Since she stood under a banner that filled the entire tent opening reading "Keeli Larsen Designs" it seemed too obvious. He flashed her his devastating smile and Keeli stepped back to give herself a bit of breathing room. She covered the moment well. "I will give you two some time to think about it."

While he and the blonde discussed the merits of the ring, Keeli studied Wyatt at close range. She was better able to see his intentional five-o'clock shadow, the length of his eyelashes, and the slash of straight brows over blue eyes cooled with gray. His hair curled at his neck. It pleased Keeli to realize that the summer heat defeated him just as she was. Now, with his head bent over her displays, she longed to finger the curls and waves.

Keeli's eye moved down to the strength of his neck and collarbone; they excited her somehow. She was staring at the open neckline of his shirt when he looked up from the ring to catch her staring. A flush of heat flooded her body, and then rose to her face in a telltale blush.

While Keeli's face flamed a heinous shade of red, the lovely blonde displayed the ring on her equally lovely, manicured hand. She turned it this way and that, stretching out her long arm to see it from afar, wiggling it in front of the small mirror on the display case. It looked fabulous on her. Keeli hid her work-roughened hands behind her back.

"I want it," she stated decisively, more to herself than either Keeli or Wyatt. Wow, this was a great sale, and a quick one too. Keeli was thrilled, except that her perfect man was about to purchase one of her favorite pieces for another woman: a beautiful woman, with sleek frizz-less hair and long elegant fingers draped over the arm of her dream man. A sleek cat of a woman batting her eyelashes and calling him "babe" while Keeli stood there a red-faced, sweating, mop-top.

Keeli swallowed down her growing jealousy and focused on the potential sale. Gratifyingly, Keeli watched as the blonde reached for her own wallet. Oh excellent, she intended to buy the ring for herself. Keeli's heart soared.

"I'll buy it for you, Missy. After all, I do owe you a birthday present."

No, no, no, no, no. Keeli's heart sank.

"Oh Wyatt," the woman responded, resting her manicured fingers on his arm as if she was incapable of standing on her own two feet. "That is too generous and it's completely unnecessary," hesitating in an artful manner. "…But of course I will let you!"

She was so damned pleased with herself, sending a smug, girl-to-girl smile Keeli's way. Keeli oozed jealousy, not sisterly camaraderie. Couldn't Wyatt see that this was her damn plan all along?

Wyatt rolled his eyes at Keeli and she realized that he fully understood what just happened. A man with this many women hanging on him must know when he is being manipulated. More important, Wyatt just shared a private moment with her, an intimate look of understanding.

The man was devastating. She cannot remember ever being so attracted to a man. She was having a mad cannot resist moment, meeting Wyatt smile for radiant smile. Keeli bent over her smart phone to swipe his credit card, but not before catching the sudden look of interest that flared in his eyes.

Keeli had him sign a receipt then efficiently wrapped the ring in a small box, despite sweaty palms and a thumping chest. She made sure that a business card containing her email and phone number was included. Just in case.

Keeli handed him the package and said a sincere thank you. Before she could say more the elegant woman pulled on Wyatt's arm and they were gone. She would have been content to stand there and look at him for hours but the entire transaction took less than ten minutes.

Head in a cloud, Keeli headed back to her director's chair, happy about her much-needed sale and frustrated that their time together was so short and so business-like.

"Ooh, girl," Clarice tracked her down in the corner, "that is one fine piece of ass."

"Wyatt Lyons Howe, IV. Wyatt Lyons Howe, IV was just talking to me."

"Earth to Keeli," Clarice waved her hand in front of Keeli's glazed stare. "I hope you charged him a whole lot for that ring, cause with a name like that he sure can afford it." Her sweat-shiny face split into a grin. "But I know you didn't, did you? And now I fear you will be useless the rest of the day."

"Huh? Oh, Clarice, you know I would never do that! Well, to tell the truth," Keeli admitted, scuffing the ground with the toe of her comfy Keds, "I was too busy staring into those eyes of his to even think of it." The two women went off into peals of laughter.

"Those eyes?" Clarice was struggling to stifle a giggle. "You were looking at his eyes when you could have been checking out that body? Did you see those pecs? And that fine ass? That is a good lookin' specimen." Clarice had raised her voice in her enthusiasm. Keeli shushed her in embarrassment, returned to her booth all serious and professional, and then was overcome with laughter again.

"As if I could miss them," Keeli hollered through the tent flaps. She heard Clarice's whoops of laughter in response.

Keeli hoped that this sale, and seeing Wyatt, portended a change of luck for what remained of the day. She picked up Shakespeare's "The Tempest" knowing that she had made several small sales as well as the ring today. She calculated that one large sale during what remained of this afternoon would do it.

Keeli should have been able to concentrate on her book and her clients now that she knew she could stop watching for Wyatt the rest of the day, but instead she rehashed every minute of their conversation, recognizing with resignation that she would need to get him out of her fantasies. The transaction had been nothing more than business. She had enjoyed his megawatt smile, but it was just polite. He was with another woman, buying a ring for her, no less.

It hit Keeli hard to admit that this man would always be out of her reach. They came from different worlds. On a whim, he bought a ring for this week's date that cost more she would spend on July rent. He was not likely to ever give her a second thought. Clarice was right. It was time to let go of her dream man and start living in the real world.

CHAPTER FOUR

Two weeks later, the scene was as different as night and day, or rather, rain and shine. This small downtown art festival was so wet and cold, more autumn weather than June. Many of the artists traveling from out of state had locked up their merchandise, tied down the flaps of their booths and given up hours ago. Keeli couldn't blame them. Attendance was understandably low and she had waited until almost 4pm to pack it in too. Only a desperate need for funds had kept her shivering in place that long.

Sales yesterday had been dismal, like the weather, so she stayed open for the intermittent opportunities that presented themselves, grateful when they came. Otherwise, she sat huddled in her cheap leather coat making a dent in "Crime and Punishment".

She stomped her feet regularly in an effort to keep them warm, but the Keds were soaked through and her jean legs had a two-inch hem of sopping material. Her hair was wild and frizzing, so that even pulled back in a band she had to keep moving it out of her face. There was no sign of a let up and it was so dark under the overcast sky that she had to squint to make out Dostoyevsky's immortal words.

All she had sold since lunch was two pairs of earrings, to two women from out of town that took her card with the promise to order more. She was fortunate to make that sale and their appreciation of her workmanship briefly cheered her up.

At 4:00 p.m., Keeli resigned herself to the quiet. This fair was not large enough to attract Wyatt, even if the bad weather wasn't discouraging enough. So, she was not watching for Wyatt at all. Instead, she began packing up. Clarice was here somewhere, trying to eke out those last few Sunday sales too. She was set up around the corner, down the entire length of tents, too far for a visit. They grabbed lunch together a few hours ago, but the warmth provided by the hearty chicken soup had worn off long ago.

Keeli texted her to say she was giving up and going indoors, but Clarice, the traitor, had gone home more than an hour earlier. She locked her jewelry, made a plan with Clarice to come back with the van after 7 o'clock and promptly at 4 o'clock she pulled down the flap and made a run for it. She braved the downpour only as far as the Cultural Center across the street.

Once inside the neoclassical building, she dropped into a metal chair in the lobby, grateful to find a seat with all the tourists coming and going. She took a moment to admire the mosaics and ceilings before watching dejectedly as her clothes left a large puddle on the tile floor. She would give it half an hour to let up and dry off a bit. She wished she had thought to run to Starbucks instead. Tea right now would have warded off a bit of her chill but she was not ready to head back outside. Instead, she hunched over her book.

Minutes later, Keeli's face was buried in her book, her hair dripping onto the table around it, when someone thrust a steaming Starbucks cup under her nose. The movement startled her and she knocked her book to the wet floor.

"Damn it, I was trying to do something nice. I am so sorry." His head was bent retrieving her book so she could not see his face. Although she had not heard that low mellow voice often, Keeli knew it was Wyatt by the reaction of her heart. She resisted reaching out to touch him before he rose back up to his full height and dropped into the seat next to her.

"I brought a coffee, but I usually see you drinking iced tea at these things, so I brought a hot tea too." He looked rugged and handsome. He was wearing a Patagonia raincoat, jeans and boots built to handle the rain. His hair was slicked back from his forehead with product but the curls sprung free near his neck.

He knows I drink iced tea? He noticed me? Keeli was staggered, delighted and flustered.

"You are an angel. Tea, I will take the tea." She reached for the warm cup greedily. "Thank you so much."

He reached in a pocket to pull out sugar and Splenda, both a little soggy. She seized the Splenda, busied herself preparing the tea, removed the protective sleeve from the cup then wrapped her hands around it.

"Mm mm, so good." Keeli sighed with contentment, sipping the hot liquid. "Perfection." She took a deep drink. Using just the tips of her thumb and forefinger, she removed the soggy book from the table where Wyatt had placed it and tried to compose herself.

What was he doing here? Who cared? OMG, he is here, now, with me.

"My pleasure," Wyatt's stormy blue eyes probed hers, seeming to ask a question, then the moment was gone. "I will replace your book. I feel terrible about it."

"Oh don't, really. First, I bought it for, like nothing, at a used bookstore. Second, I really hate it. Don't tell anyone though. I am trying to get some culture." She said the last sarcastically, pronouncing with a thick Bronx accent so it sounded like "cul-ja".

They sat close together and shared a laugh. She had never been face to face like this with him. Never been this close before or since the day in the elevator. She leaned in surreptitiously, trying to get even closer. She caught his clean outdoor aroma and the heavy, underlying scent of rain that clung to them both.

"Were you working today? I noticed you always have a pretty serious book at the art festivals. I wondered about that." He didn't ask her directly, instead leaving the observation hanging so she would explain. Wyatt seemed curious to know more about her but she avoided an explanation, answering question with question.

"What are you doing out in this miserable weather? Only people who need to be out are braving it today. You don't live around here."

"Oh, and you know that, do you? What else do you think you know about me?" His tone was accusatory, but his smile was indulgent.

As the words left her mouth, Keeli knew she had given herself away.

"I could go on for hours," she teased, "but you will think I am a stalker. Seriously, what are you doing out in this horrid rain?"

"Would you believe I came to bring you coffee?" There was a twinkle in his eye so that Keeli was not quite sure he was joking.

"Of course, my knight in shining armor." Wyatt leapt up, stepped back and dropped into a graceful bow, rising with a smile that sent her pulses racing. His flamboyant movement was as smooth as any musketeer's and his insouciance charmed her

"Seriously? I was at an appointment on the next block. I was cutting through to avoid the rain when I saw you shivering over here. So I went to grab some Starbucks and brought it back."

"Appointment on a Sunday?" Keeli was not going to slip up again. He did not need to learn that she Googled him almost daily and was well aware that he was working around the clock on a deal just two blocks south. His 23rd floor condo overlooking the lake was also less than a mile from here to the north, so he could have been cutting through on his way home.

It made perfect sense. It was logical. Or was it fate? Keeli wanted to believe in fate, since that validated her desires, confirmed to her that they belonged together.

Keeli followed Wyatt's every move in the business pages. She knew he was working on the nearby deal. She read the gossip columns for pictures of a tuxedoed Wyatt at some black tie benefit, even watched the sports pages for pictures of him in tennis garb or hockey skates. She could almost predict his favorite foods since he repeatedly took his clients to the same restaurants for meetings. She found something about him on Google almost every day, but she didn't mention that now.

"Real estate business never sleeps." Wyatt shrugged his shoulders with a little boy grin and a "what can you do" look. "What's your excuse?"

"Money," she responded bluntly. "I needed the money, so I worked the Millennium festival. Not a good choice this year."

"Well, I guess that was honest. Why not do something a bit more predictable than these fairs?"

Since he seemed interested, she continued. "This is the second year I am doing these juried fairs. I do Etsy too, since it is more year round, but I quit working for a store to pursue my own designs. It's been almost six months but, to be honest, I thought things would take off before now."

"Since they haven't, I spend my weekends freezing or sweltering and catching up on some reading. Today I had to turn off a lot of the lights, to avoid electrocution," she shrugged her shoulders in defeat, "so I gave up."

He said nothing but nodded his understanding and encouragement to continue. She found him surprisingly easy to talk to.

"As for the books..." she went on, self-conscious again, "it's hard to stay on your feet for 10 hours a day, especially when it's also a set up or take down day." Keeli explained that setting up or closing up her booth could take her a couple hours and involved a lot of loading, unloading and carrying. "My jewelry may be light," she quipped, "but the packaging and the booth display weigh a ton."

"Anyway, I hate listening to people discuss my work. It's as if they think I have no feelings," she stopped short of whining, "So to camouflage my vulnerability, I learned to bring a book. Sometimes I read it, sometimes I just pretend, but it saves me from hearing a lot of the things I find demoralizing or hurtful."

Keeli took a deep breath, smoothed her furrowed brows and shook off the bad vibe, flashing him a bright smile. "Am I talking too much?"

"Not at all. I find it fascinating. I never thought about the toll on the artist of doing so many fairs."

"I get why people sell through stores and galleries. I compare it to the pain of a mother hearing someone call her baby ugly – weekend after weekend."

"So why do you do it?" He meant it sincerely. "It sounds brutal to me."

"And we come full circle," she laughed freely again. "Money. This will all be worth it if I sell enough, or get a following or a commission."

She kept to herself that after six months of Etsy, art shows and knocking on the doors she had run out of time and options. Keeli didn't share that she had burned through the last of the dollars she set aside to buy precious metals and gemstones and wondered if she could continue at all. She said none of this, but her smile faded, her expressive green eyes grew bluer as a worried expression moved across her solemn face. She lifted a hand to smooth back her disheveled hair. Her movements told the complete story.

"Ah, demon money," he lightened the tone. "At the root of all our problems, is it not?"

"Like you have money problems," she chided him, but stopped herself from taking it further because he had a sudden, stricken look and she felt him pull away, putting distance between them in an instant.

What had she said to offend him?

Trying to recapture that intimacy, she tried teasing him. "You can afford two Grande coffees at Starbucks, so how broke can you be, really?"

"One is tea," he corrected, with some of his light mood returning.

"Yes, it was amazing that you knew I liked tea. I had no idea."

"Oh yes, I know a great deal about you, Keeli Larsen." Wyatt was looking at her like he wanted to devour her, eyes scrutinizing her green gaze, staying there momentarily before slowly shifting toward her lips and locking there.

He is going to kiss me! Please god, let him kiss me. Keeli felt that quick tightening in her belly, a tingling on her skin. The arousal was fast and fierce. If just a look got this reaction, what would the kiss do?

Keeli felt a pull toward him that was all consuming. She did not care that they were in a public place, that she strongly resembled a drowned rat. She craved him, leaned toward him, longing to feel his arms come around her and pull her to his chest, crushing her there. She moistened her lips with the tip of her tongue and watched his eyes flare with desire. She was being pulled to him with an invisible, unbreakable string. Her breath came fast between her lips, her heart threatened to explode in her chest.

Wyatt's cellphone rang at that moment, startling them both, breaking the spell that had descended. She hid her disappointment watching the heat leave his eyes. When he turned away to take the call privately, he was all business again. She knew the moment was lost.

Catching just hints of the conversation, Keeli felt her heartbeat return to normal and the heat coursing through her body cool. She could tell he was talking about a property deal.

"I gotta go," he said first into the phone, then to her.

"Thank you again for the tea. It was really thoughtful."

Really, that is all you can say?

He took her hand in his warm, larger one. She leaned toward him, but then he dropped her hand and repeated, "I gotta go. See you soon?" As quickly as she could nod yes, he was gone.

What had just happened? How had things gone south so fast?

Keeli shivered with the cold that Wyatt had kept at bay. A warm shower could not come soon enough. Giving herself a mental shake, she replayed the last half hour in her brain. Maybe the kiss had all been her imagination? He left quickly enough, and with no plans to see her again. She reinforced her resolve to move on reminding herself again that a relationship with Wyatt was a fantasy.

He was friendly, maybe he tried to steal a kiss, but clearly, it meant nothing to him. But he knew I liked tea, he knew about me. I have to stop reading something into his every kind gesture. But he did say he would see me, I think that's good. He didn't ask me out, though, and I suspect that is very, very bad.

And what about the elevator? How can he not remember me from the elevator? Or maybe he does remember, but then he should have said something. Or I should have said something. Damn, this is so confusing.

The rain was letting up and it was almost time to meet Clarice and take down her display. Good thing too. With no book to read, Keeli was very grateful to be rescued from her thoughts.

CHAPTER FIVE

Friday night at Gibson's Steakhouse. The Frog Bar was packed on weekends, but the guys had been meeting here since graduate school. The bartenders and servers knew them and treated them well and frankly, the women were very hot.

Wyatt tossed his keys to the young valet, Joe, knowing he would leave the Panamera right in front of the door. After all, a showy car attracted the "right" sort of people to the restaurant. Of course, a Maserati or Ferrari might bump him around the corner, but as a regular, he trusted Joe to keep his baby close and safe.

Pushing through the doors, Wyatt sauntered in, flirting briefly with the hostess before heading in to find the boys waiting in their usual spot. The handsome trio was huddled around a high-top close enough to the bar for great service but far enough away to be relatively quiet, considering the din. Wyatt saw some stunning women in short skirts casually lingering nearby. He knew after a few drinks that the women would be clinging to the four of them, hoping for more as the night grew later. After the long week, Wyatt intended to hang with the guys for a while but be gone before the meat market was in full force.

After a quick handshake-backslap combo with Tyler, Wyatt repeated the gesture with Randall and Alex who returned the backslap saying, "Hey, can we try to hold the girls at bay for a while? It's been weeks and it would be great to catch up." Since Wyatt agreed with Randall, he took it upon himself to address the women already moving in for the kill.

"Ladies, aren't we men the fortunate ones tonight? You all look amazing." Wyatt was implementing management 101 skills - always preface bad news with good news. "Let us buy you a round of drinks and have them sent over to your table," he smoothly herded them to the far side of the bar. "You understand we would love your company, but the fact is that we have business to conduct."

"How does he do that?" Randall said to Tyler as he watched Wyatt lead the women away.

"He reels them in, then throws them back and they never know what hit them," Alex explained. Wyatt returned alone after signaling the server to send the women a round on him. The server headed over to the cluster of giggling woman and the men were left alone leaning their heads close together.

It had been a few weeks since the four of them had been out like this. Wyatt, Tyler Winthrop, Randall Parker III and Alexander Gaines were fraternity brothers and the oldest and tightest of friends. Raised together in Lake Forest, they had played little league together, won the state tennis championship as members of the same high school team, and eventually pledged the same fraternity. Tyler and Wyatt forgave Randall for pledging Sigma Chi at Duke instead of Cornell, and Alex for doing the same at Stanford, but not until giving them both a major ration of shit. Tyler had impressed them all by going to Northwestern Law after getting his MBA. Now they called him "Professor" when he annoyed them.

The four had converged again back in Chicago to finish in the top of their class at Northwestern University's Kellogg School of Business. That had been almost 10 years ago, and all had become highly successful and remained bachelors. Family pressures to wed and have children were suffocating, but the men still managed to get together regularly for sports, drinks, vacations in Aspen or Lake Tahoe and to play the field. More like brothers than friends, they each knew the others had their back, and always would.

"What's the word, boys?" Wyatt queried as if he had not seen them this morning at the prestigious East Bank Club. They were serious about fitness and rarely exchanged more than a few words when they passed each other running track or pumping iron so this was their chance to catch up.

"That is what we want to know," Tyler started right in; Wyatt knew there is no reprieve in sight. He had been expecting an interrogation and now he would get one.

"Did you make a decision yet? Have you taken the VC offer?"

"Have you told your father?" Alex probed before Wyatt could answer Tyler's rapid-fire questions.

"Man, I would kill to be a fly on the wall for that conversation," Randall jibed.

"Do not get snarky," Wyatt warned, taking a deep, satisfying drink of a fine single-malt. To the outside world, he appeared calm but his friends watched him shred his cocktail napkin and knew how tense he really was.

They were all privy to the secret Wyatt had kept from family and others for months. He was finalizing negotiations with investors so that he could start the tech company he had dreamed of since college and the deadline to take the leap was fast approaching.

He hissed at them now to keep their voices down so it would stay secret a little longer. Wyatt had been struggling as things moved along. Go forward or can the whole idea. In three generations, no Lyons or Howe had dared to do anything but work for Lyons Howe, each eldest son trained to take over the business and maintain the family legacy. It was critical for a smooth transition when his father stepped down, and an expectation of both family and the business community.

In the early 1900's, Wyatt Howe married Meg Lyons and started buying real estate in a rapidly sprawling Chicago. What started as a home for the newlyweds and a place nearby for their children grew until he owned half the apartment buildings in their north neighborhood. Then he made purchases along the lakefront and soon owned more real estate than any individual in the city.

As the city grew, Wyatt's great-grandfather continued growing the business, branching into commercial real estate. He groomed his son, who groomed his son, who trained and educated Wyatt to expand Lyons Howe. The company was flourishing, and the family was now the largest real estate development company in the Midwest, major holders from Philadelphia to Denver.

Along the way to success, they became noted philanthropists and even more noted power brokers. The family had high expectations for Wyatt to continue the tradition. From the moment he was born, his father had groomed him for this role with the right education, exposure and training. His mother had supported her husband by introducing their son to the right families and the right social circles. In their minds, he was just months away from taking over the helm.

Of course, they had never once asked Wyatt if this was what he wanted, and he had certainly never spoken up as a boy to say he might want to do something else with his life. In fact, he had made it all the way to last year without questioning his role, accepting loyally his responsibility to his family.

However, at a conference last summer he met a venture capitalist that planted a seed that had been growing steadily. Over drinks, Wyatt had casually mentioned his idea for a real estate application, to help sell, price and appraise properties. He had visualized a tool for his work force but the investment expert saw far more. He saw a tool for the industry and suggested Wyatt pursue it.

Since that day Wyatt had been unable to get the idea out of his head, scribbling numbers on note pads, building spreadsheets and quickly coming to realize that he had the makings a strong new company. But loyalty, family loyalty, was everything so for a year he had refused to consider the possibilities. Two months ago, all that changed.

A typical family spat over Sunday dinner had escalated just enough for Regan, Wyatt's brilliant younger sister, to let her resentment show. The truth was that Regan was in love with the business and wanted desperately to run it. Just three years younger than Wyatt, she too had been raised on the family business. She had impeccable Cornell undergrad and Harvard business school credentials and real estate in her blood.

That Sunday evening it also became apparent that she had a chip on her shoulder the size of Texas. Who could blame her? It was the 21st century so the notion that a business should pass to the eldest son was, in her opinion and Wyatt's, antiquated and ludicrous. This was not the bloody British nobility; primogenitor should not apply.

Regan wanted the reins and Wyatt wanted out. He liked real estate well enough and certainly appreciated and enjoyed the spoils of the highly successful Lyons Howe empire, but he wanted to try his hand at technology. Computers, software, analytics and big data fascinated him. He believed he could successfully run this new venture, a company to design mobile business applications. He had spoken with Google already about capturing personalized data, and IBM about analytics. They were interested. Now, if he could raise the venture capital, he had research showing the market was strong and the competition was not.

He had all the plans in place, assuming he received the additional funding. He had staff ready to join him, some of it sitting around this table. He had equipment ready for purchase and a perfect location in a Lyons Howe property. He had done everything necessary to take the plunge.

More than anything, Wyatt was mentally prepared, desperate to get out from under the family name and prove himself on his own terms. He was actually psyched to take the risk and let the chips fall where they may. He had been trying to excel in sports, in school, in business, in the community, trying to find a place to stand out on his own, but always his name followed him, or preceded him, opening doors so that he could never be sure he deserved credit for his accomplishments. He knew others would kill to change places with him, would never understand the burden that came with being a Howe. He had laid all the groundwork and now he was prepared to find out if he could make it without the Howe family behind him.

What he was not prepared for was the discussion he would have first with his father, then the rest of his family, then the press. He was not sure how the business community would respond, but he knew his family would not respond well at all.

That's an understatement if ever I heard one.

"You ready to rock the old boat?" Randall queried now, breaking into Wyatt's reverie.

"Regan is definitely in a great position to take over. She would be fantastic and she is chomping at the bit for God's sake. Let her have it Wyatt, cause once she makes a few more million, I intend to marry her," Tyler laughed but Wyatt suddenly realized he might mean it.

Wyatt had never considered Tyler as a potential brother-in-law, but now he wondered why not. Tyler was a highly successful attorney, had enough money and prestige that he could never be considered a fortune hunter, and he and Regan had laughed and played together since childhood. Wyatt remembered now that Tyler had always been a little protective of her too. Their families were well acquainted and got along. Plus, they would have beautiful babies. Regan's willowy, pale beauty would be a perfect combination with Tyler's height and blond, boyish good looks. Wyatt needed to think about more than his problems, maybe help that romance along.

"Have you told her yet cause I know you have not told your father? I didn't hear the earth shake and you are not sporting major bruises." Alex socked Wyatt lightly on the arm, bringing Wyatt back to the conversation at hand.

The men were teasing Wyatt, but only in a supportive way. They all came from old, moneyed families with high expectations and they empathized with Wyatt now. There was rarely a chance to pick on the golden boy, other than missing an easy shot on the tennis court, and Alex was savoring the moment.

"Very funny, AJ. You know I am not saying anything until I know I have the investors locked in. After all, why rock the boat unnecessarily?"

"Yeah, cause that boat is gonna' rock big time," Randall rolled his eyes for emphasis. "Daddy will not be happy. Regan, dream on, Tiger. She has you totally whipped," he added in Tyler's direction.

"Mama will be even less happy," Tyler ignored Randall's dig. "No wife, no grandchildren, no legacy. What a disappointment you're turning out to be, Ivy," he said in his best Samantha Howe voice. He actually did a pretty good imitation and Wyatt visibly cringed.

"Oh yes, Ivy, dear," Alex did a weaker imitation. "When are you going to marry Sloane and make Mama happy?" After a moment's hesitation, Tyler continued in his own voice. "Or is there a new woman in the picture now? I saw Sloane and she said you were avoiding her, and Missy tells me you have stopped haunting photo shoots for the latest models. What are you up to?"

Ignoring the question Wyatt reminded the men to stop calling him 'Ivy', a nickname that he could not shake, a reminder that he was the fourth Wyatt Howe, Wyatt Howe 'I V'. It was horrible enough within the family, but his friends knew how he felt; they did it just to annoy him. It worked. At least no one called him 'Junior' which would have been so much worse, but 'Ivy' represented that family dependence Wyatt wanted to shake.

Wyatt moved smoothly into safer subjects for a short while. The men discussed the Cubs (already depressing), Bulls (finishing another losing season) and Blackhawks (thank God Chicago had one winning team). Then they speculated how badly the Bears would break their hearts come fall and how their favorites would fair at Wimbledon. The conversation shifted to business, the markets and how work was going for each. They covered real estate, Options, banking (Randall's purview) and consulting (AJ's career of choice). They rehashed their spring trip to Aspen, reminiscing about the skiing and the beautiful babes.

Wyatt took a few minutes to remind them of the Howe

Museum benefit coming up later in the month, chiding them to donate copious amounts and giving them a preview of the items in the silent auction. A sailing trip sounded enticing and they strategized to win it. Then he made the mistake of asking them who their dates would be. His date question brought his thoughts right back to Keeli, a topic he had successfully avoided to this point.

Wyatt unconsciously shredded another napkin. Three sets of eyes watched his hands before searching his face for clues. His knee, bouncing under the table, set the high top vibrating. Wyatt did a scan of the room, checking out the women who poured into the bar and encroached. They were easily recognizable. Every woman under 40 wanted a chance with the wealthy, handsome and eligible bachelors.

"So the Friday night meat market begins," Wyatt observed sadly. "Maybe it is just me, but these women look a little too hard for my taste."

"Could that be because you have a certain someone else on your mind, and no one here can compare?" Alex joked, but then he watched Wyatt take a deep breath and shred another napkin. The waitress removed the mess and left a small stack of fresh napkins. The tabletop continued to vibrate.

"OK, what is going on, Wyatt?" Alex focused his laser stare on Wyatt. His companions stared at Wyatt's face, aware that something was going on with Wyatt besides work.

As Wyatt leaned in to answer, the others lost interest in the women surrounding them. They did look a little hard - over dressed, over made-up. After years in the city and in the bar, the men easily recognized women fresh from the blowout salon with barely dry nails itching to sink into them. Despite all the effort, they had little interest in the women. Instead, they focused all their attention on Wyatt.

"Do tell, Bro," Tyler demanded.

"And don't leave out any details," Randall added with a leer, wiggling his thick eyebrows over his dark brown eyes, mimicking Groucho.

Wyatt flashed Randall an impatient smile then thought about that almost-kiss at the Cultural Center. Keeli had been wet and bedraggled but she looked smokin'-hot to him, her hair got away from her and billowed around her head like a red halo, her wet blouse clinging to her lush body. While he was honestly fascinated watching emotions move across her face and watching her expressive eyes change from green to blue, he had mostly struggled to keep his eyes from drifting down to her deep, inviting cleavage. He was pretty proud of his success.

Remembering the tip of her tongue darting out just before he would have kissed her, Wyatt felt his body stir. Damn that stupid phone call. He shook away the memories before he was out of control.

His companions were mesmerized, watching the change of emotions on his face - interest, pleasure, and lust. Something major had happened, and they intended to find out what.

"I met her at a couple of art fairs. Actually, I spotted her at a fair more than a year ago. She is a jewelry designer. Good one too. I bought one of her pieces for Missy a few weeks ago."

"Oh no, don't stop there," Tyler demanded when Wyatt hesitated. "What does she look like?"

"Red hair, pretty face, big boobs, long legs," Wyatt added as if in a trance. "And an incredible mouth - all pouty - and these exotic green and blue eyes. She's perfect. Mix of sweet and hot."

"Green AND blue?" Tyler seemed skeptical.

"Perfect?" Alex queried.

Simultaneously Randall questioned "And what has she been doing with that mouth?"

"You are a pig." Wyatt was chuckling. "Get your head out of the gutter. I barely know her."

"Never stopped you before," Randall tossed back.

"I noticed her last year and at every fair this year," Wyatt continued. "She reads Shakespeare, or Hemingway, or Dickens. Weird shit, but she is sarcastic and funny and unbelievably hot."

"That's it?" Randall sounded disappointed. "We don't care what she reads, dammit. Details, man, details"

"There are no details. I haven't even asked her out. Just ran into her at these fairs, oh, and I bought her a coffee. I haven't even called her since."

"Why not, Ivy? You obviously have it bad," Alex cut to the chase.

"Stop calling me that." Wyatt sounded a bit sharper than intended. "Please."

"That's it?" Randall sounded churlish and disappointed. "What aren't you telling us, Wyatt?"

Tyler continued, "Yeah Wyatt, you see great figures and pretty faces all the time. They throw themselves at you everywhere. C'mon buddy, what makes this one so special?"

He had to admit Tyler was right. It was not arrogant to acknowledge that Wyatt was a catch. Women pursued him, subtly and openly. He was heir to a financial powerhouse, 34 years old, well educated, engaging, interesting, easy on the eyes and single. He was not even divorced with baggage. He was really, truly single. Even at his most modest, Wyatt knew he could have almost any woman he wanted, and usually did.

Tyler hesitated, leaning in a bit closer, then lowered his voice and added reluctantly, "What about Sloane?"

"I know, I know," Wyatt sounded exasperated. "I know everyone thinks I am just getting in a few more girls before I marry Sloane, and maybe I am. But this girl feels different – unaffected - you know? She is just...something. She just does something to me, you know. It feels like she is with me, not a Howe. Just me."

"You know guys, it is easy to have women whenever we want them. We have them to take home to mama or ones we could never take home. We all know that most of time we don't care which one they are. But the truth is, I am sick of the posers and users who pretend there is a budding romance, when it is all just a game." Wyatt sounded tired and dejected.

"I want to be with someone who cares about my wants, my dreams. I do not want to just be a credit card, a name and a wedding ring. I want something different now."

"Yeah, but you have Sloane. She loves you. She wants to marry you."

"She expects to marry you, man," Alex, always logical, said it like it was.

"What makes you think this girl would be any different? She is an artist Ivy, she is probably looking for money way more than those models you date."

"Here's the thing, Tyler," he responded, "I have had my eye on Keeli for months now. Of course, you would say she is a user. Yeah, she wears cheap clothes, no designer shit. However, she never tried to chat me up or get my attention. Before last week, she barely looked me in the eye. I think she wants to but she would never have pursued it. In a world of brazen women, she is rather modest."

"OK, you win," Randall sounded exasperated. "Call the girl, go to her next art fair, just take her out, sleep with her, and get her out of your system. Can I play with Sloane In the meantime?"

"Now, why didn't I think of that?" Wyatt grinned to the guys but he knew this girl was different.

I know she is. She has to be.

The men laughed at Wyatt's comment and went back to checking out the women. Wyatt made small talk but after a respectable amount of time, he stood to leave.

"I'm outta here, guys," he said to no one in particular, waving off the women long enough to say good night to his friends.

Next to Keeli, everyone else seemed a poor substitute.

CHAPTER SIX

Here she sat, another Sunday afternoon, another art fair. It was well past two o'clock and there was no sign of him yet. Keeli had been anticipating Wyatt's arrival for two straight days although she had never seen him at a fair before a Sunday. As the afternoon grew long, she became more nervous, fidgeting with her displays and smoothing her hair repeatedly, not that she could tame the wild curls.

He was just being nice cause it was a cold, wet day. Get over yourself, girl. If he shows, you know he will have some bimbo with him. It's not like he tried to call, text, or anything. So, he might have attempted to kiss you. It didn't happen. And an 'almost' may have meant everything to you, but obviously, it was insignificant to him. He was doing what he's famous for, seizing the moment with some woman. This time it just happened to be you. Keep it in perspective.

She had dressed with more care than usual, in one of her newer bright-colored sundresses, hoping for a "Wyatt sighting", even though she was trying not to think about him. She was working diligently to forget about him, to stay rational and cool, and it helped that she was slammed with work.

The Gold Coast art fair was Keeli's best opportunity since it attracted a crowd of wealthy Chicagoans and tourists who historically bought more upscale pieces than buyers at other fairs.

The lakeshore event was already lucky for Keeli as well as most of the artists around her. Saturday was a long day, but the good weather, the location and reputation of the fair helped Keeli sell more than usual, including some big-ticket items. She was showing her new designs and they were selling well, giving Keeli the validation she needed.

She could easily pay July's rent now, unlike last month when she worried for two weeks, just making the due date. Not as frantic over money, she watched the items in the display dwindle with mixed emotions. It gave her added breathing room to stay afloat, and for that she was grateful. It also provided ready cash to purchase badly needed supplies. She would have to order right away to have adequate inventory for the Milwaukee and Port Clinton fairs coming next.

The reduced inventory represented weeks of nose to the grindstone. Keeli had put her heart and soul into this collection. Soldering and manufacturing jewelry in the heat of summer was less than ideal and she tried to avoid it as much as possible, stockpiling her inventory in the depths of a Chicago winter instead. She reminded herself to be grateful that she had work and that she welcomed it.

Still, a weekend off might make a nice break right about now.

With the perfect weather, crowds were larger than the huge numbers that experts had predicted. The lakefront setting was one of her favorites, the music carried from the band shell across Grant Park, the trails, tourists and locals whizzed by with their distinctive blue Divvy bike rentals or stretched their arms far to take selfies with Buckingham Fountain in the background. Parents checked out the fair on their way from Millennium Park to the Aquarium, dragging tired, whiney children in tow, stopping when they begged for popcorn or cotton candy.

The atmosphere was festive and complete. It filled Keeli with joyous energy. If she could just see Wyatt, the day would be ideal. It was after three already, and the crowds were thinning. The background of general noise and bustle faded out while Keeli alternated between scanning the crowd for a particular sandy-haired gentleman and pretending to read "Anna Karenina".

Just when she gave up hope of seeing him, Keeli swore that she could sense him watching her. She knew when she looked up she would see him but a discreet scan of the crowd revealed nothing. Her disappointment was tangible. She was so sure, and yet…

There he was, coming down the row of booths, sun casting an aura of light around his head. His sunglasses were hiding his eyes, but he was heading straight for her with a smile on his face and two iced drinks in his hands. He wove through the slow-moving throng and Keeli popped up from her corner to greet him.

Smoothing the wrinkles from her dress and the curls from her hair, yet again, she coached herself not to appear too anxious. If only she could control her heartbeat. She licked her lips nervously, smoothing her curls one last time.

"Hi Keeli," he spoke before he reached her. "I figured you guys don't get too many breaks so I brought you an iced tea." He hesitated as if unsure what to say next until she offered him her brightest smile. She was trying not to fidget from head to toe, but unconsciously she was digging the toe of her Ked into the soft earth.

Seeing that, and checking her out from head to toe, his voice was stronger and more confident as he put the tea on the glass display and stretched a hand toward her.

"Wyatt Howe, I bought a ring a last month, brought you tea a few weeks ago. Remember me?" He was all boyish charm.

He is definitely flirting with me. This is not wishful thinking. This is real.

She took the ice tea, feeling the warmth of his fingers and the cold of his hand where the cup rested in it. An unusual spark flew as their fingers touched. Keeli was unnerved by the sensation. He affected her too much. Keeli looked in his eyes to see if he felt it too, but those damn glasses hid everything.

He held her hand a big longer than necessary but released it to reach into the pockets of his linen shorts. He emerged with Stevia in one hand, sugar in the other. He put sugar on top of the second iced tea, while passing the sugar substitute to Keeli.

"Thanks, again. You are turning into my private catering company."

"Service with a smile."

Keeli reached for the Stevia with a grin. "You must be clairvoyant cause I really needed this. It is so thoughtful of you. Again."

"Just trying to help," he said, oozing charm. "Have tea, we deliver. The other is for your friend in the next booth, the sculptor. I noticed you two talk back and forth all the time. I figured she might need something too."

Can this guy be real?

Keeli called over to Clarice and made introductions. Clarice accepted the tea with sincere appreciation and dumped all the sugar in her cup. She took a quick sip before giving Keeli a conspiratorial look and disappearing behind her side of the canvas.

Keeli was awkward now that she was aware of how much Wyatt had been watching her. He knew she drank iced tea, not soda, and that she and Clarice were friends who often had booths next to each other. He knew about her books and who knew what else. Keeli felt overwhelmed, excited and intensely hopeful.

Could a man like Wyatt really be interested in little ol' me?

Keeli took a long draw on her straw. She was trying to collect her scattered thoughts so she could make scintillating conversation. She knew it was hopeless.

Wyatt saved her from berating herself. "Wow, this is a huge crowd, huh? I heard it was much bigger than they were expecting. I believe it. I had to circle like ten times before I found a parking space."

"Yeah, it's been bad for parking but great for sales," Keeli said, relieved to find her voice. "The weather and the setting seemed to be the magic combination cause all of Chicago showed up and most of them bought something."

"How long have you been doing these?"

"Over a year, all of last season and again this summer."

"Is Gold Coast where you do best? I know it has a history of generating huge sales and attendance."

"It is one of my best. Hey, is it my imagination or do you attend a lot of these?" She didn't admit that she had seen him all of last summer, and of course the elevator incident still went unmentioned. She was looking for answers to this enigmatic man a little at a time. Today she was trying to uncover whether he thought this was a great place to bring a date or if it was really about the art.

Of course, he IS alone today. Thank you, God.

"I own a lot of buildings that need artwork," he explained without bragging. "And I scout for the Museum of Contemporary Art and the Lyons Howe Museum sometimes. I am on the board of one, acquisition committee for the other. And of course, there is my private collection."

"Of course," Keeli mocked, her mischievous smile taking the sting out of the sarcastic retort. "Must not overlook that private collection, now must we?"

Wyatt's brief laugh left her breathless. How could she forget that rich, low and throaty sound? It was oh so sexy, and right now, it was directed at her. Keeli's legs went weak and she rested her hand on the top of the display case for balance. Wyatt saw the move and reached for her arm to steady her not realizing that the feel of his strong fingers intensified her longing.

"The heat's not bothering you?" He still had hold of her arm, his thumb moving lightly, reflexively back and forth over her skin. He looked at his hand seemed to realize what he was doing, and slowly withdrew it.

"Nah." Keeli offered no explanation for grabbing the display case. She was consumed by the warm glow moving through her body at the feel of his hand on her arm. He created a heat in her that started in her belly and crept up from there. He aroused her, causing her to move her eyes to his lips, longing for that elusive kiss.

Forcing her view back to his hidden eyes, Keeli stubbed the toe of her sneakers nervously in the grass and reminded herself where she was.

Get it together. Time to find out where he stands, once and for all.

"Speaking of buying art, how is your girlfriend enjoying her gift? It really is a beautiful ring, if I say so myself. One of my best pieces." She was fishing, but could not help herself. Unfortunately, she figured he knew exactly what she was doing.

When Wyatt hesitated to answer, she peered up at him from under her lush lashes provocatively even as she braced herself to hear his response. Instead of a disappointing answer, Wyatt removed his sunglasses, and looked her straight in the eye.

Their gazes locked and Keeli was quickly lost in the savage gray-blue blaze. Keeli's heart hammered in her chest. Her breathing turned shallow and she moistened her suddenly dry lips watching as Wyatt's eyes riveted to the movement.

Oh my, oh my.

"Girlfriend? She is not my girlfriend," his voice was husky, his teeth caught his bottom lip. His eyes drank in her face. "She is my baby sister, Missy. I adore her. I would have bought her ten rings."

The words sank into Keeli's lust-fogged brain and her face broke into a wide smile.

"Really? Your sister?" She sounded robotic, dazed.

Earth to Keeli. Snap out of this. If this is your reaction when he talks to you, how will you survive a kiss? Mmmmm, a kiss would be fantastic right now. OK, stop it. Get it together.

The fog lifted and intelligence returned to Keeli's voice as she broke eye contact.

"It would have been okay with me if you bought her ten

rings." She made the remark a snappy not greedy one, or at least she thought so. "Bring all your sisters. Bring cousins, aunts."

She was smiling at her little joke but Wyatt had that pained look on his face that she had seen flit across his face two weeks ago at the Culture Center. Something she said must have hit a nerve. "You know I am joking, right? I just want your sister to get the same pleasure wearing the ring that I got making it."

"She does, believe me," he offered. "So you consider your work a labor of love?" The pained look had disappeared. The question may have been innocent but the look Wyatt gave Keeli now was anything but. The heat between them was combustible, the air thick with tension. She was sure he must feel it when his hand started to idly stroke hers, sending shivers up her spine.

Keeli's palms grew sweaty, her breath dry in her throat.

He is here, he knew about me, he is flirting and touching me. Oh honey, this man is definitely interested in more. The 64-million dollar question is: are you prepared to let him break your heart?

Two potential customers entered the tent at that moment saving her from any decisions. She excused herself, barely hiding her disappointment that their interlude had to end. She expected him to fade into the crowd, frustrated that she would not even get to say goodbye or thank you or make plans, perhaps.

Miracle of miracles, he stayed put. He stepped back enough to allow the women access to the display cases and engaged them in conversation. They asked to see first one pair of earrings, long hoops in yellow gold, then shorter hoops in white gold. Wyatt jumped right in, giving his opinion on how they looked, suggesting a larger hoop with small, inset turquoise stones for one, large hoops with opals for the other.

Keeli was annoyed that he shamelessly flirted with the two women. She recognized that she was not special with a sharp pain in her chest. He flirted with every woman, dated supermodels. He could have any woman. He could have every woman.

He flashed her a conspiratorial wink as the women reached for more jewelry. The pain soared from her chest and began pounding. She realized that the charming rogue was helping her close the sale! This man overwhelmed her senses and she could never think clearly when he was near. Worse, she knew she was falling under his spell just as easily as the two middle-aged women he was bewitching.

Both women decided to make purchases. Sure enough, Wyatt

managed to convince them both to buy the more expensive earrings. Keeli completed the transaction, thanked them and handed them her card.

"You are a shameless flirt. Believe me, I appreciate it, but you are. You totally talked those women into spending more money – a lot more money. Perhaps you should work with me and charm all my customers." Keeli's eyes flashed with humor.

"Only the devil could separate women from their cash the way you can. You, sir, are totally evil." She stuck her finger into his chest for emphasis but the upward tilt teasing her lips gave lie to her words.

"Guilty as charged," Wyatt responded with a bow and a devilish grin. When a lock of hair fell onto his forehead Keeli fingered it back into place without thinking. He took her hand as she went to remove it, placing a light kiss in her palm and sending her pulse racing. She felt the heat of that kiss travel up her arm and settle deep in her belly. She wanted desperately to feel the warmth of his sun-kissed skin on hers, feel his strength as he pulled her tight against the broad chest she was admiring under his pale button down shirt. She pulled her hand back reluctantly, fisted and flexed her hand a few times, resisting the urge to run her hand all over him.

She was enthralled by the long strong column of his neck, the smattering of light hair revealed by the deep V in the open neck of his shirt. When he caught her staring, she quickly adjusted the Wayfarers tucked there, as if they were her purpose all along. His knowing smile told her he knew exactly what she was doing.

Ooh girl, you have it bad.

Carefully placing her hand by her side, Keeli took a deep breath to slow her racing heart. The more she watched this man, learned about him, the more she desired him. Sure, he was really good looking. Okay, she admitted to herself, outrageously good looking. The frank way his eyes bore into hers and the brilliant smile that came so easily as he chatted had her wanting to know him better. He had already shown her kindness and consideration, indicated respect for her work and for his sister. Everything she saw, she liked.

Except he is playing cat and mouse with me. I cannot be the next in his long line of women and I cannot have him on my terms. Not this man.

She kept reminding herself that he was a player, that he might have a little fun, but then he would break her less experienced heart. Her head understood all of this, but Keeli's heart was ruled by that strange pull. Her body responded to a deep longing for him. She was putty in his hands; he set her on fire.

She was barely resisting the urge to reach up and run her hand through his hair here and now, while she was supposed to be working. Her eyes returned repeatedly to the lush promise of his lips as she watched him speak and smile. She hungered to pull his head down so that she could taste a kiss.

And that damn confidence. The man looks like he owns the world. Oh, shit, you idiot, he probably does. Is there nothing wrong with this man? Oh yeah, he travels in the stratosphere, the world of museums and private collections. I travel in the world of second hand clothing stores and discount shopping.

Pulling herself together and trying to forget the electricity still warming her palm, Keeli gave herself a mental shake and tried to understand why Wyatt was toying with her. For that had to be what it was. Keeli gave herself a quick, very necessary scold to regain her composure, feeling her self-preservation instinct kick in at long last.

"Well, Sir Evil One, I appreciate the help and the tea, both were extremely thoughtful of you, but I am sure you have places to be, and I should be paying better attention to my customers." Keeli was proud of the cool efficiency in her voice. They both knew there were no customers at present though, so he had to be getting a very rude message that she was kicking him out. That was harsher than she had intended but her clouded brain was unable to conjure up a better line.

"Yeah, I guess I have overstayed my welcome." Confident, powerful Wyatt managed to pout like an 8-year-old boy, already melting some of Keeli's newfound reserve.

"I did not mean to rush you away," she quickly reversed herself, "but I figure you must have lots of other artists to see and..." she let the sentence trail off, looking down the long row of tents instead.

"Yeah, I guess I should keep moving. You're right." He was drawing out his words, following her gaze down the long rows of white canvas but not moving.

"I suppose you will be exhausted after being here all day..." his tone a bit softer, his handsome face reserved, " but maybe we could grab a coffee when the show ends, or a tea, rather. Or maybe a drink?" Wyatt was stumbling over his words a bit now and she found it totally endearing. "You could consider it my sales commission."

"I have take down around six and it will take me a couple hours but..."

He is asking me out. He is asking me out. He is asking me out.

Her heart was doing flips, hammering in her chest loud enough for him to hear.

So much for self-preservation.

She struggled to formulate a response that said yes but did not sound too anxious.

"...And it is Sunday night. Getting together at nine or ten might be an imposition."

Shut up stupid, we are adults here. It is not like it's a school night. Just grab the guy already, before he thinks this through and changes his mind!

"Oh yeah, I forgot about that..." he began as a snake of disappointment uncoiled in her belly. She was an idiot not to accept faster. Had she lost her chance?

Her regret must have showed on her face because he was quick to continue, "But if it's not too late we could still grab that drink? Would it help if I did take down with you, make it go faster?"

"That is absolutely not necessary," her face flooded with embarrassment thinking he might have thought her fishing for help. "But a drink later would be nice."

"Where do you live? I can pick you up around nine or ten or you could text me when you were ready? Whatever works for you."

Wow, he sounds anxious too. This is fantastic!

"Why don't I meet you somewhere?" Keeli responded, kicking her toe in the grass again nervously. She could not believe she was making a date with Wyatt Howe! She was working to sound calm but she felt like she could faint dead on the spot.

"I don't mind coming to get you, really."

"Well, I live in Logan Square, so I am sure that is out of your way, and I don't want to be any trouble, since it will already be so late. Besides, I figure you want to go someplace down here..." Keeli stopped babbling to catch a much needed breath.

Shut up before he thinks you are insane and reconsiders.

Wyatt gave her a reassuring grin saying with finality, "I have a new toy and I love an excuse to drive it. I will pick you up at 9:30." He gave her his cell number then stood over her like a schoolteacher until she texted him her address. Before leaving the booth, he took her hand and deepened his already low voice. "See you in a few hours then. I'm looking forward to it." His voice was a sweet caress.

Keeli stared at Wyatt's broad shoulders and tight behind as he disappeared into the crowd. She loved watching him walk, all cat-like grace and assuredness. When he was almost out of sight, he turned, caught her staring and broke into one of the sexiest, self-satisfied smiles she had ever seen.

She reached for her phone as soon as she was back in the booth and rapidly dialed her roommate, Dylan.

"You won't believe what just happened," she blurted in an excited rush. "Oh I can't tell you now," she added in frustration as a potential customer approached. But I am in big trouble. Please, please, please call that stylist friend of yours. I have a major fashion emergency." Her nerves got the best of her and Keeli hung up without waiting for an answer.

Fortunately, the customer entered the tent space forcing Keeli to push down her panic and go back to work.

CHAPTER SEVEN

"You met the woman. Keeli Larsen. The artist who made your new ring?" Wyatt was talking to his sister, Melissa, shouting into the speakerphone across the stark kitchen while he finished cleaning the remains of a hastily made ham and cheese omelet.

"Oh, the redhead? She was very pretty as I recall, but not your type, Ivy. Not your type, and not the family's type, if you catch my drift." Her voice echoed across the granite and stainless steel, sounding annoyed. "And whatever you are doing, stop it. I can't hear you over that racket."

"I am cleaning up from dinner, Missy. Ever since you fixated on that damn "Sabrina" movie, I am an expert omelet maker. I need something in my stomach before I start drinking."

He heard Missy laugh at his 'Sabrina' reference. She had enjoyed torturing him and his friends who hated sitting for Wyatt's bratty baby sister. They were just finishing high school or home from college. They wanted to be out partying. She was almost seven years younger, still in grammar school, and begging them to watch "Sabrina" when they babysat. She had them watch the Audrey Hepburn, Humphrey Bogart movie more than once, and the Harrison Ford remake over and over again.

"So, Bogart dates the chauffeur's daughter and you date the starving artist. I am seeing parallels here dear brother. You need to remember that was a movie, this is life and you have Sloane to consider. How much longer are you going to make the poor girl wait?"

"Oh man, am I in trouble. If you think I shouldn't see her how will I ever bring her home to the rest of the family?" The image of Keeli sitting at the family dining table, chatting with his parents was vivid, and astonishingly, Wyatt was comfortable with it.

"No, no, I really liked her stuff, and she seemed nice enough. I am just surprised that 'love 'em and leave 'em Wyatt' is interested in her. She seemed, now don't take me wrong brother dear, but she seemed too innocent to be your type."

Wyatt cringed when she repeated a phrase one of the local papers penned last year when he escorted a different beauty to every event. The phrase was spot on and he could not shake it.

"You know I hate that phrase, Miss," he grumbled. "You might be right about Keeli. I think she is more innocent than my usual, but I really like her. There is just something about her. I am actually nervous."

"You nervous! Where did that come from?"

Suddenly embarrassed by the confession, "Well, I usually date, you know, a friend of a friend, someone from school. There were those couple of daughters and nieces of the guys at the office, or Mom's friends. They were all known quantities. I can't remember the last time I just picked up a random girl."

"It's good for you - a change. Of course, you will have to take heat from home if you hit the papers again. There are important traditions in our family and you know you are expected to uphold them."

"Yeah, I can avoid the papers on a Sunday, but maybe not my friends. I hate to admit it, but I am concerned about her with them. You know they are all total snobs. She really is a starving artist. She is smart enough, but they will take one look at her and write her off. I am afraid they will be rude. You saw her, those clothes were awful."

Although with that body, who the hell cared? He enjoyed the image, grateful that his baby sister could not see his wolfish grin.

"You really are a snob, Ivy," Missy chided lovingly. Missy was Wyatt's favorite and the childhood nickname was sweet coming from her lips.

"She always wears those awful Keds, but she has this adorable habit of digging them into the mud when she is nervous."

"I didn't know you knew her that well, Wyatt," Missy drew out the sentence as a hint to Wyatt to offer more information.

"I really don't. She is a complete mystery. You know she makes that great jewelry, I mean she clearly has talent. I wonder if she is successful doing these shows? She seems so grateful for every sale like there is a bit of desperation lurking there. Missy, think of it, she is doing this on her own. It must be incredibly hard work." There was admiration evident in his voice as it trailed off.

"All I really know is that she likes tea, not coffee, with Stevia. Oh, and she reads the classics."

"The classics? She's a smart girl? Definitely not your usual. She is probably better read than you," Missy scolded.

"Hey, wait a sec," Wyatt jumps to his own defense. "I am no lightweight lady. I know my Shakespeare and Dickens. Besides, Sloane is incredibly well educated and you know it.

"Oh, maybe you are right. What the hell am I doing, Missy? What if she just wants the cash? I know she is poor, she's had told me so more than once – outright. I absolutely cannot tangle with another user. I cannot handle another women who pretends to want me but really wants my money or the Howe name."

Insecurity crept into Wyatt's voice and Melissa jumped in to stop it from continuing. "Are you psyching yourself out before even giving it one date, Ivy? That is not the brother I know and love."

"Here is the kicker, Miss. I think she might want the money, I know she needs it, but I just don't care. I shouldn't tell you this, but I want her bad. She has a rockin' bod under those bad dresses, long, long legs and an unbelievably tight a..."

"OK, enough Ivy," Missy cut him off. "TMI big brother. We may be close, but I am not one of the boys."

"Seriously, but she also has this wonderfully free laugh, and she just puts her emotions out there. She has complete belief in her work, and none left for herself. She hides in the back of that stupid booth, but when she comes out she is great with her customers, knowledgeable, friendly but not pushy..."

Wyatt realized he had said too much and abruptly stopped his little speech.

Then, almost as if he could not help himself he added, "And those lips, oh man, those lips."

"OK, down boy, down boy, I think I have heard enough," Missy cut him off but with the indulgence of a beloved sister. "You really like her, I can tell."

"Well..." Wyatt dragged out the word like he was setting up a joke "She is pretty damn hot."

"OK, Stud. Have a great time. Where you taking her?"

"Chicago Athletic Club."

"Into all those crowds?" Before he could answer, Missy continued, "I guess you know what you are doing. But, seriously, you better call me tomorrow with all the gory details."

"Not a chance. Love you Missy." He hung up quickly, cutting off any chance for a response.

With an hour remaining before Wyatt needed to pick up Keeli, Wyatt wandered through his apartment seeking something to occupy his mind. He was already showered and shaved. He had added gel to his hairs, hoping to control the curls he despised. The crisp button down shirt with a black/pink stripe combination that he selected was usually a hit with women. They told him the pink was a sign that he was in touch with his feminine side. All he knew was that they told him he looked good. His jeans were hip, his Italian loafers were buffed to a high shine, and a Rolex on his wrist was his only jewelry.

He added the last of the dishes to the dishwasher. Assured that the countertops were clean, no giant fingerprints on the stainless refrigerator, he flipped off the lights. He slid the stool he was sitting on earlier under the dark wood breakfast bar as he left the room headed down the short corridor to his office. Perhaps he could accomplish something to keep from watching the clock.

Oh what the hell, it's one drink, not a damn marriage proposal.

Wyatt picked up a trade magazine determined to concentrate. Throwing it down in exasperation, he grabbed the remote to catch up on the Cubs game instead. It managed to hold his interest – barely – for the necessary time. Checking the clock that had pride of place on his deck, Wyatt grabbed his cellphone, glad to see it was time to go. Hours ago, he had Googled directions, then, just to be safe, run Mapquest too.

One last check of the apartment; nothing was out of place. The home office door was closed, safely off limits, the living room was perfect, but then he almost never used the professionally decorated space. The modern square-cornered cream sofas and leather ottomans, carefully scattered pillows and magazines left the room feeling a bit cold to him. He admitted that the earth tones were a perfect setting for his art, all hand picked by him from local modern artists and photographers. The room had been featured in "Chicago Architecture and Living Magazine" but he still avoided the room unless he had company, preferring the casual warmth of the kitchen or the comfort of the media room.

Moving down the corridor, again admiring his art choices, an Asian sculpture, a large colorful modern painting, he knew the guest room would be spotless. He never used it and the housekeeper kept it company-ready. His bedroom was another story.

He pulled once more on one corner of the hastily made bed and plumped the red pillows that brightened the otherwise neutral tones. The sheets were changed Friday and the press would have been surprised to learn that only he had slept on them since. There are no shoes or clothes on the floor or chair. Satisfied, he turned to leave the room, then returned to switch on the table lamp, keeping the light low for ambiance.

Just in case I get lucky. You never know.

He checked the master bath one last time. He splashed himself lightly with spicy cologne, noticed the Rolex and swapped it for a less prestigious watch, kicking off the shoes and quickly donning a slightly scuffed pair of Nikes.

Satisfied at last he grabbed his keys and the poorly wrapped parcel on the front foyer table and headed out. He punched the elevator button and checked his reflection for the umpteenth time in the large mirror over the hallway table.

Wyatt had lived in this condominium for more than five years, loved the building, it's great location right off Michigan Avenue, but the elevators were slow, and he fidgeted while waiting. It finally arrived and he hit "P2" descending to the second of the garage floors where his cars were parked. The doors opened with a jarring 'ding,' and Wyatt headed for the far corner with a jaunty step.

"Hey Wyatt, we on for hockey Tuesday?" Wyatt was startled to hear his old friend Geoff Willis shout his name from down the garage row. Preoccupied with Keeli, he almost walked right by without seeing him. "7 o'clock as usual?"

The brief question helped Wyatt realize he needed to get his head back in focus before he got behind the wheel of the car. "Yep, I am going to kick your ass, as usual."

"Yeah, you try!" Geoff hollered back good-naturedly. "But piss me off and I might have to stiff you at your little fundraiser."

Oh shit! The gala for the Howe Museum is in one short week. Time flies…

Wyatt knew Geoff was always generous so he ignored his idle threat. "Ass-kicking or not, man, you had better bring your checkbook" Wyatt volleyed back with a wave as he ducked between his Land Cruiser and his Porsche.

Lately, every conversation with friends had ended with the 'bring your checkbook remark," as the Howe Foundation was hosting the art museum's annual fundraiser. He had been overseeing committees, making phone calls and sending letters for close to a year to assure a grand success. It would be a major moneymaker for the museum and a grand event for the society magazines. He would have to get Keeli out of his system quickly and concentrate on the benefit.

With the beep-beep of the car's unlocking, Wyatt got the contented look of a lion that spotted his prey. His new Porsche Panamera SE was a decadent purchase, but Wyatt had not a moment of buyer's remorse. Even after a month, he still admired the sleek machine, part sports car and all luxury. He considered it Porsche at its best. It has all the luxury of a top-of-the-line BMW married to all the high performance and sleek speed that had earned Porsche its reputation.

It was not easy to keep the white car clean in the grime of Chicago, but for Wyatt, this was his new baby and taking care of the vehicle felt like a true labor of love. The leather interior was dust free and still had that new car smell while the exterior had been waxed to a polished shine. Wyatt ran his hand over the surfaces as he slid into the driver's seat.

WXRT roared to life blasting over the purr of the engine, reminding Wyatt of how loud he had played the radio earlier. He savored the fabulous sound system a moment before reluctantly turning down the volume to a reasonable level. He was clearly a man who loved his rock and roll, and loved it loud. Being exposed to Lyric Opera, Joffrey Ballet, the Chicago Symphony and jazz quartets had helped Wyatt gain an appreciation for them, but his first love remained his true love. After a moment, he cranked back up the volume and sang along with the Eagles.

"Living it up at the Hotel California, what a lonely place..." The words came unconsciously as Wyatt wound his way up from the bowels of the building toward the city lights. Wyatt took the sharp turns of the parking garage a little too quickly, savoring the responsiveness of the high performance vehicle. It had become an addiction to drive, so much so that Wyatt had even visited his family in the suburbs more than usual in the last month. His mother had been unable to complain that she never saw him.

Wyatt hollered a polite "have a good night" through the open window, waved at the garage attendant and edged into the sidewalk foot traffic carefully. A June Sunday night on the Magnificent Mile meant plenty of tourists still cramming the sidewalks. The numerous restaurants and small playhouses always attracted crowds here and it was close enough to Oak Street Beach that on a night like this the hearty souls who stayed until the moon rose were just heading home in sandy beach attire and flip-flops, towels and totes on their arms.

Wyatt inched past all of them and onto side streets, cutting across town to Keeli's address quickly, making great time, only to struggle for a nearby parking space. A summer heat shower threatened and Wyatt anticipated a run to or from the car in the rain.

He was planning to take Keeli to the Chicago Athletic Association. It had been renovated just a few years back into several floors of restaurants and bars. The spaces were massive and very popular, but the owners had retained the original woodwork, fireplaces and ambiance in the Drawing Room that made it feel quiet and private. The lovely space was divided into conversation areas by plush rugs and held small tables surrounded by leather chairs or high backed love seats where people could be cozy and feel alone in the large space. Wyatt was targeting one of those loveseats for tonight.

Wyatt knew they had food if Keeli was hungry, unobtrusive service and a valet to help avoid the rain that was suddenly in the revised forecast. In addition, it was very hip and Wyatt was hoping to impress her. He ran the risk that his friends would be hanging out in the adjacent huge Game Room, but he figured on a Sunday night he could avoid them by staying in the Drawing Room. They would be unlikely to be looking for him at all, and certainly not there. He wanted to keep them from meeting Keeli.

It is not that I am ashamed of her, cause I'm not. I just want to save her the hassle...and me all the questions. Wyatt did not want to examine that thought too closely.

A beat up Honda just two doors down from Keeli's address pulled out and Wyatt maneuvered his Porsche into the spot easily. He hated leaving it on the street even briefly but the spot was large and, assuming most people were at home this time on a Sunday night, he figured it would be safe for ten minutes. Hopefully, Keeli was the type of girl who is ready on time.

He had it all planned out. He would avoid his friends and use this private time getting to know Keeli. So far, she had been friendly but a little flirty too. She was most likely looking for him to help her get ahead, fund her little operation maybe, or open the right doors for her. He had been with enough women looking to use him. He could read their intentions almost immediately and would know about Keeli quickly. Then he could decide whether to dump her fast or whether to get lost in that luscious body for a few weeks first.

If she were just innocent and friendly, he would move on after tonight. He had enough friends, and she might complicate his feelings of friendship if he let her.

But what if she was not a user, not just a friend? What if that pull he felt was matched in her? He knew he could get lost in her laughter, hypnotized by her unusual eyes. He knew the feel of her skin burned his and that her lips tempted him to kiss them for unending nights. He wanted her with a primitive, uncontrolled longing. Keeping his hands off her was torture. He feared that she was under his skin, that he might want more than a few weeks.

He had felt that luscious ass almost six months ago, and thought about it ever since. He knew he should have said something about it by now, apologized.

However, something held him back - a fear of spoiling this budding relationship.

She hasn't said anything either.

Oh yeah, she had been in the back of his mind since that January day. He had been furious when he discovered he had been thwarted, that she was gone with no phone or email contact. He had been an ogre around the office until his frustration subsided almost a month later. He could not ride the elevator without reliving that moment, could not buy a coffee without longing for her presence. He was afraid of what he was starting with Keeli, but he was unable to stay away. He was in unchartered waters with her.

It's one drink Wyatt; get out of your head. One drink. One night. Do what the boys said. Go get laid and get over her. Don't forget about Sloane, for God's sake.

Sloane was the furthest thing from Wyatt's mind. He was envisioning Keeli, naked and warm in his arms, red hair spilling over his arm as he rose above her. He envisioned her lips rosy from his kisses, her cheeks lightly chafed from his beard. His body instantly responded to the image and with a deep breath, Wyatt sprinted through the rain and up the stairs to Keeli's apartment like a general leading the charge.

CHAPTER EIGHT

$\int$he wanted to meet somewhere instead of allowing Wyatt to pick her up at the apartment, but she knew that would never fly. She was not ashamed of the place exactly, but she knew the apartment would look shabby and cheap, because it was. It was also crowded with stuff since she had moved in and taken over two bedrooms, one now her tiny sleeping space, the other her design studio.

Keeli's roommates, Dylan and Theo, had started out as friends, then roommates. Now they were planning a wedding, recently legalized in Illinois. They moved into one bedroom and sought two roommates. Instead, they got Keeli, who took both of the inexpensive rooms and now paid just under half of the rent.

The space worked and so did the relationship. The three were a match made in heaven, hitting it off instantly, becoming BFFs. Keeli sometimes felt like the third wheel, but the boys were smart, kind and hilarious to be around, so she moved in and paid her rent as best she could. In addition to everything else, they were great about helping her out when her she struggled to get the rent on time.

Dylan, chef at a hip Wicker Park restaurant, was gone most nights, Theo ran a catering company and both she and Dylan helped him out when they were able, Dylan in the kitchen, Keeli as wait staff. Theo was gone some days and some nights, and Keeli was gone most weekends. The crowded space worked well until all three were in it at once, like tonight.

This was Keeli's first date since moving in with the boys over a year ago and now they were commenting on all her clothing choices. The boys had great style and Keeli was grateful for their advice if not their torment. She wanted to rely solely on the stylist friend of Dylan's who had brought her an armload of clothing options.

"Please just be polite, and then disappear," she rudely

suggested when the two salivated about meeting Wyatt. "And do not tell him all my secrets," she begged.

"Are you kidding? This is Wyatt Lyons Howe, honey," Dylan responded. "His family has their name on universities and museums and every building in town. And he is a hotty. No way am I missing this. I plan to bask in his exalted presence for a few minutes. Besides, we made a deal."

The moment Wyatt walked away that afternoon, Keeli had phoned Dylan, begging him to get some help from his stylist friend for her date. Sofia had arrived to help her, but in exchange, Keeli had to promise to introduce the boys to Wyatt. Keeli loved Dylan like a brother, but she was terrified to leave him alone with Wyatt for even a minute. You had to know Dylan awhile before you really got his offbeat sense of humor.

Keeli had planned to be ready so that she could introduce the three men quickly and make a dash out the door, but Wyatt would be there any minute and she was still putting the finishing touches on her appearance.

She knew she looked her best; she had a professional with great taste dressing her. Still, when she looked in the mirror she saw too much red hair, too many curves, legs that were too long, giant lips and deer-in-the headlight eyes. The only things Keeli liked about her body were her nose, which was mostly straight and tilting up slightly at the tip, and her eyebrows, not too thick, not too thin, not too red. She knew other people found her eyes fascinating, being forest green totally rimmed in blue, but she just thought they were strange.

Tonight, with some help, this combination of features was dressed to impress. She wore a pair of designer jeans she could normally not afford, faded to a perfect pale-blue and hugging her long legs like a second skin. The stylist paired them with a jade green scoop neck blouse, sleeveless, flowing to the waist before hugging her hips. It was low at the neck but not revealingly low, tight in the bust but not excessively tight, solid in the front and back but stitched so that just the tiniest hint of skin showed on both sides. It was a blouse to tantalize, not tease. The outfit, finished off with her shined up black leather sandals, made her look curvy but not overblown, sexy but not overtly. Although, she kept telling herself she had nothing planned, the gorgeous lavender push-up bra and panties underneath everything made her feel feminine and seductive.

The blouse provided a hint at her tiny waist without making her hips seem large, the push-up bra contributed a wonderful glimpse of cleavage and she knew the shoes, with three inch heels and a platform, would make her a better height for kissing this tall man

Yes, that much I am planning on. I have imagined it over and over since we were interrupted at the Cultural Center - weeks of imagining a kiss. Could the real thing live up to my make-believe kisses? I intend to find out.

Keeli was just relieved that her hair was behaving. The last thing she wanted was a bad hair night. Her mop of curls was hard to tame with even a little humidity but today had been dry and clear. Keeli returned from the fair, washed and dried it quickly so that now – still warm from the flatiron - it laid to the middle of her back, thick and sleek like a red waterfall.

Standing in front the dresser, wishing for a full-length mirror as she did everyday, Keeli stood on tiptoe trying unsuccessfully to get the full effect. Giving up in frustration, she gave herself a reminder that she could not compete with Wyatt's usual dates so she would just be her best.

Keeli focused on selecting the one piece of signature jewelry she would wear. This was what she - and not the stylist - got to choose and the small independence thrilled her. She also admitted that the jewelry was designed to distract Wyatt's eye from her cheap purse and shoes. The stylist had not thought to bring purses and shoes were a no-go. After a day on her feet, Keeli went with a pair she had already broken in.

With this neckline, the bib necklace she created last month would work. The five strands of green-tinted steel cable with the South Sea intermittent pearls was one of her best pieces, with real commercial appeal. She tried it on, then took it off and opted for a new silver cuff bracelet. It left her neckline and cleavage bare and was a great statement piece. The sterling bracelet was weighty, about 2 inches wide with jasmine blossoms framing rows of silver braids. The cuff showed off her lean, muscular arms and represented hours and hours of her time. She took one last look, reminded herself to hide her work-roughened hands, and prayed she was appropriately dressed for wherever they were going.

Please God; do not let me make a fool of myself, or worse yet, humiliate this proud man.

Right on time, Keeli heard the knock then the chatter and

laughter coming from the living room. It sounded like Wyatt and Dylan were hitting it off, which would be great.

Why does it matter if your friends like him and he them? Do you really believe this will be more than a one-time thing? Don't answer that!

With heart pounding in her chest, Keeli reapplied enough tinted lip-gloss to replace what she had nervously chewed off. The heels on her sandals sounded deafening against the scuffed hardwoods and echoed in the narrow corridor. She cringed a bit, knowing they could hear her clomping down the hall like an elephant.

Then he was standing there, fresh shaven, gloriously tall and manly in a button-down black and pink (pink!) striped oxford shirt and black jeans. His sandy hair looked freshly washed and lightly styled off his face. Keeli's fingers itched to dive into those waves. His lips looked kissable and his blue eyes were piercing as they lazily and thoroughly scanned her from top to toe.

The heat in that gaze sent a blush moving through Keeli, moving inexorably from her shoes to her hairline. His gaze on her was stripping her naked. Places on Keeli's body heated, melting. Keeli became aware of places that had been dormant coming awake from his look alone. When his eyes hesitated at her cleavage, her heart skipped a beat or two, and when they lingered on her lips, she parted them on a sigh.

Finally, he made eye contact, but by then Keeli's brain was mush. Wyatt's lips turned up, his eyes sparkled with laughter. He knew exactly what effect he was having and that realization brought Keeli back to her senses. She remembered to smile and find her voice. She remembered, too, that they were not alone.

"Will I do?" She just passed some unwritten test with flying colors. She realized it sounded like she was fishing for a compliment and got flustered, blushing again. "I mean is this ok for wherever we are going?" She tried to recover from the awkward moment.

He gave her a nod.

Was he speechless too? I mean this is Wyatt Howe and he has asked her – HER – out for drinks.

The butterflies in her belly collided with the warmth of seduction. Keeli, Wyatt and Dylan were still standing in the doorway. He had said not one word, but Keeli was ready to drag him down the hall, Neanderthal style and make love all night. She wanted to feel the weight of his naked body crushing her into the mattress. She wanted to feel his kisses on every inch of her body.

He looks good enough to eat.

"Right on time." She sounded inane, but it was all she could think of while she shook away the sensuous image. " And I see you have met Dylan." For once Keeli was grateful for Dylan's presence. Although she feared he might say something embarrassing, Keeli was speechless and needed the help.

"Yeah, actually we've met before," Dylan said seriously and mysteriously. Suddenly Keeli was concerned that Wyatt had a dark past that Dylan was aware of, or that perhaps they hated each other.

"Wyatt is active in that arts community where Theo caters. We just agreed that he is one of the best caterers in the city, so he passes my test. You can go out with him with my blessing."

"Well, if we have your blessing, then it's all good," Keeli quipped finally feeling her mushy brain return to its former intelligence.

"Yeah, and Wyatt says you guys keep meeting at art fairs. I had no idea you were one of us, Wyatt. Around here we love artists."

"Oh no," Wyatt was quick to correct. "Not me. I do not have an artistic bone in my body. Wish I did. I am a patron of the arts." He said "patron" in a way that clarified quickly that he was not a viewer but a buyer. The statement highlighted their myriad differences reminding Keeli of their backgrounds. He had not said it to be a snob, it was just who Wyatt was, a part of him.

Happiness warred with a feeling of inadequacy when Keeli thought of spending the evening with this witty, charming and sophisticated man. He was out of her league, but he was here, with her, for now.

"So, shall we get going? Where are we going, by the way? I never bothered to ask. Drinks, right?" Keeli almost clamped a hand over her mouth to stop the inane chatter. Why, oh why couldn't she think of something witty? She always wished she could be wittier, smarter and more educated. Another difference.

"You might want a coat, just in case." Keeli watched Wyatt look around the front entry, perhaps for a coat closet, maybe just ready to escape the cramped space. She saw his eyes move from the bare hallway to the living room filled with consignment furniture before he found the coat rack in the corner and moved toward it.

She would rather have died than be seen in her shabby fake-leather jacket. Instead, she insisted she would be fine.

Baby, you are putting off more than enough heat to keep me warm.

She blushed at the thought, turned away to grab her hobo bag, but not before she saw a look of confusion cross Wyatt's face. She could have no secrets with the way she blushed all the time.

He stepped aside smoothly, allowed her to precede him through the door, and grabbed Dylan's hand for a firm handshake on his way out. Keeli breathed an audible sigh of relief to be out of the ramshackle apartment and away from Dylan's unpredictable humor. Wyatt caught her eye, looking concerned that the sigh was indicative of a problem. Keeli flashed him a wide, reassuring smile and he gave her a slightly cocky grin. She could not have explained why, but she felt suddenly that she and Wyatt were on the same page, ready to focus completely on each other.

He moved to stand close to her, saying not a word. Wyatt wrapped an arm about her waist, strong and sure, turning her until they were face to face. She felt the heat of his skin, the strength in his large hand on her small frame. She could smell his clean, masculine scent in the small space and feel his heart thumping. Her breathing sped up in response.

"You look fantastic," he whispered on a breath. Keeli lifted her face toward his, looking straight into his eyes almost, but not quite, level with hers.

"I have been looking forward to this ever since you suggested it." Her voice came out low, husky and seductive.

"Me too." Their lips were almost touching. She could smell his minty breath mingling with hers. She wanted to close the gap, feel the velvet touch of his lips. The sexual tension was palpable. They had barely exchanged ten words, had not made it out of the stairwell but Keeli could see where this was headed.

Suddenly nervous, Keeli pulled back as much as she could with his arm around her, and started down the two flights of stairs to the first floor, trying to regain her equilibrium.

OMG he is so hot, how the hell will I get through drinks without losing it? At this rate, we will never make it out of the building.

"I really would have been okay coming down to meet you." She cut off her thoughts and reverted to friendly banter. "I didn't hear the rain from my apartment." Keeli stepped into the night air, "but now I feel especially bad for making you come get me."

Rain! Where did that come from? My hair is doomed. So much for thirty minutes with the flat iron. Just my luck. No wonder Wyatt thought I might want a coat.

"You didn't 'make' me do anything. I never do anything I do not want to. Never. And that is something you might want to remember about me."

Suddenly Wyatt was this icy cool man she had not seen before. He was emphatic, almost as if he was scolding her. It captured her complete attention. Keeli figured she was seeing the real-estate-mogul side of Wyatt. She liked the playful side of Wyatt, respected the intelligence and wit, but this confident side of him turned her on more.

Keeli loved that he was so commanding, so self-assured, but now her butterflies were back in full force and she realized how enthralled she was with him. She responded instinctively to his strength, sensing a strong character and directness that touched a chord in her.

His hand still held her waist, the warmth spreading and intensifying. The combination of his arresting presence, powerful demeanor and polished veneer was overwhelming her senses. Keeli realized that she was definitely not prepared for the onslaught of delicious appeal that was Wyatt Howe. She was not prepared, but she liked it.

Oh yes, I like it very much.

"Chicago Athletic Association?" he suggested. It was the hot spot for drinks overlooking Millennium Park and the Art Institute.

"Sure, perfect," Keeli responded, grateful that she had heard of the hip bar and did not have to ask about exercising. Of course, she had never been there. She knew that it had undergone an extensive renovation and reopened as the top location for twenty- and thirty-somethings. She pictured noisy and crowded, and tangible disappointment deflated her anticipation of a cozy couch and conversation.

"You've been there?" She shook her head no and he smiled. "It's hip, but it's Sunday so the crowds shouldn't be too bad. The Drawing Room should be great this time of night. We can find a comfortable couch and grab food too. I thought you might not have had time to eat."

"I didn't," Keeli replied, "I would love some food." So, he had pictured a couch too. Delighted they were on the same page, Keeli realized that beneath all her nerves she was hungry.

"Nice car," she drawled in sincere appreciation when they stopped in front of the Panamera. "Really nice car. I see now why you want didn't mind driving." He flashed her a wide smile. "I have brothers who trained me to appreciate fine machinery when I see it. And this is certainly fine machinery. Your new toy, I gather?"

Wyatt helped her into the car, handling her as if she might break. "Glad you like it, Ma'am," he drawled sarcastically, but she could tell she had just scored points.

The door closed softly and she sat back in the hushed interior, running her hands along the supple leather until he slid into the driver's seat. His eyes dropped to watch her hand stroking the leather; looking into her face, he met her gaze with a heated one of his own. Becoming aware of what she was doing, she forced herself to stop, but the sexual tension was overflowing the intimate space.

"I want to know everything about you, Keeli. Tell me everything." His eyes stared into hers. She felt herself falling under his spell. She felt his thumb stroke her leg lightly, rhythmically. The feel of his hand on her thigh was burning into her skin, large and solid. His voice, low and melodic was that of a hypnotist pulling at her soul. The space was small; the man was larger than life.

Ah, that touch. I love that touch. What did he ask me? Shit, what did he ask me? You are so in trouble, girl.

CHAPTER NINE

*I*t took Keeli a few moments to respond. Perhaps she was deciding where to start. It was a broad question after all. Wyatt was hopeful that the delay was due to that confused look on her face, and he was arrogant enough to think he might be the cause of that confusion. He loved this part of a date, when the sexual tension was thick, when the relationship was full of possibility.

"Let's see. I am a jewelry designer obviously. I have been doing it for about six years now. I love it. The working with my hands, coming up with ideas, seeing people wear my designs. I love everything but the selling. I hate the selling." No surprise, she started with a safe topic, her work.

"I went out on my own this year after working for other jewelers, first downstate, then here. I came up from Gilman, IL. Do you know it?" Wyatt shook his head no and she continued, "Mid-state, on the interstate, lots of corn, not much else. I could not wait to get out of there, although I love, love, love my brothers. I have two. They still run a farm there. And, of course, I miss my mom too." It sounded to him like mom was almost an afterthought.

"I have a brother too, and two sisters, all younger. You met Missy last week, so you know already that she has me wrapped around her little finger." Wyatt managed to make eye contact with Keeli, keep his hand on her thigh and maneuver the car through the light traffic on the dark, damp streets.

"See how much we already have in common? We both have brothers. It is meant to be," Wyatt flashed Keeli a playful grin.

"Oh yeah," Keeli bantered back, "and my Porsche is parked right down the block too. Didn't you see it when you drove up?"

"You may not drive one, but you can certainly appreciate one. I like that," he kept the conversation light when it could have moved quickly into that 'you have lots – I have nothing' territory. They traveled in completely different worlds. He would have plenty of reminders of that, no need to start yet.

Her grin faded. She continued more quietly. "Seriously, I am just a starving artist. I am committed to making this work but it is pretty hard to make ends meet selling my own designs. I have no name recognition yet, no stores carrying my stuff. I rely on me, just me. Well, and fortunately Theo helps me out by getting me jobs filling in as a server when he does big jobs."

"You do the fairs on weekends and work nights for Theo? When do you create your jewelry? Or sleep, for that matter?" When she ignored the question, Wyatt probed further. He loved hearing her voice, wanted to keep her talking. She was very matter of fact, not feeling sorry for herself. He really liked that about her. "Do you make the pieces yourself or just design them?"

"I don't just anything," Keeli's clipped response was indignant before she backed off. "Sorry, I get a little defensive about my work. I am challenged about it all the time. I do all the designs, select all the materials but I only do about half of the actual construction, the rest goes to wonderful manufacturers in the area.

"I sell my small stuff on Etsy, do the art fairs for the higher end pieces," she explained. "It is slow going. My goal is to get representation in some stores. No one has signed on so far but I am pretty determined."

When Wyatt asked about going out on her own without a store lined up Keeli continued. "I got tired of selling other people's jewelry." She grew animated as she told him about working for Mr. Weinberg, and a large retailer before that. She shifted, turning in her seat to face Wyatt more fully, giving him an opportunity to move his hand where it rested on her leg.

Wyatt seized the opening to slide his palm further up her thigh, the warmth of her skin heating the jeans. His thumb began making lazy circles on her denim clad leg, sending sharp quivers of desire through his whole body. She did nothing about it, perhaps unaware he was doing it, but he could think of nothing else.

"Go on," he encouraged Keeli to continue, bringing her back to the moment. He needed to concentrate on what she said, not how warm and strong she felt. Otherwise, he feared he could not drive safely. He was moments away from pulling to the nearest curb and kissing her senseless.

"I came to Chicago six years ago to take some metalsmithing

classes and never left. I worked at the small retailers, worked up to the big names, but in January decided to try it on my own."

"So you work totally alone? What if you need help? Aren't you ever lonesome?" Wyatt probed, flatteringly interested. "I am surrounded by people all day, meetings, conference calls. I cannot even fathom working alone."

"I cannot afford a whole store, or employees obviously. I considered sharing studio space with other jewelers and designers but I cannot afford it, so I turned our third bedroom into a studio, and do heavy work in the basement, for safety. If things don't turn around soon I won't be able to pay for the apartment rent either." Keeli continued sadly. "This weekend was great, but up until now it has been a very slow summer for art fairs. I could design from Gilman, move back home, but frankly, I would rather die."

So, she doesn't want to go home. Is that a Gilman statement, a family statement or a failure statement?

Wyatt knew she had just given him a major glimpse into her, if he just knew how to interpret it.

Keeli put a positive spin on her work and finances as best she was able. The conversation moved to the remaining art fair season. Wyatt was very knowledgeable about all of them, the type of clientele they attracted, the fees for a booth, which fairs were juried for entry, which were open. He liked her choices for the rest of the summer, the juried fairs in Milwaukee and Highland Park. She basked in his approval openly and he preened with importance.

I am so glad I know this stuff. She values my opinions, wants my input. This is so cool. A woman who can have an intelligent conversation about art without being a groupie. Intelligent and hot.

Before she knew it, they were pulling up in front of the wide Chicago Athletic Club doors and a liveried valet was opening her door. Wyatt jumped out to come around to her and quickly ushered her out of the rain and into the lobby. The smell from Shake Shack was delicious and overwhelming. Wyatt placed his hand on the small of her back again, guiding her toward the stairs to the second floor. He watched her look toward the burger joint with longing.

"Do you want a burger first?" Wyatt He offered her the choice but they agreed to split a burger upstairs instead. He selected a high-back loveseat off to the side of the empty fireplace. Keeli looked around briefly before settling into the seat, wide eyed as she took in the large room, original woodwork and tall windows overlooking Michigan Avenue.

"We can tour later. There is a game room that is worth seeing." There was still a good crowd despite the late hour on a Sunday night. Wyatt flagged down a server before dropping gracefully onto the couch beside Keeli. He was careful to leave enough room between them not to be sitting on her, but little enough space to easily wrap his arm around her shoulder and pull her close.

"I hadn't thought it would be so crowded," Keeli observed, "this late on a Sunday, you know?"

"The bar stays open late, they have the game room and our crowd, as you know, operates on very little sleep if offered a good alternative."

"Of course, you are so right. I don't usually have the friends or the funds to party a lot. Most of the time, I am waitressing anyway. So, is this is your new pick up spot? Oh shoot, forget I just said that. I have no idea why I brought that up." Keeli was flustered, looking everywhere but at Wyatt.

Saved when the server appeared, Keeli dove behind the cocktail menu for reprieve and inspiration. It was a hectic scene but the waitress was not too busy to chat with Wyatt. He was a regular, he tipped generously and they slipped into easy conversation. Keeli looked unhappy about it, possessive and jealous and Wyatt enjoyed the moment. He helped her pick a glass of red wine, pointing to one on the menu when she confessed they were all unfamiliar and overpriced. Wyatt ordered an 18-year-old scotch, the most expensive on the small menu and a burger for them to split.

"Hip joint, hip prices," Keeli observed and for a brief moment, Wyatt was concerned about her continually returning to the topic of money. Then he remembered what she had said about partying and decided it was not aimed at him. He let it go…for now.

Even tucked away somewhat privately, people stopped by to say hello to Wyatt. Otherwise, he nodded or waved to a few people while keeping his distance. He seemed to know everyone and he had certainly garnered the interest of many women in the room.

"Are you always the center of attention?" Keeli's question was honestly curious, no bite to her voice and he considered his answer carefully.

"You know, I guess I am. I never really thought about it before because it has always just been the case. First, my father was the important one in every situation, then he introduced me and I became the de facto second in command. No dad, I rise like cream."

"Do you like it?"

Wyatt was stunned by the question. No one had ever asked him before it he enjoyed being 'big man on campus'. He had taken for granted that he would be, but did he actually like it? The question made him squirm a bit causing him to consider how much easier another woman might be. This one challenged him and he was not sure he liked it.

Wondering if another woman might be an easier option for tonight, he let his eyes meet those of a couple beautiful women scattered about the room. They all signaled their availability with a look or a smile. Then his eyes rested back on Keeli's insecure countenance.

She is so on to me! What are you doing idiot? You have the hottest woman in the room sitting here. You like looking at her, you like talking to her. She is into cars and maybe into you.

Wyatt immediately lost interest in everyone and everything else, turning his full attention to Keeli.

They chatted about the bar, the food menu, and shared some people watching while awaiting the arrival of their drinks. Wyatt heard Keeli's stomach growl and they were able to laugh about it comfortably. He rested his arm behind her, his hand idly playing with a lock of her hair. He knew it was a cliché, but it felt like ropes and ropes of silk.

"You have straight hair tonight," he made the observation and Keeli launched into a small diatribe about her unruly curls and the color of her hair. Before she could say more, Wyatt stopped her by putting his hand firmly on her leg. She quieted, those blue-green eyes staring into his.

"A man could lose himself in those curls, Keeli. I miss them."

Wyatt reached out to pull her gaze back to his, softly caressing her jawline, then slowly stroking the length of her bottom lip with his thumb. Her lips were so soft and velvety. They were the most erotic things Wyatt had experienced in a while, especially when instinctively she opened her mouth and reached for him with the tip of her tongue.

Wyatt watched as she snatched up her drink, effectively putting a barrier between them. He gave up, placing the burger in front of her, knowing that she needed it more than he did. The moment had passed, for now, but as she raised her glass he lifted his own, clinking it with hers, toasting in a low, seductive voice, "to us."

"To us," Keeli responded, locking eyes with Wyatt over the rim of their glasses and taking a sip of the deep, ruby liquid, allowing it to rest on her tongue before swallowing. He watched in fascination. "Yum. This is delicious."

"Yes, you are," Wyatt smiled at her as he lowered his glass and pushed the burger closer to her. "Try this."

Keeli took a small bite and savored it briefly. "Oh, this is so good." As expected, Keeli proceeded to demolish three-quarters of the sandwich before apologetically offering the last few bites to Wyatt. He ate the last of the burger in two huge bites, wiping his hands properly on the napkin in his lap and pushing the empty plate out of the way.

"So, I guess you were hungry. Should I order more?"

"Oh, how embarrassing. I am so sorry, I was just hungry and it was so good. Do you need more food? I, of course, am good now." She went from sorry to silly and they shared a laugh.

"What about you? I have been monopolizing the conversation, but tell me more about you, Wyatt."

Oh damn, we are back to friendly.

"There is really not that much to tell," he began modestly. "I grew up in Lake Forest..."

"Sorry I don't know where that is," Keeli interrupted.

"Really, you really aren't from around here. It is about 20 miles north along the lake. Pretty, wealthy, insular. The town went nuts years ago when Mr. T moved in and cut down all his trees. No? Doesn't ring a bell?"

"Sorry," she mumbled.

"Anyway, I got out of there when I went to Cornell, then Kellogg for the MBA, just like dear old dad. Family tradition is very important to both the Lyons and Howe families so I got a double dose of it." Wyatt tried to keep the derision from his voice.

"But those are great schools. I would kill to have the opportunities of a Lyons or a Howe. Think of the advantages you have." Her enthusiasm was unmistakable.

Suddenly introspective, Wyatt scowled at Keeli and went

quiet.

"What did I say? I obviously said something wrong. Did you not like school? Did you have a bad experience?" Her concern was touching and Wyatt thawed.

"Actually I loved school and being away from home, on my own. I studied business, of course, but I minored in engineering. Software engineering. I was fascinated by the technology behind a business, and with actually writing code. My friends had to keep my secret, cover for me when I was playing in the computer labs if anyone was looking for me."

"You're a geek? I would never have guessed. I would have loved to study at places like that, to learn business or English lit. I went a community college instead but I studied some business too." Keeli said the last with bravado, proud of her educational achievement, not intimidated by Wyatt.

"I went to community college near Gilman at Kankakee Community College. I had to work part time to pay for it, and live at home to make ends meet. I managed to sneak in some metalsmithing and metallurgy classes at the U of I."

"Ok, so it wasn't Cornell but they were tough classes and I was juggling a lot. I focused on business, on everything I needed to get a job. That is why see me reading all the time now, cause I never got to take English Lit in college."

Jumping up in his seat, Wyatt rummaged in the large pocket of the jacket slung over the couch arm beside him.

"That reminds me. I have something for you." He presented Keeli with a small parcel poorly wrapped in newspaper, copious amounts of tape holding the corners shut, looking as if a five year old had wrapped it.

Keeli laughed, first at the wrapping, then at the parcel, obviously a paperback book from its weight, shape and size.

"To replace the one I ruined," Wyatt explained as she tore open a new copy of "Crime and Punishment."

"You shouldn't have, really. You didn't ruin it. I dropped it. Nevertheless, thank you. Thank you so much." Her sincerity moved him. She seemed more pleased by the gift of a paperback book than Sloane did when he gave her designer bags, vacations or even jewelry.

"It's no big deal," Wyatt was a bit embarrassed by her response.

"It is to me," she was looking at him with such admiration

that it was hypnotic.

"You must not get a lot of gifts."

"You aren't kidding," came her heartfelt reply.

Wyatt was speechless. He took a fortifying swig of scotch before putting his glass on the low table and turning to her fully again. He reached his arm behind her again, fingered a lock of her hair bringing his other hand to rest lightly on her leg. He started sliding his thumb back and forth mid-thigh, watching her reaction, and seeing the blaze of heat in her eyes. He let the conversation lag, concentrating on the intoxicating feel of her.

"Well, you already know that I came up here about five or six years ago, etc., etc. I moved here with my friend Meg but last year she went home to get married and I moved in with Dylan and Theo. My mom was appalled when she found out I live with two guys. I tried to take the sting out by telling her they were gay but that just made it worse," They both laughed.

"Living with them has been fantastic. I found them on Craigslist and could not have asked for better luck. I thought Dylan was a girl when I replied to the ad. They did not say if they were looking for male or female so how was I supposed to know?" She turned up her hands in that questioning way. She liked to talk with her hands, he realized, very animated.

"Anyway, we have become great friends now."

"Holy shit! You moved in with two strange men you found on Craigslist?" Now Wyatt sounded appalled and remarkably parental. "Don't you know how dangerous that is?"

"I am not an idiot," Keeli replied with some fire. "I did background checks and got references for them. You sound worse than my mom."

"Sorry. Who am I to get on your case?" Wyatt quickly backed down and flashed that disarming smile again before turning back to the table, and savoring a sip of scotch. "I have not had roommates since Cornell. I forget how hard it is to find good ones."

"So, on to you now," Keeli threw the conversational ball back in his court. "Do you like your work? What about hobbies? You must travel a lot." Wyatt heard the longing in her voice on the word travel. They might be talking about him, but her questions were revealing as much as when she talked about herself.

"What else can I tell you?" Keeli watched as he gathered his thoughts. "I collect modern art, preferably by local and up and coming artists. My job," he sneered, "My job is a bit of a joke. I spend all day in meetings and keeping my father happy. That is the most important part of my work. I work for my father, who worked for his father and so on and so on. I go to too many meetings. I spend time working with architects and builders which is okay, but then I spend hours fighting with the city on zoning. The usual. It's a job."

"A job?" Keeli could not believe her ears. "You are second in command at a huge real estate conglomerate and you call it a job?"

"Yeah, I guess that sounds pretty stupid, when you put it like that," Wyatt conceded with a cheeky grin. "But it really is a lot of routine stuff. One building is usually just like another, one deal like the next. In addition, my dad oversees everything like we are all two year olds that need a babysitter. It's pretty annoying after all this time."

"But the business will all be yours some day, right?" Keeli was really trying to understand Wyatt's seeming lack of enthusiasm for his work. "And you are a power broker about town, that must be pretty cool. I mean you know the mayor and stuff."

"Don't be too impressed. Yeah, I guess I know important people, but Keeli, they are still just people."

"Only someone who grew up like you did could say that," she chided but the slight up tilt to her lips and way she placed her hand over his helped take the sting out of her words. "I mean what do you want that you can't have?"

"You," he whispered causing her face to flame and her green-blue eyes to flare. "And the ability to create something completely on my own and take full credit for the success or failure. Like you."

"Then why do you do it? What not go do something you love? Go be a geek somewhere."

"This is Lyons Howe Real Estate we are talking about. Four generations have gone into the business and made it bigger and better. My brother and one of my sisters work there too. There are family expectations.

"You wouldn't understand, you do it all yourself, but I am completely tied to my family. From the moment I was born. I was groomed to take over this business. I have the CIO title because my father wanted to placate me but I do not do enough around the technology. I never make a difference. Then I get to run around the city letting everyone think I am a big-deal, sitting on the board of this corporation or museum or college because of my name, because we donated lots of money," he took a deep breath and looked deep into her eyes. "I want to prove myself Keeli, that is what I want."

Keeli was clearly caught off-guard by Wyatt's impassioned statements but recovered quickly. "In truth, I can relate. It is why I started my own business in the first place. Moreover, I did it with six months savings and a prayer. You have everything you could want at your disposal, Wyatt, so what on earth is stopping you?" Keeli's was challenging him.

"Family," Wyatt spit the word at her. "Family. No one goes against the family. It would break my parents' hearts if I said I wanted to do anything other than work at Lyons-Howe. My father is not well; he is counting on me to be ready to take the helm. If I said I was is leaving, I sincerely believe it would kill him."

Keeli saw the conversation tie Wyatt in knots and she carefully considered her next statement. "Wyatt, you have a brother and a sister in the business. Maybe they would like to step up if you gave them the chance. Did you ever think of that?"

"You are so wise, Keeli." Wyatt felt comfortable having this conversation with Keeli, more so than with his friends who voiced concerns over dashing family expectations, or worse, having less money and prestige. Everyone else seemed more concerned about Wyatt's status than his desires. Keeli, the woman he thought might be an opportunist had never once mentioned living with less money. She just focused on his goals and desires.

"I actually think my sister Regan would love to take over the business. And she would be so good at it. My brother Ethan is still pretty young and inexperienced."

"Have you discussed it with her?"

"Not yet, because once she knows, the whole family knows. I have to find a way to discuss it calmly with my father first. As is, he will never forgive me, but if he found out from someone else, he would be furious."

Keeli nodded her head in understanding. Wyatt watched as she worked on a solution to his problem, teamed with him in a way Sloane never did. Actually in a way no one else did. Of course, Keeli was not part of his larger life; she would not understand all the risks, all he would have to sacrifice. Sloane could see that aspect of the issue in ways Keeli would never understand.

"I know it's not the same, but I had some family expectations I had to deal with too. Much less significant than yours, I am sure. My dad died a few years ago and my brothers put a lot of pressure on me to stay home and take care of my mom, so she would not be alone and so that the farm work would continue. The farm supports the whole family, my mom, my brothers and now their families too. They were very angry when I left; they accused me of turning my back on them. It was ugly.

"So I can just imagine what it is like to be the fourth generation with such high expectations. My brother's wife stepped in for me, and perhaps Regan and Ethan could step in for you. We kept it in the family, and you would be too."

Keeli impressed Wyatt. She was giving serious consideration to his issue, paying attention to him, not his status, not his money, not his name. In fact, her suggestion that he hand things to Regan and take a chance on his own company would risk all of his privileges. She didn't seem to care. He appreciated her empathy. He felt comfortable talking to her, aroused touching her and proud to be seen in the company of such a beauty.

Wyatt slowly slid his hand from Keeli's hair to cup the back of her neck. The hand that had been drawing lazy circles on her leg reached across her to pull her toward him. Keeli's heart sped up; he could feel it, see the flush rising above the low cut blouse.

Her neck felt small, his hand was large and warm, and her skin was unbelievably soft. He was touched by her story, by how hard she must have worked to do it all alone. He dropped her work-roughened hand to return his to her leg, his lust-filled brain focused on the heat traveling into his hand as he moved back and forth. Wyatt stared into Keeli's face, deep into her eyes. His gaze dropped to her mouth and lingered there. His hand pulled gently coaxing Keeli to move closer toward him as he leaned toward her.

He heard Keeli's heart hammer in in her chest, her erratic breathing. Excitement and anticipation were coursing through his veins. She kept her eyes open as long as possible, caught in his clear blue gaze, but at the last moment, they fluttered shut and so did his.

The kiss was soft at first, enticing. His lips were firm and sure against hers. Hers were soft and pliant. He teased her mouth open with his tongue, allowing him in to explore. She tasted of mint, mustard, and moist warmth. Her tongue danced against his as he probed slowly and gently before deepening the kiss. She released a small sigh that was his undoing.

Wyatt pulled her closer, his strong arms tightened around her and Keeli reached her arms behind his neck in return. Her palm rested against his nape, cool against his warm, fingers stroking his neck erotically, pulling gently on his curls. Her breasts flattened against his chest. The feeling was so arousing that he tried to draw her into his body, needing to be even closer.

His teeth nibbled at her bottom lip, his tongue explored every corner before returning to dance against the roof of her mouth. His hand slid up Keeli's back and around to graze her breast with his fingertips. Then slowly he backed away with a last nip at her lower lip and they both dragged in a deep breath. Keeli looked disoriented, her gaze unfocused and yearning.

Jeez, what is wrong with you? You were about to feel her up in the middle of a restaurant, in front of God knows whom. And, unbelievably, she was about to let you.

"So where were we? You were telling me about moving here from Gilman," Wyatt leaned back with a satisfied grin, watched Keeli respond to his touch, her tongue slipping out to moisten her lips as a flush rose into her cheeks.

"Are you going to pretend that didn't just happen?" She was confused and indignant, and adorable.

"Yes, for the moment, I am. We are in a public place after all, and I am trying to regain my equilibrium. For the moment..."

He watched understanding dawn across her beautiful features and nodded encouragement for her to continue talking, while he continued to stroke her thigh distractingly.

After a deep drink of her wine, hand shaking slightly, she was searching for conversation, clearly still rattled by the kiss.

Holy shit the girl can kiss. Oh no, no, no, this is definitely not okay. I cannot bring a farm girl home and leave the family business too. One or the other maybe, but certainly not both. She will never live up to the family standards, my friends will eat her alive. Just get her in bed and get over her.

"Bro," a dark haired,clean-cut, well-dressed man about Wyatt's age approached, checking Keeli out from head to toe – not subtly. It broke the conversation and serious mood when his strong handshake almost pulled Wyatt off the couch. "I almost didn't see you hiding over here. You should have let us know you would be here tonight. Aha," he said spotting Keeli, "no wonder you are hiding. Introduce me to your fiery beauty?"

Wyatt was incredibly relieved not to have been interrupted just one minute sooner. He pasted a tight smile on his face, and then exchanged pleasantries with Randall. The two waved to Alex and Tyler across the room, but they did not approach. Alex gave him a shrug. His expression let Wyatt know they had tried to keep Randall away. Wyatt was open and friendly a moment more, disguising as best he could his strong desire for his friend to disappear.

"Keeli Larsen," Wyatt made introductions when it became clear Randall wasn't leaving, "I want you to meet one of my oldest friends in the world, Randall Parker. This is Keeli Larsen. She is a jewelry artist I met recently." Keeli stood and the two shook hands, Randall relinquishing hers reluctantly.

They exchanged pleasantries. He politely asked about her jewelry, she asked if he too was from Lake Forest and how long he had known Wyatt, but his constant perusal of her body and use of sexual innuendo obviously disturbed Keeli so the conversation lagged. Wyatt tried to steer Randall away from being his usual self, sweet but rough around the edges. When he wouldn't take the hint, Wyatt jumped in to talk about getting together Tuesday for hockey and signaled the conversation was over.

Instead of leaving, Randall put an unwelcome arm around Keeli's shoulder, his hand dipping uncomfortably close to her breast, the smell of alcohol strong on his breath. "How 'bout I get the guys to come over and hang for a bit?" he suggested. Keeli wriggled out of his grasp and moved closer to Wyatt.

"How 'bout you get lost," Wyatt responded raising one eyebrow. Randall looked mildly surprised but not offended.

"Ok, ok, I can take a hint." Laughing and giving Wyatt an encouraging slap on the back, he said his farewell to Keeli. "Cute, let me know when you are done with her," he mumbled under his breath to Wyatt, and giving him a significant look returned to his friends. Wyatt stood seething at Randall's audacity and grappling with another more protective emotion.

"Sorry about that, Keeli," Wyatt apologized. "I thought we could be alone over here."

"No problem. We are alone now," she quickly reassured him, "It was nice meeting a friend of yours."

"You are very gracious. Randall is a good guy, but maybe he should have stopped a few beers ago. So where were we?" Wyatt used a low, seductive voice he hoped would capture an earlier, intimate mood along with a blatantly carnal smile.

"We were talking about your work," Keeli's sensuous voice gave lie to her words.

"Yeah, let's save that conversation for another day." He signaled for the check. "It's late. Let's get out of here."

It was well after midnight as Keeli and Wyatt emerged into the rainy night air. It had cooled off considerably, and Wyatt quickly wrapped both his jacket and his arm around Keeli, to keep her warm and to continue touching her.

He handed the ticket to the valet while they stood huddled under the large canopy doorway. Wyatt pulled Keeli even closer, tight up against him and began nipping at her lips first teasing then demanding. His warm hand was stroking up and down her back, around her sides, sliding a hand against the underside of her breast as if by accident. Under the cover of his jacket, he boldly slid a hand into the top of her blouse, cupped her breast and fondled the hardened nipple between his thumb and forefinger. He felt her thrust her hips hard against him, but she did not stop him, opening her mouth for his kisses.

Lust rushed through his body, settling tight in his groin. He loved the sensation of her skin, her full breast overflowing his large hand and the hard nub of her nipple. He loved how responsive she was, fully giving herself over to his mouth and hand. He was savoring every sensation; all he could do was feel, as he became increasingly aroused. He deepened the kisses, his tongue exploring every warm recess of her mouth, encouraging hers to do the same. His body pressed her up against the wall, taking her mouth hungrily as his erection pressed hard against her.

The sound of a car stopping just feet from them and an embarrassed "ahem" brought him back to his senses and he recalled where they were with a start. He could have taken her right there on the street, pressing her into the rough brick.

So much for friendly. This is just where I want this woman, in my arms and in my bed. She bewitches me with her allure and her laughter, but once we have sex, I will get her out of my system. I need her out of my head.

They ran through rain that fell hard and steady now. Always the gentleman, he got soaked opening her door for her. He nabbed his jacket and threw it over his head before he sprinted around the car, tipped the drenched valet and slid in to the darkness and hushed quiet of the Panamera. They watched as each of them dripped rain on his gorgeous leather interior. Seeing her stricken face, he reached to turn on the seat warmers and the heat.

"It's just water Keeli, and this should warm us up pretty fast," Wyatt said innocently before he realized the double entendre with a wolfish grin. "I guess we are already pretty warm, huh?"

"I think that is the understatement of the day."

They sat in the car a moment, not moving into the now sparse traffic. He hadn't asked her yet where to take her, not sure the best way to phrase it.

A break in the traffic opened up and Wyatt pulled out from the curb and turned the car north. He still said nothing except to ask her if she is warm enough before again adjusting the temperature and airflow in the car.

Wyatt stopped fidgeting with the dials and turned the radio on low. Eric Clapton serenaded them.

"I want to take you home with me," he took the direct approach, "and make love with you all night."

She sat there, no response, looking like a deer caught in a headlight. He waited the span of two breaths but she still looked uncertain. Keeli sat silent, staring, mesmerized by his hands as they rested on the steering wheel. Those hands were on her not too long ago, but now he was not touching her at all. The loss was acute.

"But it was a long day for you, and we both work tomorrow, so I think it would be better if I took you home."

Where did that little speech come from? You could have convinced her, and right now you could be minutes away from being deep inside her.

He waited again for her to contradict him but she remained silent. Not sure why he offered her the out, bewildered by himself, he took the next left driving toward Keeli's neighborhood, weaving around the buses and few cars, putting the performance car through its paces intuitively.

Keeli still said nothing, watching his hands or perhaps staring into space, maybe just listening to the music. He had no idea what she was thinking. The silence would have felt surprisingly comfortable, two people quiet together after a long day, if the unresolved issue of sex didn't hang in the air.

As they drew closer to her apartment, they started the small talk that ends a date - how nice the wine was, his friend seemed nice, thank you and the usual pleasantries.

"Well, we're here," Wyatt said too soon, regret obvious in his voice. He should have said something about the kisses, mentioned another date.

Instead, he reached for the umbrella behind his seat while Keeli quickly opened her door and bolted into the rain. "Wait," he shouted at her back until the closing door cut off his words. He jumped out and ran to catch up with her.

"Don't bother, really. I am wet already," she replied a bit too sharply. The heat of the blush rushed into her cheeks. He replayed her words, trying to understand the blush and caught the double entendre. They share a smile – his appreciative, hers embarrassed.

Holding the umbrella over them both, Wyatt lightly touched his lips to hers, nibbled at her lower lip slightly then kissed her more deeply. He was not touching her anywhere just offering slow, drugging kisses over and over until she pulled back and fumbled for the sleek door handle. He leaned into her, sandwiching her between the door and his erection. Grabbing her damp hair in both hands, he pulled her mouth to his again, probing every crevice with his tongue, tasting her like a starving man.

He pulled back to look into her lovely face, raindrops looking like tears on her cheeks, her mouth lush and pink from kissing. He could drown in this woman. Something made her different, less grasping, more insightful, and so damn sexy. He wanted her until he hurt. Literally. Maybe he should take her home after all.

Before he could form a coherent sentence, Keeli rushed through the downstairs security door and looked back to see Wyatt standing there, a look of consternation on his face.

Wyatt stood in the rain, dropping the umbrella to let the water hit him like a cold shower.What the hell man? What just happened to you? An empty bed was definitely not the game plan. You had better figure out what you want from this woman before she wrecks everything.

CHAPTER TEN

It was Saturday night and, after months of planning and hard work, the Howe Art Museum fundraiser was finally under way. The modern building had been converted to a ballroom filled with flowers and greenery, crystal and china and crisp white linens. Champagne flowed along with top shelf liquor, while wait staff efficiently passed through the crowds guaranteeing that everyone's glasses were filled, and that the scrumptious tidbits were available to tantalize the guests' palates.

The Lyons or Howe name was on auditoriums, museums, concert halls, senior centers, parks, universities and prep schools, and of course, lots and lots of other buildings. However, this museum may have been their crowning achievement. It consistently ranked in the top five modern art museums in the world. Tonight they celebrated the 25th anniversary. They had accomplished a great deal, but Wyatt was now chairman of the board, and he had far more ambitious plans that required generous donations from the people in this room. A lot was riding on tonight's success.

Benefits and tuxedos were not new to Wyatt. Galas were regular weekend events and had been since he served on the youth board for Children's Hospital at age 20. However, this was the first time his name was on everything. LHRE had hosted events before, but usually with his father at the helm. This time he would be in charge, his father watching with a critical eye. It was time for him to carry on the family tradition, while upping the stakes, just as his father did to his grandfather, and his grandfather did to his father before that. Improving the family position was one of the key ways to honor family traditions in the Howe household.

As the oldest, Wyatt understood that the burden fell more to him than to his siblings. He was never allowed to forget the opportunities given to him, the education, training, introductions, everything designed for the moment he would be the patriarch. He was happy with the prospect of being patriarch, but not being president of LHRE. How he could make his father see eye to eye with him on this remained a mystery, but he hoped a roaring success tonight would ease the conversation at least a bit.

Wyatt stood amongst the crowd still hovering near the entrance, greeting guests as they arrived and thanking God for good weather after the rain last week. Events here were so much better when drinks and dessert were served in the courtyard and dancing was under the stars. It really was a great venue and Wyatt longed to increase funding any way he could. The museum's collections were some of the finest in the world, but they could always use more. Wyatt spent much of his time combing art fairs and galleries in hopes of finding the next Picasso, Pollack or deKooning. He looked around the room to see their works proudly on display, drawing the eye from the peacocks strutting the room.

The room was a picture as well, flooded in light, inky black night outside except for a twinkle of tea lights forming a canopy on the terrace. Urns overflowed with flowers in shades of white, green and pale lavender, their fragrance perfuming the room, their leaves thick, green and velvety.

People had been pouring into the space for almost an hour, filling the open space with colorful dresses interspersed with penguin-like men. The noise had been steadily increasing so that Wyatt could only barely hear the strains of the string quartet off to one side of the room, playing Mozart, Shubert and Bartok.

Wyatt had a team of assistants flanking him in case he needed anything managed at the last minute or to help him identify the big donors he needed to greet by name. He had used them to run errands but had recognized everyone without prompting. Not a small feat in a room of over 500 people.

Wyatt watched with satisfaction as his fellow trustees moved about the space, assiduously working the crowd. He saw his father's white hair just over the heads of the tuxedoed men and elegantly coiffed women and could tell, even from afar, that he was in his element. His uber-fit mother, the epitome of elegance, leaned on her husband's arm as if unable to stand without the support.

They made an elegant couple, even now, after almost 40 years of marriage. They had common interests and one common goal –

the preservation of the Lyons Howe family and fortune. Everything they said and did instinctively served that single purpose. Looking at them now, stately, elegant and clearly in their element, Wyatt realized he wanted a woman to spend his life with that shared his goals too, who stood side by side with him during important events, who helped him raise a caring, loving family. He may not share his father's business interests, but he shared his love of family and his desire to be a leader in his community.

Wyatt Howe III clearly loved these moments, his chance to work a room as a king among Chicago's elite. Trey - a nickname given to third like Junior or the dreaded Ivy - lived to see the moneyed and powerful pay homage to him. Wyatt saw him throw back his head and a moment later heard that unique guffaw of a laugh.

He must be separating someone from his or her money. He does it so well and enjoys it so much. He has had years of practice, in business and in philanthropy. Wyatt was hoping to be half as successful tonight as his father was at raising much-needed funds for worthy causes.

Who am I kidding, I have to beat what he delivered last year or never live it down.

Wyatt's date for the evening, the lovely Sloane Huyler, sidled up beside him, slipped her arm through his possessively, took a sip of champagne and comfortably joined Wyatt's conversation with one of Chicago's powerful aldermen. The three chatted comfortably for a minute. "...Isn't that your idea, Wyatt?" Shit. Sloane was talking to him, putting her hand on his arm to draw him back to the conversation. Wyatt's mind had been wandering all night and she had saved him from embarrassment more than once.

"Wyatt," Sloane repeated while squeezing his arm significantly, "Alderman Myers was just saying that extending the hours at the museum was helpful for the restaurants in the area. I reminded him that you pushed for that, didn't you, darling?" Sloane knew he hated when she called him that, but together with the arm squeeze, it worked to smoothly draw Wyatt back into the conversation.

Thank God, dinner is only minutes away.

"It is wonderful for the tourism business overall," she continued. "And that is good for advertising dollars, and hotels too. And that makes all of us very happy." She waved her elegant hand between Wyatt and herself, indicating that her marketing consulting business and Lyons Howe, as well as the museum and the city, benefitted from the increased revenues.

"A win-win for us all. You two make an excellent team," the alderman agreed as she excused herself politely to work the room. Wyatt had heard that line before of course. He understood that everyone assumed he would finish sowing his wild oats and settle down with Sloane. Many close to him had hinted that they expected an announcement soon. Sloane too never missed an opportunity to remind Wyatt that time was passing, threatening not to wait much longer; she behaved as if every date was just the prelude to a proposal.

Wyatt considered her seriously for a wife. She fit in well with his family, was successful in her own right and came from money, overcoming his fear that she might just want him for his. The two met when Wyatt was a regular speaker and mentor for her Kellogg MBA class over three years ago. She had caught his eye at the time with her cool beauty and her pedigree. She came from the right family. Her life of privilege showed in her taste and her confidence. She was a classic beauty. Her pale skin, dark hair and ice-blue eyes made a compelling combination. She was a bit skeletal, but who wasn't in their circle, and she knew how to accentuate her features so that she had a quiet allure underneath her aloof exterior.

She was hard working, joining her father at Huyler Industries, a consulting company specializing in marketing, helping him triple his business and gain large clients including Lyons Howe. She had hinted that she could hand over the reins to raise a family, although Wyatt had never asked. No one would call Sloane the 'little' woman, but she would happily be the big woman behind the big man. She had always been great at sending business his way using her connections on those rare occasions when his had failed. They did in fact make a very good team.

Oh yes, the business loved her and so did his family. Their fathers worked closely together in various business arrangements over the years, their mothers did garden clubs and charitable luncheons together. Everyone would be happy with the arrangement. Moreover, Wyatt sincerely liked Sloane. She was smart, beautiful, polished, accomplished, and willing to experiment now and then to keep things lively in bed.

He joined her now, determined to pay more attention to her

this evening, although she did not demand it.

"You look stunning," he told her belatedly. Wyatt knew her dress was some designer, it always was. Usually he made an effort to know 'who' she was wearing and comment on it since that mattered so much to her. Tonight he asked about her jewelry and about other women's jewelry instead. Not usually something he noticed, she raised an inquisitive eyebrow before she helped him identify the goose egg sized pieces the women wore. He knew his newfound fascination with jewelry had everything to do with his newfound fascination with a certain jeweler. He waited while Sloane finished her descriptions then determined to drop the subject and his thoughts of Keeli. Only later did he consider that he might have given Sloane the wrong impression with his sudden jewelry questions.

"Well, your father is certainly enjoying himself, isn't he?" Sloane would know, having seen his father at both his best and his worst over the last three years. She had been welcomed to dinners, parties and to lounge by the pool with the Howe family as many times as Wyatt had been part of her life at her parents' elegant Glencoe home. They had dated on and off. Wyatt relied on her to be the perfect hostess or date at these types of events and she took him everywhere as her 'plus one.' She was connected with all the 'right' people and had the grace, poise and confidence that came from growing up a Huyler.

Despite all that, she had never gotten his blood as hot and his cock as hard as a few public kisses had last week. Wyatt had confided to the boys after hockey Tuesday night that he felt like a teenager being with Keeli, unable to control himself, hands straying, pulling at her and nibbling on her despite the public setting. He confided this with a measure of embarrassment mixed with pride, and then concluded his story by admitting he took her home to avoid having her turn him down.

The great Wyatt Howe confessed to his buddies that he was going to strike out with a naïve, small-town artist. He wanted her, he explained to the men, but he was not sure she wanted him. Oh, sure, he told them, she kissed him back readily enough; let him fondle her a bit, once she got over her shock. However, he explained, when they came up for air, he felt her repeatedly pulling back.

The boys could not believe he didn't 'go for it' and he took the gentle ribbing from them and acknowledged his insecurity. They were astonished that "love 'em and leave 'em Howe" had not even tried.

"You need to do this girl before you settle down, Ivy, or she will always haunt you as the one that got away," Randall had commanded melodramatically. They had all laughed and changed the subject at the time, but the thought had stayed with Wyatt all week.

Putting Keeli back out of his mind, Wyatt made one more circle of the room, encouraging people to participate in the silent auction, to write that extra check. "Remember why you are here, Howe," he mumbled to himself. "It is not so you can think about lush lips and pillowy breasts."

"Did you say something?" Sloane was looking at him strangely and he knew she at least heard the word "breasts." Thinking quickly, he said, "Yes. Let's get everyone into dinner. I think that would be best."

CHAPTER ELEVEN

$\int$aturday night. Date night. Well, date night for the rest of the world. Not me.

Catching a glimpse of herself in the reflective glass of the long museum window, Keeli saw her grim face and practiced her server smile. Her thick curls were tightly pulled back, the low chignon already giving her a headache. She was shoved into a slightly too tight black and white uniform and extremely uncomfortable 1-inch heels. The uniform accentuating her busty form, she hunched her shoulders slightly to compensate. An extra inch at the bottom would have made her more comfortable too. Well, she could not do anything about that now.

Keeli berated herself for the thousandth time, cursing her lack of backbone. It had taken Theo all of ten minutes to talk her into working tonight despite her objections. The Howe Museum fundraiser was a guarantee that she would see Wyatt but Theo had been relentless.

"I know you think he doesn't want to see you, but I don't care. Five hundred people will be there, and he will not be looking at the servers. If you don't want him to see you he won't, but I need the help, Hon. I lost three of my best servers today and I can't replace them all on such short notice, you would be a godsend."

"My uniform isn't even clean Theo, my pants are still crumpled in the hamper and I have no time to run to the

Laundromat." She thought that would stop him in his tracks.

"I borrowed one for you, it should fit pretty close if not perfectly." That was her last excuse so she gave in. She loved Theo like a brother, knew this was a big night for him and wanted to help. If only it was any other event but this one.

She looked at her reflection again. If she kept her shoulders hunched and her head down she could blend in with the servers. She was sure she could get away with this. She just had to because she would be horrified to run into Wyatt.

First, there was the whole week with no word. No text, no email, no phone call. Second, she knew their positions tonight would be the final nail in the coffin. She would never have a chance with Prince Charming once he saw her in the role of Cinderella. He was the host. She was the server. The gulf between them was enormous.

She had rehashed the date repeatedly. Was she too easy? Not easy enough? Had she been too unsophisticated? Said something stupid? Had his friend not liked her? His kisses had been unbelievably hot, but the night ended so coldly.

She had been mortified; looking in the mirror once she was safely in her bedroom. She looked like a drowned rat - hair wet and straggly, blouse plastered to her wet skin, mouth ripe and red from Wyatt's onslaught of kisses, the soft skin around it pink from chafing against his rougher male scruff. She felt like Cinderella to his Prince Charming then too. Even wet he had been handsome as hell.

So where is my fairytale ending? You idiot, you idiot, you idiot. Why the hell did you have to let him kiss you? And kiss you, and kiss you.

Keeli had been punishing herself since the moment she bolted from Wyatt's car. She never behaved like that on a first date – not ever. She was old enough not to let lust rule her decisions and she knew that at least for her, sex always muddied the waters. She had let his hands roam too far, then run from him without even saying good night and thank you, too confused because he brought her home instead of bedding her.

She was so confused. Keeli knew she would have felt worse if she had slept with him. She knew this was Wyatt Lyons Howe IV. He took a different woman to bed every weekend, women far more sophisticated and beautiful than she could ever dream of being. He was a player, she had read the stories, seen him with the women. She didn't want to be another notch in his bedpost.

Then she was angry and hurt because he didn't want to sleep with her. The man slept with everyone. Why not her? She had been on fire for him. Thought he felt the same. He had cooled so suddenly and then nothing, not a peep since then. What did all those other women have that she was lacking?

The clashing viewpoints had already caused her six sleepless nights, nights waiting for him to contact her, to want to see her again. Six nights and just when she had come to terms with it and convinced herself to let it go, she was about to be in the same room with him.

For a full week, she had questioned her judgment. How could she let him kiss her like that, touch her like that? She had decided he was just copping a quick feel while she had felt a real connection. The conversation had been witty, well matched. At least she had thought so. She had actually believed they might have a chance, a connection that could turn into something real.

Wyatt had been her fantasy man for two years, since the first time she saw him in the lobby of his office building. For two years, she had debated with herself about him. Her heart believed he was the man for her, her head knew he was out of reach. Her head always won, but her heart refused to let go.

Well, it was letting go now. Serving wench and Greek God cannot build a future together.

Keeli moved away from the window, plastered on her server smile and grabbed a tray. Using her hip to push through the kitchen door she moved through the crowd. It was just another catered event.

Keeli was not so jaded though. She recognized that this was a gorgeous, no expense spared party. She was wowed by the elegance, admiring it as she circled the room. Keeli coveted the centerpieces, admiring the skill of the florist and enjoying the mild floral scents. She wondered what would happen to them after tonight, wishing she could take one home, knowing she could not.

The smells in the kitchen were heavenly and Keeli was blissfully aware that at the end of the night she would get to sample all the delicacies. It was one of her favorite things about helping Theo, that and the money. Dylan was here tonight too, taking a night off from the restaurant since Theo was especially nervous. The Howe Museum event attracted the elite of the elite and presented big possibilities for Theo if all went well.

Feeling the pressure, Theo was barking orders like an episode of "Hell's Kitchen". Keeli felt grateful to escape, even if it meant circulating with hors d'oeuvres while wearing too-tight shoes. She wished now that she had gone with her dress flats. So it was a dress, who said she had to wear heels with it? What had she been thinking?

Putting her sore feet out of her mind, Keeli concentrated on the women instead. She knew that these galas were the best place by far for her to see extraordinary jewelry all under one roof. The huge stones were the bluest blues, the reddest reds. The pearls were the size of gumdrops and had the most beautiful luster. They were done in the best of taste, of course, to match the elegant designer dresses worn by Chicago's upper crust. She recognized the Armani gown from the window at Sak's on one woman and the Monique Lhuiller from the Neiman Marcus window on that gorgeous brunette. Both dresses were the perfect backdrops for their jewels. Perfection.

No Carrie Bradshaw in this crowd. All subdued elegance like Charlotte. If Keeli had just one or two of these women as clients, she knew she would have it made. She was finally cognizant of how this business worked. Getting into the inner sanctum was nearly impossible, but once there it would guarantee her success.

When she saw a David Webb bracelet on someone's wrist, she was so mesmerized by the black enamel and diamond snake that Keeli almost dropped a full tray of hors d'oeuvres on a man's spotless shoes. She saw that bracelet just last week in a trade magazine selling for over $50,000. Now, she realized in wonder, she was in the same room with it. At moments like this, she almost missed working at Tiffany's. But, she reminded herself; she had never seen anything there like this David Webb.

Okay, she admitted as she returned to move through the crowd with her tray, she also missed Tiffany's when she remembered the steady paycheck. She missed Mr. Weinstein then too. Her stomach growled, and she realized this would be the first real food she would eat this week. Besides earning some extra cash, the catering food sure beat ramen noodles and peanut butter sandwiches. Theo always did a fantastic job and tonight looked to be the height of luxury.

The alcohol was flowing; the passed trays were filled with wonderful bites of panko-crusted shrimp and little baby back ribs all sourced from local farmers and merchants. She really admired Theo's sustainability policy, but it helped more that he was great to work for, was a good friend and paid pretty well. In addition, he always made sure there was food enough for the worker-bees.

So, the uniform was a bit snug, and shoes hurt on these concrete floors. As long as she avoided Wyatt, the payoff was worth it.

Keeli moved out of the way, as everyone was ushered to his or her tables, moving back to work her station. Keeli was laying out the schedule in her mind. Dinner, then the speechmakers would drone on for a while, the guests would write their big checks, the dancing would start, and the caterers would finally set up the dessert buffet.

Damn, at least three hours before I can get out of these shoes.

Keeli watched as Chicago's one-percent took their seats, 500 people moving smoothly through the room without missing a beat in their conversations. A few women lifted their dresses daintily, displaying the red soles of their Christian Louboutins as they avoided tripping over hems.

I wonder if their feet hurt too. If they do, at least they hurt in fab shoes.

Keeli had been assigned tables 1 and 2. Usually these would

be the big shots, the biggest donors, the speakers, and the hosts. She figured she might even be serving Wyatt's father and mother. While normally she might be curious about them, tonight she just wanted the longest distance possible between her and any Howe.

These people would know just what tonight was costing them and tallying profits in their heads. This needed to be a big moneymaker to be a success because last year was a record breaker and expectations were high. Keeli was relieved she was not in charge. She certainly didn't envy the guys running this show. Their names and their results would be plastered all over tomorrow's Trib, side by side with pictures of the beautiful people.

Keeli knew that Theo demonstrated a lot of confidence in her by asking her to handle these tables. He employed her for enough weddings and parties to know that he could count on her to keep the patrons happy, the service impeccable and the all-important wine flowing. More wine, more dollars. Never failed.

Tonight she did not want the bigwigs tables. She wanted the back of the room, the nobodies, anyone but Wyatt. After losing the battle with Theo about changing tables, Keeli realized that she would have a hard time avoiding Wyatt. The least she could do was give him a heads up, so she bit the bullet and sent him a warning text. She kept it short and sweet. "Wkg museum. Will try to avoid u. Pretend we r strangers if paths cross."

Now that dinner was about to be served, she pushed Wyatt out of her head and focused on doing her job beautifully. She wanted the guests to have a wonderful time, Theo to get kudos and the event to be successful. She was professional about serving, through and through.

The conversations swelled across the formally set tables as the final guests took their seats. Keeli moved toward Table 1, juggling a huge serving tray laden with a tantalizing appetizer of roasted pepper ravioli. Her mouth was watering from the aroma as she weaved between Tables 3 and 4 to get to her diners.

And that is when she saw him. There stood Wyatt Lyons Howe IV in all his tuxedoed glory. He could be the next James

Bond. He had the looks, clean-shaven, icy blue eyes, hair tamed with only the slightest curl at his neck, megawatt smile. He had the body too with his height, wide shoulders and trim hips shown to advantage in what had to be a custom made tuxedo.

He has the ego of course. Maybe he has the killer instinct too. After all, he is killing me. I wonder what he would make of me dying a slow death checking my phone constantly, wishing for something I can never have.

Clearly, he was seated at Table 1. How could Theo have let this happen? Wyatt was helping a gorgeous brunette into her seat. She was obviously his date. Keeli felt her jealousy like a live snake, coiling around her mind.

Reminding herself she was a professional, Keeli considered anyone at her table as her boss for tonight. It was her job to serve them impeccably. Her heart plummeted with the realization that she could not do that and still avoid Wyatt. There was no way to avoid him.

At least she had spotted him first, so she had the advantage, an extra moment to steel herself and control her shock. Starting as far out of his vision as possible, Keeli worked her way around the table until she was serving his date, standing almost directly behind him where he could not see her. She was saving him for last, buying herself as much time as possible. Once he saw her, she knew all her dreams would be dashed, so she was stalling as long as possible.

Wyatt was speaking animatedly about the museum funding to the couple beside him. He was clearly knowledgeable about the museum and its collections. He was definitely one of the hosts, and Keeli wondered how she did not know this before tonight, wondering if he was on the Board of Trustees. Perhaps his date was a board member, because she was almost finishing his sentences, supplying facts and figures as if she had penned them on her palm in preparation for a final exam.

They made a great couple, undeniably. He rested his arm along the back of her chair, and she leaned into him frequently, resting her hand on his muscular thigh. The green monster of envy rose up in Keeli. They laughed together and the brunette leaned close to give Wyatt a soft butterfly of a kiss.

I will remember this as the exact moment my bubble burst. He was a fantasy. I just needed to really see it this clearly. She is perfect for him. She belongs. I am the interloper.

Then he was looking at her as if she was the serpent in the Garden of Eden. The shock was evident as a faint flush colored his cheeks. Their eyes locked for a moment but he broke his stare quickly. That she outstared him pleased Keeli, for some immature reason. And then it was over as if it never happened, he was continuing his conversations while Keeli moved away to her serving station, ever efficient and reliable, getting the remaining appetizers to Table 2.

They both got a short reprieve. Keeli used the time to calm her drumming heart and do her job, praying the worst was behind her. She knew now that he would pretend not to know her, or her him. It was a good plan. Like last week never happened. In her distraught state, she wondered briefly if she had dreamed their whole date. She shook her head to get it together and moved back toward the kitchen.

Keeli leaned against the kitchen wall, bent over trying to catch her breath and resisting the urge to throw up. She eyed a nearby glass of wine with longing. She sounded as if she had just finished a sprint. She resisted the wine and the urge to burst into tears.

"You ok, Keeli?" Dylan's concerned voice came from her friend kneeling in front of her, trying to see her face. "You look like you've seen a ghost, Sug." Even at this moment, Keeli couldn't help but smile. When Dylan called her 'Sug' with that southern drawl of his, it was so sweet. If he called her Sugar, Keeli knew she would lose it, but somehow the shortened version worked for them.

"Wyatt, Wyatt is at Table 1," she stuttered between breaths. "He's at my table with a stunning brunette. Oh, I wish I was dead."

"Miss Melodrama, cool your jets. You barely know the guy; he is certainly not worth dying over. He is Wyatt Howe, for pity sake.

You knew he had a stable of women."

Dylan was not being harsh, just realistic, trying to remind her that they both knew Wyatt was a player when he asked her for drinks.

"It's not like you let him get close or anything, Sug. It was just drinks."

OK, so I might not have mentioned the major face sucking that Wyatt and I did last weekend.

"Show me the brunette," he demanded so she walked over to the kitchen entrance with Dylan and pointed across the room toward Wyatt and his gorgeous date.

"Over there."

"Holy shit, Girl, that is Sloane Huyler. They are a serious couple, I think. He brings her to all of these things. I've seen them on the society pages. I did warn you that Howe was way out of your league. I warned you not to go there, Keeli. He will break your little small-town, no-money, innocent heart. Those folks stick with their own and you know it."

He's right, he's right, he's right. Keeli steeled herself to the tough words. Dylan was not telling her anything she did not know logically, but emotionally those kisses were still wreaking havoc.

She had told herself she was ready but she had not been prepared to let go. Keeli had convinced herself that they were starting something so special that he would overlook her background. She had believed that they both felt something special, that she mattered to him.

Then.... he just dismissed me. No phone, no email, no texts. Maybe I meant nothing to him. I probably meant nothing to him. It was one night for him, one drink. I was the one who thought about him for two years.

"OK, Keeli, go be professional. Back to work."

"You are right Dylan, I am just overreacting."

Giving herself one last stern lecture, Keeli pulled it together reminding herself she was at work, and she needed the job. "Stop thinking, stop feeling and just work," she muttered to herself. She grabbed another loaded tray and headed back out to deliver salads to her tables.

Do not look at him. Just don't look at him and you can get through this.

Keeli started with Table 2 this time working up the courage to go back to Wyatt's table. She was back in her waitressing groove when she returned to Table 1. She felt totally ready now, pretending they were strangers. She just wanted to get through this horrible night.

"So," the white haired gentleman across from Wyatt was addressing Wyatt and his perfect date as she approached the table. "When are you two going to make your parents proud and announce a damn wedding date?"

I swear, the plate just slipped.

Keeli would repeat all night and well into the next day that what happened had not been intentional. She insisted she was too professional to spill a salad right down the back of the brunette's chair and onto her pale pink dress.

"Oh God, Oh God, Oh God."

If there was a God, he was not helping tonight. Say something coherent you idiot.

"Good thing there is no salad dressing on that," Sloane said without missing a beat, smiling up at Keeli, all kindness and patience. As if she wasn't perfect enough already, she was busy saving Keeli's ass by laughing it off. Keeli blushed beet red, stammered several incoherent apologies while her co-server ran to clean up the mess.

Keeli made a beeline to the kitchen fighting back tears. She had never screwed up like this at an elite event, and to do it in front of Wyatt was even more humiliating, beyond bearing.

The bastard is engaged!! What the hell was he doing kissing me like that if he is marrying her?

Keeli was beyond pissed, hands clenching and unclenching along with her jaw. She would obviously have to change tables for the rest of the night. She was done here. What about Wyatt? He just sat there, helping Sloane clean up, fussing over her. He was treating Keeli as the insignificant paid help that she was.

Engaged! I swear, when I see him again... next art show I will give him a piece of my mind and a swift kick in the balls. I swear I will.

CHAPTER TWELVE

Wyatt had been accepting congratulations for well over an hour.

The gala exceeded all expectations, breaking the previous year's fundraising records by an unprecedented 24%. It was a major feat in these economic times or so everyone was saying. No doubt the papers would call it a great success all around – the fundraising, the glitterati, even the speeches were a hit.

Wyatt's speech received the laughs he hoped for as well as rapt attention and a standing ovation. His parents' pride had been particularly gratifying. They would never guess the strain he had been under to pull this off; only Tyler was completely aware of the nerves that had consumed Wyatt all week. Wyatt presented the cool façade of an experienced host to everyone else.

Now he accepted his kudos in stride; he was a natural at this, a chip off the old block. He heard the murmurs through the crowds milling around the museum, reluctant to return to their lives and leave the elegant fantasy created for the gala. They said he would outshine his father as a philanthropist and as a fundraiser. They praised both him and the lovely Sloane ever present by his side, repeatedly calling them a 'power couple.'

Sloane had noticed his distraction all evening, but she gently brought him back each time to focus on the moment at hand. Now she was taking credit as the evening's hostess, saying good night and thank you as people straggled out of the museum to the waiting taxis, cars and limousines snaking their way to the entrance. She regularly drew Wyatt's attention back to the diminishing crowd to assure he said the appropriate farewells.

Sloane peeled herself away from him long enough to join Wyatt's sisters Regan and Missy and Missy's husband, Stephen. Stephen had loosened his tie slightly, but the women were still unwrinkled in their pastels and jewel tone designer gowns, gems glittering against the elegant backdrops. If their feet hurt, they were not showing it.

"What a success tonight turned out to be," a leading industrialist said to the small group. "The evening was flawless, and the auction was truly a marvel. The Mayor was telling me he thought it a brilliant idea to focus on local artists."

"Yes, my Wyatt is clever that way. He is an avid collector. We focus on local artwork, you know." Sloane gave Wyatt his much deserved due while somehow managing to take the credit too.

"Wyatt has developed quite a reputation for the artists he's discovered haunting art fairs and galleries," Sloane explained now. "He has a real eye for potential."

"Yes," the industrialist concurred, "I heard he has amassed quite a collection."

"Wyatt has been purchasing pieces for the last few years, many of which he donated for tonight's silent auction." Sloane could not keep the pride from her voice as she confessed Wyatt's secret to the small crowd of contributors. "Wyatt, of course, is too modest to take the credit, which is why so many of the auction items were donated anonymously."

Missy flashed a scowl in Sloane's direction, knowing Wyatt would not want his contributions made public. Sloane saw the warning but chose to ignore it. "Oh yes, Wyatt has been very modest, but the hard work he put into tonight definitely paid off."

Wyatt joined them at that moment, silencing Sloane with a sharp squeeze to her arm. Ignoring her beyond that, smoothly picking up the thread of the conversation, he told the group that the success was a direct result of a large group effort by dedicated individuals, naming several and pulling a few into the conversation as he extricated himself.

Sloane, hanging on his arm like a leech, finally stopped him as he tried to move away. "What is wrong with you tonight?" she whispered under her breath with obvious exasperation. "You have not been paying any attention to me all night, except to be annoyed, of course. You have been a million miles away. What the hell is going on?"

Wyatt, recognizing he would not escape without providing a response whispered back, "I was just nervous."

"Then what is your excuse now?"

"The adrenaline is still pumping like mad," he explained. "I really need to wind down."

Sloane must have been satisfied with his answer for she released her stranglehold on his arm and flashed him a seductive smile. "I can certainly help you with that," she purred, stroking his back suggestively.

"If it is okay with you, I will put you in the town car and stick around a bit to finish things off. I just need to be alone tonight."

"Of course, Ivy," Sloane agreed despite her obvious disappointment. "If you think you need to do that, I completely understand."

She moved through the remaining throng to say her last good nights, circling the remaining guests before turning back to Wyatt in a feigned afterthought.

"Oh, and do be sure to let management know about that stupid, incompetent waitress. Make sure they fire her."

"I thought it surprising that you hardly reacted to having a salad dropped down your back. It is not like you to laugh off a mishap like that." Wyatt wondered how long she had been biting her tongue, since the demand for Keeli's firing would be a normal response for Sloane.

"Darling, I would never disrupt your lovely event like that," she drawled.

"You don't care that she might need this job, to feed her family perhaps?"

"Oh please, like I care. She may have ruined my dress. It cost much more than she makes in a day. The big loss was mine. She needs to go. Be sure you deal with her now."

"I intend to do just that," Wyatt responded.

Wyatt helped her into the limousine and gave her a perfunctory goodnight kiss. Tyler saw him sending Sloane home and cornered him on his way back into the building.

"Flying solo my friend? If so, let's get out of here and go celebrate properly. You earned it, Ivy. Tonight was an incredibly success. You hit it out of the park, my man."

"I have some loose ends to tie up, Ty, so let me text you in a little while." Wyatt remained non-committal and the two men parted ways.

Now, time to deal with Keeli. After all, he promised Sloane. Smiling to himself he picked up his pace and headed for the kitchen.

CHAPTER THIRTEEN

*D*ishwashers were hovered over the sinks while chefs packed up their knives when Wyatt stormed into the kitchen. Theo caught his eye and motioned with his head toward the rear of the kitchen where 10 people were bent low over the table, laughing and relaxing. They were eating like sumo-wrestlers. He watched undetected by all but Keeli as they shoveled ravioli into their mouths or roast beef or Crème Brule. They crammed the food in around their rapid-fire chatter.

"Yeah, that is the same food that your guests slowly savored in the museum this evening," Theo said with a sad smile as Wyatt watched the wait staff. "May as well be McDonalds."

Keeli hunched lower, trying to avoid Wyatt as he approached the table.

"That smells so great. Any dessert left for me?" he pushed his way toward the table and a seat next to Keeli. She stopped eating, watching him warily as she slowly put down her cutlery. At least he had not caught her earlier tears and temper, both of which she now had under control.

The son of a bitch is engaged.

The look she gave him was far from friendly, but she shifted over to make room for him at the table. Someone slid mocha panna cotta along the tabletop toward Wyatt. He reached for it with a nod and a smile and dug his spoon into the creamy confection.

While he let the flavors explode on his tongue, the staff watched him. Realizing how much he was savoring the sweets, someone passed the crème brule and flourless chocolate cake his way too. Wyatt leaned toward Keeli so that their shoulders rubbed, reaching across her breasts for the desserts, saying nothing. She pulled away sharply, as if burned by the contact. Her coworkers watched the scene unfold, forks in midair. Wyatt ate in contentment, enjoying the sampling of desserts while Keeli quietly seethed.

What the hell is he up to? He has not called in a week. He shows up here with another woman, a woman he is engaged too. I am not, not, not falling for this man's charm.

"Dylan, how's it going?" Wyatt was talking across the table to her roommate, ignoring her except for the shoulder touching hers again. "How do you think it went tonight?"

Wyatt and Dylan began a rehash of the evening's highs and lows from the kitchen perspective, others around the table adding their opinions and stories. The rumors of the successful night had reached the kitchen and Wyatt accepted the staff's compliments with deprecating humor.

No one seemed to care that Wyatt was wearing a beautifully tailored tuxedo. He was just eating leftovers with the rest of them, as if he belonged at the table.

"I am so glad to hear it. Up front it appeared flawless...well almost flawless." Keeli heard him saying now, Wyatt was looking straight at her and she knew that damn flush was moving across her cheeks. "There may have been a tiny mishap, but nothing I can't deal with."

"Finished?" Without waiting for an answer he grabbed her arm and pulled her from her chair, her fork clattering to the table. "Good night all and thank you again."

Shoving a wad of bills into Theo hand he muttered "tips" and continued dragging Keeli from the kitchen. Despite her obvious reluctance, no one moved or said a word as he pulled her from the room.

He took long strides out of the kitchen to a dark corner of the gallery. They were both spoiling for a fight, spitting like cats, eyeing each other like fighters in the ring.

"Let go of me, damn you." Once they were out of earshot of the kitchen, Keeli tried to break free from his vise-like grip on her upper arm. "Wyatt, you are hurting me. Let go. Go be with your skinny fiancé. Damn it. Go away." Keeli heard the tremor of tears in her voice and clamped her mouth shut.

"What the hell happened in there tonight? Salad! You dropped a damn salad down my guest's dress? What were you thinking? Were you thinking at all?" Wyatt was fuming, barking questions but giving her no chance to answer.

Getting to the darkest corner of the room, Wyatt forcefully pushed Keeli into a dining chair, releasing her arm only long enough to trap her by placing his hands on the table on either side of her chair. She tried to stand, but he pushed her back into the chair, just stopping himself from shoving her. Realizing how angry he was, Keeli opted to quiet down and stop struggling.

"What they hell were you thinking?" He spat the words at her. "You just about ruined the dinner, destroyed a couture gown, not to mention get yourself fired."

"I swear Wyatt," Keeli heard the pleading in her voice and scolded herself to stop that immediately. In a cooler, more professional voice she continued, "It was an accident, purely an accident. If you want Theo to fire me, you know he will. You are too important a client." She said the last with more conviction than she felt, trying to placate Wyatt. It would kill Theo to fire her, knowing how badly she needed the job.

"Damn, I wish I hadn't had that last scotch," Wyatt muttered under his breath, more to himself than to Keeli. She looked up at him with confused green eyes, the blue, outer rim wider and bluer than normal, even in the dark room. He was staring at her, apparently trying to calm himself down a bit. She had no idea what he was thinking.

The silent stare continued until she felt uncomfortable. A nervous Keeli snaked her tongue out to lick her bottom lip. Before she understood what was happening Wyatt hauled her to her feet, yanked her tight against his hard frame and began nipping that bottom lip between his teeth. He was stealing her breath, kissing her wildly.

She smelled like the kitchen and a touch of floral perfume almost completely worn off. He tasted of scotch and warmth. His arms were wrapped tight around her, squeezing off her air supply then providing it with his mouth. Neither could let go, and the kiss went on until Keeli finally roughly pushed him away.

"What the hell are you doing?" she blurted out, as if she had not returned his kisses with equal passion. "Stop kissing me, damn it. Go back to your fiancé." She spat the last word at Wyatt with loathing.

"Sloane is not my fiancé. She is an old friend." Wyatt let the words come in an exasperated sigh. "When I need a hostess for these things she comes to the rescue. What kind of asshole do you think I am? If I had a fiancé would I have been out with you last week?" He stared deep into Keeli's eyes.

"Then why did that man call her your fiancé and ask about your wedding date?" She stabbed the question at Wyatt, highly suspicious.

"People have been unsuccessfully trying to marry me off, Keeli, and you know it." He appeared sincere and his eyes, locked on hers, appeared to be searching for understanding.

Can I believe him? Do I dare trust him? It is true that the tabloids always say he is engaged to this one or that one. Besides, I want this. There is definitely something between us.

Keeli had talked herself into forgiving the misunderstanding. Still, she tried to think straight.

Of course it might just be lust. Lust is not a relationship, girl. You want to believe him, don't you? Your want your Prince Charming cause you never ever learn. Oh what the hell.

"I believe you and I am pretty sure you aren't an asshole. Or at least a total asshole," Keeli heard herself say, curving her lips flirtatiously. She intended to make him suffer, at least a little, so she surprised both of them with her quick words of forgiveness.

"Of course, you also didn't call all week?" She put the statement out as a question, and then berated herself for mentioning it.

"The gala. This damn gala has taken up every waking minute this week. I asked Sloane to attend with me months ago, or I would have invited you." Keeli heard both the truth in his statement and the doubt. Would he have invited her to sit at the table with his family, with moguls of Chicago politics and industry? She doubted it. "By the way, why didn't you let me know you would be here? A heads up would have been nice."

"Come on, Wyatt. We both know you're not in a position to invite me," Keeli opted to confront Wyatt now, before they went any further. "Look at the two of us, for God's sake. I am a friggin' waitress at your event. You are the host. We are living in two completely different worlds. You would never have invited me and we both know it. And I texted you hours ago. I gave you a heads up."

"Well, I am inviting you now, dinner tomorrow night? Would that work for you?

Pick you up at 7:30?" He waited with confidence, knowing Keeli would accept, checking his text messages while he waited and cursing under his breath when he found her earlier message.

"What's the point? We should just stop this now." Shut up idiot. Just say yes.

"Come on," he cajoled, turning on the Howe charm, "you know there is something between us. Let's give it a chance and see where it takes us."

"I am working for Theo tomorrow night," she responded reluctantly. "I can't duck out at the last minute, even if I wanted to."

"And you do want to, right?" Wyatt picked up on her last statement. "So Monday? How 'bout dinner Monday night?"

"Monday works." Keeli responded carefully, as if she is reviewing a mental calendar. "It will have to be after seven. Ok with you?"

"Sure, I will pick you up at seven," Wyatt was quick to agree.

"No, don't pick me up, I will be out. Just text me where to meet you and I will be there," Keeli said cryptically. Appearing not to probe while probing Wyatt asked what neighborhood she would be coming from, so he could pick something convenient.

"Oh, I will still be in Logan Square, just not at home." Keeli was providing no additional information. She could tell he wanted specifics and enjoyed the moment, feeling briefly like she had the upper hand at last.

"OK, I will text you, seven o'clock Monday. I better get out of your hair and let you get going." He started to walk away, "wait, how are you getting home?"

"Dylan and Theo will take me."

"Oh yeah, okay," Wyatt accepted her answer but she could sense his disappointment as they said goodnight.

Monday night. OMG Keeli-girl, you are getting a second date! I hope my heartbeat returns to normal before then.

Keeli laughed as she returned to the kitchen. Luckily, the team had finished cleaning up but left her some food. Giving Dylan thumbs up, she dropped into a vacant chair, wide smile on her face as she dove into the goodies with gusto.

CHAPTER FOURTEEN

Wyatt met Tyler a little after 2:00 a.m. He was exhausted; knew any sane person would go home and get some sleep. However, the adrenaline was pumping, both from the gala and his confrontation with Keeli. He was too wired to sleep. One drink and a little quiet rehash of the night with Tyler would be the perfect way to wind down although he hoped to wind down with Keeli in a much more enticing way. That hope was now futile.

Entering the Seven Lions, Wyatt recognized several people he knew sitting in the restaurant. He nodded an occasional hello as he moved straight to the wood and leather bar. The large square space had four good corners in which to get some privacy and would be open as late as the patrons were drinking.

He found Tyler nursing a scotch at the bar and ordered one for himself, arranging to have it brought to a quiet corner. Comfortably ensconced at the high table in the shadowed space they only stood out slightly in their tuxedos.

"I wasn't sure you would show," Tyler began with an accusing tone as he leaned forward conspiratorially. "Were you holding out for a better offer?"

Wyatt was reluctant to discuss Keeli and Sloane with his friend, but figured Tyler might offer some beneficial advice.

"I was chasing down Keeli. You know, the redhead from last week. She was a server tonight - at my table of all things. She was the one who poured salad down Sloane's back."

"I heard about that," Tyler was chucking. "So sorry to have missed seeing it first hand. Sloane must have been spitting mad. Did she demand to have her fired?"

"She kept her cool when it happened, but as you would expect, she demanded Keeli be fired." Wyatt wondered even as he said the words why he remained involved with such a cold-hearted woman.

As if reading his thoughts, "She really is a cold bitch, Ivy, you know that right? Tyler probed. "She is beautiful, and she makes a good hostess, but why do you keep her around? I have never understood why you didn't break it off before now. The longer you date her, the more she will expect from you."

"I hear you, man, and you are right. I need to cut her loose once and for all. But we have a history, you know? And now our families are tight."

"Yeah, but sometimes history is just history. You have to let it go to have a future." Sometimes Tyler said the most obvious things. He was like Yoda, with great delivery of wisdom. This was one of those moments, cutting through the alcohol and landing like a rock in the pit of Wyatt's stomach.

"You are so right. I want Keeli, not Sloane. I need to break it off with Sloane once and for all," Wyatt said with determination.

"Wait a sec. Not so fast," Tyler interrupted. "You cannot date a waitress, Ivy. Think of your family. Shit, think of your friends. We would all be hanging around at some event while she waited on us? That would not be cool."

Before Wyatt could reply, Tyler continued, "I've seen her, Ivy. She's pretty. She has a girl-next-door look and I know you can be a sucker for that. But you need someone who fits into your world. Not a waitress. Someone with the right style, with the right education and breeding."

"She is not a damn horse, Ty, and she is not a waitress either." Wyatt was getting annoyed and it was apparent in his rising voice. "She is an artist, a jeweler, and a good one, damn it."

"Okay, okay," Tyler put his hands up in surrender, "She is a jeweler who does a great waitress imitation. The result is the same, Ivy. What else do you know about her, really? Is the little jeweler girl any better a choice for you than a waitress would be? Really, you cannot make this work. With everything else you are about to do with you father, it is not a good time to bring home a girl from the wrong side of the tracks."

"You are not being fair, Ty. So what if she's a farm girl? That does not make her uneducated or from the wrong side of the tracks."

"Well, it sure as hell doesn't make her one of us."

Wyatt's head sunk lower over his scotch, knowing that Tyler's words are absolutely true. "Yeah, I hear you, man.

"I can't explain it, Ty. She completely disarms me." He pulled his shoulders back and looked Tyler In the eye. "When I am with her it is like everything falls away and it is just the two of us." Wyatt had a far-away look in his eyes as he continued, "She has blindsided me. She is sarcastic, and witty, and sexy as hell. She has enough education and street smarts to be an interesting conversationalist. We just fit somehow. Like we can finish each other's sentences. Most of all, it seems like she really cares about me, you know. Me, not the name, not the money. Like I can trust her."

"Holy shit," Tyler could not hide his surprised reaction. "When did you fall so hard for this woman?"

Embarrassed by his confession and Tyler's reaction to it, Wyatt looked down briefly, fiddled with his drink and shredded the cocktail napkin beneath it before finally making eye contact again with Tyler.

"She is hot, man. Smart, funny and hot as hell. Any man with two eyes would want her. She kisses unbelievably and I just know she will be amazing in bed." Wyatt knew the best way to survive this grilling was to downplay the romance and emphasize the sex. Otherwise he was certainly in for a lecture from Tyler along with the third degree.

"Okay, yeah, she is hot," Tyler conceded. "But can't you pick a hotty with the right pedigree instead? Someone like your sister

Regan, for example? Now that is a woman who..."

"Do not go there." Wyatt barked, cutting Tyler off. "That is my sister you are talking about so I would tread lightly, my friend," Wyatt gave him a friendly warning but it halted the conversation just the same.

"Noted," Tyler acknowledged the warning and changed the subject to safely review the night's events, giving Wyatt richly-deserved accolades, sharing anecdotes about people's comments or behaviors and eventually coming back to Wyatt's family.

"Seriously, Ivy, Regan came alone tonight?" Tyler had been chasing Wyatt's younger sister since their high school days. "No date, huh?"

"You know Regan thinks of you like her big brother, right? You have no hope there," Wyatt told his friend bluntly, "You need to let that go, once and for all."

"Yeah, like you are letting go of Keeli?" Tyler came back at Wyatt with the snide remark.

Having no response, Wyatt fell into silence. Finally Tyler restarted the conversation with a new subject. "Your father, he looked so proud, but he did not look too healthy. It was good you were in charge this year. I am not sure he could have handled everything. He looked so damn proud of you though."

"Yeah, my father," Wyatt looked sad. "The cardiologist says he is doing much better, but I thought he looked pale too. Maybe we need to invite him for a round or two of golf, get him out in the sunshine. Get him out of the office a bit more. Or suggest he get away for a while."

"Yeah, we could do that. Randall would play too, or my dad maybe. I will pick a day this week and invite him if you want?"

With the subject safely in neutral territory, the two men considered one more round. Wyatt determined it was past time to stop drinking and get some sleep. Despite the late hour, Wyatt decided to walk up Michigan Avenue, his long strides eating the pavement quickly, and the image of blue-green eyes dancing in his head.

Good thing he could rest tomorrow. He had big plans for

Monday for which he would definitely need some sleep.

CHAPTER FIFTEEN

Keeli woke well-rested and optimistic Monday although it took her brain a few minutes to work through the haze and remember why.

A date! I have a dinner date with Wyatt tonight.

Lying in bed, Keeli basked in anticipation while stretching tired muscles and mentally planning her day. She needed a game plan so she could get everything done. Most days she just mixed work with more work but today she looked forward to mixing business with pleasure.

She had some phone calls to make. Mondays always began with calls to at least five boutiques asking to show them her jewelry, looking for someone to consign her work. She was still focusing on Chicago area retailers, in case one or two would agree to let her bring something by to show them.

Next, she needed to build up her inventory after her success at the Gold Coast Art fair. That would be the better portion of her day. By four, she would have to get cleaned up to be ready for summer tutoring at the library by 5:00. And then, her glorious, glorious date with Wyatt Howe.

Picking up a pillow from the floor, Keeli returned it to the messy bed, along with all the covers she had kicked off during the night. She wished again for air conditioning, but it was a luxury she could not yet afford. The window fan just could not keep up with Chicago's heat and humidity but the window unit would have to wait until she could buy supplies and pay her share of rent and utilities.

Maybe next summer, she planned optimistically, drawing on her light robe over the camisole and bikini panties she'd slept in. She figured she was alone in the apartment, but the robe was a precaution in case she was wrong. She headed for the bathroom.

Dylan had been gone for hours. He had a lunch shift to prepare at the restaurant, but it turned out Theo was still sleeping although it was almost nine, later than Keeli liked to start.

At least she didn't have a battle for the single bathroom today. She ran through her morning ritual at her leisure, her mind already designing jewelry.

Padding on bare feet to the kitchen, she fixed a cup of tea and then threw on tired, soft jeans and a faded t-shirt while it steeped. Lacing her Keds, she went back to grab her mug and took it and her cellphone through the middle door off the long hallway, closing it quietly behind her.

Keeli turned on the window fan in her "studio" and sorted through her designs. She planned to work only in sterling silver today. She looked forward to finishing her calls and heading to the basement of the building where the storage lockers and coin laundry were and where she did her soldering and metal work.

At least it will be cool downstairs.

Keeli pulled a dog-eared hand written list toward her and scanned her notes. The paper looked like chicken scratches at this point but it had originally held the names and numbers of over 100 Chicago-area boutiques and galleries that she knew carried designer jewelry. Now more than half were crossed off her list, the scribbles in the margins just confusing her as she looked for numbers she had not already tried. She had started adding names and numbers of shops that were smaller, less exclusive, or further away.

She was on page three of the six-page list, halfway finished, and so far, she had been able to take her designs to about one-third of the places she called. No one had been willing to strike a deal with her. Part of her issue was the commission. She had talked to very successful retailers but she was an unknown with no leverage so they wanted 50% or more from each sale. She could not survive on less than a 70/30 split.

Think positive. You have a date tonight after all. It will be a very good day.

Someone she met in the kitchen Saturday suggested she reach out to a florist/gift shop owner in Evanston, so she tried there first. Pay dirt! The woman invited her to come later in the week to show her some designs and Keeli set up the meeting for Wednesday. Of the remaining calls, one woman hung up on her with a curt "no thanks"; one politely suggested she call back in November with her holiday collection, a stall tactic she had heard several times before. The next person asked her to call back later when she could talk longer. That one might be promising.

The last call, to a small gallery/store also in Evanston, showed potential. The manager explained that they were always looking for new talent and suggested she come in with at least 10 pieces later in the week. Keeli was ecstatic, thanked her – perhaps a bit too effusively – and scheduled an appointment for Wednesday afternoon. Then she sifted through the pieces she had left after the last few art shows, identifying ten pieces across a mid-price range, and checked to be sure her portfolio was handy. She was ready for Wednesday with two appointments a scant two miles from each other.

Feeling pleased with herself, Keeli picked out several designs for rings, earrings and bracelets, pulled the colorful beads and semi-precious gems she needed for the work she hoped to complete that day and put them in her toolbox to carry down to the basement.

She had taken stock after Gold Coast, as she did after every festival. Earrings and rings were selling the most this summer, so that was where she would focus this week, until her stock was replenished. Sketching a few modifications based on the materials she had available, Keeli was finally satisfied with her plans.

Today she would focus on the selections she would make in

sterling, saving the more detailed designs and wax molds for the gold pieces she will send out for manufacturing. Someday she hoped to have the equipment – and confidence – to do it all herself, but she was not there yet.

Grabbing a second cup of tea, Keeli heard Theo moving around at last. Keeli hollered to him that she was heading downstairs, grabbed an apple from the fridge and her keys from the counter. There was a bounce in her step as she descended the three flights to the cool, damp basement with her toolbox of supplies. Switching on the overhead light and her worktable lamp, Keeli was quickly immersed in her work, laying out stones, soldering settings, working with opals, beads and black pearls, forming shapes and etching designs in metal.

When her stomach starting growling seriously she glanced at her watch surprised that three hours had passed. Keeli wandered upstairs, thrilled to find a gorgeous Greek salad with grilled chicken, courtesy of Theo. There were such advantages to living with a caterer and a chef. Left on her own, Keeli would forget to eat, or make boxed macaroni and cheese, but the boys always fed her well.

It was almost three; the apartment was sunny and hot. Closing the shades to block out what heat she could, Keeli inhaled the delicious food and then peeled off her sweaty clothes, dropping them in the corner of her bedroom before wandering down the hall to take a shower. Piling her hair high on her head, she waited the requisite five minutes for the water to be hot and then jumped in and washed quickly. Keeli remained under the stream an extra minute before jumping from the rapidly cooling water. The cool water felt good on a day like today, but a cold shower was not desirable. Getting a hot shower in this apartment was something of an art.

Soon Keeli was standing in front of her meager wardrobe struggling with what to wear. Her choices were pitiful and she knew it. She could ask Theo for advice, but opted not to although she had little confidence in her own choices. Grabbing her phone, she called upstairs hoping to solicit help from her wonderful neighbor, Lynn, but got no answer. She would have to do this on her own and she felt perspiration gathering between her breasts at the thought.

Not knowing Wyatt's plans, she was doubly unsure what was appropriate. Wrapped in her towel, she held up blouses and dresses waiting for something to click. Fortunately, after about six tries she was content, if not elated.

Keeli looked at herself critically in the dresser mirror. The colorful print dress was cool and cute, appropriate for a summer Monday night and not too faded. The scoop neck was more alluring than sexy; the snug waist showed off her curves and the length was not too short. She tested to be sure it didn't ride up too high when she sat down and was satisfied. Grabbing a pair of flat sandals and a sweater for the air conditioned library, she added some smoky eye shadow and mascara, brushed her teeth being careful not to spill toothpaste on her dress, grabbed her sketch pad and headed out the door while still applying lip gloss.

Keeli walked the few blocks from her house to the library slowly, not wanting to overheat, looking forward to working with the kids. She loved volunteering two days a week. It got her out of the house and allowed her to give to the community. She had started working at the library as soon as she moved to the neighborhood. With the mayor's summer reading initiative and literacy programs and now with art programs for teens, the library was bustling.

Many teens were in the program because their parents hoped to keep their children out of trouble while they worked. These kids mostly participated grudgingly, until Keeli won them over. A few were really talented though, showing excitement, interest and promise. It was those kids that kept Keeli coming back from 5:00-6:30 week after week.

She arrived and dropped her sketchbook on the back counter, carefully buttoning the sweater over her scooped-neck dress so that no cleavage was showing. These teenage boys didn't need to be getting any ideas.

Keeli pulled out supplies for collage making - today's project.

Kids trickled in

for about fifteen minutes, the last around ten past the hour. Jose was always late; it was a game he played with Keeli, trying to get a reaction. Eventually the small group of 14 settled around tables to rip pictures from magazines and lay out their designs. Keeli encouraged them to select a theme, something they cared about or were interested in exploring. She explained that their best work would come from feeling passion. The teens giggled, so she changed tactics.

"Pick something important to you. Tell a story with your collage. I expect to know your stories when I look at them." This direction got them moving, focused on their work, tongues between teeth with concentration. Keeli circled the room, providing encouragement and advice, watching their works come to life.

The time passed quickly. When 6:30 rolled around Keeli was very proud of herself. The teens had done outstanding work, enjoyed themselves and she had only checked her phone about a dozen times.

She wandered the room slowly, reminding everyone to finish and clean up their tables. Alone finally, she put away the supplies and went to the ladies room to check her appearance one last time. The full-length mirror was a welcome treat and she twisted from side to side to check the dress with the shoes. Too late now to wear heels, although she knew she would be sorry. Touching up her lip-gloss, she moved toward the outdoors. It was still warm and beautiful, a perfect summer night except the humidity.

Wyatt texted just before five asking if Dunlay's on the Square would work for Keeli. It was perfect, she loved the restaurant and bar and it was only about a ten-minute walk from the library. They served a terrific house-made Sangria that would be perfect for this warm night. She texted 'perfect' with a smiley face and confirmed that she would be there at 7:00.

Now, she just needed to control her jitters and kill fifteen minutes so she would not be early. She contemplated stopping back home for higher heels, but it was in the wrong direction so she resisted. Instead she did some deep breathing to help calm down and doodled in her sketchbook. At 6:55, she walked to Dunlay's, arriving eight minutes later to find Wyatt sitting at the bar looking devastatingly handsome.

"Right on time. I like that," he greeted her with a wide smile, showing his approval. He jumped off the barstool and took her small hands in his before leaning down to chastely kiss her cheek.

His sandy hair was rumpled as if he had run his hands through it several times, perhaps in exasperation, but otherwise he looked flawless. He was wearing an elegant custom suit in a shade of gray that cooled his blue eyes. His crisp white shirt looked fresh and the beautiful patterned tie looked expensive.

He looked fresh enough to be starting his day, not as if he had come from a full day of work. He was so polished. Someone else in a suit might look overdressed but Wyatt just looked like he belonged

"You look great," he mumbled under his breath as his eyes scanned her appreciatively from the riot of red curls haloing her face to the tips of her painted toes, peeping out of the open-toed flats. "Any trouble getting here?"

"I walked from the library, so it was easy," she responded, self-consciously smoothing down her skirt as he signaled the hostess that they were ready for their table. They followed the skeletal woman in her painted-on jeans to a quiet table. Keeli felt like an amazon next to the wraith checking out Wyatt. Keeli was relieved to see that he never gave the woman a second look. When she saw the privacy surrounding the table, Keeli was comforted. The restaurant was full of women eyeing Wyatt like dessert and she was happy to have a buffer zone around them, even a small one.

"The library? Getting more classics for your upcoming shows?" Wyatt teased, holding out her chair, waiting patiently for her to slide in. She caught him peeking down the cleavage of her dress. He was frozen there and she got a moment of feminine power from the effect she had on him. The hostess left them menus and slipped away. Once she was gone Wyatt leaned over and gave Keeli a slow, breathtaking kiss, then took his seat as if nothing happened.

Keeli was nonplussed by the action, sitting stunned while Wyatt picked up his menu and perused it.

"What's good here?" Without waiting for an answer he returned to their earlier conversation. "Okay, back to the library," he prodded. "I am anxious to get to the bottom of this mystery."

"No mystery," Keeli explained regaining her equilibrium by studying the menu a moment. "I volunteer two afternoons a week, helping teens with art." Wyatt raised an eyebrow, impressed and she took a few minutes to describe the work and share some anecdotes about some of her favorite kids.

"I mentor kids about the same age. Hockey," he explained. "They are so interesting, volatile sometimes, emotional, sensitive. I know exactly what you are talking about with your kids. And talented; some of them are so talented."

Keeli latched onto Wyatt's empathy and talked more about her time at the library until the server came to take their order.

"But this must be boring you to death," Keeli said after several minutes, although Wyatt did not look bored at all. He had been laughing at her funny stories, helping with ideas for her problem kids. In fact, he was being the perfect date, she realized with surprise. She was so sure they would have too little in common to get through a second date. She was gratified to discover how wrong she was.

"What about the rest of your day," he interrupted her musings. "How does Keeli Larsen spend a typical day?"

"Well," she dragged out the word, collecting her thoughts, "I guess I don't really have a typical day. Most mornings I work in the studio, to take advantage of the light. I make sketches, wax molds, and try different stones to get ideas. However, some mornings I read other jeweler's brochures, magazines, that sort of stuff.

"And I have all the business stuff to do – read up and apply for juried shows, tax and inventory paperwork, web updates, mailing lists. The stuff I hate."

Keeli checked to be sure Wyatt was still paying attention. He smiled, encouraging her to continue.

"Afternoons I build, solder, etch. I do the heavy lifting in the basement of our building and that is nice and cool in summer, which I need by afternoon. No air conditioning," she responded to the question on his face.

"That is the routine, and then I have stuff I do weekly. Monday I call stores and galleries trying to get placement. Tuesday I update Etsy and deal with orders there. Wednesday I call on galleries and shops because it is the day I have a car, Thursday I am in the studio all day and Friday I do design stuff, unless I have a show that weekend. If I have a show, Thursday and Friday are dedicated to packing, moving and set up. Pretty boring, I guess."

"Not boring at all," Wyatt assured her. "In fact, I would love to watch you work sometime." He watched as the statement raised a blush to her cheeks. "Not one for an audience, I gather?"

"Oh no, I would be so nervous if you were watching me. It is hard enough trying to sell in front of you. You make it look so easy, but I get shy trying to hawk my own stuff. It sounds so egotistical to me. It comes so naturally to you though."

"Number one rule of sales," Wyatt slipped into lecturer mode, "believe in your product and let it sell itself. I believe in your jewelry." He said this last sentence very matter of factly, but watched across the table as Keeli's eyes grew wide with surprise, their blue-green pupils dark and expressive.

"You have no idea how much that means to me," she confessed with a small break in her voice. "No one believes in me. No one." Getting her emotions under control, Keeli tried to change the subject. "What about you?

He shook off her effort and insisted she explain her last statement. After trying to avoid answering, Keeli finally revealed a little more of herself to Wyatt.

"When I left Gilman my family pretty much turned their backs on me. Oh, they love me, don't get me wrong, but they think I belong at home, with them. My brothers don't like the idea of me alone in the city, for one thing, but they also believe I should be caring for my mom. Since my dad died, she lives alone in that big house and they like to guilt me about it.

"So they undermine my efforts when they can. First they questioned my ability to complete school, slowing me down when they could by requiring my help on the farm. Then they tried to tell me I had no talent, suggesting I try beading, small pieces that I could sell at the farmer's market. They have no clue about my ambitions."

"They have no clue how good you are," Wyatt answered forcefully, anger simmering below the surface. "You are a grown woman, entitled to make your own choices. Are they really that small-minded?"

"Oh no, I am painting them black and white, when it is really so gray. They love me. They want me near them. They want to be able to keep an eye on me. They want me to settle down and have a family. If I have to hear one more crack about turning 30 with no husband and kids, though, I may explode. All my friends are in Gilman, married to local men, raising children. It's not that I don't want a family, because I do someday. However, not right now, not with any of the boys from Gilman and not at the expense of my career. They just don't understand my choices, so they don't support them. If I didn't have Clarice, Theo and Dylan, I think I would go crazy.

"And maybe everyone back home is right, Wyatt." She looked stricken. "After all, I was doing this a long time before striking out on my own. I am almost broke and getting nowhere. Why should they believe in me? All indicators are that I am not good enough." She clapped a hand over her mouth to stop chattering. "Sorry, it's just hard to keep going when no one wants to show my work. It's obvious that the experts don't think I have what it takes. I guess they are right."

"Don't give up yet," Wyatt encouraged her now. "I believe in your talent, your strength and your determination, Keeli. You are an inspiration to me. You have done what I only dream of doing."

Blushing, Keeli murmured an awkward thanks and shifted

direction. "Enough about me already, tell me about a typical week for the famous Wyatt Lyons Howe, IV."

"So formal? First, I am not famous." She watched as he cooled to her instantly and knew she had hit a nerve, but not sure how. "My life is about meetings mostly, with sellers, with buyers, with architects, developers, city planners. Otherwise, I am looking at spreadsheets then meeting with investors, bankers, and lawyers. It's pretty dull stuff."

Keeli knew that Wyatt was playing down the significance of his work, so she asked questions to find out more about his current projects - two large buildings being developed for Chicago's up and coming South Loop neighborhood and a huge office complex in the western suburbs. These represented tens of millions of dollars, he explained nonchalantly, and a lot of time with his father.

"The whole family is involved in the business," he was explaining now. "My sister Regan would love to run the show, but my father won't hear of it. He rules with an iron fist and questions and reviews everything we do. I feel like I am still in first grade with him, still on trial. It annoys the crap out of me."

Keeli heard the heat in his voice, but then he reined it in and continued, "My brother Ethan trained as an architect and is involved with project design. Regan and I run the offices with my father. She is strategy. I am finance and technology, such as it is. We both do acquisitions. We all do the development work. Regan and I make a great pair behind the scenes but she loves the work more."

"And Melissa?" Keeli noticed he never mentioned the sister she met at the art fair. "She didn't strike me as the real estate mogul type, somehow."

"Missy? She did a short stint running our HR department. She is really good with people and great with personnel issues, but right now she is a stay-at-home mom to my two perfect nieces."

Wyatt's face took on an indulgent sweetness as he thumbed his phone before proudly displaying a photo of two adorable, sandy-haired girls.

"The older one is Alden, she is three and just discovered 'Frozen'. The little one is Abigail. She just turned one but she already wants to do whatever Alden does."

"They are so adorable." Keeli loved watching Wyatt's face as he showed her a few more pictures with such obvious love and pride. She could tell he loved his nieces, wondered if he might want children of his own. Keeli knew to bite her tongue rather than ask him. It was way too soon for those questions.

"Do you see them often?" she queried instead.

"They live up north, in Glencoe, but now that I have the Panamera, I see them more than before. I like taking the drive up there more than I did in the truck, so I visit pretty regularly."

"A truck? You drove a truck!" Keeli could not believe her ears. "I cannot picture you in a truck."

"Yep, mud flaps and everything," Wyatt responded with pride. "I work at construction sites, remember?"

"I didn't realize. I usually see you in suits," Keeli reminded him, gesturing to his beautiful gray suit. "From now on though, I will think of you like a 'Wild West' Wyatt. I have a completely new image of you. Less Wyatt Howe, more Wyatt Earp."

"Well, technically it is an SUV," Wyatt laughed. "But it is a Land Cruiser, and so it handles like a truck. Does that make me suit guy or cowpoke?"

They were both laughing as the server came to deliver their order. Keeli stole a quick glance at her phone and was surprised to realize they had been sitting over drinks nearly an hour. Wyatt ordered another round of drinks then reached across the table and took Keeli's hand, removing the phone from her grip gently and running his thumb over her palm seductively.

"Have to be somewhere else?"

She quickly reassured him. "There is nowhere else I need or want to be." He flashed her a relieved, cocky grin and his thumb glided up to her wrist, then back to her thumb in a hypnotic rhythm. Keeli's thighs tightened against each other in sudden arousal as she searched her now-empty brain for speech.

Wyatt was searching Keeli's eyes with his icy blue ones and

she could see his lust there. He knew the effect he had on her, even here in a crowded restaurant. Keeli had that feeling she often got with Wyatt - that she was out of her depth.

Her lips parted slightly and her tongue peeked out to moisten her bottom lip. Wyatt released her hand with a smug lift of his lips.

Oh yeah, he knew exactly what he was doing to her. Exactly.

"So, tell me what you do for fun, Keeli." He was all politeness.

He must have felt that right? He must know we keep sharing these incredible moments. How does he keep so damn calm?

Keeli took a deep breath, mentally shaking off the desire that was consuming her completely from just that small stroke on her wrist.

"I work two jobs, as you well know. I work art fairs on weekends and work in the studio during the week, so there is not much time for fun." She sounded so wistful until she caught herself and changed tone, not wanting him to think she was complaining. "Not that I am unhappy, mind you. I just wish I had more free weekends. I have only been in Chicago a few years really, so I love to go to the art museums, the parks, the stores, ride my bike along the lake. I jog pretty regularly, watch movies, read, and hang out with friends - the usual."

"The usual," Wyatt repeated, cynically. "None of that would be my usual, but I am thrilled to hear you like the art museums."

"Yes, I read that you raised a lot of money for them Saturday. Fine job, Mr. Howe, very fine job." Keeli dropped her chin and her voice to sound like a pompous, old man and Wyatt laughed at her bad imitation while acknowledging her well-deserved accolades with shy pride.

"Yes, thank you, that is more like my definition of 'the usual.' My usual is black tie fundraisers, a little tennis and golf with business associates, family dinners." None of these sounded like fun as he said them. Keeli called him on it.

"Those sound like obligations to me," she voiced her opinion with a bit of trepidation. "What about fun, just plain fun?"

"Hockey," he said without missing a beat, "Playing and

watching hockey. Great food, great music, great women." Wyatt raised his eyebrows in a perfect Groucho Marx imitation, taking the sting out of the last words. "Spending time with you."

"Speaking of great food..." Her heart was hammering in her chest. Keeli felt a blush creep into her cheeks and changed the subject. She had never been one to pick at her food in front of a man but she backed off a bit from her usual habit of bending low over her food and shoveling. It was a bad habit she picked up living with brothers on a farm. Putting her fork down she reminded herself she was not on the farm anymore.

"Mm, this is delicious," she raved around a mouthful of chicken potpie. "Is the fish good?" She noticed that he was eating his fish and chips with a fork. "You idiot, just pick it up with your hands and make a mess. It tastes better that way."

Unlike Keeli, Wyatt did not speak with a mouthful, swallowing before answering. "I have never been here before but the food is very good. I picked it from Yelp because it had good reviews and it was convenient for you. Is it a regular spot for you?"

"Not too regular, but I have been here before. Just pick it up," she goaded him again, until Wyatt finally picked up the flakey fish and took a huge bite.

"OK, it does taste better this way," he laughingly admitted. "Don't tell my mother."

That allowed for an easy segue and the conversation flowed. They conversed easily over their food, about restaurants, Logan Square and how Keeli liked living there, about his friends and family, a little more about hers. When the server offered dessert, he checked with her before declining for them both and suggesting one last round of drinks instead. They agreed to move back to the bar.

The server delivered the check and Keeli reached for her oversized bag. "What do I owe?" she asked sincerely.

Wyatt looked shocked. "Nothing, of course, I can buy dinner." She had obviously offended him.

"I know you can," Keeli offered, "but you bought last time

and I thought it would be right if tonight I paid at least my fair share."

"Do you know how ridiculous you sound?" He was very offended, Keeli realized. "I have more money than God and you are offering to split the check?"

Wyatt's voice was rising. Keeli was not sure what she had done wrong, but she knew she needed to diffuse the situation.

"I don't date much, Wyatt. I thought this was the right thing to do." She thought the excuse was lame, but it was all she could come up with. "Besides, just because you have money doesn't mean I can spend it for you."

"Are you for real?" Wyatt's anger dissipated as quickly as it had appeared. He handed his platinum card to the server and asked him to bring the receipt to the bar. He planted a kiss on the top of her head, well below his in her flat shoes.

"Thank you for dinner," Keeli offered in a small voice.

"It was my complete pleasure," Wyatt responded and gave her a quick kiss on the lips. "My complete pleasure," he repeated. "And Keeli," he waited until she made eye contact, "I will always be the one to buy dinner. Got it?"

Keeli nodded mutely understanding that something had shifted in their relationship. She could not tell if he was still angry but at least he had implied there might be a next time. She held on to that notion to get past the awkwardness of the moment.

They found two stools at the bar and Wyatt helped her onto one before sitting facing her on the other. Her legs were caught between his strong thighs and he placed one hand on them lightly, the other idly stirring the ice in his scotch. His thumb started those lazy circles on her thigh that he seemed to make unconsciously.

"I like you, Keeli," he stated bluntly. "I really like being with you."

"I like you too Wyatt, and I like being with you," she responded carefully wondering where he was going with the statement.

"I would like to spend more time with you."

Nothing like just putting it out there. "I would like to see more of you too."

"Good. So, what is your schedule like? I am asking because I would like to take you to Ravinia for some music. Would that appeal to you?"

"Oh definitely," Keeli bounced with excitement. "I have never been to Ravinia, but I imagine it must be fantastic to listen to music under the stars on a beautiful summer night." Since moving to Chicago, Keeli had seen the ads for Ravinia, a 36-acre park with an open pavilion and musicians from the symphony to heavy metal bands performing all summer.

"There are some jazz greats in concert this Saturday. We could go?"

"Oh I wish I could," Keeli sounded so disappointed. "But I have the Milwaukee art fest this weekend so I can't make it. It's Milwaukee, so it is a big deal for me as well as a very late night."

"Another time?" He sounded less confident.

"Definitely another time," Keeli replied, "although I don't know much about jazz."

"It's a deal. So...Do you have plans in Milwaukee?"

"Well, it depends on whether I rent a car or ride with Clarice I guess."

"Let me take you. I will drive you up and get us a place to stay, or do you already have one?" Wyatt was taking control of the situation a little quickly for Keeli's taste, although the offer sounded fantastic. He was caught up in the planning, speaking faster and faster.

A weekend with Wyatt. It would be paradise, but I have so much work to do. Ahh, screw the work Keeli. Take a chance.

"Oh wait, I can't do the whole weekend." Wyatt was thumbing his phone as he spoke. "I promised to be in Lake Forest Sunday for dinner. I could still take you up Friday and stay over until Sunday morning, if you could get a ride back? Lake Forest would be on my way home. And...If I can make it late enough, we can both go to my folks, then I could bring you home."

Even as the words left his mouth Keeli could see he was wishing he could take them back.

Take her to meet his family after knowing each other a week? Well, knowing each other a year, but only dating a week? Besides, she was not his typical date and they both knew it. She would appall his family.

"I could not impose on you like that," she said now, helping them both save face. "It will be crazy for me Friday, leaving at the crack of dawn and setting up. I will miss seeing you but maybe we can do something the following week instead."

"We'll see." He sounded dejected.

Maybe he is rethinking the whole 'I like you' thing. I guess I blew this one after all. Maybe he is just relieved that I turned down that dinner invitation. He dodged a bullet. We both did.

"Actually," he offered after a pause, "I was thinking it was time to talk to my father about leaving the business. Sunday dinner would be a good time for that, so maybe it is better if I go alone."

"Wyatt, that is such a big step. Are you ready?" When he nodded yes, she continued, "I think it will go really well. You have a plan, potential investors, and they are your family. They love you and want you to be happy, right?"

"Oh Keeli, you have no clue, do you?" He asked, no bite to the words, just an observation. "They may love me, but they love honor, duty and family tradition a whole lot more."

"So do you, you believe in all of those," she encouraged him.

"Really? Then why break with tradition and shirk my duty? That is the question he will ask me. My father will want to understand why I am willing to break his heart. It will not be pretty."

The mood was suddenly somber. Wyatt was shredding a damp, cocktail napkin, so Keeli put her hand over his, calming him. Wyatt folded his hand around hers, and wrapped his legs around hers pulling her to stand, leaning against him for balance.

Wyatt tightened his thighs around her legs and reached his hands around either side of her face wrapping his fingers in the curls at the nape of her neck. Pulling her firmly toward him he kissed her softly, leaned back to look into her eyes. He must have seen what he was looking for because he hauled her still tighter against him, kissing her deep and hard, demanding for her to respond in kind.

Keeli's world was turning upside down. Wyatt had her surrounded with his hands on her face and neck, his legs holding her in a vise grip as his mouth plundered hers. The kiss was strong, warm and compelling. She returned it from the depths of her body, pressing her breasts hard against his unyielding chest, matching his tongue stroke for velvety stroke. There was a fluttering low in her abdomen as she slid even closer so that their bodies were touching from lips to hips. She could not get enough, did not care that they were in a public place. If he had tried to make love to her right there on the floor, she would have let him. She wanted him with her whole being.

Fortunately, or unfortunately, he was aware of their surroundings. He slowly broke off contact, leaning back slightly, dipping in for one short last kiss, and then releasing her so that she fell back onto her stool. Her eyes cleared of their dazed look to find him smiling down at her like the cat that stole the cream. She gave him a shaky smile in return. She was still in a sensuous haze so he took her hand and helped her from the barstool as if she was a precious porcelain doll.

"Let's get out of here." He was standing behind her, hand on the small of her back, pointing her toward the door. His hand slipped lower as they maneuvered through the crowd, coming to rest on the curve of her behind. It was a longer version of that brief caress in the elevator last winter, but unlike the elevator encounter, she knew his hand was there intentionally, savoring her curves through the thin material of her dress.

"Feels so good," he mumbled under his breath. "Feels familiar."

Did he just say that or did I imagine it? Does he remember the elevator the way I do?

When they were standing on the street in front of the restaurant she came to herself again. "I live that way," she pointed north.

"I am parked that way." He pointed south. In unspoken agreement he took her hand and they walked toward his car. He stood tall and imposing above her. She shuffled a bit closer to him as they walked. There was nowhere she wanted to be more.

The summer sun had set and the sky was shades of deep blue and black. Keeli and Wyatt stepped in unison, hands clasped, hips touching, moving from shadows to the halo of a street lamp, to shadow again. The air was warm and humid, a typical summer night. Wyatt had his suit jacket slung over his shoulder dangling from one finger. Keeli's sweater was draped over the top of her hobo bag. She could feel the warmth of his skin through the fine cotton of his shirt; see the ripple of his muscles when he moved. She longed to run her hands over his taut body. They moved silently through the night, totally aware of each other.

With a 'beep beep' Wyatt unlocked the car then he opened the passenger door, casually tossing his jacket behind the seat. He took her bag and sweater and dropped them onto the passenger seat, pulled her to him, closed the sleek door and leaned her against it. He rested his body against hers, sandwiching her between his warm skin and the cool metal.

She loved the weight of him pressing against her, found his commanding presence an incredible turn on. He was looking at her like he wanted to devour her but he didn't move, just pressed his body from hips to shoulders tight against hers, seeking something in her eyes.

"You know how much I want you, right?" There was a challenge in his husky voice.

With his erection hard against her belly, Keeli knew exactly how much. She nodded yes, unable to speak, incredibly aroused, longing for his kisses, wanting his hands all over her. Only a tiny corner of her brain was able to remind her that this man was a player, that he would not stay interested in her for long. She tried valiantly to listen to her foggy mind telling her he would break her heart, telling her not to go to bed with him.

No matter how loud her brain was screaming, her body was shouting louder. Her breasts were smashed against Wyatt's rock hard chest, hardening her nipples. She could feel his heart pounding in a staccato that matched her own. She smelled the scotch he breathed, longed to taste it on her tongue.

He was holding her hands low and tight against her thighs, fingers laced with hers. Her heart was racing with anticipation of his kiss, and after what felt like eons to her she finally watched his head dip slowly toward hers, lips resting hot and full against her own, pinning her tighter still between his rugged form and the sleek car door, demanding she give him everything.

His mouth ravaged hers relentlessly, his tongue seeking every warm crevice. The rough stubble on his cheek rasped against her smooth skin, making her insides tingle. She tried to push her body still harder against him, restrained by his hold on her hands. She craved even more contact. He brushed gently against her swollen lips with his own, catching her breaths. She felt as if she coming up from beneath the sea, grabbing air only to return below, hungry for more.

Keeli was unsure how long they kissed before a voice called from the sidewalk "get a room!" Breaking their embrace, Wyatt gave her the shy smile of an embarrassed teenager. Keeli avoided eye contact with Wyatt until her lifted her chin with his finger, forcing her to look in his eyes.

"He has a point I guess. We should take this indoors." Wyatt was leaving the choice to her but he was obviously asking if she wanted to go home with him or invite him to her place. The latter was out of the question. She would be mortified to have him make love to her in her old, creaky, single bed with the boys right down the hall. Nothing seemed less romantic to her.

Look at you, thinking not if but where. So much for protecting your heart.

Keeli felt that internal battle, brain versus body. Could she go back to his place? Was it too soon? Was it too much? Lust was still coursing through her veins.

Waiting for her response but sensing her hesitation, Wyatt backed up and away from her body, adjusting his clothing a bit as he did.

"I suppose I better get you home," he stated with conviction. Keeli felt her ambivalence give way to disappointment.

Didn't he want to try harder? Why was he being such a gentleman again?

"I suppose," she said, backing up to open the car door, only to find he'd reached for the handle as well. He brushed her hand, then held it, and squeezed it gently. She slid into the cool interior, calming her breathing and contemplated changing her mind before it was too late.

What to do? What to do? Am I just doing this to play hard to get? Is hard to get even an option? I want him. He wants me. It's obvious. It's inevitable. You are a grown woman Keeli Larsen. What the hell are you waiting for?

Wyatt leaned across the console to give her a light kiss on the lips. "Why so serious, gorgeous?"

The question sounded too polished and rehearsed, like a line he said to all the girls. It helped Keeli make up her mind. Deciding he was too much of a player, she resigned herself to sleeping alone until she knew him better.

"Just sad to see our lovely evening end," she told him with a shy smile. "But it has been a long day. For both of us, I imagine." Done. She had made it clear she planned to go home.

Wyatt took the hint, bringing the engine purring to life before turning to her in the intimate space.

"I can tell you're not ready, Keeli. I can wait – not long – but I can wait."

They made the four-minute drive to her house in silence.

"So you are away this weekend?"

"Yes, in Milwaukee," she reminded him.

"Yeah, I really hate to wait a full week to catch up again."

Catch up? Catch up? Is that what we are doing here?

"So, how 'bout coming to watch me play hockey tomorrow night? A lot of wives and girlfriends come and we go out for a beer afterwards. It might be fun for you to meet everyone and I would get to spend more time with you. What do you think?"

"That could be a lot of fun. Sure," Keeli was trying to hide her excitement.

He wants to see me again tomorrow! This is a dream. This must be a dream.

"I really hate to ask but is there any chance we can meet there? I can bring you home after but I have meetings right up to seven." Keeli could tell that this bothered him a lot. It delighted her that he was so chivalrous.

"Well, I guess, just this once," she allowed, smiling.

"I will text you the address. Seven o'clock and you should wear something warm. It gets cold in the arena."

Wyatt double parked in front of her apartment, and went around, opening her door and helping her out of the car. He did not release her hand, holding it tight and swinging her arm a little as he walked her to the door.

"I'll walk you up," he offered as she inserted her key in the lock.

"Totally unnecessary. Save your strength. You will need it on the ice tomorrow."

Wyatt wrapped his warm hand around her cheek and neck, pulling her close for several hot, deep kisses before releasing her with obvious regret.

"Until tomorrow." His voice was husky with desire.

"Thank you for a wonderful night," she responded in a low, breathy voice before stealing yet one more kiss, rising on her tiptoes to catch him unaware.

"Until tomorrow." She turned, moved quickly through the door and headed upstairs in a sensual fog.

Tomorrow could not come soon enough.

CHAPTER SIXTEEN

Tuesday went by in a blur for Keeli although she knew she was productive because her inventory was replenished and ready for the Milwaukee art fair. She was completely out of money and gems at this point. She would need a big success this weekend in order to buy more materials and to eat. Although she was proud of the pieces she created, she knew that Milwaukee offered a lot of competition and she not entirely confident that people would buy. If they didn't, she had two options: a lot of catering work or moving home with her tail between her legs. Neither option appealed. This would be a make it or break it weekend.

Needing to get that pressure off her mind, Keeli cleaned up the last of her work for the day, and went to take a much-needed shower before going out tonight.

How did one dress so that they were warm enough for the ice rink and cool enough for the summer heat? And how did one do that with a tiny wardrobe of mostly work jeans and tees? Keeli wished she had more girlfriends, or at least one friend her size that she could borrow clothes for tonight. Oh well, she would have to make do.

She piled her hair high on her head to keep it dry and took a quick shower. Then she indulged herself, slathering her skin in a lovely floral-scented lotion she had received from Theo for her birthday last August. The bottle was almost empty so she made a mental note to hint for more next month.

Wow, my birthday is approaching fast. Twenty-nine and on the verge of running home to Mommy. How depressing is that?

Giving herself a mental and physical shake, Keeli took down her curls and let them hang loose and wild around her oval face. Her eyes looked very green and very wide as she added a touch of liner and mascara and some lip-gloss. She headed down the hall to fight with her closet.

Standing in her best skinny jeans and a pink lace bra she held a top or blouse up against her body, made a face and put it back in the closet. She repeated the process, unhappy with them all. She dug through the small dresser of drawers for an alternative, coming up with a pink camisole that was ok for wearing as outerwear, if slightly low cut. Digging in the bottom drawer for a sweater to wear over it she rationalized that she would be covered by a sweater, so the camisole, with its lacey edge and ribbon, could help capture the dressy/ sexy/casual look she was going for.

She grabbed a black sweater, pinching a few pills off of it to make it look a little less worn, pulled it on and checked herself out from front and profile. Deciding it would have to do, she pulled on warm socks to keep her feet warm and her Keds.

Next, she turned to the jewelry haphazardly scattered on the dresser and hanging on the doorknob, selecting a pearl and onyx looped silver necklace hanging from a sterling chain. It was perfect, very contemporary, small enough not to overwhelm but large enough to make an impression. Pairing it with a pair of black pearl earrings, Keeli felt as ready as she would ever be.

Keeli yanked off the sweater, standing briefly in front of the window fan to cool off. After a few minutes, she felt human again, grabbed her keys and her purse, wishing the hobo looked better. Keeli headed for the bus stop with just a few minutes to spare.

Moving quickly two-thirds of the way down the bus, Keeli was grateful to find a seat for the 30-minute ride. She took out the "Hockey for Dummies" book she had checked out of the library that morning. Sure, she had Blackhawk fever during the Stanley

Cup playoffs just like every other person in Chicago, but that didn't mean she understood much of what she had been watching.

When she arrived, the arena was almost empty making it easy to find her way to the cluster of women. They were gathered at middle ice about eight rows from the Plexiglas partition. Trying to decide where to place herself, Keeli stayed toward the edge of the group, approaching shyly.

"Hi, I'm Keeli," she reached her hand out to shake that of the first woman she came upon. A lovely, pixie of a woman turned toward her. She appeared to be a bit younger than Keeli, hair sleek, makeup perfect, dress, boots and wool coat all designer. Keeli saw her eyes travel from Keeli's mass of untamed curls to take in her faded jeans and worn Keds before extending two fingers into Keeli's as if afraid to make contact.

"Joan," she said briskly. "Bud's wife. And that is Leslie, Sue, Barb…" at this point Keeli knew she wouldn't remember the names of the fifteen or so women sitting there, although she would remember the names of the two adorable toddlers she met, Cole and Amanda. About half the women were older, half younger, half wives, half girlfriends. All looked at her like she was a homeless person who walked in off the street carrying a dreaded disease – maybe two.

"I am a friend of Wyatt's," she said now and watched a few women relax and warm up to her a bit. One in particular, whose name she did not catch, motioned her to come sit with her. The larger group returned to idle small talk - the weather, which bar to go to after the game, a bit about home decorating or gardening. Keeli noticed with interest that no one spoke about a career.

"I am Tyler's latest," the woman explained, self-deprecatingly. "You've met Tyler I think? At CAC a few weeks ago?"

"CAC?"

"The Chicago Athletic Club. The bar."

"Oh, of course, I think we waved from across the room. I'm Keeli." She extended her hand in greeting. "I guess I am Wyatt's latest."

"Molly." Molly offered her hand in a warm handshake and Keeli let out a breath she did not realize she was holding.

"So, how long have you two been dating and where did you meet?" Molly was wasting no time grilling Keeli, as two other women sitting in the row above them leaned forward to eavesdrop.

"Oh, that night I met Tyler was actually our first date. So, three weeks or so, I guess." Keeli was mentally counting as she spoke. "We actually worked in the same building for a couple years, but Wyatt would never have noticed me. Then we met again at the Wells Street art fair. We have been touching base at art fairs ever since."

Jeez, did I say too much? What has Wyatt been telling them?

"Well, Ivy certainly kept you a secret. We all thought he was still with Sloane," one of the eavesdropping women piped up in a snarky voice.

"You knew he broke up with Sloane a long time ago," Molly retorted to Keeli's relief. "Don't start stirring up trouble now, Sam."

"Not completely," Sam's voice dripped with venom. "He took her to the gala just last week."

Turning to face completely forward and lowering her voice Molly continued, "Samantha and Sloane are friends but she is just making trouble cause she likes to. Totally ignore her."

"I will, and thanks," Keeli gave Molly a grateful smile as the guys took to the ice in full gear. She couldn't really tell them apart under their helmets and padding but by reading the names on their jerseys, Keeli could find Wyatt, and determine he was a defenseman. "Are they practicing or playing?"

"Playing. It's a city league, mostly for fun. Of course, they are guys so it's always competitive too. They can't help themselves." Molly laughed before turning her full attention to the game.

Keeli followed as best she could, understanding the rudimentary rules and penalties, asking for help from Molly now and then. At the end of the first period, Wyatt's team was down by one goal, looked exhausted and was huddling to strategize. He gave Keeli a brief wave from across the ice, but nothing more.

The boys were in better form for the second period, preventing their opponents from getting more than a few shots on goal and scoring three goals themselves. At the end of the second period, they were visibly pumped and many came over to say hi to the women. Wyatt motioned Keeli to come away from the group, meeting her at a small break in the Plexiglas.

"Having fun?" He was shouting to her before she even reached him. She could see that he was enjoying himself and preening a bit for her.

"Yeah, I am. You guys are good."

"Tonight, but not always," he offered modestly "You meet the girls?"

"Molly seems to have taken me under her wing."

"Great, cause Tyler is my best bud. If you two get along we can see more of them. You know, double date or something."

"That would be great," Keeli watched the teams taking their positions again on the ice. "You better go."

Wyatt leaned over and planted a quick kiss on Keeli's mouth. "Later. Wish me luck." He was already skating away.

Back at her seat it became apparent that the kiss changed Keeli's position with the women. Some of them warmed up a bit more but Samantha was predictably frostier.

"So, where did you buy that adorable camisole, Keeli?" her voice was dripping with sarcasm. "And are those Keds I see you wearing? "

"I don't remember, Sam, sorry. And yes to the Keds, I live in them. I am on my feet a lot, so they are perfect for me," Keeli was not going to be dragged into a designer war that she would only lose.

"What about that necklace?" Barb leaned in. Sitting on Molly's other side she had been acting friendly if a bit reserved but with this query she was either trying to help Keeli or hurt her more. Keeli wasn't sure.

"Oh, I made it. That is what I do. I am a jewelry designer."

"You made that?" three voices chorused. "Really?" "It's

fantastic."

"Wow, you are really good," Molly chimed in. Keeli relaxed in her seat, gratified by the compliments. She felt better about being there as she turned her attention away from the women and back to the game. At that moment, Wyatt was slammed into the boards by a huge forward from the opposing team. Keeli cringed at the rough contact but Wyatt slammed back with equal force then skated away as if nothing happened.

The third period was decidedly rougher with both teams under pressure as the clock wound down. The score had not changed but the tension was palpable on the ice and in the stands. The cheering sections for both teams grew louder, with the two toddlers screaming until their faces were red and their mom scolded them to 'cool it a little.'

The body checks grew in number and a fistfight broke out pulling in five of the 12 players on the ice, and two from the benches. It stopped the action briefly, but the anger burned out quickly and they returned to the game after a brief word from the referee. A few players made trips to the penalty box but that was to be expected. The game ended with Wyatt's team winning 3-1. Cheers erupted from the ice, the toddlers and with a bit more reserve, from the women as well.

"Now what?" Keeli followed behind Molly and Barb as they gathered their belongings and began moving toward the exit.

"We meet the guys by the back door in about ten minutes and head out for drinks which leaves us just enough time for a bathroom break. Come on."

Sure enough, the entire group of women headed to the ladies room as a single unit, used the facilities, freshened hair and lipstick, and divested themselves of sweaters and scarves. Then, again as a single unit, they headed toward the side entrance to the facility and gathered on the sidewalk, rehashing the game and making driving plans to wherever it was agreed they would go.

Five minutes later, the men trickled out, hair still wet from showers, large duffle bags in hand. Hugs, kisses and congratulations went around from the whole group. No one made an effort to introduce Keeli so she hung back on the outer fringe of the crowd, waiting.

One of the last to exit the building, Wyatt came out laughing at something Tyler said and headed over to Keeli. He dropped his bag and twirled her around with joy.

"We won! Great game, huh?" He bent to steal a swift kiss. He was like a five year old, elated by his victory and grinning from ear to ear with male pride.

Tyler nodded his recognition before sweeping Molly up in his embrace and shouting to no one in particular, "So team, where we headed?"

"The usual," several people responded as either question or statement and 'the usual' was agreed upon as Wyatt led Keeli toward his car. She was walking beside him, holding hands when he stopped behind a black Range Rover and it beeped to unlock. Lifting the tailgate window, Wyatt lobbed his bag into the back, slammed the door with some force and turned to see Keeli looking confused.

"No Panamera?"

"My sweaty equipment in the toy? Not a chance," he explained as he opened the door for her. "I save it for hot dates instead." The man was oozing boyish energy and charm. Keeli found the combination irresistible, falling under his spell, grinning like a lovesick fool.

"So, just where is the usual?"

Rather than answer, Wyatt pulled Keeli against the center console, pushed his hands into her hair and soundly kissed her, thrusting his tongue to taste her moist warmth, sucking gently on her bottom lip and sighing with contentment.

"I missed you last night," he confessed unabashedly. "You should have been in my bed all night, losing lots and lots of sleep."

Keeli's face flamed in response. She chewed her bottom lip and turned to face the front windshield.

How the hell do I respond to that when I agree completely?

Fortunately, Wyatt didn't seem to expect a response. He

maneuvered the SUV into traffic and headed toward her neighborhood. "Revolution Brewing," he told her, answering her earlier question. "This late on a Tuesday we can usually have most of the place to ourselves. Plus, they have killer burgers. Are you hungry? I am positively famished."

"Sure, food sounds great. You should be famished; you worked your butt off for three periods without a break. Shouldn't someone have come in to give you a rest?" Keeli thought with pride that she sounded like someone who knew what they were talking about.

"Oh yeah, definitely. But we were short a few guys tonight."

They rehashed the game period by period during the rest of the short ride to the brewpub, easily parking the SUV on the street. The manager jerked his thumb toward the corner obviously recognizing Wyatt as a regular.

Keeli and Wyatt made their way through the crowd and to an intimate corner of the large space. They were not the first to arrive and pitchers of beer and plates of wings and large pizzas were magically appearing at the tables before immediately disappearing into the hungry mouths of the men. Refills would be needed soon as the plates emptied in moments.

Between bites of pizza, Wyatt took Keeli around and made introductions to men from both teams as well as their wives and girlfriends. Some were pleasant and welcoming, many sized her up openly and were chilly but unfailingly polite. Keeli had a hard time getting comfortable with the group despite the warm reassurance of Wyatt's large hand tight around her waist.

Wyatt leaned in regularly whispering phrases like 'I can't wait until later' or 'we are going to have one hot night'. He regularly trailed little kisses across her cheek or neck. He knew how to get to her, and quickly. Each little touch or whisper warm across her earlobe sent a corresponding clench into her lower belly.

Offering her something other than the fast flowing beer, Wyatt kept Keeli close, pulling her along with him to order her a glass of wine from bar. "Pinot," he said to the young female bartender, who nodded her understanding, checked Wyatt out thoroughly then went down the bar a few steps to get the wine. She returned quickly with the ruby liquid and a come-hither smile. Wyatt took the glass, ignored the smile, and placed two crisp twenties on the bar, mumbling "keep it" under his breath.

He never even looked at her, and she is very pretty, but really, forty dollars for one drink? That is either some wine or some tip. Keeli, you are out of your league here.

She couldn't hold her tongue, "Forty dollars for a glass of wine?"

"Nah, but she needs the tip." He offered nothing further as Keeli felt jealousy snake through her, wondering how Wyatt knew what the woman needed.

Was there a woman he didn't know? A woman he hadn't had?

The transaction at the bar just added to Keeli's feelings of inadequacy. She could see that everyone knew each other, so she felt like an outsider. In addition, the women were all so much more elegant than she was and not particularly interested in getting to know her better.

Wyatt either didn't notice or didn't care. Standing close, he was touching her repeatedly. If his hand was not tight around her waist, his arm was about her shoulders. He was constantly pushing a stray curl from her face or making small circles on her palm. It should have been enough to make her not care what other people thought, but this mattered to Keeli. These were Wyatt's friends and she wanted them to accept her and eventually to like her. She understood that she was new to the group, recognized that they came from different backgrounds, but if she could not bridge this gap with people who wanted Wyatt to be happy, she worried that those who wanted to keep them apart would easily succeed.

This was her proving ground, and so far it was not going well.

Just when she was ready to throw in the towel, working up the nerve to tell Wyatt she wanted to leave, Barb came over, singling her out with small talk before managing to detach her from Wyatt.

"I was resisting bothering you tonight. I mean who wants to talk shop when they are celebrating a win, but I really wanted to ask you about your necklace again." Barb was being apologetic while still pressing her goal. "Do you sell them or is that a piece you made just for yourself?"

"I sell them," Keeli responded. "Everything I make is for sale, unless it is a custom piece commissioned by a client as a one-of-a-kind."

"Would it be rude or inappropriate to ask how much a piece like that costs?" Barb asked, pointing at Keeli's necklace.

"This piece sells for about $600 plus the chain, which would be priced by length."

"Well, with that chain for example?"

"With this chain it would be $720, plus tax of course. The state has to get its cut." Keeli's heart was racing at the possibility of getting someone in this crowd interested in her designs. They were just the customers she was trying to reach. Still, she held back, allowing Barb to make things happen. She wasn't here to sell jewelry, but…

"Really?" Barb dragged out the word so that Keeli could not tell if that was a high or low figure in the woman's mind. Keeli knew it was a fair price considering the cost of the gems alone, and she suspected it was not a figure that would make a dent in Barb's budget. Again, she held her tongue.

"I would really love to buy it from you."

"Great," Keeli was working hard to hide her elation. "It will look beautiful with your coloring." She calmly offered to send it to Barb along with an invoice as early as tomorrow. She asked Barb for an address, realized she would have to dig for a pen and walked over to the bar to rummage through her hobo bag.

"Oh, I was just planning to take it now. I could give you a check. But perhaps you prefer to wait." Barb sounded disappointed making it clear to Keeli that she did not intend to wait. Keeli suspected that Barb, and the rest of this crowd, got exactly what they wanted, when they wanted it.

"You could have it tonight, I guess," Keeli wanted to be

accommodating but felt uncomfortable about handing over the necklace. "You would have it by the weekend otherwise," she offered instead.

"Oh, the weekend. I would still prefer it tonight." She was already reaching for her checkbook, writing in the date and amount, not even bothering to get Keeli's name to include on the check. "You can fill in the rest," she tossed over her shoulder as she put on the necklace and wandered away without a word of thanks. Keeli noticed with annoyance that there was no tax included. She would have to pay taxes from her profits.

Wyatt rejoined her as Barb walked away, wrapping both arms around her and pulling her close for a scorching kiss.

"What was that about?"

"Barb just bought my necklace," Keeli answered with pride, expecting Wyatt would be excited for her.

Instead he got a thunderous look on his face, lowering his voice to a husky accusation.

"You are using our date to sell to my friends?" he spit the words at her. "How dare you? You need to leave." When Keeli hesitated, looking at Wyatt with confusion, he grabbed her arm. "You need to leave NOW!"

He was fuming at her, dragging her toward the door, obviously planning to send her home. He was vibrating with fury.

"She asked me, Wyatt," Keeli was trying to calm him down, not sure what just happened. "She asked me if it was for sale." Keeli resisted his strong pull before he pulled her too fast for her to remain upright. "I just said yes, and she bought it. Damn it, Wyatt, stop pulling my arm. You're hurting me."

Wyatt pulled up short and Keeli plowed into him. He turned, holding her tight and taking several deep breaths. "I misunderstood. I thought you were using this opportunity to sell your jewelry to my friends."

"I wouldn't do that. And frankly, I am hurt that you would think I would."

"My mistake," Wyatt conceded without apology. He took another calming breath and ran a hand through his hair in frustration. "It is time for us to leave anyway," he said, suddenly sounding exhausted. The playful hints about their night together were forgotten.

"Yeah, I guess so," Keeli tried to keep the hurt from her voice.

"Come on, I'll take you home."

"I think I just want to walk," Keeli said now, knowing an argument would ensue with chivalrous Wyatt. "That way you can go back to say your goodnights at least, and finish your beer. You need to unwind with your buddies."

Surprisingly, Wyatt did not argue. He simply walked her to the sidewalk. There, without discussion, he handed her into a cab, gave the driver two twenties and kissed her briefly on the cheek before shutting the door.

So much for walking.

She was not irritated with his high-handed behavior, Keeli realized. She was too caught up in being confused. She had never seen anger like that, so quick to flair and so quick to dissipate. She had clearly hit some hot button, but he was in no mood to discuss it, and frankly, neither was she.

Keeli sat back in the taxi for the short trip home, realizing that she had made a big sale tonight and should be enjoying the moment. She wasn't. She was realizing that Wyatt had made no overture toward seeing her again, no effort to be with her for the rest of tonight. What had started out so promising had fizzled in a matter of moments, and she still didn't understand why.

Shit. Shit. Shit. I have lost him for sure now. Do not dwell on this. Do not dwell on this. It was just a couple weeks of your life – ok, and two years of fantasies, but who's counting? You can get over him. You knew he would dump you eventually.

Keeli felt the tears flowing down her cheeks before she realized she was crying.

That's it. Just keep telling yourself you can get over him Keeli, and eventually you will. Dammit though, I think eventually might take a very long time.

CHAPTER SEVENTEEN

Wyatt returned to the bar alone. He looked shell-shocked and still simmered with anger.

"You look awful, man. Who killed your dog?" Tyler approached warily. "Where's Keeli?"

"She left," Wyatt barked.

"She left? I thought for sure you were going to get lucky tonight. What the hell happened?"

"I thought so too until I jumped down her throat," Wyatt admitted freely. "I believed she was using me to sell her jewelry to my friends and you know I will not tolerate that. Now I know that Barb approached her. Keeli was blameless. She makes fantastic stuff; I should have expected someone would notice. I should have celebrated the sale, been proud of her success. Instead I was a dick and threw her in a cab."

"Wait a sec. How do you know she wasn't working the crowd, Ivy? She might have been encouraging Barb. It wouldn't surprise me one bit. It's not like she fits in here. It is obvious that she needs cash, just look at her." Tyler planted doubt back in Wyatt's mind. Was he trying to make Wyatt feel better or warn him off? Either way, the comment did not sit well with Wyatt.

"She fits perfectly," he defended. "She is smart, funny, talented and beautiful."

Rolling his eyes a bit in a typical 'you know what I mean'

expression, Tyler responded simply. "Ivy, she is not one of us and you know it. She isn't now, she never will be. I think you might be confusing your need to get in her pants with a desire to actually be with her."

"Fuck you, Tyler," Wyatt fired at Tyler with a contemptuous sneer. "I never knew what a total snob you were."

"I'm just saying." Although he knew Wyatt almost never lost his temper enough to swear, Tyler threw caution to the wind and continued. "She's no Sloane. She could not be a hostess for you at a business dinner or a fundraiser. She doesn't have the background, the education or experience. Be honest. We both know she is not the girl you bring home to your mother. Your family will have a cow, and you know it. You know I'm right."

"Where's Keeli?" Molly joined the conversation, not realizing how heated it was. She had Barb and Samantha in tow, forcing the men to stop their discussion. Wyatt ran his hand through his hair, distracted, and tried to focus on the women.

"I wanted to talk to her some more - get to know her better. I like her, Wyatt, I really do. She needs the "Fashion Police", but I rather like that small town, innocent way she has about her."

"She is really talented too," Barb added. "I had her sell me the necklace she was wearing. Asked her to just take it off here and sell it to me now." She proudly fingered the stones of the necklace now resting in her cleavage.

"I will concede that she has talent, "Samantha chimed in. "but she is no Sloane, Wyatt. She has no class, no conversation. You guys know what I mean," Samantha lectured the small group. "She is not one of us."

"Like I said…" Tyler added, giving Wyatt a smug "I told you so" look.

"Oh shut up, Sam," Molly and Barb said in unison.

"Yeah, just shut up," Wyatt echoed. He slammed his empty beer mug down on the nearest table. "I am done. I am so done here." With that, Wyatt turned from his friends, taking long strides toward the door without a backward glance. He could not get away from them, and his thoughts, fast enough.

CHAPTER EIGHTEEN

Wednesday dawned overcast and rainy again. The humidity was terrible but at least it was cooler. Keeli laid under the sticky sheet trying to decide whether to close the window and sweat or leave it open and grab a towel for the incoming rain. She was too tired to decide so she just lay there, feeling blue. She was too tired to do anything.

She tried rubbing the crusty itch from her eyes but after hours of crying she knew it would take more than a few passes with her fists to fix this mess. She had sales calls to make and acknowledged she would have to get moving soon, but lying there without moving helped her hold to illusion that last night had not happened. As long as she stayed in bed, she figured she could pretend there was still hope. The moment she started her day she had to deal with reality once more. Unfortunately there was no Wyatt in reality. At least no Wyatt for her.

She was grateful the boys were still working when she got home last night. She still did not know how she would explain what happened. She wasn't sure she could explain it to herself. She would have to say something eventually but by then she hoped to have her act together.

After another fifteen minutes, Keeli finally got up, closed the window and went to the bathroom. She emerged with a fresh washed face, clean teeth, a low ponytail, a towel for mopping the floor and a new attitude.

The puddle dealt with, Keeli took a quick shower and donned her one 'business call' suit, added her gold cuff with turquoise stones and grabbed the low-heeled shoes with the recently replaced soles.

She prepped an Earl Grey tea, zapping it in a to-go mug and clutched her portfolio to protect it from the rain. She rapidly walked three blocks to pick up a Zipcar for the next few hours. The hourly rental option had been a godsend for Keeli, who grouped her business calls around renting the car one day a week. Driving it more destroyed her budget. Today would be tight but she had laid out a plan of action. First the two stops in Evanston, then a trip to her manufacturer and if she still had time, a short trip to the bank to deposit the check from last night.

Driving north in the compact rental, she reached the unique florist/gift shop in less than thirty minutes. She was just finishing her tea as she put money in the meter. Checking her hair, reapplying the lip-gloss she had chewed off, she grabbed her large hobo bag and small portfolio and entered the exclusive shop right on schedule. It was ten in the morning, as overcast as night outside, but inside it was like springtime, filled with bright light and the intermingled fragrance of a dozen types of flowers.

Introducing herself to the owner, she gratefully accepted a slightly chipped mug of weak tea while the woman pulled a small boudoir chair over to a table strewn with papers. The computer on the tabletop looked out of place in the charming shop. Keeli accepted the proffered chair and surreptitiously slipped off one painful shoe.

With a minimum of small talk, the two established a cordial relationship while Keeli unpacked the samples she had in her hobo bag. Offering up a selection of twenty items –rings, bracelets and necklaces – in yellow, rose and white gold as well as sterling, she thoughtfully displayed the items. Keeli had carefully selected the pieces to represent a good cross section of styles and prices.

The manager examined her work carefully then thumbed through Keeli's portfolio asking questions about delivery times, where else she sold merchandise and her background. She took a copy of Keeli's resume, wrote some notes and circled her email address. Finally, when Keeli felt she would burst with curiosity the owner looked Keeli full in the face and announced was interested in carrying Keeli's merchandise for the Christmas holidays. Keeli would need to deliver forty items in specific styles with specific price points by October 1.

Keeli stifled her panic at having to produce forty pieces by October in addition to maintaining adequate Etsy and art show inventory. There was no cash advance, of course, and Keeli was unsure where the money would come from to buy materials or to pay rent until October. She said none of this, asking calmly

about percentages, deciding she would live with the 60/40 split, although not happily.

The manager promised to forward a consignment contract for Keeli to review with her attorneys and suggested they talk again in a month. Keeli thanked her warmly and headed back to the parking space in a downpour.

Keeli knew she should be thrilled to have someone consigning her work; it was what she had been working toward for six long months. But she had no idea how she could survive until October. She needed someone else to buy a lot – for cash - before then. She went running through the rain already planning her next call in her head.

Oh great, now I look like a drowned rat too.

Keeli knew that she was holding her emotions together by a thread and her dripping hair threatened to push her over the edge. First Wyatt, now a 60/40 split and no sales before October. Keeli literally felt the black cloud over her head.

However, once in the dry car, air conditioning cooling her warm face and drying her damp hair, Keeli realized she had finally acquired a sales partner. It was a first for her. Someone finally said yes. After all the rejection, Keeli realized things might be looking up.

Pulling her phone out, Keeli added a calendar entry to check back in one week if no contract had arrived, she fired off a quick note to herself to replace the necklace she sold last night and begin the 40 consignment pieces and yeah, she checked her email and texts. There was nothing from Wyatt.

Chiding herself for even checking, she navigated to the gallery/shop in north Evanston for her 11:30 appointment. Waiting while the manager finished with a client, Keeli had time to compare her work with that on display throughout the store. Her work would compliment the inventory they had, but not compete directly. It would be a great location, the right clientele. She crossed her fingers and approached the manager as the client took her bag and left the shop.

An hour later she had a definite 'maybe' from the manager who had to review Keeli's work with her partner before committing to anything. They agreed to get back together in two weeks. It was not the answer Keeli had hoped to receive, but the door remained open. It was the best day Keeli could remember since she began hawking her wares. It was the first day with no one saying "no". She would take it, and be grateful.

Back in her Zipcar, Keeli failed to resist checking her phone again. Nothing from Wyatt, but a missed call from an unknown number caught her attention and she listened to the message immediately.

"Keeli, hi. This is Melissa Howe Wallace, Wyatt's sister. You may remember me; I bought a ring from you a few weeks ago. The nanny has the kids today, and I was hoping we could make a plan to meet? Call me at your convenience, please. I look forward to speaking with you."

The message was lovely and welcoming, triggering a stab of regret that Keeli would never get to know this woman. She may not be with Wyatt anymore, but Keeli knew she had to return the call. Good manners dictated that she do so.

Taking a deep breath, Keeli waited four rings then heard the same lovely voice at the end of the line.

"Hello? Wallace Residence."

"Melissa? It's Keeli Larsen, returning your call."

"Keeli, hi! Thanks so much for getting back to me quickly. I wanted to make a plan to meet for lunch. I am not sure what your schedule is like but Wednesdays are usually best for me. Can you find the time?"

Choosing her words carefully, Keeli responded. "Melissa, I think you should know that I am not dating Wyatt any more."

"I see. I didn't realize." After a brief silence, Missy continued, "but this is not about Wyatt, this is about us, and lunch. I am in the suburbs, but I could come to you in the city perhaps?"

"Actually, I am in Evanston right now," Keeli offered.

"Fantastic, let's meet in say thirty minutes? Please, call me Missy. All my friends do." Missy suggested a small Italian restaurant halfway between her home and Evanston, gave Keeli the simple directions to get there and was gone.

Keeli sat stunned, not quite sure what she had just agreed to, but looking forward to it just the same. Keeli would have to delay her plans to visit her manufacturer until later in the week. Today was certainly turning out differently than she had imagined. Thank God she had decided to get out of bed after all.

Following her hastily scrawled directions, Keeli had no trouble finding the charming Italian bistro/market right along the lakefront. Missy was waiting just inside the door looking tall, lovely and untouched by the rain. Keeli had forgotten just how beautiful she was.

Beaming a broad smile, Missy linked her arm through Keeli's as they followed the host to their table. "So, Keeli Larsen, I have grand plans for you. Let's eat and then let's talk."

CHAPTER NINETEEN

Keeli did the short walk home with her portfolio under one arm and her hobo bag and a small bag of leftover four-cheese fettuccini in the other. The rain had subsided to a lovely, refreshing drizzle.

At her door, she juggled her packages and dug out her key but was arrested mid-reach to the mailbox by the sight of a huge floral box in the corner of the small foyer. Hoping against hope she dropped her portfolio and reached to turn the box until the card was visible. They were for her and could only be from one person.

Resisting the urge to tear open the card right there, Keeli maneuvered her portfolio and keys so that she was able to carry the long box as well. Beaming with pleasure, itchy with anticipation, she fumbled with the lock, threw open the door and gently placed the flowers on the small table in the living room.

She had savored the moment long enough and tore off the lid and reached through layers of tissue to discover an enormous bouquet of pink roses and lush greenery. Keeli did a quick count, before inhaling the fragrance and burying her nose in 24 long-stemmed blooms. Finally she reached for the card.

"I am an ass." That was it, no signature, nothing but the brief contrite phrase written in a bold masculine scrawl. Keeli read it three more times before holding it high above her head and dancing around the kitchen like a moron.

Ending her jig, Keeli reached for her phone, stood there in

157

careful thought and eventually typed "Hey Ass, thanks for the beautiful flowers." She hit send, listening to the whoosh sound to assure herself it was sent and then waited. And waited. And waited.

Telling herself that watching the phone would not help, Keeli went to change out of her suit and uncomfortable, damp pumps. She returned to the kitchen in comfy work jeans, a ratty t-shirt and her Keds, put her leftovers in the fridge and poured a big glass of water before checking her phone again.

Nothing.

She gathered her tools and materials to get some work done. She needed forty new pieces for October. She was behind schedule for creating a new collection. She sketched listlessly, knowing she needed to head to the basement and get busy but also aware that she couldn't get a phone signal down there. Keeli dragged out her time upstairs another thirty minutes before giving in. Refilling her water glass, she gathered her supplies to head downstairs.

He's busy. He's an important man, lots of meetings. He sent flowers for God's sake, what more do you want, selfish girl? Who am I kidding? I want him to call!

Checking her quiet phone one last time, Keeli filled her arms with materials and opened the door.

CHAPTER TWENTY

Wyatt enjoyed watching Keeli jump a clear foot off the ground.

Standing there, hand poised to knock he had obviously surprised her. She had surprised him but he managed to hide it better, a smug grin on his face.

He looked gorgeous in a tailored navy suit, hair glistening with raindrops, watching Keeli check him out slowly, seeing the admiration in her eyes.

Bowing slightly from the waist he gave Keeli a disarming smile and pronounced, "Ass extraordinaire, at your service."

Dropping her armload, Keeli stammered, "How did you get in downstairs?" Wyatt had more important business than discussing the lack of building security. Rather than answer, he gathered her close, tasting the sweet honey of her lips and mouth, ravaging her with his tongue and squeezing the breath from her only to replace it with his own.

After what felt like several long, satisfying minutes, he stepped back to admire her dirty work clothes, kissing her nose, then the top of her head.

"Aren't you going to invite me in?" He was pouring on the charm. He could not get over how good she felt, how scared he had been at the idea of losing her. Just thinking about it again, he pulled her close, running his hands up her back. He reached under the dusty t-shirt to stroke her silky skin before wrapping his

159

large hands around her tiny waist to tug her up against his growing erection. She felt so damn good.

Keeli kissed him back, pressed herself tight again him, pulled him fully into the apartment and kicked the door shut with her foot. She broke the kiss, breathing like a sprinter and pulled him toward her bedroom without a word. She took a step, ran her tongue along his lips, took a step, nibbled his neck, and took a step. She was intoxicating. He kept his hands about her waist, following her halting steps down the hallway, keeping her lips tight against his, her tongue entwined with his.

She shut the bedroom door behind them, rattling the necklaces hanging there. He heard several hit the floor, but she motioned to ignore them, and pulled him back into her embrace. Their hands brushed as they both lifted her shirt, breaking the kiss long enough to pull it over her head before clinging to each other again.

Wyatt pushed her against the hard planks of the door, leaning into her with his body, pinning her in place. His hands stabbed into her curls, grasping them lightly, holding her head in place as he plundered her mouth. Gasping for air, he pulled back, kissing her hair, her cheeks, her lips, her eyes and then her lips again, settling there with a groan of satisfaction as her lips part and her tongue sought his.

Their mouths danced the dance of lovers, stroking, dipping and tasting every moist inch. First Keeli demanded from Wyatt, her mouth drawing from his until he took command and pulled from her all she had to give. She tasted sweet and tangy, making him briefly think of what she had for lunch before losing the thought again.

Keeli reached her hands under his lapels, rubbing the hard muscles of his chest through the fine, cotton of his shirt and he carelessly shrugged his suit jacket off his shoulders. She caught it before it hit the floor and moved to drape it over the back of the upholstered chair in the corner but Wyatt kept her pinned against the wall, tossing the jacket in the general vicinity of the chair without concern.

He loved the feel of her pressed tight against him, tight muscled and small except where her full breasts were flattened against his chest. He felt a rapid heartbeat, not sure if it was hers or his. He was moving against her, a slow hip movement, grinding her gently between his hard body and the door. His erection was bursting against his pants, pushing hard into her softness, and he mimicked the movements of sex.

She was so responsive, pressing against him, touching him everywhere, up his arms, his back, pulling his shirt from his pants. Keeli fluctuated between kneading his hard muscles and skimming his skin, heating him up and leaving him wanting more. Her hands cupped his ass pulling him harder against her, leaving him no doubt of what she wanted.

Keeli made small sexy sounds as Wyatt caressed her everywhere, his hands in her hair, sliding over her breasts, her arms, and her hips. He stopped long enough to pull his shirt over his head and yank off his elegant tie, letting both fall to the floor forgotten. She responded to the delicious sensation of skin on skin running her hands from shoulder to waist along the sides of his body, snaking into the top of his belted pants.

Wyatt stepped back, pulling her with him. She wrapped her legs around his waist and he lifted her, his hands sinking into the taut muscles of her behind.

"I have thought of sinking my hands into your ass again every day. You are such a temptress, taunting me in the elevator, and then disappearing. I thought I would go mad trying to find you."

"You remember," Keeli's pleasure was tangible and she peppered Wyatt with tiny kisses all over his face. "I thought you didn't remember me. Why didn't you say something?"

"I'm saying something now," he growled in her ear before capturing her mouth in a heart-stopping kiss. He continued to hold her with one strong arm leaning back far enough to unsnap the tops of her jeans, stroking her abdomen before sliding his hand around the side of her body pulling the jeans lower. Leaving them hugging her hips, Wyatt traced lazy circles on her back, first small provocative movements, then larger movements, his fingers skimming over her bra, over her sides, resting on her abdomen, fingers stealing lower. All the while she pulled him tight to her with her strong, lean legs wrapped tight about him, her sex hot against his stomach.

Cradled in his arms, she felt small, vulnerable and sexy as hell. He wanted her, craved her, but felt protective at the same time, trying to slow down this freight train driving him to possess her. His thumbs skimmed her breasts over her bra, touching the bare skin below, then her breasts through the lacey material, then skin. It was heavenly torment and he felt power coursing through his veins watching her unbridled response.

He took the remaining two steps until her knees connected with the edge of the bed and gently released her, his arm wrapped behind her to ease her down. His drugging kisses were endless. Her eyes were lust filled, glazed with desire, and locked with his deep blue gaze.

She threw two small pillows roughly to the floor just before she landed on the threadbare quilt. He followed, laying on her heavily, his body driving hers into the mattress. Keeli wrapped her arms about his muscled torso, her hands stroking every chiseled inch. When her small hands slid along his waist and he felt her small fingers brush against his erection, Wyatt drew a shaky deep breath and reached for her jeans, concentrating on getting her undressed while he could still think.

She released a small sigh of pleasure when Wyatt unsnapped her bra and removed it with one hand while reaching for her pants with the other. Wyatt continued his slow kisses, savoring the velvety feel of her lips, the moist warmth of her mouth. He was bruising her mouth with crushing kisses that she returned with equal force.

Wyatt rolled away from Keeli only enough to start slithering her jeans down her legs. Her hands were draped over him and she clung to his body so that when he moved she followed, almost pushing him over the edge the bed.

"Damn single bed!" he growled.

"Sorry," Keeli replied before he captured her lips again in an intoxicating kiss. "Next time, my place. " He saw the excitement ratchet up in her smoking green eyes. "Does it please you, Keeli, knowing that there will be a next time? Believe me, there will be too many 'next times' to count."

"Okay with me," she barely got the words out before sucking in her breath, aware of Wyatt stroking the area he revealed by opening her pants, smooth fingertips teasing the top of her panties, dipping lower.

He began kissing Keeli harder, sucking on the fullness of her bottom lip, drawing her tongue from her mouth to his while his hands pushed against the denim of her jeans sliding them lower with his long arms. When they were below her knees, he broke the kiss long enough to remove them completely. They were caught, wrapped around her Keds sending both of them into peals of laughter. The sexual tension broke as Wyatt struggled to remove both the jeans and the shoes trapped beneath them. The clumsy work completed, Keeli laid back in nothing but the small swatch of lace smiling up at him self-consciously.

He stared at her body with hunger and admiration and heart-stopping lust.

"You're so beautiful." Wyatt's voice was raspy, full of longing.

"You make me feel beautiful when you stare at me like that," Keeli shyly replied.

Keeli reached for his belt but Wyatt brushed her fingers away, instead breaking his scrutiny to undo it himself. With a smirk he kicked off his shoes noisily, then removed his pants in one fluid motion. His erection tented the black boxer-briefs that hugged his hips, his manhood on proud display.

Laying skin to silky skin, he wrapped a large hand around her bare breast, feeling the weight of it in his hands, his long fingers tweaking her hardening nipple. Her body arched up from the mattress at the combination of soft and tough. She was so responsive, so free. It sent a lightning rod of desire shooting through him. Keeli reached around Wyatt, trying to draw closer, hold him tighter, running her hands along the tight muscles of his toned body, feeling the uncoiled power. She reached up into the hair along the nape of his neck, trying to tug him impossibly closer.

Wyatt trailed moist kisses down Keeli's chin, sucking gently at her neck and shoulder, finding a small spot that sent sharp desire pooling in her belly and eliciting a moan from between her lips. He slid further, wrapping his lips around her tight nipple, laving it with his tongue, swirling the wet warmth around his mouth before lightly biting down. Keeli let out a small yelp, followed by a little mewl of contentment.

"Oh my god," she sighed with contentment and desire. "That feels incredible." Keeli clawed at him, as if she was trying to crawl under his skin. "My body is on fire, Wyatt." He could feel her heat; see the light sheen of moisture on her upper lip as she strained against her own longing. A light floral scent and the aroma of his expensive aftershave mingled with the earthy smell of arousal. Her feet were shuffling against the quilt. He recognized her restless desire, her unconscious reach for more. It made him feel powerful.

Wyatt's mouth licked and sucked as he paid equal homage to her other breast, fulfilling a longing Keeli had not recognized she had. He brushed his rough cheek against her stomach, and listened to Keeli's heart pound as she held her breath.

Keeli touched every inch she could reach. Wyatt felt her small hands rub his pecs; slide over his shoulders and around to his back. He felt her fingers dig into the taut muscles of his ass, causing them to tighten reflexively. He ground his pelvis harder against her softness, pulling her tight against him. He was devouring her with his mouth, pushing her into the mattress in a slow, carnal samba.

"You are so beautiful," Wyatt whispered in awe, his voice husky "I wanted to take this slower, savor it, but I am desperate for you. You ready for me, babe? I can't hold back any more." Wyatt looked deep into her eyes, seeking assurance.

"Yes," came her breathy response. "We can slow it down next time, Wyatt. Just make love to me. Now," she begged, breath coming in short gasps, hands roaming over his skin uncontrollably, pulling him hard against her.

As soon as the words were out of Keeli's mouth, Wyatt was up; yanking off his boxer-briefs while Keeli threw off the scratchy quilt and lay back on the sheets. Wyatt bent his body over her, touching only mouth to mouth while his hands slowly slid the lacey bikini down her legs. Tantalizing anticipation coursed through his veins while Wyatt tried to cling to sanity, trying to prolong the moment. A fine sheen covered his body from the effort.

"Shit, hang on." Wyatt sat bolt upright, shaken. He stood, flashing Keeli an apologetic look. Keeli wasted no time admiring his lean hips, powerful legs and proud manhood jutting erect and ready. Wyatt preened under her adoring eyes.

Wyatt looked stricken a moment, glancing around the sparsely furnished room before his eyes settled on his pants, in a heap on the floor. He grabbed them, reaching first into one pocket, then another, then a back pocket, growing increasingly frantic.

"Shit." He was obviously losing his patience when Keeli flashed him a disarming smile, leaned over and riffled through the drawer of her bedside table.

"Looking for this?" She asked nonchalantly dangling a condom between her thumb and forefinger. Flashing a grateful wide grin, Wyatt grabbed the condom without ceremony, ripped it open with his teeth and slid it over his impressive length.

Kissing Keeli hard on the mouth, he laid his body upon hers from shoulder to knees, reaching under him to wrap her legs around his hips, raising her up to meet him. She was wet and ready. Wyatt had hoped to slide in slowly but the sweet feel of her around him was too tempting. He plunged forward, burying himself deep inside her. Lying still, he reveled in the feeling, listening to Keeli's sigh of pleasure. Keeli squeezed her legs harder around his slim hips, enveloping him in her tight body, her arms and legs holding him firmly in place, their mouths melding in a scorching kiss.

Giving Keeli time to adjust to the feeling of Wyatt deep inside her, he tried staying still for a moment longer, listening to his heart bursting in his chest. His traitorous body took over, and he withdrew almost completely before stroking deep into her.

"You feel so damn good," he repeated like a litany, over and over with each slow thrust. She rose to meet him, kissing his shoulders, his collarbone, his chest, his mouth, making little breathy sounds again and again.

The bed creaked under them loud and obvious. "Thank god the guys are out," Keeli said in a moment of clarity.

"I plan to make plenty of noise," Wyatt laughed, "and then I want to make you scream."

Already so aroused before sinking into Keeli, Wyatt struggled to hold back, watching her face, working his magic on her body. He sucked her breast hard into his mouth, nipped at the hollow between her neck and collarbone, thrusting into her with mounting speed, watching her spiral out of control.

As she approached her climax, Keeli's hands held tight to Wyatt's butt, her breathing more erratic, and her grasp tightening. He was restraining himself, waiting for her to achieve her pleasure, his arms straining to hold himself above her, his face tight with his need for release.

Just when the pleasure could not get more intense, more wonderful, he sensed a tightening begin in her loins. Little moans and breathy sounds were spilling from her lips and her eyes were on his, unfocused. He moved his hips in circles, dipping into her welcoming body, watching her lose control. A loud "ohm" burst from her mouth as raw pleasure coursed through her being.

Wyatt, smug smile on his face, probed her mouth with his tongue, warm and insistent as his movements gained momentum. He was moving hard and fast into Keeli, her last spasms squeezing tight around his manhood as he released into her with a satisfied groan.

Wyatt held himself over Keeli briefly before rolling off and to the side, bringing her with him in the small space, tucking her tight under his arm. Their skin was slick with sweat as they lay crammed face to face in the small bed.

He kissed her gently, searching her eyes for an unsaid

message.

"Okay?"

"Very okay," Keeli tilted her head up to kiss him gently. "You?"

"Oh yeah."

Wyatt rolled to his back placing his hands behind his head and staring off into space. He and Keeli worked on catching their breath, coming back to earth. After a long pause, he kissed her lips softly, then the top of her head. He felt like a God. She did this to him.

CHAPTER TWENTY-ONE

Once their breathing had returned to normal and after a few gentle kisses, Wyatt broke the comfortable silence.

"This is your space, huh? Where you live?" Wyatt looked about the room as if only seeing it now.

"Not really. I just sleep here. My true space is next door, my design studio."

"You really love what you do, don't you?" Wyatt sounded wistful and sincerely curious.

"I really do."

"And you believe in yourself? That you can do this all on your own?"

"I am starting to believe. I finally see light at the end of the tunnel. I had a good day today."

"I had a great day today, " Wyatt responded with a lecherous grin. " And it's not over."

"Really," Keeli dragged out the word, "What did you have in mind, Sir?" Keeli was running her fingers through the course hairs on Wyatt's chest, pulling them slightly, teasing. He played along, feigned pain, alarming her before laughing at his little joke. She laid her hand safely on his chest, gently tracing the structure of his bones and muscles with her fingertips.

Wyatt started running his fingers through the ends of her hair, twirling a tight curl around his index finger repeatedly. He seemed unaware of his action as if he couldn't stop touching, connecting. She understood. She was not ready to break the sensual spell they had created.

"Well," Wyatt picked up on her question after a moment of quiet, "We could do this again." He motioned to the rumpled bed. "Or maybe we should think about some food?" Keeli leaned away to check the clock on her bedside table surprised that it showed it was almost six. At the same moment, her stomach growled loudly and she went off into girlish laughter.

Wyatt could not help laughing too, until their eyes met, held steady and he started kissing her again, holding her naked body against the warmth strength of his own. She leaned into him, molding her curves to his hard muscle.

"So, more?" he lifted his brow in a sinister expression.

"Food," Keeli responded without hesitation. Wyatt grabbed his chest as if mortally wounded and fell back against the pillow. They laughed together again.

"In the mood for anything special? Order in or go out?"

"In. I would rather order in. Pizza? Chinese?" She had no idea what he liked and, with a little shock, realized how little she really knew about this man.

"Hmmm. What about we go back to my place for the night and pick up a couple steak dinners on the way? I worked up a big appetite," he smirked at her. "We could call ahead and grab something fast?"

Steak dinner for take out? Oh yeah. This man knows how to live.

"Can I bring my flowers along?" Keeli questioned coquettishly.

"Absolutely. I wouldn't have it any other way," Wyatt was suddenly bouncing with energy, ready to get moving.

"Okay, then. Let me get a quick shower and some clothes and we are out of here."

"No shower," Wyatt commanded imperiously. "Shower later, my place. Just throw something on, bring a toothbrush and we are outta here."

Keeli flashed him an enormous smile when he said toothbrush, but Wyatt missed it while he rummaged around the floor for his clothes.

"Aye aye, Captain," Keeli gave a salute, stopped to admire Wyatt's tight ass and long strong legs as he moved about the room and bent for his clothes. Without the veneer of a custom suit, he was a he-man, all height and muscle. Keeli smiled to herself at the thought then remembered to grab her jeans, panties and bra from the floor, reaching into the closet for a clean shirt.

Looking past her shoulder Wyatt's gaze was focused on her jewelry. There were chains, bracelets and mesh bags hanging from the closet rod taking up most of the small space. More hung from the doorknobs and was piled on the dresser top too. Her jewelry filled all available space. There were five pairs of shoes thrown haphazardly on the floor: flip flops, sneakers, a pair of outdated black flats, black heels and the sandals she was wearing for their first date. On hangers, there was one black dress, two sundresses, four shirts and a faded leather jacket as well as her waitressing uniform. On the shelf above were folded about six or seven pairs of jeans in a variety of washes and disrepair.

"Is that your whole wardrobe?" Keeli could tell that Wyatt could not keep himself from asking the question. She was sure he failed to recognize the insult in his tone.

"Well, I have more in the dresser," she pointed at the small beat up bureau defensively. "Sweaters, tees and winter stuff."

"But that's it?" Wyatt's expression moved from appalled to enlightened. Keeli saw the exact moment when Wyatt became aware of how little she had, how simply she lived, how different she would always be from him and how far from his world.

She tried putting a brave face on it, wondering how to recapture the previous connection. They needed to move beyond this gulf again.

"Well grab whatever, we're outta here." Whatever Wyatt was thinking, Keeli was relieved to see that he still wanted her to come to his place for the night. She had feared for a moment that he might try to wriggle out.

Keeli disappeared into the bathroom giving Wyatt time to snoop into her design studio. He could see that the light was better here, the shades pulled high to maximize it. He wandered the small room, checking out the pictures and sketches pinned to the walls, running his fingers over the supplies covering the table before stopping before her drafting board. A cheap box fan sat on the floor aimed at the board and two high voltage lamps were targeting it as well. The room was almost twice the size of the small bedroom next door.

Keeli watched Wyatt move about the room, knowing he was unaware she had returned. "Any questions?" she asked, startling him with the question.

"No, but I can see some of your inspiration, and your talent. You really are so creative. These are good," he pointed to her sketches. "Really good. Where are the soldering and other dirty work done?"

"In the basement where it is cooler. And some I have to send out."

She had smoothed her mass of curls although they were already getting away from her again, her face was fresh scrubbed and she smelled of minty toothpaste. He slid against her body with a quick hard kiss, passing in the narrow hallway to make his way to the bathroom.

Keeli could only imagine what Wyatt must be thinking now. The old bathroom was small, typical of a vintage apartment. The subway tiles were a bad turquoise blue, chipped here and there. The window placed in the wall next to the ancient tub was an old sash type that was painted shut with twenty or thirty coats of peeling paint. The floor of mismatched tiles was cool under his feet but didn't look too clean. They had added shelves to cover every inch of floor and wall space to hold towels, shampoos and the products that made up the daily life of one woman and two exacting gay men. There were lots and lots of products.

Wyatt was back in the bedroom in no time, saying nothing more about how she lived, pulling his pale blue shirt onto his still damp body, haphazardly stuffing his beautiful tie in his jacket pocket. Keeli was still standing in bra and panties, staring into the closet. She had picked up her clothes from the floor, but hadn't wanted to put them back on. Wyatt looked so polished; she wanted to look good for him but was stymied on how to manage.

"Clothes, woman," he directed her. "This man needs food."

She smiled over her shoulder, nodded and grabbed a pair of jeans from the shelf, sliding them up her long legs. Wyatt watched as she shimmied them over her tight behind and she could tell he enjoyed the view.

"You know," his voice was the hypnotic timber of a storyteller, "I'm still thinking about your ass that day I grabbed it in the elevator."

"And...?"

Wyatt took the two steps needed to cross the room and swatted her playfully on the butt. "I could not believe I was that brazen, but you just lured me in."

Laughing and unsuccessfully trying to swat him back, Keeli returned to the closet, shoved her feet into flip flops and turned to the dresser, grabbing a plain white V-neck t-shirt, pulling it over her head. Keeli knew the cotton clung to her curves and enjoyed watching Wyatt discover that too, basking in his admiring glance.

"Ready?"

"Just let me grab a bracelet. I am naked without jewelry." Keeli was already sorting through the metals and gems scattered on the dresser. She grabbed a silver openwork cuff, about two inches wide and slid it onto her wrist. Suddenly her outfit seemed elevated above the cheap tee and jeans.

"I like you naked," Wyatt flashed her a wide smile. "But you look great in clothes too. Okay, ready. Let's blow this pop-stand."

Grabbing her hobo bag and dropping her toothbrush and a clean pair of panties into it she closed the bedroom door behind her and followed Wyatt into the living room.

Scooping up the keys and the vase of flowers, she led him to the door and out of the building. He held her hand as they moved quickly through the drizzle to his Panamera, parked at the curb.

After starting the engine and fiddling with the radio stations,

Wyatt handed Keeli his phone. "Just scroll through the contacts, or use Siri. I have Rosebud, Ditka's, Gibson's and Morton's all ready for speed dial. Just pick one. They all know my standing order."

Keeli was thumbing through Wyatt's contacts list, noticing all the business names interspersed with way too many women's names. She was feeling overwhelmed, perhaps by the dinner choices but more likely by the women.

The silence stretched for a moment too long before she caught up with what he had been saying and he gave her a quizzical look. She gathered her wits again.

"You have a standing order?" Keeli didn't try to hide her astonishment. "I have never even been to these places."

"What can I say? I am a meat and potatoes guy," he laughed. "Just call Rosebud, it's easy. Get yourself a steak and sides or a steak salad, which ever you prefer."

"What do you get?" she asked as he maneuvered easily through the heavy traffic, approaching the Gold Coast neighborhood.

"I get a bone-in sirloin, but you can get a rib eye or filet, or something Italian, pasta or chicken. Just think of what you want, they will figure it out for us."

Keeli decided to review the menu online while Wyatt drove. She called the restaurant.

"I want an order for pickup please. Wyatt Howe, yeah, he'll have the usual and I will have the skirt steak salad. Yes, Gorgonzola is fine, thanks. Ten minutes?" She caught Wyatt's eye, repeated the timing and he nodded yes.

"Yes, good, ten minutes. Thank you."

"Perfect," he offered. "Will you need dessert?"

"Why, do you have a standing order with a bakery?" she sniped gently.

"Don't get smart with me, young lady." Wyatt responded in a parental tone. "I will take you over my knee then send you to bed with no supper."

"I like the 'send to bed part'," she retorted, humor lighting her eyes.

"That you shall have, my dear. Your wish is my command."

"In that case, I would like dessert please," she responded as a blush climbed into her cheeks. "I have a terrible sweet tooth."

"Totally my pleasure." his smile widened indicating his approval as he pulled around the corner of Rush Street and parked illegally in front of the restaurant.

"Do you mind running in? They have a credit card on file, just sign the slip and leave a decent tip, ok?"

Keeli slipped from the car, her mind fixated on how different their lives were, moving to consider the huge number of women's names stored in his phone, and finally obsessing over her appearance as she walked into the restaurant. She was not appropriately attired for the white tablecloth interior. Keeli felt decidedly out of her element, on every level. How had she gone from the joy of receiving flowers from a sexy, virile man, not to mention post-coital bliss, to this horrible embarrassment and insecurity?

The maître 'd approached as if Keeli was elegantly dressed saying "How may I help you ma'am? One?"

"No, a pickup order for Wyatt Howe." Before she could finish saying his name the gentlemen was whisking her to the bar, calling for the order. With a flourish the bartender handed her a receipt and pen. A strange woman signing a credit card was certainly not out of the ordinary for these people. With a slightly shaking hand she calculated a tip and signed his name. Picking up the hot packages carefully, she returned to the car. She needed the reassurance of Wyatt's admiration for her but instead she found him deep in a business conversation.

"I forgot, ok, I forgot. It's no big deal. I'll just reschedule it for tomorrow." After a minute of hesitation while the other person spoke in his ear Wyatt responded, "Oh yeah, not tomorrow. Then Friday? I can squeeze it in in the afternoon, right after our lunch meeting, and if we do that the contracts can still be signed this week."

Keeli could hear the garbled voice of an unhappy man on the

other end of the line shouting as Wyatt held the phone several inches away from his ear, mimicking the disembodied voice.

"Relax, Father, really. You will give yourself another heart attack. I missed a meeting. The world will not end and the deal will close. I promise. I know this is important. Yes, Father, I am aware. No Father, I have not forgotten. Yes, Father, I understand my responsibilities. I will call their office and fall on my sword. It will be fine. I promise. Go catch your train, read a magazine or something and I will make it all okay."

Wyatt sounded like he was talking to a petulant child, repeating the same phrases over and over, calming his father. The voice grew fainter; the rage apparently over, and after more of the same, Wyatt disconnected the call with a frustrated mutter, running his hand through his hair.

"My father. He seems to think I belonged somewhere other than your place this afternoon." His voice was heavy with irony, his smile disarming, but Keeli was not fooled. Wyatt had work to do today and instead he had been in bed with her. He did not strike her as the type of man to blow off work, quite the opposite in fact.

"I'm so sorry." She didn't not know what else to say, feeling somehow at fault, although she certainly hadn't lured him to her place. "I know how important your work is."

"Are you? I'm not sorry at all. Not at all," and with one sentence he recaptured the earlier mood. Wyatt made a sharp turn into the underground garage of a luxury condominium building just off Chicago's "Magnificent Mile". She had a vague idea of where Wyatt lived but could not help being impressed now with the location.

He kept making hairpin turns lower under the building until he effortlessly slid the Panamera into a tight parking space between the SUV and an imposing concrete post.

Keeli grabbed her hobo bag from behind the front seat along with the beautiful flowers, while Wyatt took the food and a gorgeous leather briefcase. Keeli was anticipating Wyatt's condo with some trepidation.

Another way to highlight our differences. I hate being reminded.

Feeling insecure already, Keeli knew that her apartment juxtaposed with his condo would not be helpful. She knew that the relationship was a whim for him, but she wanted it to last as long as possible. She wanted to know this man and she lived in fear of his leaving her. One night had felt like a lifetime already. Now that she had experienced Wyatt in bed, she knew she would be devastated when he left.

Ultimately he will have to be with someone from his social circle – some skinny bitch like Sloane. Yeah, probably Sloane.

Keeli knew that Wyatt leaving would be hard enough let alone picturing him with Sloane. She tried to have Keeli fired and Keeli would never forgive her for that. Keeli hoped when the time came for them to part that she would be gracious about Wyatt falling in love and marrying. She knew his family expected it, that he wanted it.

She wanted it too. Someday. And with a man just like Wyatt. He was tender, smart, funny and incredible in bed. Keeli, when she was honest with herself, knew that Wyatt could break her heart.

I am totally falling for Wyatt. No matter how hard I try not to, no matter how many times I remind myself he will leave me, the guy is just captivating to me. He is storming his way right into my heart.

CHAPTER TWENTY-TWO

Keeli was roused from her thoughts by the elevator bell signaling their arrival at the 28th floor. There were four doors opening off the wide hallway and she waited to see which way to go. Wyatt took her hand in his, doing those lazy thumb circles that drove her to distraction as they walked to the end of the corridor and he entered a code on a keypad to open the door.

"These two are mine." He indicated the door he was opening and one halfway down the hall.

"Two?" Keeli could not afford a closet in this building and he owned two units.

"I wanted the extra space so I put two units together. It gives me a good guest room, plus an office and some privacy. You'll see." He announced all this as if it was nothing but Keeli's trepidation was growing by leaps and bounds. How could she ever have thought she might fit in his world?

As they entered, he indicated a heavy marble table in the foyer for her purse then moved straight ahead into a large kitchen, dropped the food on the counter and took the vase of flowers from her to place them prominently on the counter. He pulled her into his arms and gave her a slow, thorough kiss that left her pulse fluttering.

"Come on, I'll show you around. Then we'll eat cause I am famished. Somehow or other I managed to work up quite an appetite," he lifted a single brow and gave Keeli a leering grin. She couldn't help but laugh.

Standing in the modern kitchen, Keeli was overwhelmed already. The kitchen seemed to be the size of her entire apartment, or at least it felt like it, all open space and stainless steel. It had a high ceiling and a view over the tops of buildings all around them. One wall held cabinets and what appeared to be a brand new double oven. The next wall had the sink, dishwasher and refrigerator, also looking shiny and unused. In the middle was an enormous wood and stainless island with a gray countertop reflecting the five lamps hanging above it.

The entire room looked like something out of a magazine.

"How about some wine?" Keeli looked to see Wyatt holding up a bottle that he must have extricated from the wine refrigerator right behind him. She nodded yes and he pointed to a cabinet near her, asking her to get two glasses. Instantly she went from feeling like an observer to a helper in the kitchen. Keeli felt her nerves ratchet down a notch.

Keeli looked past the cabinet to see a second island containing another oven and a wet bar. Grabbing two glasses from the bar, she turned to Wyatt, catching a glimpse of a glass and metal dining table centered in the dining room. Walls of windows on two sides and the entrance to a balcony on the third all reflected her mane of red hair surrounding a pixie face with her mouth hanging open. Shutting it immediately she schooled her features and admired the sense of the table hanging over the city on air.

"Whoever designed this place did an amazing job," she admitted trying to contain her awe.

"That would be me," Wyatt replied, a hint of pride in his voice. "Except the living room. I hate the living room, but it was designed for a magazine article, so I just left it when they finished shooting. You'll see."

He poured some fragrant red wine into the stemmed glasses, handed one to Keeli and took her hand.

"I'll give you the ten cent tour." He started leading her from the room. "Obviously this is the kitchen, and the dining room is over there." He was pointing toward the 'floating' table and then pulling her from the room. The gray tile floors sparkled, the white and wood cabinets kept the space from being cold. It was large and modern but inviting somehow.

Impressive.

"We'll come back to the living room in a sec," Wyatt explained as they walked past the opening to the dark room. Moving down a corridor lined with modern paintings and sculptures, Keeli's feet sank into a gorgeous blue oriental rug. Somehow the contemporary and traditional worked perfectly together alongside deep, rich wainscoting. Walking past two doors on the right, Wyatt flicked on and off the lights quickly and said succinctly, "guest room, guest bath," before opening the last door on that side.

"This is my home office. Nothing personal but it is hands off to guests, so I would appreciate you respecting my privacy on this. I have client financial reports and the like so I am protecting their privacy as well." The statement could have been construed as cold and suspicious but he said it so matter-of-factly that Keeli just understood that this was his sanctuary.

"Sure, of course, I respect that completely."

Wyatt closed the door to the office after Keeli got a brief peek into the dim space. More dark wood, many books and a massive desk covered with two computer monitors and stacks of papers. She thought she saw a low white sofa, maybe leather, against the wall but the door closed quickly and Wyatt was moving away.

Opening the door across the hall he announced "our room" as he thumbed the light switch and the two bedside lamps lit gradually.

Our room? Did he just say our room?

Again, the room was huge, dominated by a large bed with a gray leather headboard with brass studs all around it. The bed had a crisp white quilt bordered in gray and the bedside tables were pale gray wood. One was empty; the other held a small stack of papers and books. Gray curtains in a heavy fabric covered the large windows that ran from floor to ceiling along one wall. A low, long bookcase overflowing with small artifacts and books ran the length of the windows, more modern art was displayed on the walls and Keeli was itching to look at all of it more closely.

Wyatt had crossed the large room, pulling her along to another door.

"This place just goes on and on, doesn't it?" Keeli was overwhelmed. "It's enormous."

"Yeah, it is a lot of space for just me, but I wanted this configuration. Besides it was a great buy in the right neighborhood, and I am in real estate, so…"

"Location, location, location," Keeli quoted the mantra of all real estate agents before stepping forward into a bright white space.

"Now I see why you said we would shower here. This is a little nicer than my place." Keeli's understatement got a smile from Wyatt. The bathroom was enormous - a marble palace the size of Keeli's living room. The walls were stark white with recessed lighting reflecting off every surface. Keeli wandered further into the room, running her fingers lightly over the long countertop. The two square sinks sunken into it were spotlessly clean and the countertop was bare of toiletries. Turning around she drooled over a two-person tub that resembled a small swimming pool, with the updated version of a chandelier hanging in the private alcove.

Next to the tub, surrounded by dark wooden shelves overflowing with towels, was a shower big enough for a sports team to share. Inside were a thermostat, too many handles to count and at least three showerheads. There was even a marble bench large enough to lie down on.

Ooh, we could have some serious fun in here.

"OK, now I am suitably impressed, Wyatt. I could live in this bathroom if you could arrange for a small refrigerator and microwave?"

"Yeah, it's pretty nice. There is a small refrigerator in that corner," he pointed to a cabinet across the room. "Just kidding."

Keeli gave his triceps a friendly punch allowing Wyatt to take her in his arms again and kiss her soundly.

"Let's eat," he surprised her by saying while dragging her back to the kitchen.

Wyatt was a whirlwind in the kitchen, grabbing plates, silverware, refilling wine glasses, setting out placemats and even lighting a pair of candlesticks all in a matter of moments. He scooped the food from its containers to beautiful china plates and carried it all to the table, tasking Keeli only with grabbing napkins from a nearby drawer. In less than three minutes they were seated at the dining room table, her flowers a lovely centerpiece, for a candlelit steak dinner.

"This must be the best restaurant in town, Wyatt. Thank you so much," Keeli took Wyatt's hand, squeezed it lightly and looked into his eyes. She wanted to be sure he understood that she took none of this for granted and his proud smile in return indicated to her that he did.

Raising his glass to her, Wyatt spoke softly, "To many more dinners together. To many more lots of things together," he added with a mischievous grin.

"To lots more," she responded sipping the fine wine. He dug into his steak heartily and they ate with limited conversation for several minutes until he finally put his fork down when his meal was half gone.

"Keeli, you know how to give a man a serious appetite." Wyatt realized the double entendre after a moment and started to laugh. She took another moment to understand the joke before joining him sputtering "my pleasure".

"I didn't mean it that way," he backpedaled finally, catching his breath. "Or maybe I did."

"So, tell me something about yourself, Wyatt." Keeli was determined to get to know this man on every possible level. "I know you have a birth mark just above your butt, that you play a mean game of hockey, but I don't know what makes you happy, or sad, or proud. I don't know your favorite color, your interests, your likes and dislikes, except steak."

"Not true, you know a lot about me. You know I collect art,

you have met or seen most of my friends and family, you have seen where I live. You know more about me than I do about you," he accused.

"Oh no, you are not going to do this to me again. You always manage to turn the tables so I end up talking. Not happening. Start with something simple. Tell me about your plans for your new business."

Wyatt cringed slightly, stalling while he took a huge bite of steak and chewed thoughtfully. "That is anything but simple. Right now that is something of a sore subject for me actually," he began slowly. However, he put his utensils down and Keeli could tell he was about to open up to her.

"I think I have told you that I want to run a technology business. I was a closet geek in college, did you know that? I was afraid it would ruin my jock image, make it harder to get girls. What did I know? Anyway, I am supposed to meet with potential backers in a few weeks, venture capital folks who might be prepared to fund my new company, and I have yet to tell my father that I am leaving. How do I tell him now, when he is sick? I was about to tell him when he had a heart attack." He jumped in to reassure Keeli before she could ask. "A mild one, but still. So here I am caught in this mess.

"You know I work for my dad, and you know I want to leave to start my own company, but I am not sure how if you understand how hard it will be telling my father that I want out. My father worked for his father and my grandfather worked for his father, and it was always believed that I would continue – and grow – their legacy. As the eldest son, I would be expected to protect the business and use it to provide for everyone in the clan, to be the patriarch someday. Telling him I want out is a very big deal and right now my father is not in the best of health, which makes it a bad time to leave and a bad time to tell him I am leaving. It's just a lousy combination."

"I am sorry to hear he is unwell," Keeli murmured.

"Yeah, thank you for that.. Real estate is okay, don't get me wrong, and we certainly are a successful company. There is even a lot of opportunity but…"

Wyatt went silent, his words hanging between them while he idly twirled the stem of his wine glass, lost in thought.

"Oh Wyatt, how awful for you. I think I finally understand the pressure you are under but I am sure your dad will be supportive of your dreams. He is your dad after all." Even as she said the words, Keeli knew she was not sure at all. Wyatt had spoken repeatedly about his family's traditions and expectations. He was in a tough spot.

"The ironic part of this whole thing is that you were right when you suggested that my sister Regan might want to run the business. I believe she really does. I haven't discussed it with her, and obviously, I haven't discussed it with the rest of my family. Except Missy. She knows everything about it. She and I have no secrets."

"I have one month to figure it out and everyone has been walking on eggshells around my father since his attack. The doctor says he is fine now and he is back at work part time. He is getting out, but we all still worry. My mother would fall apart if something happened to him."

"I am sure he will be fine Wyatt. I saw him at the gala and he looked very fit. So did your mother. They make a great couple."

"They should. They have been married nearly forty years. They can finish each other's thoughts. He takes care of her and she supports his goals. Both of them put family honor and tradition first. They make a unified front. Family is absolutely everything in our house and I worry that if I go out on my own, it will be considered a betrayal."

"Come on, really? It's the twenty-first century." Keeli tried not to sound skeptical or judgmental but a bit of cynicism crept into her voice. "I would think your family would love to see your pioneering spirit, your willingness to take a chance." Keeli wanted desperately to be supportive to Wyatt in his venture, to see him succeed.

"I know you think you understand, Keeli, but you really don't," Wyatt responded dejectedly. "You do not know my family. Loyalty, family, closing ranks, we are born understanding these things. Each generation passes the torch to the next whose responsibility it is to go to the right schools, know the right people, marry the right girl, and live in the right neighborhood. Of course you must continue the empire that supports it all, make it larger and more successful with each generation. We are like the Kennedys – lots and lots of money, lots and lots of expectations."

"You're right," Keeli jumped in, "I don't know what it's like to be born with a silver spoon in my mouth and a lot of traditions to uphold. But I do understand the price you pay for breaking with family, for failing to live up to their expectations."

Wyatt rolled his eyes at Keeli, so she rushed to continue. "I understand family, I really do. My brothers all work the farm my father worked before them. My mother still hounds me to come back home. She thinks I am some kind of lunatic for leaving Gilman. I belong at home with my family, she would say, married to a Gilman boy.

"You want to know what that life would look like? I would get a job or help on the farm days and make more babies to carry on the tradition. She thinks my jewelry designing might be a nice little hobby, something I do in my spare time. I could sell my 'beads', as she calls them, at the country fair, but make a career at it? No way. My family has no intention of entering the twenty-first century and they are angry that I defied them to do so." Keeli shut up realizing she had hijacked the conversation again.

"Anyway, I just said that to show you I understand," she continued. "Notice, Wyatt, I left anyway to pursue my dreams. I walked away from their expectations to live up to my own. And I had a lot less going for me than you do. You can do this, I am sure of it. I bet you are a genius."

That was all Wyatt needed to segue from sullen to stirred up. For the next ten minutes he described the variety of real-estate-related solutions he had designed into full-blown software applications. He described the prototypes he created for the investors to review, the market research he had completed. Even without much knowledge of software or real estate, Keeli could see that there was a real opportunity for the programs Wyatt described. They could help homebuyers, people moving to new cities, brokers and agents and even renters and commercial property developers. He had covered all the bases.

It all sounded fabulous to Keeli. She found herself peppering him with questions, occasionally having to slow his enthusiasm down so that she could understand. He really was a geek, she realized, when she repeatedly asked him to speak in words she could actually understand instead of computer jargon. Finally Wyatt caught a deep breath and grabbed Keeli's hand.

"Enough," he announced. "I have other plans for us tonight." Keeli started to clear the table. "Leave it," Wyatt commanded as he leaned forward to blow out the candles before dragging Keeli by the arm so that she had to jog to keep up with him. "And my favorite color is red, like your hair," he told her with a leering grin as he pulled her down the hall to his room and turned down the bed, leaving the lights glowing softly.

"Don't move," he ordered. "Don't move until I say you can." With that he left her standing, toes digging into the softness of an elegant oriental rug. She heard him run back to the kitchen. He returned in moments carrying the two wine glasses and a fresh bottle of wine. Placing them carefully on one side of the bed he pointed a finger at her.

"Do not move," he admonished and disappeared again, this time returning with a large glass of water, which he placed, on a coaster on the opposite bedside table.

Bounding over to stand in front of her he slid his hands up and down her bare arms, flashing a sexy smile that sent her pulse racing.

"Okay, now you can move, but only to kiss me," he warned seriously. He moved his hands from her arms to her waist, lifting the hem of her tee to run his fingers lightly over her skin, side to side low across her stomach inching higher. Keeli struggled to stay immobile under the erotic onslaught. She lifted her face to his for a kiss and he crushed his lips down upon hers.

Wyatt's mouth claimed Keeli's as his hands splayed across her stomach and torso, tilting her off her feet until she fell back onto the bed. Soon he was pulling off her jeans, never breaking the kiss. His tongue was devouring her mouth relentlessly, his hands sure in their movements. He had her divested of all but her panties before raising his head from the kiss. Her mouth was swollen and bruised with kisses. Her eyes looked drugged and her hair was wild about her head.

"I have never seen anything more beautiful than you are right now," he said in a husky whisper before dropping his head to suckle her breast. Keeli could not breathe, could not think. Instinctively she wrapped her bare arms and legs around his still fully clothed body, clumsily pulling at his shirttails to help him undress. He got the message, rapidly undressing, haphazardly tossing his elegant suit to the carpet.

Reaching into the nightstand, he pulled out a string of condoms ripping several from the chain, keeping one in hand while dropping the rest on the tabletop. "For later," he shared, the corners of his lips lifting. Then he was removing the last of her clothing and tonguing his way from lips to breasts to naval and back again. Keeli was moaning and thrashing with desire as Wyatt sheathed his length and drove into her wet, waiting body.

"So much for taking it slow," he laughed. "You okay?" Keeli nodded yes, adjusted to the sudden fullness of having Wyatt deep inside her. Wyatt took the pace down a notch, making love to her slowly, kissing her hair, her lips, her eyes, his hands tracing her features, her arms, her body.

"You feel so good," he kept repeating, "so good." Much as she loved the ferocity of their earlier lovemaking, Keeli was savoring this slow sensuous dance until she found herself urging Wyatt on, speeding up her responses to his thrusts, clawing his back to drag him closer.

Her breath came in quick pants as Wyatt took Keeli to new highs, holding her there, hovering on the brink until she thought she would explode, then taking her higher.

"Please, Wyatt, please," she was begging. Wyatt picked up the pace even more and took them both over the precipice. Keeli's panting took on a frenetic quality, as she pulled harder at Wyatt, shuddering with her orgasm, pushing Wyatt over the edge with a satisfied moan.

Keeli could barely catch her breath, disappointed when Wyatt rolled off her until he pulled her tight against his hot skin. Wrapping one arm around her shoulders, his other hand made lazy circles around her breast. She loved that he kept touching her.

"Good," he said, kissing her soundly, "that was so good."

"It was amazing," Keeli agreed when she could finally find her voice. "You are a wild man and I am exhausted."

"Exhausted? Does not mean you don't want to try out the shower tonight?"

Keeli barely mumbled a response, snuggling closer into Wyatt's side.

"Huh?" he asked her. "What did you say?"

"Just give me a few minutes, okay?" Wyatt translated her mumbling at last and leaned back with a contented sign. Keeli felt his hand leave her skin only to find him handing her a wine glass a moment later. Taking a sip, he offered her the glass and she perked up a bit, sat up, dislodging his arm reluctantly and took the wine.

The two stayed together like that, sharing the wine, bits of conversation and light kisses. Wyatt moved his hand from her skin to her hair, from her hair to her breast, over and over in a soothing pattern.

"Mm, that's nice," she uttered in a voice lulled with sleep.

"Morning shower it is," he said softly. "What time do you need to be somewhere?"

"I need to work tomorrow, my place, whenever," her voice faded.

"Sleep," he whispered. "Sleep."

CHAPTER TWENTY-THREE

Keeli sat up in bed, looking around her, remembering last night with a rosy blush. She rolled to face Wyatt only to find herself alone in the big bed. The alarm clock indicated that it was only 7:15. The heavy curtains kept the room dark but Keeli could see strong sunlight peeking around the edges. She could not remember falling asleep, but she felt well rested.

And slightly sore. A good sore. A great sore.

Hearing no sounds Keeli wandered into the bathroom, caught a glimpse of herself in the large mirror, and tried to tame her hair unsuccessfully. She splashed water on her face and went digging for her toothbrush in her hobo bag. She brushed her teeth noticing that her lips were much fuller than usual, bright pink and well kissed. She rummaged in his dresser drawer, finding a clean white t-shirt and yanking it over her head. It was long enough to pass for a short dress.

Good thing I work at home today. Anyone looking at me, even a stranger, would know what I have been up to.

Although she heard no sounds, Keeli assumed Wyatt would not have left her in the apartment alone. She wandered past the living room, now lit by the large windows to display a pair of white leather sofas separated by a low modern table. There was a magnificent bright colored rug covering the hardwood floors. A statement art piece displayed prominently over the fireplace looked suspiciously like a Miro. Shaking her head in disbelief she continued on to the kitchen.

The smell of coffee was strong as she got closer and Keeli saw an espresso machine tucked into the corner of the counter. There was a lovely Japanese style teapot sitting open beside it. Looking in it, Keeli saw teabags with their tags dangling out the opening, waiting for hot water. Padding back down the hall, she went in search of Wyatt, finally hearing faint sounds of music coming from his office.

Knocking quietly on the door Keeli waited for permission to enter. She knocked a bit louder the second time and the door was quickly yanked open. The sound of the Rolling Stones was quite loud now. Wyatt stood there in a pair of lightweight sweatpants looking well muscled, powerful and downright irresistible. His hair was sticking up slightly on top and curling against his neck in back. Longing to run her fingers through it, Keeli rose on tiptoe, shyly pulling his head down for a kiss and fingering the soft curls.

"Good morning," her voice was husky and sexy. "Good morning," she repeated in a clearer voice.

"Hey sleepyhead," he kissed her again, lingering on her lips, wrapping his arms about her and pulling her t-shirt clad body against his shirtless one. Sliding his hands under the shirt he cupped her butt and pulled her tightly against a growing erection.

"Tea, or back to bed?" He was being boyish and provocative.

"Tea first, then bed? How long have you been awake?" she followed him down the hall.

"What time is it?"

"About 7:30, a little before," Keeli estimated.

"A couple hours. I am an early riser," and with that he took her hand and moved it toward the tented front of his sweatpants with a laugh. She gave him a very brief caress before he moved away to get hot water for her tea, starting the espresso machine as he passed it. He turned to her with a large, airtight metal canister.

"I didn't know what kind of tea you would like so I bought a bunch. I threw Earl Gray in the pot, but feel free to change it."

"You must have thought I was a sure thing," she said with a

pout, digging through the canister of Earl Grey, Chai, English Breakfast and assorted flavored teas.

"I hoped," Wyatt replied with a swift kiss to the top of her head. He was so tall and powerful standing next to her at the counter, both of them in bare feet. He made her feel small, a rare thing for a woman of her height. She liked it.

"I'll stick with the Earl Gray. Good choice, this is really good selection, Wyatt. I appreciate the effort you went through."

"Absolutely my pleasure," he responded, pouring water over her tea and frothing steamed milk noisily. She added a touch of the milk to her tea, he added sugar to his cappuccino and they moved as one to the dining table to enjoy their morning brews.

"No dirty dishes?" The kitchen was spotless despite last night's feast.

"I took care of it this morning," he volunteered and she chided him gently for not letting her help clean up last night.

"I had better plans for you last night," he smirked.

The light coming in the dining rooms windows was really white and pure. Keeli sat with the sun bathing her face in contented silence. Wyatt broke her reverie with a light touch of his fingers caressing her arm.

"You seem far away, what are you thinking?"

"I was thinking that this is exactly the way I picture morning light in Paris. I was imagining sitting at an outdoor café, sipping my tea on a perfect morning."

This is a perfect morning." Wyatt stroked her arm again, slowly up and down, up and down. "Have you been to Paris?" Keeli shook her head. "You would love it. We should go some time."

It's just a figure of speech, Keeli reminded herself when her hopes soared and her heart sped up. He is not planning a future with you. He is just caught up in the moment.

"So, what will your day be like? Mine will be filled with boring meetings that I will not be able to concentrate on." Just like that, Wyatt had moved from musing about Paris to the mundane realities of a workday in Chicago.

"I have an incredible day today actually." Keeli's excitement was palpable and Wyatt could not help grinning in response. "I get to pick the jewelry that I will take to Milwaukee Friday. It is a juried show, so the pieces they reviewed must be included but I get to pick the rest. Tomorrow I will pack them all up and get everything organized for the weekend."

"I wish I could go with you, help you set up or whatever, watch you in your element for awhile. The art museum is fantastic too; I love the architecture and the setting. A few romantic nights away with you would be a lovely bonus, of course."

"I totally love that plan, but I understand you have your own life too. I have tons of work and long days and no chance of a romantic hotel in my future. Clarice and I will share a room at the Motel 6. It keeps our costs down so we can afford to do a few away art shows. Usually I just turn them down but Milwaukee is my favorite art fair to go to and to show at. I love the lakeside setting, the access to the art museum, the crowds, just everything. In addition, the artists there are fantastic. They help raise my game."

"Well then, I better get you moving so you can get organized and on your way." Wyatt checked to see that she had almost finished her tea, gulped the last of his espresso and grabbed her hand, pulling her down the hall toward the bedroom.

Get her on her way? What happened to going back to bed? Keeli tamped down her disappointment when Wyatt pulled her past the bed, still rumpled and inviting, and into the brightly lit bathroom.

"Time for us to christen the shower, don't you think?" With a wicked grin, Wyatt threw an oversized towel onto the edge of the tub, within easy reach of the shower, stalking towards Keeli like a leopard and lifting the shirt from her body. Running his hands slowly up her back and back down to cup her butt he pulled her tight against his body, gave her a slow, coffee-flavored kiss then reached in the stall to turn on all those confusing dials. Three showerheads sprang to life as a warm mist quickly fogged the room.

Adjusting the temperature, Wyatt directed Keeli to stand under the rain shower from above, following her in as he maneuvered the double jets on each wall. Soon they were being sprayed evenly from shoulder to thigh, despite their height differences. Wyatt wrapped Keeli in his arms and she sighed with pleasure.

"This is sheer bliss," she gushed, turning to face him.

He was sliding his hands over her slick body, a forest scented soap in hand. "Yes, it certainly is."

Keeli stole the soap from Wyatt and started working her slippery hands down his back before turning him to lather his chest, arms and abdomen. As her hands moved lower, Wyatt took the bar back from her to do the same luxurious massage on her soft skin, moving lower to caress her thighs and calves with his sliding hands. She used him for balance when he lifted first one foot, then the other, growing drowsy from the heat and aroused by his hands. Turning in his arms, she rested against him, her back to his front as Wyatt continued his seductive movements. When he reached her breasts he trailed small kisses along her hairline and cheek until Keeli turned in his arms to demand a more satisfying kiss.

Pulling his head toward her, Keeli rose to her toes and pressed her body against his, sliding skin to skin. Her mouth sought his in a deep kiss, exploring his mouth thoroughly. Her hands grazed over his damp skin. She felt like she was trying to climb inside his skin, trying to get ever closer as he pushed her from beneath the overhead spray and against the wall. Lifting her legs to wrap around his waist, he slid easily into her moist heat.

Murmuring incoherent phrases, Wyatt slid his length in and out of Keeli, holding her between the wall and him with ease. The tile, at first chilly to her back, had warmed and served as a slippery backdrop, easing their movements. Their kisses were hungry, deep and demanding as Keeli climbed quickly to completion. Keeli moaned her pleasure, her body pulsing around Wyatt as her legs and arms constricted about him of their own volition. She moved as if to encourage Wyatt to orgasm but he shook his head.

"Again, Keeli. Do that again. I love watching you, babe. You are so incredibly hot." His words, his kisses, his touch and the hot hard length of him soon had her losing control, a soft scream escaping her lips. Almost immediately Wyatt was moaning his pleasure as well, quickly pulling out of her to spill his seed down the shower drain.

Arms still entwined, Wyatt leaned against Keeli where she lay slumped against the wall. They regained their equilibrium and their breath slowly, peppering each other with small kisses. Wyatt pulled Keeli back under the overhead spray, matter-of-factly reaching for shampoo to lather his short curls, rinsed off and stepped from the shower.

Still coming down from her high, Keeli took the shampoo in a daze, washed her red mop unconsciously, rinsing from head to toe before fiddling with the dials until the spray shut off. Stepping from the moist heat, she found Wyatt holding up an oversized white towel before he quickly cocooned her in the expensive Egyptian cotton.

It was so comfortable and natural for Keeli to stand beside him at the double sinks, taking the toothbrush she left by the sink, running a comb through her wet and tangled locks while watching from the corner of her eye as Wyatt shaved the face she had come to hold so dear. They behaved like a couple, and she reveled in the sensation.

Don't get ahead of yourself, just try to enjoy it while it lasts. You need to keep your head on with this guy, much as you want to just let go.

Getting all the snarls from her hair at last, Keeli wrapped it again in the towel, squeezing the last of the moisture from it before following Wyatt from the bathroom in search of her clothes. Digging clean panties from her bag and sliding into her jeans and top, Keeli turned to find Wyatt emerging from his walk-in closet in a crisp white shirt and perfectly pressed dark trousers. He was wrapping an elegant blue tie about his neck without a mirror, the knot flawless. His bare feet looked so sexy to her, peeking between the dark pants and dark carpet, and for a brief moment she wanted to grab him and pull him back to bed. Instead she moved from seductive to practical.

"What time do your meetings start?"

"Not 'til ten, so I have time to get a little food in you and take you home."

"Not necessary, Wyatt. I never eat this early although I appreciate the thought. I can keep you company and then grab the bus home. I know you have lots to take care of."

"Absolutely not. I will take you home even if you don't let me feed you. The office can wait. Except for a four o'clock conference call with my potential investors, I really don't care anyway."

"Really? What will the call be about?" Wyatt heard Keeli's excitement even with her head half buried under the bed searching for her shoes.

"Let me at least fix you toast and I will tell you," he negotiated.

"Okay, but only if you have peanut butter."

"Really? I had no idea you were a peanut butter girl. We are in luck because I can indeed feed you peanut butter toast." Wyatt was mocking her so she attempted to swat him with her towel. He sidestepped her efforts easily and headed down the long corridor, his laughter trailing behind him. True to his word, within two minutes he had bakery bread toasting and a jar of chunky peanut butter sitting on the counter.

A second cup of tea and warm peanut butter oozing over her fingers, Keeli listened attentively as Wyatt explained today's call. He would be discussing financing requirements based on the five-year business plan he sent his investors for review. It sounded complicated to Keeli, but she understood the basics from her own entrepreneurial efforts, and followed along as best she could.

She asked insightful questions, leading him to ask her where she got her financing.

"Oh no, there is no financing. I refuse to be beholden to anyone. I put aside enough money to buy supplies and support myself for six months before I left my job. I am determined to do this entirely on my own."

"But that's crazy, Keeli," Wyatt chided. "You must have learned about shared risk in school? And what about money for expansion? It is ridiculous to refuse funding."

"Do not call me ridiculous," Keeli responded defensively. "I really want to prove to my family that I can do this on my own. They were such skeptics, so unsupportive. It's important that I prove myself to them, and to me."

Wyatt was empathetic, especially about proving yourself to your family. It was something they had in common and it led to a conversation again about his feelings of disloyalty and fear of discovery. She remembered how hard it was to stand up to her mother, how her brothers had encouraged her to guilt about leaving Gilman. Wyatt made it sound as if he would be killing his parents and siblings.

"Okay, I may not understand the generational expectations of a rich family like yours," she finally admitted after going back and forth about it a few minutes. "But I do understand how hard it is to do something they think you shouldn't do. I really get it, Wyatt. But family tradition be damned, you have to decide how much you want this, don't you? You have to choose."

"Independence be damned then too, Keeli. You could ask for help, get investors for your business too."

"That's different." Even as the words left her mouth, she knew it was no different. They were both choosing to go against what they were comfortable with in order to succeed on their own terms. She conceded his point.

"Did I mention, I love being right?" he skillfully lightened the mood.

As soon as she swallowed the last bite of toast, Keeli was on her feet, reluctantly offering to get going. Wyatt had shifted from boyfriend to businessman in front of her eyes, checking the time and his incoming text messages frequently. She could tell he needed to get his day started.

While Wyatt reached for his briefcase and keys, Keeli ran to retrieve her toothbrush and run a comb through her wild curls one last time before they dried. Emerging from the bathroom, she walked right into Wyatt's open arms. Keeli was relieved to have a moment of romance before parting ways. She wanted to hold onto this feeling for as long as she could.

"I'm going to miss you this weekend. Funny how quickly I have gotten used to having you around," she confessed.

What are you doing, idiot. No possessiveness. It's just fun for him, remember?

You cannot say stuff like that.

"Me too. We'll have to do something about that."

Oooh. Or maybe you can.

CHAPTER TWENTY-FOUR

Clarice and Keeli had been inching forward in the crowd of vans and U-hauls for more than an hour, the sun beating relentlessly into Clarice's Chevy van, taxing the air conditioning beyond its capacity. Fearing that the car would overheat, they had sweated without the engine for fifteen-minute intervals twice already and there were still eight vehicles ahead of them waiting to unload before they could move into position. This was the part of street fairs that both women hated the most and they had been whining non-stop since entering the end of the line.

"So, enough whining, we sound pitiful," Clarice admonished in her no-nonsense way. "Tell me something cheerful. How's your love life? You have been pretty quiet on that front all day. Any recent sightings of the wealthy and wonderful Wyatt?"

A blush moved up Keeli's cheeks adding color that had nothing to do with the sun. Clarice, always observant, pounced instantly.

"We have been in this car for more than two hours and you didn't think to mention this to me? Spill, girl. Now!"

"We have been on a few dates. Clarice, I like him."

"You like him? That is all you are giving me? I thought we were friends."

"OK, I really, really like him. Is that better? I am afraid to jinx things by saying too much."

"And the dates?" Clarice pumped her for information.

"Well, I told you about him stopping to buy me coffee a couple weeks ago, and going out for drinks. Last week I went to see him play hockey and Wednesday we got together again."

"And..."

Keeli knew that Clarice would keep at her until she shared everything. "And, I stayed over at his place Wednesday night."

"WHAT? Do not leave me hangin' here, Keeli. I mean it." She inched the car forward, "We are stuck in this line at least fifteen more minutes, so you better start talking."

Keeli gave Clarice an overview of the dates, describing Wyatt's friends, his apartment, his bathroom, avoiding details of their conversations and sex. Clarice kept questioning Keeli, trying to get more information until the two were laughing and joking about it.

"Girl, I suspect that what you are not telling me is way more interesting than what you are telling me. However, if you want to keep it private, I can respect that, not! Come on Keeli, give me something."

Keeli was saved from providing details as the women finally reach the front of the unloading dock. They worked well together, rapidly emptying the van of display cases, banners and sculptures as well as two pad-locked cases of jewelry and the dollies for moving it all. Keeli would stay with these while Clarice searched for the closest thing to shade in the exhibitor parking lot.

The exhibition actually opened at 10:00 this morning, but Keeli and Clarice agreed that they would take their chances setting up on Friday instead of Thursday, hoping for smaller set up crowds. Despite the long wait, their plan had actually succeeded, shaving a couple hours from their usual wait to unload their goods. The downside was that now it took Clarice a long time to return. Spaces in the exhibitor lot were scarce and she had to return from quite a distance.

The two women were pros by now at piling the materials and moving them into the booths. They carefully loaded Keeli's gear under Clarice's, stacking everything so that it was stable for rolling the hand trucks to their tents. This season Keeli was well positioned in the center of the long aisle of booths. Being near an opening to the sound stages and food, she would be right in the path of a lot of foot traffic. Unfortunately, the two women were not located near each other this weekend. Clarice's booth was closer to the museum entrance, also a prime space, but all the way at the other end of the long exhibition tent.

The two wished each other well with a hug and waved as they separated to tackle the hard work of set up. Keeli had her display cases put together in moments, their wrap stored out of her way in the trunks behind the booth. She hung the black velvet boards on the wall, her banner behind them and set up the lighting to shine precisely. Then she began the critical task of placing her jewelry just so, adjusting the lighting, rearranging pieces, adjusting lighting again until she was completely satisfied.

Content at last, she grabbed Flaubert's "Madame Bovary" from her bag and gratefully sank into her director's chair. She had placed the chair in the aisle today, not hidden in the booth. She was alongside fellow artists if she wanted to chat, with a perfect view of her booth and the traffic from both directions.

It was almost noon and Keeli was anxious to make a few sales. The crowds were swelling and adrenaline was pumping through her veins. The Milwaukee Lakefront Festival of Art was an impressive show, connected to the award winning Art Museum with its winged roof, gorgeous gardens, modern fountains and spectacular lakefront setting. It attracted local crowds but also the wealthy Chicago suburban crowd she was desperate to reach.

The judging was known to be tough for this show, so attendees knew they were seeing the finest artists from all over the country. Completely enclosed, the artists were protected under a long white tent with additional space in the museum. There were two music venues to attract additional crowds from the street or the lakefront trails, assuring high attendance.

The energy in both the artists and the crowd was palpable and the afternoon flew by in a blur of activity. When Clarice wandered by close to 4:00, Keeli was able to report that she doing well, steadily moving smaller items as well as a few more expensive designs. Clarice had a tougher audience but she had sold several garden sculptures already, so both women were pleased.

"We are here until 10 tonight," Keeli reminded Clarice as they started planning for a dinner break. They agreed to delay dinner until just before six, when the afternoon crowds would diminish but before the evening crowd swelled. Each woman brought a sandwich that they devoured hours ago, so Clarice was thrilled when Keeli shared a fruit salad from Theo as a late afternoon snack. Inhaling the food quickly, both returned to their posts.

At six, the women were hot, sweaty, tired but happy with their first day's sales. They headed to the food area for some dinner. Clarice was buoyed by the honorable mention ribbon that the judges had attached to her booth an hour ago. She kept reliving the moment for Keeli, her pride evident. Keeli was overjoyed for her friend and telling her so for the umpteenth time when a deep voice sounded from over her shoulder.

"Ladies, I thought I would never find you. But here you are, of course, stuffing your lovely faces."

CHAPTER TWENTY-FIVE

For a heartbeat, Keeli was certain she had conjured up the elegant man now standing in front of her. His hair was curling slightly along his perfectly pressed collar. Several buttons at the top of his shirt were unbuttoned, exposing the strong column of his neck. His suit jacket was long gone.

"What are you doing here?" She was sputtering and sitting paralyzed when Wyatt scooped her from the plastic lawn chair and folded her into his embrace. She recognized the aroma of his expensive shampoo faintly clinging to his hair as he tilted his head lower to give her a chaste kiss on the cheek.

"I had to check on my girls," he announced casually, as if he did not just drive through at least two hours of rush hour traffic to be here. He squeezed Clarice's hand in greeting,

"Don't get up," he told her. "I imagine you must be tired."

"We are - tired but happy," Clarice confirmed, shifting in her seat to give Keeli a sly glance from under her lids.

"Seriously, Wyatt, what are you doing here?" Keeli was growing insistent. "I thought we agreed you were too busy to get away."

"We agreed I could not set up or stay until Sunday, but we never agreed I would not be here at all. How could I miss my favorite show of the summer?

"Well, when you put it like that...so you came for the show, not for me?" Keeli was shamelessly flirting, surprising both herself and Clarice. Keeli never flirted.

"For the show, of course. But... since I am here anyway..." Laughing, the three settled in for a short break together, the women eating fast food meals, Wyatt sipping a Wisconsin microbrew. He was comfortably talking about sculpture with Clarice like they were old friends, idly stroking Keeli's bare arms with his fingertips. Too soon the women needed to return to their booths.

After giving Clarice a tight hug, Wyatt lagged behind Keeli who had moved back toward her booth. She was easy to follow despite the growing crowds, dressed in her usual bright colored sundress and Keds, hair flaming in the waning sunlight.

"Do you mind my being here," Wyatt caught up to her and fidgeted awaiting Keeli's answer.

"Of course not. I am thrilled. I was just surprised." Their eyes met, Wyatt's lips lifting in a sexy, lazy grin. He was running his fingers up and down the creamy skin of her upper arm, the rays of the sun still warm on it. The sexual tension grew between them quickly so that Keeli could not look away.

"I hope you won't object, but I thought Clarice might want that Motel 6 room to herself tonight. I got a room for us." Wyatt's husky voice signaled he was having the same response she was.

"Hmmm, I might mind. I was looking forward to all that luxury." She was teasing him comfortably, falling in step with his mood. She saw that he too was comfortable with the ribbing, was in fact enjoying it.

"I got us a suite at The Pfister," Wyatt casually mentioned the name of a century old luxury hotel in the heart of the city. Keeli had never even been to their bar for a drink, always too underdressed when she worked the festival.

"The Pfister? A suite?" She was overwhelmed, looking at Wyatt with wide eyes trying to regain her composure with a tiny laugh. "I might be able to handle that."

Wyatt broke into an enormous grin, knowing he had blown her away with both his arrival and the promise of a night in the opulent hotel. "We can invite Clarice over for breakfast in the morning, before you head back to work. Okay?"

"Yeah, sure, okay," Keeli remained stunned until Wyatt swooped down and gave her a hard, swift kiss. "Back to work for you," he swatted her on the behind. "I'm going exploring and will be back before ten."

Before the kiss or the words registered, he was gone; she fell into the director's chair with a thump, as if the last thirty minutes were a figment of her imagination. She had to work, to come down from this dazed high, let go of the heat scorching her from the inside out and return to her professional demeanor.

Get it together. You have a job to do. At that moment several people entered her tent. Keeli jumped up to assist, leaving her sensuous fog behind.

Back in her stride, the evening flew by in a whirlwind of activity for Keeli. She was selling rings and bracelets in large numbers. Earrings and necklaces were moving more slowly but still selling well. She kept a running tally of sales in her head, excited to realize she had sold enough to place an order for new gemstones. Her mind was wandering to pictures of new work, a new collection forming in her mind that she believed she could complete before summer's end.

What a week! Two stores are interested; Missy reached out, now this. Wyatt must be bringing me luck – among other things.

Around 9:30, Wyatt returned with a bottle of water for her in one hand, her small overnight bag in the other. Before she can ask, he explained "I met up with Clarice and retrieved this, along with her promise to meet us for breakfast at 8 am sharp.

"Has it been going well? I heard some great music and saw a modern art exhibit in the museum that you just have to see. Maybe we can go on a break tomorrow and see it together? They have a huge Lichtenstein and an Andy Warhol near each other. The colors of one set off the other perfectly. You just have to see it," he gushed with enthusiasm.

The crowds had thinned by now, mostly moving to the music stages and beer vendors outside as the tents shut down for the night, guards moving conspicuously into position. Keeli turned off her lights, locked a few very high-end pieces into the trunk, locked the remainder into the cases and tied down the flaps of her booth.

Wyatt, helping where he could, checked the locks on everything twice, sliding her chair across the dusty floor into the dark booth before taking her overnight bag and oversized hobo and settling both on his shoulder. Holding hands and walking close together they moved as one toward the parking garage. It was a beautiful night. Bright city lights prevented them from seeing many stars, but Keeli reflexively turned her face to the sky when they emerged from the tent.

"Stargazing?"

"Can't help it. On the farm, at this time of night, the sky is amazing. You can see a million stars. I always forget how bright it is in the city. I always forget." She repeated wistfully.

"Missing the farm?"

"Sometimes. I miss my brothers, for sure. And the peace and quiet."

"You never talk about your parents," Wyatt probed gently. "Just your brothers."

"My dad died when I was thirteen. He had cancer. It was pretty awful, but quick. I think we felt like we had just enough time to say good-bye and poof, he was gone. My mom never got over it. She was still young, you know? Anyway, it just made my mom cling to us tighter. She was not a big fan of my moving away, to say the least."

"But she can see your talent. She must?"

"If she does, Wyatt, she sure isn't saying so. I told you, she has been critical of my choice to leave since the day I made it. It is torture calling home. She loves to plant doubt in my brain. She thrives on undermining my confidence."

"But why, what is the point in that?"

"Wyatt, think about your own situation. She wants me to toe her line. And her line is coming home 'where I belong' instead of struggling in Chicago. That is one of the reasons I can't ask for help. It would just be another reason to say, 'I told you so.' She tells me that there is too much competition, that I don't have what it takes. Oh yeah, she is a joy to talk with."

"But she's wrong. You certainly have what it takes." Wyatt was visibly angry on Keeli's behalf.

"Not according to her. She says I don't have the talent, the experience. I especially love when she tells me she is my mother and just being honest with me since no one else will be. That one really hurts."

"That is just cruel."

"But effective. Whenever I talk to her, for the rest of the day I believe I should just give up and go home. But I get over it, make more jewelry and start again. I am not going home just so she can have her way. I am not working the farm, being a waitress, and watching the boys play video games and pool on the weekends. I did that to pay for my education, and now I plan to use it. I am a damn good jewelry designer." Keeli had worked herself up as she spoke.

"Yes you are." Wyatt spoke calmly and authoritatively, bringing Keeli back from her ledge.

"I miss hanging with my brothers. We had some raucous times that were really fun. And they did spoil me since I was the only girl. That was nice too. But going back now would mean I was a failure and that is just not happening."

"I am sad that you don't have the support of your family," Wyatt sympathized. "I know how awful that feels, believe me."

"You know, I had convinced myself I had something special. When I was in high school my art teachers were really encouraging, and my design teachers in college were too. Promise you won't laugh. This is such a cliché." Keeli looked over at Wyatt expectantly and he nodded his assent. "Against the advice of all my friends and my mom, of course, I hopped on a bus to Chicago with $400 in my pocket, my jewelers tools and two changes of clothes in a backpack. I knew no one and I had no job. Looking back now, I know I was an idiot."

"But look how far you have come. Maybe you were not so

idiotic?"

"Enough. Maybe we should change the subject?"

"If you like."

"But you know," she continued despite wanting to move on," you would have liked my dad and I think he would have liked you too. He spent my whole childhood telling me I could be anything I wanted when I grew up. He told me I could be president and I believed him. My mom thinks small. She has been in Gilman her whole life. Not my dad though, he saw more of the world. He made me believe I could have the world."

"He really sounds like the kind of dad I wish I had. Both of my parents are overprotective. Everything is family, family business, family loyalty, family name."

"But I am sure they love you and want the best for you. And they must be so proud."

"Don't get me wrong," Wyatt stated as he pulled in front of the hotel. The doorman sprang forward to help Keeli from the car, "They gave me everything."

By necessity, the conversation shifted to check-in information and baggage discussions before Wyatt handed the keys to the valet and the bellman led them into the grand lobby. Keeli spun around to admire the high ceilings gilded with gold, the quiet luxury of the oriental carpets and charm of large wooden furniture. While Wyatt dealt with registration, Keeli admired the artwork scattered along every wall and poked her nose into the leather and wood restaurant.

"We are on the club level, but we can have breakfast here in the morning if you prefer?"

"No, upstairs is fine, I guess," Keeli only vaguely understood what it meant to be on club level, but assumed from Wyatt's words that it came with breakfast.

"Want a nightcap, or just to head up? We can get drinks up there too, if you prefer."

It was obvious to Keeli that Wyatt was accustomed to club levels and old, luxury hotels but it was all new and overwhelming for her.

"What about our bags?" She was clearly confused.

"What about them? The bellman took them up." Wyatt did not even seem to understand Keeli's question. Then, understanding crept into his face. "Oh, yeah, I have the key to the room. So we can choose. If you want to stay down here we can sit in the bar or we can grab a glass of wine or a beer from the lounge on club level, admire the view from there, then take it to our room." He was helping her get the lay of the land at last.

"Oh, I am exhausted and filthy, so how bout we just grab something upstairs?"

"Perfect." Wyatt led her to the elevator, pressed the button for the 23rd floor, inserting his key to make it work, and then they were alone in the quiet of the elevator.

"You don't look filthy to me. You look sexy. This makes me think of the first time I touched you," he murmured as his lips descended on hers. He captured her mouth in a slow, searing kiss, leaning his body to trap hers against the wall of the cabin. She returned his kiss hungrily and they were caught up in the moment. It was a surprise when the doors opened on 23 much too soon.

"Damn, I hate a quick elevator," Wyatt smirked at her and ran his index finger slowly along her bottom lip, already bruised with his kisses. "After you, Madame," he bowed with a flourish before stepping back for her to precede him.

Following the signs to the Club lounge Keeli pulled open the double doors before Wyatt could assist. She walked straight across the room to admire the view of Milwaukee laid out before her. Wyatt stepped behind her, wrapping his arms around her waist and pulling her close.

"Beautiful," she breathed.

Yes," he responded, turning her to look at him. He bent to suck her bottom lip into his mouth, running his tongue along its wet warmth. She checked to assure that they were alone then gave in to the moment, wrapping her arms about his neck and moving as tightly against him as she could.

"Red or white?" he asked after a minute or two, adjusting the bulge in his trousers as he moved across the room to the bar. The plush carpeting absorbed his footfalls and she followed, the toe of her Keds catching in the deep nap. Falling forward, she reached to catch herself, but Wyatt was there before she could grab a nearby chair.

"Careful, Keeli!" he held her tight while she caught her breath after the narrow escape. "Maybe you are more tired than I realized?"

"No, I'm just not used to such thick carpeting."

"We need to fix that." Another cryptic response from Wyatt set Keeli's heart racing. "Let's grab a bottle of white. It will be light and crisp. We can take it to our room, okay?"

Nodding her agreement, Keeli reached for two glasses, Wyatt took the wine from the small refrigerator and they meandered their way to the room stopping along the way to kiss and embrace. Wyatt trailed hot kisses over her bare shoulder and the nape of her neck, shooting waves of longing straight to her core.

Pressing the small key card into the slot and getting the corresponding beep, Wyatt opened the door and flipped the light switch as Keeli moved into and around the luxurious suite. She wandered slowly, running her fingers over the beautiful wooden tables and four-poster bed, the suede sofas, the heavy fabrics of the curtains. Her beat-up bag was sitting on a chair in the corner beside a small bag in black leather that must have been Wyatt's.

He packed so light, just one night I guess. Stop moping, Keeli, he is a very busy man who drove all the way to Milwaukee to spend one night with you.

"What are you smiling about?"

"I am just realizing how lucky I am to spend the night here with you rather than the Motel 6 with Clarice."

"Is it the suite or the company that has you smiling?" Wyatt flashed her a cocky look, obviously fishing for compliments.

"Well, if I am being totally honest...." Wyatt tackled Keeli to the bed and started tickling her sides. She dissolved into a fit of giggles before shouting, "the company, it's the company" until he relented.

After lowering himself to the bed for a few sultry kisses, Keeli begged for a quick shower and Wyatt let her up while he opened the wine and poured two glasses.

He left her to shower in peace. It had been a long day for them both and was now approaching midnight. When he heard her emerge from the shower, he knocked and entered the steamy room to find her swaddled in an oversized bath sheet, her hair piled in a mass of curls on her head, damp tendrils curling about her face.

"I wish I was an artist instead of a collector," he mused. "I would paint you just like that, flushed with heat, hair damp, skin moist. You are so beautiful."

"Don't embarrass me, Wyatt. No one talks like that." The blush rose in her already pink cheeks and a blissful smile widened her lips.

"Okay, no romantic stuff. How 'bout instead we hit the mini bar and the bottle of wine I opened while I check the Cubs score? Is that unromantic enough for you?"

"That sounds perfect." Keeli emerged from the bathroom, now wrapped in the hotel supplied terry robe that reached to her fingertips and was tightly belted, overlapping quite a distance around her tiny waist. She looked like a child playing dress-up and Wyatt could not help chuckling as he helped her roll the sleeves a bit.

She dropped exhausted to the bed, jostling the candy bars, nuts and chips that Wyatt had neatly arranged for her perusal. She selected a bag of potato chips and wolfed them down, followed by a deep drink of the crisp, cool wine.

"Should I order room service instead? Are you really hungry?" He was fiddling with the remote control, shifting through the available channels impatiently looking for the sports stations.

"Nope, this will do it. Thanks anyway. This is perfect and I am too tired to wait for room service."

A huge yawn stretched Keeli's mouth confirming her statement as she finished the chips and slipped her feet under the blankets. She ran her feet over the luxurious, cool sheets, and propped a pillow behind her back with a contented sigh.

Wyatt finally found the ball game, stopped channel surfing and swept the remaining food into his hands. He padded barefoot and silent, returning the uneaten food to the minibar. He peeled off his clothes, dropping them in a pile onto the corner chair and crawled in beside her in the large bed. He reached an arm behind her under the pillow grabbing both to pull her close for a long kiss. He was stopped by another large yawn from Keeli. She laughed in embarrassment as he settled for a kiss to her forehead.

"Okay, sleepyhead, what do you say we just cuddle and fall asleep? You have to get up in a few hours and do another long day's work."

"I'm so sorry, Wyatt, but I just can't keep my eyes open. I really want to," but her voice was already fading and she was snuggling into the blankets like a child.

Wyatt set an alarm, muted the TV and turned off the lights. Not his night to score it would seem. Lying in the dark a few minutes, he listened to Keeli's quiet breathing before shutting off the television and wrapping himself around her sleeping form.

At least the Cubs scored tonight.

CHAPTER TWENTY-SIX

Clarice and Keeli were back in their booths setting up for a long day by 9:30. The weather promised to be perfect and they were well rested and very well fed. Clarice had told Keeli at least four times how impressed she was with Wyatt, how polite and generous he was, how thoughtful, and how incredibly hot.

"And I love the way he looks at you, girl, like you are the best thing he has ever seen." Keeli had seen that look too, a cross between lascivious and loving. She basked in its glow. He really seemed to care about her and she knew she was falling hard.

Clarice had been working for a year to get Keeli to forget about Wyatt, reminding her that he was a player and that he was not going to give her a second glance. Now she was telling a different story, encouraging Keeli to go after this prize.

The feelings she and Wyatt shared were still new and fragile, but Keeli believed in them. She sensed real promise. When she confided those feelings to her friend, Clarice agreed. Keeli felt her hopes soar and her little warning voice go silent.

She was encouraged by the way he opened up to her about his work, his dreams and his family. She got the impression that he was telling her things he didn't share with many people in his life. She counted herself as a member of his inner circle now, an intimate group, she knew, and she was grateful to be included.

He supported her dreams as well. He believed in her in ways

even her own family didn't, boosting her confidence and propelling her forward. This was of great significance to her because Wyatt was knowledgeable on the subject, he knew talent, so his good opinion held more weight.

She loved waking up close to him this morning; hated having to leave the cocoon of their beautiful suite. He was efficient moving her out the door for breakfast and the art show, lingering over kisses only a few times, especially when he told her that he would be leaving to head south around noon. She had hoped to have another night with him but he had business meetings this afternoon and family commitments tomorrow so she was graceful about letting him go.

He said his farewells earlier, but she knew that he had wandered off to explore the art fair, always in search of new talent. Her mind was lingering over the ease and comfort they experienced together, brushing their teeth side by side, getting coffee, getting dressed and out the door like they had lived together for years. He was easy, but exciting - the perfect combination – and she hungered to spend more time with him. She hoped he would stop by one last time before heading home although she knew not to expect it.

Instead, she focused her full attention on the festival, enjoying the interactions with customers and potential customers, explaining her techniques, helping people select just the right piece for their face, for that special occasion or for the perfect gift. The hours flew by and soon Clarice was bringing salads from one of the food stands.

"Just something to tide us over until later," she explained. "I thought we could eat German food later, or at least bratwursts, and maybe listen to some music."

"I am okay with staying here and eating brats," Keeli agreed. The bands looked promising, the crowds were thick and engaging and once they were done working it would feel good to mingle and enjoy a little of the festival as observers, not exhibitors.

By 8:30, neither woman could stand any longer so they headed to the Motel 6 for the night. After last night's luxury, Keeli was initially crabby about the lumpy bed and scratchy sheets but she enjoyed the time with Clarice, comparing stories from the day. Both women had enjoyed excellent sales. Clarice was particularly excited about a potential commission for several works to display in a corporate lobby. This was exactly the opportunity she had been longing for, and while she had no details yet, she was still giddy with possibilities.

Keeli was too sapped of energy to be appropriately thrilled for her friend, and she was disappointed by Wyatt's silence. She had texted several times during the day, first to say 'thank you', then to ask if he arrived home safely, finally to say 'good night'. No response to any of these. She tamped down her concern, hugged her dear friend good night, begging her forgiveness when she quickly turned out the lights and tried to fall asleep.

Tossing and turning for a short while, Keeli wondered why Wyatt never texted back, where he was tonight and who he was with. Finally, she gave in to her exhaustion and slept.

It seemed only minutes had passed when Clarice's phone blasted Motown music, waking Keeli from a deep sleep. Just thinking about another seven hours on her feet today, followed by breaking down the booth and the two-hour ride, Keeli was worn out.

Checking her phone, she was crushed to find nothing from Wyatt. She thought they were doing so well together, but insecurity bubbled up in her, leaving her unsettled and edgy as she donned her last clean sundress and her Keds, ran a brush through her unruly curls and pulled them back in a loose ponytail for the day. It promised to be hot and sunny, perfect for fair-goers but hot and sticky for her inside the tent.

By opening time at ten, Keeli had laid out everything she had left to sell, including her best, most expensive pieces and the small items she threw in at the last minute to assure she would not sell out. She had struggled to display them together, arranging and rearranging the items in the cases, never fully satisfied.

She knew the dissatisfaction was not about the display. She was anxious about Wyatt, checking her phone frequently. Her mood worsened as the day – and the silence – wore on.

By three, she was exhausted, her inventory was picked over and she went in search of Clarice, who agreed to closing up an hour early so they could beat the crowds. By six, they were on the road, stuck in traffic with all the weekenders returning to the city after a lovely retreat to Wisconsin. The two hour drive stretched to well over three and Keeli's nerves were shot by the time Clarice dropped her at home and helped her drag her trunks to the basement for storage.

They hugged each other goodbye and promising to talk tomorrow when both recovered from the long weekend. Keeli could not wait to eat and shower. She had planned to take a final stock and see how her weekend had gone, but instead fell to the sofa exhausted, deciding to leave the inventory review for tomorrow.

After shoveling in the leftovers from last night's catering job, delicious appetizers and salmon, Keeli took a quick shower and wandered back to the empty living room with her hair dripping down. There was still nothing from Wyatt and Keeli was growing increasingly concerned. It was late enough for him to have finished dinner with his family hours ago. She decided to try texting him once more and was relieved to get a quick response.

'Is anything wrong?' she texted and within minutes he responded 'all good, just busy.'

'You home? I am. All good here too.' She hesitated over her fingers. What to say next?

'TTYL.' That was all she got back and it took a few minutes for even that response. He must be busy, Keeli rationalized. She flipped on the TV randomly selected a program and pulled paperwork into her lap to summarize the weekend results and plan for the coming week. She figured she might as well get it done now.

The weekend was a resounding success and Keeli was excited to realize that she would need a lot of new inventory. It would be a week to crack down and create for shows several weeks away. She would need to shop for supplies first thing tomorrow, right after a trip to the bank.

At 11 o'clock, she checked her phone one last time and dejectedly headed to bed.

CHAPTER TWENTY-SEVEN

At 9 Chapter, Wyatt finally headed to the city. Traffic was light and he was enjoying the Porsche engine revving under him at higher than legal speeds. He watched his mirrors carefully for police, but everyone around him was speeding, leaving him confident he would go unmolested blazing down the expressway.

He needed the speed to help diffuse the anger pulsing through his blood. He had been simmering slowly, working to a full boil over the course of a very long day with his family. Right now he hated them, wondered how he would ever forgive them for their insular attitudes and snobbery. He could not believe they were his flesh and blood. He was actually embarrassed to be a Howe, ashamed of his parents, infuriated at Tyler, and confused about his future.

His phone began playing Maroon 5's "Moves Like Jagger" - Missy's ringtone. She could not get enough of Adam Levine. Usually the song, Missy's favorite, brought a smile to his face. She was his favorite sister after all, but he was even avoiding her now. She had already called three times without him picking up. Obviously, she was not giving up.

Punching the hands-free button Wyatt barked, "Missy, just leave it. I am so done!"

"Just shut up and listen," Missy jumped in before Wyatt could hang up on her. "Okay, so they are snobs. You knew that already.

Okay, so Dad doesn't want you starting your own business. Seriously? Did you think he would jump at the opportunity to let you go?"

Missy stopped to catch her breath. "And don't you dare hang up on me, Wyatt."

"I'm here," he was resigned to listening to her since she wouldn't stop calling anyway. "I know you are right. It is what I should have expected, but I hoped for so much more. Even Regan didn't help much, and you know she wants my job. She should be helping me."

"She did what she could, Ivy. She wants to stay in Dad's good graces especially because she wants your job."

Wyatt eased his foot off the gas pedal a bit, taking a few cleansing breaths to overcome the adrenaline racing through his system.

"It is a nightmare, Missy. You know it is. I could kill Tyler for showing up with his big mouth and setting things in motion. I may never forgive him."

"Stop, Wyatt. You are just going to get worked up again. Leave it. Sleep on it. Let Dad sleep on it and see how you feel in the morning. And stop speeding so you get home in one piece," she finished.

"I am not speeding.... much." He could not help a small lift to his lips. "Love you, Missy."

"Love you, too." Then she was gone, having done the job of calming him considerably so he could get home safely.

Wyatt drove on autopilot, remembering the disastrous afternoon and evening. Usually family dinners were proper and polite, the food excellent, the house comfortable and spotless, and the family, while not exactly warm, were a known quantity. More over, the little ones running around added a lively distraction from too much business and money talk, or too much pressure to marry.

This day had started the usual way. It was a lovely summer day perfect for a relaxing, scenic lakefront drive from downtown to Lake Forest. The views of the crowded beaches gave way to high rises but then the road started twisting, fun for driving in the Panamera and the homes grew stately, larger, better landscaped, and more exclusive. Finally, the twisting roads along the ravines cut into the hillier landscape of Chicago's far northern suburbs. Here there were long gated drives, manicured lawns, and houses invisible behind shrubs precisely clipped.

Wyatt loved this drive, leaving behind the hubbub of the city for the peacefulness of the remote suburb, the cool crisp air quality after the suffocating city heat. Since he had learned to drive, he had taken this route for pleasure or when he needed to think. He found it soothing somehow.

Turning into the driveway of his childhood home, he proceeded down the curving drive to park beside the numerous luxury cars, grabbed the confections he always brought his mother from her favorite city bakery and took the steps two at time.

Pulling open the screen to let himself in he hollered, "Does anyone care that the door is open and the a/c is on?" No one answered so he closed the door behind him and walked through the center hallway oblivious to the elegant décor he had known all his life. The house might look like a magazine spread, but to Wyatt it was just home. He moved past the refined living room on one side, the formal dining room on the other to enter a beehive of activity in the kitchen and family room.

Wyatt kissed his mother, who stood perfectly coiffed, made up, and dressed in white linen as if they weren't having a barbeque. She looked ready for a formal luncheon at the country club. Moving past her, he found Regan and Missy mixing drinks and putting chips in bowls, cheese and crackers on platters. Kissing cheeks and exchanging pleasantries, he stepped into the family room, shaking hands with his father and brother, neither of whom looked up from the baseball game.

"Uncle Wyatt" came the squeal of young a voice just before a small body hurled itself into his arms. Wyatt happily accepted the sloppy kisses of the two year old before gently pushing her back outdoors.

"Abigail, you are soaking wet!"

"I swimming. You watch," the chubby little girl commanded, pulling Wyatt by the arm to follow her outside. He accompanied his niece willingly, greeting his brother-in law and watching for a few minutes while the girl showed off her new aquatic skills, such as they were. The inflated water wings were clearly doing most of the work.

"Outstanding. Don't forget to breathe though," he coached before turning to head back inside. Barely one foot in the door another small body ran to Wyatt, begging "pick me up, pick me up, Uncle Wyatt."

"You are getting so big, Alden," he told his niece, lifting her high in the air before carefully returning her to her feet. She squealed with joy then ran out to join her brother in the pool. He could hear Stephen shouting "no running" then the splash of a little body entering the water and the muffled sound of the two children's giggles.

"A drink, my lord?" Missy handed him a scotch on the rocks in a beautiful cut crystal tumbler, mimicked a servant's curtsy and pulled him to sit by her on the stately, cream sofa. "Your buddy Tyler called to say he is stopping by around 5," she informed him, brows rising in question.

"Really? Why?" Missy shrugged in answer, satisfied that Wyatt had not broken with tradition to invite his friend to dine on family night. It had always been a family-only event. The rare exception had been when Wyatt brought Sloane, something he had not done in months. "He's staying for dinner?"

"He didn't say."

Turning to the men, Wyatt again queried the status of the game. "Eighth inning. Cubs up by two" followed by silence until a commercial break. Then his father began an inquisition on all the meetings held that week, deals made, not made, how construction progressed at this site or that.

"Enough shop, Wyatt. It's Sunday," His mother scolded her husband. "Ivy hardly ever gets here these days and you can talk shop at the office. He is mine for now." She sat close to him after this proclamation, taking his hand in hers.

"Tell me how you are dear," she began politely, but Wyatt knew an inquisition was coming. "What is happening with you? Did you invite Sloane to join us? There is plenty of food, if you want to call her."

"Actually, I am not seeing Sloane, but you already knew that Mother. I am actually seeing someone new."

The room went silent, the game suddenly forgotten as everyone turned to Wyatt. He had their complete attention, whether he wanted it or not.

"Her name is Keeli Larsen. She is a jewelry designer."

"Really, dear, " his mother drawled "An artist? How charming. Who are her parents? Do we know them? Wyatt," she queried her husband, "do we know any Larsens?"

Trying to save her favorite brother, Missy jumped into the fray. "Oh, she is a lovely girl, and you would love her jewelry, Mother. You and Regan would want to buy everything."

"She is from downstate, Mother. I do not think you would know her parents. They own a farm."

"Farmers?" His mother was almost shrieking, "A commercial farm? How many acres? Is it very large?" She emphasized the word "large" very strategically.

"I don't think so, Mother. A family farm."

During this exchange, Tyler had arrived, helped himself to a drink and – however unwelcome - joined the conversation.

"Oh, Mrs. Howe, nothing to worry about. Trust me. This is not serious. I met her. Pretty, actually," he conceded, "but certainly not relationship material. Maybe you saw her?" he looked at all of them as he continued, "She was our waitress at the Howe Museum dinner."

"A waitress?" his mother queried in a deadly calm voice that the family knew was the precursor to all hell breaking loose. Wyatt sent Tyler a scathing look. Tyler did not even have the courtesy to pretend to be abashed. He knew exactly what he had done.

"Yes, she is a waitress. Part time. Her roommate owns the

catering company and she helps out from time to time." Not the complete truth, but not a complete lie either, and Wyatt hoped to kill the uproar resulting from the waitress remark.

Not so lucky.

"Her roommate is male?" Regan was asking.

"He's gay."

"This just gets better and better," his brother chuckled from the corner, one eye still on the game.

"Where on earth did you meet this waitress, and how long has this been going on?" His father's voice was imperious.

"Artist, Father. I met her at an art show. Actually, I met her when she worked for a jeweler in our office building, but rekindled the relationship several months ago at an art fair. Missy was with me, buying jewelry."

"Oh yes, that ring you like so much, Regan, it is one of hers." Missy chimed in and Regan agreed, "I love that ring."

But Tyler was not done fueling this fire.

"You would have laughed to see her at our hockey game last week. She just couldn't fit in with the group. No education, no conversation, but she is attractive. I can see why Ivy might find her fun for a bit."

"She is educated, Tyler. And charming, Mother. And she runs her own business, Father. You would like her very much if you got to know her." Wyatt heard the defensiveness in his response but could not find a way to regain control of this conversation.

"I found her delightful. I met her at the Gold Coast Art Fair. And we had lunch last week too," Missy offered.

"You had lunch with her?" Wyatt's head nearly swiveled off his neck turning to look at Missy after that remark but her face gave nothing away.

Why was Missy meeting with Keeli, and why the hell didn't either of them tell me about it?

"Ivy, you wouldn't really get serious with an artist, would you? I mean, could you take her to client dinners? What kind of hostess would she be?" His mother had always been the perfect partner for his father at that type of event; of course she would worry about that now.

"That won't be an issue with the new business," Tyler piped up. "Geeks have different standards." Six sets of eyes bored into Wyatt.

"Explain please," his father demanded in a frosty voice.

"Tyler, what exactly are you doing here?" Wyatt had commandeered his father's cold demeanor and clipped tones causing Tyler to jump quickly to his feet and head toward the door.

"Actually, I am not sure why I stopped by. I never meant to interrupt family dinner. Forgive me." He was out the door with one longing look at Regan as he went.

"Son. I want to speak to you in my study right now." Wyatt's father ordered as soon as he saw Tyler's back.

Knowing that his father would not be sidetracked, Wyatt reluctantly followed his father's slower gait to the wood paneled room. Always one of Wyatt's favorite places in the large house, the study had the smell of books and paper. It was dark and cool on this summer afternoon, serene inside with an open view across the manicured lawn. Wyatt caught a glimpse of orange lilies, blue hydrangea and roses artfully placed to look random before taking a seat in front of the imposing desk.

"Sir," Wyatt began. "You know I am committed to the success of Lyons Howe. I have been there for you and the company since I finished school. I helped to grow the commercial business and expand our reach beyond the Midwest. I believe you have no complaints about my work." Wyatt tried to set the tone before his father could take control. He had never intended to talk about both Keeli and his new company in the same night. He understood he now had an uphill climb to earn his father's support.

"No, son, I have no complaints - at least not until now. Just spit it out. What the devil's going on?"

"Father, I have a great opportunity to start my own tech company and I want to take it. I have venture capital firms asking to meet with me. They are pursuing me. I believe I will have the necessary funding within a few months. I want to develop real estate software. It would benefit Lyons Howe but it would be my dream. We would still work together, just in a new manner."

Wyatt stopped to catch his breath. At first, his father responded with stony silence, not a good sign.

"You are part of this family, the next in line to run this business and you want to pursue some dream of yours?" His father's face was blazing with fury. "Do you know what I am handing you? Are you that ungrateful? First some down-on-her-luck artist, now a tech company?"

"Leave Keeli out of this," Wyatt suppressed his anger. "These are two completely separate issues."

"No, Ivy, they are not. They are both examples of your reluctance to accept your responsibility to this family. You are 34 years old, you should be anxious to assume control of Lyons Howe. You should have an acceptable wife and family. You should be a responsible member of this family and this community instead of a constant disappointment to your mother and myself."

"A constant disappointment? Is that what I am?" Wyatt was out of his chair and pacing like a panther, voice rising with each circle of the room. "This is not what you have said in the past. If I am so awful, give Regan the damn business. You know she wants it. Please Father, just set me free."

"Free! Free! You ungrateful miscreant. Regan is a girl for god's sake. She will not run Lyons Howe. It goes to the first-born son. It has always belonged to the first-born son."

"Then give it to Ethan."

"Ethan is still wet behind the ears, damn it. It goes to you, you have known that since infancy."

"Father, this is the twenty-first century. There are women running far bigger corporations than ours. They run countries. You need to rethink letting Regan run things. I love software. You love real estate. Just let me try this, please."

Wyatt had promised himself he would not beg or cajole, but he could hear the whining creeping into his voice. He was the little boy seeking daddy's approval. Wyatt tried to regain control of the conversation. "Father, I am concerned about your heart. Please can we just discuss this calmly and rationally - man to man?"

"You are not behaving like a man. You are not behaving like my son. You are behaving like a spoiled brat. Are you prepared to give up everything? If you are not vice president of Lyons Howe, you will have nothing, no salary, and no benefits. Are you prepared to give them up? Are you prepared to support yourself? And just how long do you think it will take your little artist to run once she knows you are poor?"

"Poor? C'mon Father, who are we kidding. I have enough investments of my own to last a lifetime. Also, I do not intend to allow my software company to fail. This is a win-win, Father. I want to create real estate selling and valuation apps that Lyons Howe will want to buy. There is real synergy here. Please cut me loose and then partner with me."

"This will kill your mother." Wyatt's father predicted, his voice low and ominous. "I am sure your grandfather is spinning in his grave right now. I am ashamed to call you my son. Get out of my sight."

Wyatt slammed the cut-glass tumbler he had been holding in a death grip to the cherry table and stormed from the room. Moving past everyone he headed for the front door in a fury. Missy hollered his name and came running from the kitchen. Clearly, she had been watching for him to emerge from the study.

"Ivy, wait. Mother will kill you if you leave now."

"Yeah, well Father will kill me if I stay. So what do I do now?"

"Get another drink and calm down. Then go find Mother and she will smooth things over. You cannot leave before dinner. It is just not done."

Wyatt knew she was right. No one walked out on his mother's dinners, ever. She might behave like a fragile flower but she ruled the family with an iron fist. Wyatt III might have the booming voice and tall presence, but his slender wife had him wrapped around her little finger. If she wanted her son at the dinner table, he would be at the dinner table.

Taking Missy's advice, Wyatt grabbed a fresh drink and Regan's hand, dragging her out the front door and away from prying ears to let her know that he had just asked to leave the family business. Once over her shock, she was thrilled at the idea of leading Lyons Howe. They discussed the steps needed for a smooth transition and Regan was quickly excited about bringing some of Wyatt's new applications into what would be her business. Wyatt carefully avoided telling her what their father had said about her running Lyons Howe.

"I can see how this can modernize our sales approach dramatically," she was bouncing on her toes with excitement. "It would give us an amazing competitive advantage. You, big brother, just may be a genius. How soon can we have prototypes?"

"Well, Madame President, first get your father off my back, let me complete my deal with the venture capital team, and then maybe three months after that you can have alpha code. Work for you?"

"If I have to wait that long, I guess I will. It may take that long to bring Father around anyway."

"Yeah, no kidding." Wyatt locked arms with Regan and they returned to the house. Wyatt's mood was greatly improved. Keeli had been right about Regan; she really wanted this opportunity so she would look out for him.

"Dinner is on the table. Where have you two been?" his mother was herding the children into the dining room, motioning everyone else to follow. "Wyatt, dinner," she called in the direction of the closed study door. "Ivy, go get your father while the food is hot."

"I'll go," Regan volunteered and Wyatt headed for the seat furthest from his father's, waiting for the inevitable fireworks to begin.

A perfectly sliced slab of beef fresh off the grill sat on the table along with horseradish sauce, a large colorful salad, fresh corn, tomatoes and a steamy loaf of sour dough bread. It might be family barbeque but the china was Royal Crown Derby, the crystal was Waterford and the silver was polished to a high shine. The platters surrounded a professionally designed floral centerpiece that was replaced semi-weekly by the premier Lake Forest florist, and the linens were fresh pressed by a local laundry service.

The table easily accommodated the family of nine. The room was large enough to entertain twenty or more. Tonight, Wyatt wished for more leaves in the table since the distance between him and his father was clearly not big enough.

"I will not sit at the same table with Ivy," his father pouted. "He is not welcome in my home."

"Well, he is welcome in mine, Wyatt, so sit down and serve the roast please." Wyatt Senior did as he was bid by his wife, but not before sending her and his eldest son each an angry scowl.

"What the hell is going on with you two? Is this about the girl? Ivy, your father is right. The girl is probably overwhelmed by your money and status. They always are. You know what to expect from those types."

"Those types? Seriously, Mother?" Wyatt's response dripped with sarcasm. "What the hell is wrong with you people?"

"How dare you speak to us like that Ivy? Apologize this instant."

"Don't worry dear, Ivy no longer has money and status."

"What?" A chorus of voices rang around the table, eyes bouncing between the two men trying to understand what was going on.

"Oh yes, sweetheart. Your darling boy just quit Lyons Howe to pursue his dreams. Forget our dreams," his arm swept the room indicating that he spoke for the whole family, "he only cares about his own selfish desires."

Wyatt's mother looked like she was about to faint, gripping the edge of the table with her manicured fingers. She looked as if someone just died.

"Why are you doing this to me, Ivy. Don't you love us? Don't you love your father? We built all of this for you."

At this point, the conversation became a free-for-all. Wyatt's brother instantly sided with his parents. He could see additional unwanted work and responsibility coming his way if Wyatt left the firm. Regan and Missy were siding with Wyatt though. The children just wanted the attention of the adults while Missy's husband stayed safely quiet. The lovely dinner sat untouched as sides were drawn for the protracted battle.

After thirty minutes of raised voices, no one was listening to anyone else. Wyatt's mother began to cry softly but conspicuously. "You are destroying your father, Ivy. And me. You are destroying this family. Do you understand?"

"Oh please. I am so done with this conversation. I just want to start a software company for god's sake. I am a grown man who wants to do something on my own. The business is in Regan's very capable hands. Nothing is destroyed. No one is destroyed."

"I wanted you to follow in your father's footsteps. I have always wanted that for you. You are my first-born. It is your responsibility to take care of your brother and sisters. And marry. And give me grandchildren. How do you know Sloane will still have you if you run some little software company?"

"Mother. I do not want Sloane," Wyatt spoke to his mother as if speaking to a child, slowly clipping each word. "I want Keeli. I may be falling in love with Keeli. Do you understand? This is a woman who will want me even if I have nothing."

"Well, Son," his father piped up. "You have nothing as of right now. No job. No family support. And for the record, that girl is not welcome in this house. So, looks like you don't have her either. I hope you are proud of yourself. You have made a complete mess of your life and broken our hearts. You are no longer welcome at Lyons Howe, but by God you will honor your mother's wishes and marry an acceptable girl."

"Or what?" Wyatt's anger was rising uncontrollably as Missy laid her cool fingers on his arm to hold him back. He had risen from his chair, staring down the table at his father with venom shooting from his eyes.

"I will grudgingly allow you to pursue your software dreams, Ivy. Lyons Howe will invest in your company and purchase your products when they become available, but not without Sloane. This is a package deal, Son. Sloane comes with the investment. She is good for your future and you will need all the help you can get."

Wyatt leaped back, knocking the chair over in his haste to get away from his family. "Thank you for a lovely evening, Mother," he mocked, placing a dry kiss on her cheek before striding to the door without a backward glance. The door slammed behind him.

What the hell just happened? What a mess. They don't even know Keeli, have not met her. Why are they so set against her? And why are they so set on Sloane? I am the one who has to live with her, not them.

Reliving the evening now, Wyatt took the turns too fast, furious with the night's events. This was marital blackmail. Yet even now he realized he was considering sacrificing his fledgling relationship with Keeli for his family's support of his professional goals. He hated himself for it. Yes, it was still early days with Keeli, but what did it say about his principles if he agreed to marry Sloane?

I am a grown man, damn it, and whom I love should be my choice.

His father was playing hardball with his dream and Wyatt knew who would win. After all, he had learned all his negotiating skills from his father. He wanted to understand what was driving this demand before he agreed to it, but he knew his father did not make demands lightly. Wyatt felt his relationship with Keeli slipping through his fingers.

After talking to Missy, Wyatt knew she was right. They all just needed to sleep on it. Wyatt would find a way for his parents to meet Keeli. They would come to care for her and appreciate her, just as he did, and then his father would forget his stupid ultimatum.

Of course he would. Wouldn't he?

CHAPTER TWENTY-EIGHT

By Thursday, Keeli could no longer fool herself. Wyatt was not just busy; he was avoiding her. He had returned none of her texts since his terse reply on Sunday and she had finally stopped writing. She did not want to be a clingy pest who couldn't take a hint. She had shed a few tears; okay, a lot of tears. Theo and Dylan had been great listeners and wonderful at making up excuses for the silent phone.

"Didn't you say his dad was sick? Perhaps they had a health emergency."

"He works so hard Keeli, and travels a bunch. I bet he went out of town without taking your number," Theo offered. "Or his phone died," Dylan added.

"His phone fell in the toilet and he doesn't have your number now." Theo got her to smile briefly with that one.

They had plied her with yummy food from the restaurant and the caterers, lots of wine and had even given up the bathroom for a full hour so she could soak uninterrupted. None of it helped.

"I was a fool, wasn't I?" she kept asking anyone who would listen. "I knew he was a player. I knew he was with a different girl every week. I should have realized he would throw me over too, right?"

The upstairs neighbors, Lynn and Mark, had come down to keep her company three evenings in a row, but finally even they agreed with her assessment and told her to move on. Clarice seemed as confused as Keeli. Disagreeing with her about giving up, Clarice insisted that something was wrong, saying she knew he felt something special. Neither answer made her feel better.

The one good thing about the silence was that it was paying off in her work. She was creating like a lunatic, being incredibly productive. No new designs were percolating in her brain, but she was quick to complete her existing designs with new stones that she had purchased using the money from the Milwaukee sales. She had a huge inventory ready for the Port Clinton festival in August and half of what she would need later in the year for consigning with the Evanston stores.

She and Missy were still in touch and by unspoken agreement, neither mentioned Wyatt. Missy invited her to meet for lunch again, but Keeli made up an excuse. She could not go out without showing her blotchy face and red eyes. She really had to stop crying herself to sleep.

Keeli worked through the quiet weekend, hiding in the basement with her tools, waitressing for a large, backyard bar mitzvah Saturday night. She took a break Sunday long enough to share pizza with Lynn and Mark, who did their best to make her laugh a bit, but otherwise she stayed heads down over her worktable.

She actually enjoyed the waitressing gig. It was a beautiful summer night and the kids were cute. The party ended at a reasonable hour and she made decent money. Of course, she did tear up a few times. Tonight she was supposed to be at Ravinia. Right now, she should be with Wyatt, listening to music under the stars. Keeli cried herself to sleep again.

By Monday, Keeli gave herself a stern talking to, deciding she was over Wyatt. She had moped for a full week after only dating the man a month or two. Enough was enough. It had been a fun interlude. She learned a lot about herself, got to go places she would otherwise never have seen. She learned about hockey and had a tentative new friendship.

And, for a few wonderful weeks, she had felt sexy and

desirable. Now she would chalk it up to experience and move forward.

Two weeks later, Keeli decided to use the bar mitzvah waitressing money to get a really good haircut. New hairdo equaled new outlook. At least she hoped so. It had been almost a month since she last saw Wyatt. There had been no word, but she had bonded with Missy. At least now she knew that he was not tending to his ailing father or out of town. He was just not interested. She scheduled an appointment at a posh salon recommended by Missy and made plans to meet her after for lunch.

Although she couldn't afford it, and thought more than once about cancelling, here Keeli was, taking the small elevator from ground level to the glass enclosed salon and girding herself to lose her signature red curls. She was instantly overwhelmed by the bustle of activity, the posters of gorgeous models and the elegance of the clientele. She knew she looked out of place - gauche and frankly, poor. She pulled her shoulders back, lifted her chin and determined to brave this strange, chic world.

Her appointment was with someone named Aaron. She sat in his chair with trepidation, sipping the plastic cup of wine handed to her by his assistant and fidgeting with the slippery smock covering her from neck to knees.

"So, my dear, what do you have in mind?" A tall, lanky fair-haired man came to stand behind her chair. He was handsome, clean cut and in his late 30's. He had kind eyes and an over-the-top way of speaking that made Keeli trust him immediately.

"I have no idea, something less wild maybe? A bit more professional?"

"Really, you want to tame this lusciousness?" He was wonderfully melodramatic. "You know a man could get lost in these curls. Well," he added with a giggle, "a straight man."

He ran his hands through her hair, twisting the curls around his index finger, testing their weight, combing her hair this way and that. "We could do a treatment to make it straight, of course," Aaron finally offered. "But, sweetie, I think you will miss these curls. So how 'bout we shape it up? We'll get rid of some of the fullness and then let your natural curl do the rest. I want to emphasize your eyes more and let the shape of your face come through, too."

"Whatever you say."

"Ooh," he shrieked like a child on Christmas morning, drawing attention of those around him, "I love when I have free reign. You just leave this to me."

Keeli was shuttled to the shampoo station, lathered, rinsed, lathered again and then left with a "mask" on her hair.

Who knew such a thing existed?

They offered a second glass of wine but since it was it just 11:00, Keeli declined, fearing she would be too drunk to get through lunch. A statuesque woman dressed all in black delivered a bottle of water instead.

When Keeli was sure her neck would break from laying back over the basin, another black clad woman with blue-streaked blonde hair rinsed her hair and escorted her back to Aaron's chair near the front windows. Aaron combed out her hair, turned the chair so that she was unable to watch him in the mirror and began to snip, chatting the whole time. Before she realized it, she was sharing more about herself than usual. She had described moving to Chicago, talked all about her jewelry designs and the difficulties of finding buyers. She had even confessed a bit about her broken heart.

What was it about stylists? She always told them too much.

"My clients would probably love your jewelry if we could just find a way to put you together," Aaron was pondering this dilemma while he blew her hair dry, then feathered the bottom with a special scissors.

"Do you have a catalog or pictures or a web site? Maybe I could get my next client to host a trunk show. Can you stick around and meet her?"

"That would be fantastic. And my hair will look great for her too." Keeli raised an eyebrow in question, frustrated not to be able to see what Aaron had been doing.

"Okay, Miss Nosey, you can see it in two minutes." He was smearing some kind of gel into her hair and fussing with a few select curls. "Voila!"

Keeli was speechless when he spun the chair around, running her hands along the smooth tresses, poking at a wave here and a curl there in awe.

"You are a total genius." She was gushing with pleasure and Aaron's face spread into a satisfied grin.

"I guess you like it?"

"I love it. But will I be able to recreate it?"

"It's not hard, let me show you." Aaron made it all seem so easy and he snapped a picture of her with her new smooth, beach-waves. The look was soft and easy, less messy than her natural curls, full but not too big for her face. Her eyes looked enormous now and her hair was silky and shiny. She felt beautiful.

"I couldn't be happier, really." Keeli praised the stylist again while they schedule a follow on appointment for seven weeks later.

"Sure you could. You could be happier with fabulous hair and a trunk show. And here come's my next client now, so be on your toes, Keeli."

A woman of indiscriminate age walked toward them. Her movements were of a young woman, her face of someone over 50 but maybe only by a few years. She had that recognizable look of wealth and confidence. Her handbag was easily worth thousands. She was wearing a simple pear-shaped diamond on the second finger of her left hand that Keeli estimated at an eye-popping eight or nine carats. Keeli loved the ring. Despite the obvious wealth, the woman was wearing jeans and little black leather flats and seemed very approachable.

Aaron introduced his client, Linda Stuart, explaining that he knew her whole family. Her two daughters and her two sisters were included in his clientele. They chatted like old friends and it took him only a moment to mention that Keeli was an up and coming jewelry designer. In one more minute, he had planted the idea of a trunk show. As he had anticipated, she jumped on the idea and the women exchanged emails to set up a date.

Keeli floated from the salon as if she was on top of the world, feeling pretty and poised to break into a new customer market. Everything felt new, fresh, and full of possibilities. The sun was shining on this early August day and for the first time since returning from Milwaukee, Keeli believed that her life was good, that she would be happy again. She had just enough time to buy a small thank you gift for Missy before meeting her for lunch. After all, it was she who suggested she call the salon and get a new look. That had led to meeting Linda and new possibilities. What a great day!

She scanned the street for a shop that she could afford. There were not many. The low-price point merchandise at Prada, Hermes and Barney's was still out of her reach. Heading for Bloomingdales around the corner, Keeli was horrified to see Wyatt ten paces away, arm in arm with Sloane. It was too late to duck back inside somewhere so Keeli steeled herself for the meeting.

At least my hair looks fantastic.

"Wyatt, hi. And it's Sloane, right?" Keeli was cool and poised, extending her hand to shake Sloane's. "Lovely to see you again." Her voice betrayed none of her panic.

"Oh, it's the clumsy little waitress, Wyatt," Sloane rudely ignored the extended hand and addressed herself to Wyatt, not Keeli.

"Keeli Larsen, Sloane Huyler. I am not sure you were ever introduced." Wyatt made the awkward introductions looking very uncomfortable, as if he wished he were anywhere but here. "Keeli is a jewelry designer, Sloane. She just waitresses to help her friend, who is a caterer."

Keeli appreciated Wyatt's effort to increase her standing with the chilly brunette, recognizing instantly that it made no difference. As if to confirm her suspicion, Sloane responded, "Well, that explains why you were so clumsy. You are not doing your friend's business much good if you spill his creations."

I can't believe I thought she was being so nice the night the benefit. She is obviously a cold bitch. I hope she makes him miserable.

"Yes, well, then I guess it is a good thing it's not my full-time job," Keeli responded with a tight smile. "Nice to meet you, good to see you Wyatt." Before she could lose it completely, Keeli lifted her chin, straightened her spine and walked away at a brisk pace.

Do not turn around, Keeli Larsen, whatever you do. Do. Not. Turn. Around.

She got only about 10 paces before a strong hand on her arm slowed her movement. Wyatt had followed her down the sidewalk, but Sloane was watching them like a hawk and still within hearing distance.

"Keeli, wait. Please," Keeli looked at the hand on her arm as if it was a serpent and Wyatt removed it self-consciously.

"I can explain. Please, let me explain. It's complicated, but I can explain. Can I call you later?"

"Nothing has been preventing you from calling me, Wyatt." The frost in her tone was bone chilling.

"Yeah, I guess you are right about that. You look fantastic, by the way."

Always the charmer, isn't he? Maybe he just can't help himself.

"Thank you. You don't owe me an explanation, Wyatt. I am a big girl. I knew the lay of the land when I agreed to go out with you. Sloane is waiting. You don't want to be rude."

"I'll call you in a couple hours," he said plaintively, but he was speaking to air. Keeli had walked away.

CHAPTER TWENTY-NINE

Four hours later, Keeli was a little tipsy and giggling with her roommates. They have finished a bottle of pretty good champagne and half a bottle of even better Chardonnay. That was in addition to the two glasses of wine Keeli had over lunch, too.

She had been celebrating her new look, a possible trunk show and the biggest news of all, Dylan and Theo's engagement.

"I knew things were getting serious, but I confess you caught me by surprise," Keeli repeated. She had been telling them this for the last hour, over and over. "I should have seen it coming, huh?"

"We weren't completely sure last year when the law changed, but now we know we want to spend the rest of our lives together."

"I am just so happy for you both. I had better be a bridesmaid. And no ugly dresses, promise me," and the three begin giggling again. "I think I might be drunk."

"Oh, Keeli, you are definitely drunk," Theo laughed.

"We do want to give you a heads up that we want to move after the wedding," Dylan took the conversation in a more serious direction. "We want to buy something, not rent."

"Moving, you guys are moving?" Keeli wailed. "When? Where?"

"Well, the wedding is set for eight weeks from now. Dylan reserved the restaurant without any problem, the benefit of working there. I am calling in favors from everyone I work with. Then a couple weeks of honeymoon, so you have at least two months. Lots of time."

Keeli sobered up quickly. "Two months? You call that a lot of time? Where will I go?"

"You could stay here," Dylan offered, "with some new roommates. You should have no problem with that. Logan Square is hip now."

"Yeah, maybe." Keeli was less than enthusiastic at the prospect of randomly finding new roommates among Chicago's millions. "Not your problem, boys. Tonight we celebrate." Pasting on an obviously forced smile, Keeli raised her glass to Theo for a refill.

"Oh no you don't. You are cut off, my tipsy friend." He refused the refill and took her glass from her as the buzzer went off indicating someone was at the downstairs door.

"Expecting company?" Dylan asked. Looking at them both, he was met by bewilderment. He struggled to get off the floor and went to the intercom. "Who is it?" he shouted into the machine. He had never gotten the hang of it and they all began laughing. "You can talk normally," Theo was already correcting, so that they did not actually hear a voice respond before Dylan hit the button to release the downstairs door.

The three waited expectantly listening to footfalls on the creaky stairs. When the sound grew closer, Dylan stepped into the hallway. Theo and Keeli heard him speaking to someone he knew. Perhaps Mark, from upstairs, had forgotten his keys.

"We're celebrating, come drink with us," they heard him offer. Then Wyatt's large frame was filling the small entryway. The boys were welcoming him, sharing their exciting news, pouring him a large glass of the crisp, cool wine.

"Congratulations guys. This is so exciting. I am so happy for you both." The three were doing those backslapping, non-hug hugs that men do while Keeli remained frozen in place, cross-legged on the floor.

"You said you were going to call, not show up." The words

came out sharper than she intended. In her drunken state she was unable to hide her hurt and anger.

"I tried calling a couple times but got no answer," he shrugged. Keeli lay across the floor, stretching for her hobo bag just out of reach and dug for her cellphone. Sure enough, she had three missed calls and two text messages, all from Wyatt. She also saw that she already had an email from Linda Stuart with a list of possible dates for a trunk show. Her heart, already pounding uncontrollably since Wyatt entered the room, did an extra little flip of joy. She couldn't wait to reply.

"What do you want, Wyatt? You are intruding on our little celebration."

"Oh, no intrusion, man. We are about done with the booze anyway." Dylan missed the scathing look Keeli fired his way. "You're just in time to share the last of it with us."

The three men drank and laughed together like old friends while Keeli did a slow burn watching them. After several minutes, Theo took Dylan by the hand to lead him down the hall. "We'll just leave you two alone then."

Wyatt took Keeli's hands, easily lifting her from the floor and settling her on the tired, lumpy couch. Leaving her there, he wandered into the kitchen, emerging moments later with a large glass of water, which he pressed into her hands.

After three large, unladylike gulps, Keeli put the glass on the scarred side table, not bothering to put a coaster under it. Wyatt reached for a coaster, and reaching across her, placed it carefully under the damp glass. His proximity as he leaned across her body almost made her faint with desire. Moving slowly back to a sitting position he stopped halfway back to upright, gently touching her smooth waves, then her face, with his fingertips.

"You look so beautiful." He sounded awed, looking at Keeli with his heart on his sleeve. "I have missed you so much."

She responded to his confession with stony silence until he was forced to continue.

"I wanted to call you, I did."

"Yeah, I can tell."

"I did. All hell broke loose with my family the day after I saw you in Milwaukee."

"Is everyone okay?" Keeli could not help asking with concern. "Your father? He's okay?"

"Yeah, sorry, everyone is healthy. That is not what I meant. I didn't mean to scare you. It is this damn family loyalty crap. I told my father I wanted to start my own company."

"Is he thrilled?" Keeli had forgotten her anger now, turning halfway toward Wyatt in her excitement.

"Thrilled? Not the word I would use here." The sarcasm was heavy in Wyatt's voice. "He threatened to disown me."

"Are you kidding?" Keeli could not believe it. "He should be so proud of you, of what you have already accomplished and about what you want to achieve in the future. I don't understand."

"It's that family thing I have tried explaining. It is not about what I want to do. It is about abandoning the company, the family, and the name. He wants to cut me off without a cent, which is okay. I don't care about the money. Then he played his ace. He threatened not to be a customer of the new company. My investors will jump ship if I cannot bring them Lyons Howe."

"Oh Wyatt, this is awful. I am so sorry." Keeli started making suggestions, different investors, and other potential customers. "You have thought of all this already, I am sure."

"Yeah. Anyway, he came around in the end, sort of."
Sort of?"

"If I agree to marry Sloane, who is my mother's choice for me, he will not only promise to be a client, he will be an investor."

Keeli moved to put some distance between their bodies as a distinct chill came over her.

"So, you are with Sloane now. Congratulations. I hope you will be very happy."

And I get sent back to the wrong side of the tracks.

"It's not like that, I swear."

"Seriously? Then what is it like?"

Wyatt had no answer. Keeli had understood perfectly.

"I am so embarrassed, Keeli. My family would love you if they got to know you, but all they see is that Sloane has the money and connections to help the family and the new business. And my father has some contracts with her father that really complicate things further."

"… While I am a useless gold-digger who cannot help you at all." She flung the words at him in disgust. "I get it. Believe me, this is not new for me. Let's be honest, Wyatt. They see what you told them to see in me. What you saw in me too, if you are honest with yourself. I was just someone to kill a little time with. I think you should leave."

Keeli stood a bit unsteadily and moved toward the door. Wyatt reached to stop her and in her attempt to shake him off, she lost her balance, landing hard on him, hearing the sofa leg make a definite cracking sound.

"Oh great, now I broke the sofa too. Shit. Look, just go, ok, just go." She was pushing against the hard muscles of his chest, trying to rise to her feet again. He was holding her in place though, and she was no match for his strength.

"That is not what I see, Keeli. I care about you, I do. However, I have wanted this company since college and now it is in reach. I can't jeopardize it now." He was pleading with her to understand. In fact, despite her hurt and anger, and a lot of alcohol, she did understand and sympathize.

"My family is closed minded, and old fashioned. They live in their tight little world with people from the same cloistered little world and they like it that way. I can't challenge the status quo right now."

"I understand, Wyatt, really I do. I wish you all the luck in the world."

"Just let me get my financing and then we can talk."

"No we can't. It's over. You will see that too. We barely knew each other. Go marry Sloane. She will make you a perfect hostess and a good wife. She will fit in and help you succeed. I could never do that for you, Wyatt. Just go be happy."

Keeli wanted him to leave before she started crying, but he wouldn't let her go. She wanted desperately to lean into his neck and sob. She was not going to be able to keep up this charade must longer.

"I care about you, Keeli. I am falling for you and I believe you feel the same way about me. I know it's only been a few months, but we have something here. You know we do. Just give me a little time to bring my folks around and launch my company."

"Sure, Wyatt. You go do that. Just bring them around and we will see what happens."

Say it like you believe it, Keeli, or he will never let you go.

Perhaps she had convinced him that it would work out, because he was holding her now like things would be fine. He believed that he would get his family to see that she belonged with him. They would invest in his business and then Keeli and Wyatt could live happily ever after.

What damn fairy tale has he been reading?

He was kissing her hair and her face and she needed him to give her space. Panic was rising in her uncontrollably. "Wyatt, stop, please. I am drunk and tired. You cannot jeopardize things now. You need to go."

"Let me stay tonight, Keeli. Better yet, come home with me. We need to be together. We need to talk. It's been too long."

"Not tonight. Call me tomorrow." With that, she rose to her feet, leading Wyatt to the door. She turned her face up and accepted his kisses. Let him believe she would be there tomorrow if he needed to. She knew that this was the end. She loved this man with her whole being. She would not risk his success even if he would. She would let him go.

Her heart was breaking anew as she closed the door softly behind him and listened to him recede from her life.

CHAPTER THIRTY

"Sloane, I cannot stress this enough." Wyatt was pacing Sloane's perfectly decorated vintage apartment. "These meetings with the investors will be make it or break it for me."

Sloane patted the seat next to her on the overstuffed blue sofa. "Darling, I am well aware of what is at stake here. I know perfectly well how to behave with a group of businessmen. Have I not played hostess at enough parties for you yet? Don't you know you can trust me?"

Her little speech, which started with a powerful, independent voice ended in a flirtatious pout and Wyatt remembered again why she annoyed him. He was incredibly nervous about taking her with him to Las Vegas for these three days of meetings.

What if she gets too strident, or too flirtatious? She had been a perfect hostess in the past, but then she was trying to win him. Now she had him over a barrel and she knew it. The balance of power in their relationship had shifted.

"Seriously, they are bringing their spouses. Try to hang with them, ok? We both know you like to be in the middle of the business discussions, but please just resist this one time." Throwing his hands in the air in frustration, he began pacing again.

"Stop pacing, I have this. The car will be here any minute. You just have to relax."

"Hah!" That one word contained all the anger and bitterness that Wyatt had been feeling for the last four weeks, since the family dinner disaster when his father gave him that awful ultimatum. He had met with his father the following week, understood now that he had entered into deals with Sloane's father that could compromise Lyons Howe's reputation and business. Wyatt was in a position to protect them all, but to do so he would have to marry Sloane. He was furious with his father for overreaching, for his greed and shortsightedness. But his father had been ill, anxious and less than cautious.

He had not seen anyone from his family since that meeting except Missy. She came for weekly dinners with him and sometimes brought the kids. He got all the news from her about things at home. His mother was hurt by his absence but standing by her husband. Regan was thrilled to be in charge at Lyons Howe and his brother was falling into line behind her with no questions asked.

Each week Missy tried to bring up the topic of Keeli, but Wyatt refused to discuss her, saying only, "I can't do this, Miss, I cannot talk about her." Since Keeli was saying pretty much the same thing, Missy was staying out of the middle despite her misgivings.

The buzzer brought Wyatt back to the present. He picked up his overnight bag and Sloane's heavy tote bag, nodding to her to indicate that she would need to pull her large rolling bag herself. She checked her apartment quickly to see if she forgot anything, left on a light in the long hallway leading to the bedrooms, and locked the door behind them. Wyatt was already fidgeting at the elevator when she joined him.

The driver loaded their luggage into the waiting Lincoln Town Car. Wyatt squirmed in the back seat until Sloane laid a perfectly manicured hand over his.

"Would you feel better if we reviewed it one more time?" Wyatt nodded the affirmative. "There will be three couples from the VC company, all from the Silicon Valley. Edward is the president, Cary the VP of finance and Sydney is the strategy person, right?"

"Yes, and she is very powerful," Wyatt cut in. "The men are bringing their wives, Sydney is bringing her husband who also happens to own a software company."

"And we are meeting them for cocktails tonight at 6:30?"

"Yep, and dinner afterward in the hotel, I think.

"I am sure they picked some heavy French food place where they can impress you with their money." Sloane said with derision "I don't know what I will eat if it is all carbs."

"Don't be so sure. This is a California crowd remember? They said it would be casual."

"So why didn't we meet in San Francisco?" Sloane whined. "I would have much preferred that over Vegas."

"They were heading to a conference in Vegas already, Sloane. I explained that to you twice." Wyatt concentrated on keeping his patience. It was still early and he had three more days with her.

"We could have waited for them to get back to San Francisco, Wyatt. I don't understand the rush."

Wyatt turned to her, shock evident on his handsome, tired face. "Are you kidding me? I have been waiting weeks to talk to these guys. Without them I am finished, do you understand that? I am poised to launch a complete line of real estate software, I have my father pledged to beta test everything, but I cannot open my doors without capital and a lot of it."

"But you funded your business, sweetie. You hired those people and got office space already, I don't understand why you can't just keep doing that." Sloane rested her hand on Wyatt's thigh, smoothing the exquisite fabric of his suit pants over the strength of his thigh.

"I have used all the money I have Sloane. It would be good to have something to live on, right? After all, you like to live well, my dear." His voice dripped sarcasm that was not lost on Sloane.

Sloane moved her head away from his, flipping her straight hair in his face as she turned to look out the window. This was her way of indicating that she was done talking. Wyatt knew that if he saw her face right now she would be pouting like a two year old.

By tacit agreement, they said as little as possible for the rest of the trip, operating in tense silence, speaking only when necessary.

At the airport, they whisked through the first class lines, and then sat silently in the Admiral's Club until their flight was called. Wyatt noticed that Sloane slipped two magazines from the lounge into her bag. Despite his encouragement to leave them, she would not, so Wyatt gave up the fight.

Once on board, Sloane cuddled against Wyatt across the wide seat divider. "Honey, I am sorry. Let's go get you your money and have a lovely few days poolside in Vegas, okay? I don't know why I am being so difficult. Forgive me?"

After that, they operated companionably, getting their luggage and driver in Vegas, checking into The Cosmopolitan and unpacking in their suite. Sloane removed her creased white linen dress and slipped into a tiny white bikini. Wyatt threw on surfer shorts and called housekeeping to arrange for his suit to be picked up by the hotel for pressing, along with his shoes for a quick shine.

"Sloane, would you like to give them your dress for pressing?" Wyatt offered, "The staff has promised to have everything back before dinner."

Sloane gave him the dress to have pressed without pointing out that she had brought three others for the two-night trip. She probably would not wear the dress again, but Wyatt took it and paid to have it pressed without complaint.

"Now that's done, Wyatt, can we please go to the pool?" Sloane was whining but Wyatt figured the sunshine and fresh air would help improve her mood. They wandered down to one of the many hotel pools.

Wyatt preferred to sit near the pool's edge, but Sloane cajoled him into spending the extra hundreds for one of the shady cabanas. She efficiently draped herself upon a chaise, ordered cocktails and began reading the stack of magazines by her elbow, ordering the staff around like a queen. Wyatt disappeared to the bar without her noticing.

"Coke," he said to the waiting barman, gulping it down before heading for the pool. It was in the mid-90's if not hotter and Wyatt dove smoothly into the busy pool, rising and sluicing the water from his toned body like a seal. Somewhat refreshed he walked gingerly on the hot pavement, made his way back to the cabana and flopped on a mostly shaded lounger. Sloane did not acknowledge his return.

The sun had shifted when Wyatt woke with a jolt. The last weeks had been exhausting and the warm sun finally took its toll. Making sure he still had time to lie around and finding it only 3 Chapter, Wyatt moved to a shadier spot and reflected on the last month's efforts.

Almost immediately after leaving Keeli's apartment that night, Wyatt began making calls. He had already eyed the space for his offices. They were, of course, in a Lyons Howe building he owned and once managed. He called meetings with the people he had been coordinating with for the last year, software developers, engineers, accountants and real estate sales people and offered them jobs.

The meeting at the bank had been sticky, but they did advance him the cash to get started, taking his trust fund and personal investment accounts as collateral. If he didn't make a success of this venture, he would be broke.

Lyon Technical Solutions Software officially opened two weeks ago and already they had a rough design for two products and a prototype for a third. Things were moving faster than Wyatt could have imagined, the small team operating like a well-oiled machine. He had no need for marketing staff yet since he had offered Lyons Howe a six-month exclusive deal. Instead, his product designers were meeting with people from Lyons Howe in a marketing capacity for now. It kept the team smaller, and cheaper, and got the staff closer to their end users too.

All this activity meant 12 to 14-hour days for Wyatt, who slept little. In the few hours he did rest, he dreamed about money problems or software designs.

If things went well tonight and tomorrow, it would all pay off. He had concrete prototypes and designs to share with the VC people and a strong indication that they would invest the millions he needed. Best of all, his father seemed to have come around about Wyatt's new venture. He was offering to match the VC investment dollar for dollar.

He just had to keep his cool around Sloane and get through these meetings. His temper had been flaring more than usual since they had reconciled. It wasn't her fault his father had forced them together. She was thrilled with it of course – making wedding plans for early spring, basking in a role to which she had always believed she was entitled.

At 4:30, the couple headed back to their suite. The air conditioning was too cool on Wyatt's skin and he realized that he had gotten a bit too much sun. His sun-kissed cheeks confirmed this, but only make him look more rugged and devilishly handsome. The pink would be a golden tan by morning. His hair had acquired streaks of blonde over the summer and the overall look of a sun god was not far off the mark.

Sloane demanded the shower first and after a lengthy time in the steamy room she emerged wrapped in a sumptuous terry robe. She sat on the end of the king-size bed to dry her shoulder-length hair while Wyatt slipped into the bathroom to shower. When he emerged, she immediately took back over the space to do her makeup and preen.

He knew she would be at least another 30 minutes, giving him time to catch the scores on ESPN and check his email. Stopping to follow a tennis match for a few minutes, Wyatt lost interest and surfed channels until he found the Cubs game. His team was up by three runs in the bottom of the eighth inning. It would be their fourth win in a row. Wyatt gave a small 'whoop' drawing Sloane from the bathroom.

Wyatt had a sad realization that when he was alone in the room, he was calm; but as soon as Sloane reentered his tension ratcheted up She didn't even need to speak, just being in the same room with her caused his mood to worsen.

I have to get over this. I am going to face this woman every morning for the rest of my life. I used to like her. I just need to recapture that feeling. Yeah, why did I ever like her? She is everything I always feared in a woman – she would run if I were not a Howe, if I lost my money. In an instant.

"We need to leave in15 minutes." Her muffled voice rose from the closet. Wyatt stepped into the bathroom, fixed his hair, brushed his teeth and emerged to find Sloane looking elegant in a red MaxMara dress that perfectly suited her height and her extremely slender figure. She was even taller in the strappy sandals she was fastening into place. She was the perfect picture of the executive wife doing casual.

Oh yeah, this was what I liked about her.

Wyatt grabbed his recently pressed Zegna suit from the closet, added a crisp white shirt but no tie, grabbed his shoes, now polished to a high sheen and after pocketing his phone, wallet and room key turned to give Sloane his arm. They made a gorgeous couple, both tall, elegant, fit and good looking.

In the few minutes he had taken to get dressed she had added a statement necklace to her bare neck. The floor dropped out from under him when he saw it.

"Where did you get that necklace?" His voice was a bit too sharp and accusatory.

"I borrowed it from Missy, don't you like it?"

"Ah, that explains why I thought it looked so familiar," he mumbled to himself, regaining his composure. When did Missy buy more of Keeli's jewelry? He would recognize it anywhere. Now he would be thinking of Keeli when he needed to be focused on business.

Like there is ever a time I am not thinking of Keeli.

"I like it fine. It goes well with the dress."

Wyatt sounded confident, but the butterflies in his stomach would not subside. He had a bad feeling about this dinner.

CHAPTER THIRTY-ONE

Keeli was actually enjoying herself. She thought she would feel overwrought and out of place, but Linda had been the perfect hostess, and that made Keeli more comfortable. The women invited to the trunk show turned out to be fun to be with, much more like friends. The conversation flowed easily and Keeli was delighted to find that they had much in common.

If you exclude their millions, of course.

Linda had been a dream come true to work with, inviting 20 guests she knew were likely to buy, setting up the food and wine, sending out hand-written invitations, following up with phone calls. Then, as icing on the cake she had blithely announced at the beginning of the evening that Keeli "only works with a very elite clientele." The phrase had worked like catnip on kittens. It would seem that snob appeal was critical to selling expensive jewelry.

The women were mothers, writers, and philanthropists. They were doctors and lawyers, well educated, well read and up on current events. Their conversation was lively and engaging. The time flew by while they nibbled on sweet and savory finger foods, sipped expensive wines and tried on jewelry. Keeli anticipated being underdressed, small town and unsophisticated, but this group of women had shown up in jeans and sundresses. They were impressed by her efforts to work through the classics, her determination to educate herself. They had been nothing but warm and supportive.

The response to her jewelry was outstanding. She took orders for several custom pieces using gems including pearls, sapphires, and diamonds. She sold most of the inventory she brought as well. Best of all, she scheduled two more trunk shows. This group of twenty or so women represented precisely the clientele she had been trying to reach.

As she wrote up her last order of the night, sipping fine Bordeaux and laughing at the pictures one of the women was sharing from Facebook, she wondered what she could send Aaron to thank him for opening this door for her. Earlier, when she had seen Linda admire a lovely bracelet, she deftly removed it from the table and put it aside as a thank you for her hostess. Aaron and Linda may have been the key to turning around Keeli's entire business.

Ready now to call it a night, she was packing the last of her displays and mirrors when Linda suggested they sit for a few minutes before Keeli headed home. Normally Keeli would be watching the clock, anxious to return her Zipcar, but tonight she had borrowed Theo's car so she gratefully sank into a plush armchair and kicked off her heels.

"I think we were a success," Linda announced with pride.

"We were indeed. How can I ever thank you?"

"Stop doing art fairs, my dear. These women will be your bread and butter from now on. I would be happy to invest, to help you open a storefront if you like, or at least support your efforts to sell in boutiques. You make beautiful pieces, but they need higher quality stones to appeal to this crowd. Let me help you pay for them."

Keeli was speechless, overwhelmed by the generosity of this virtual stranger. "I couldn't let you do that, Linda. I would be sick if something happened to your investment."

"Oh, please. I don't know what else to do with my money but spend it, make it and lose it. Lately I have been making a lot, spending a lot and losing nothing. There is no hardship here. Take the offer, please. Let me be your benefactor. I want to be able to brag to my friends."

This last was said with such glee that Keeli found herself agreeing that she would at least consider the remarkable offer. They rehashed the evening for a few more minutes before Keeli took her bags of merchandise and said good night. The two women shared a fierce hug.

Keeli loaded her much lighter baggage in the trunk of the car and pondered Linda's offer while driving the few miles from the Gold Coast condo back to Logan Square. Keeli was dealing with so much change it made her head spin.

She had confirmed with the two Evanston stores last week. One would consign a large order in October. She was delivering a smaller order to the other store next week. She had one trunk show under her belt and two more scheduled. She had Missy talking to several boutiques on her behalf and now Linda offering to invest in her future.

She knew she should turn down the offer but she also recognized that it would allow her to get an apartment on her own. The concern over housing after the upcoming wedding had been foremost on her mind. With business so busy, the last thing Keeli needed was to be homeless and without a studio.

The temptation was great, but Keeli stifled her excitement. She had vowed to do this completely on her own. What if she lost Linda's money? What if Missy introduced her and she disappointed the boutique owners? She strengthened her resolve to do this on her own. That way failure affected her alone.

Of course, she could create some spreadsheets, consider the amounts involved, discuss it carefully with her neighbor upstairs, Lynn, who was an outstanding businessperson, and then decide. Keeli went back and forth in her mind – taking help from anyone was not her strong suit.

Pushing the idea aside for the moment, Keeli enjoyed the quiet darkness around her. The streets were almost empty this late on a weeknight and she had the windows open to enjoy the heat and smell of August in Chicago. She was tired of air conditioning and ready for autumn, now just around the corner.

The night reminded her of driving home with Wyatt late at night after their first drink. She allowed herself to feel the pain and heartbreak for a few minutes. She had made a pact with herself. She kept herself as busy as possible, not allowing thoughts of him to intrude in her day. Then in the quiet of nighttime she gave herself no more than 30 minutes to mourn her loss.

She missed him terribly. On a night like this, she wished she could share her news with him, ask his advice, and celebrate her success. She wondered what he was doing, sure he was somewhere with Sloane.

Keeli had been scouring the Internet for news of his new startup. A big story announced the opening, but she had read nothing since. She thought perhaps she would see him at the Port Clinton Art Festival but he failed to show, crushing her last hope of running into him.

Okay, 30 minutes is up. Time to think about other things.

Turning to happier thoughts, Keeli planned what kind of dress she would buy for Theo and Dylan's wedding. She had made enough money tonight to buy something chic. She wanted something fun and pretty, something feminine and not cheap looking. Something classy. She was looking forward to shopping in the better stores. Maybe she could get Missy to come along to help her.

She reminded herself that what she really needed to think about was jewelry - lots and lots of jewelry. She had to complete the custom wedding rings she designed for Theo and Dylan, and the custom pieces ordered tonight. Keeli began building her list of to-dos in her head, itching for a notepad to write everything down. She really needed inspiration for a new winter collection, because her fall collection was almost all sold out or committed.

It's time for me to get happy, and get creative. Just keep moving forward. Keep moving forward.

CHAPTER THIRTY-TWO

Wyatt could breathe at long last. Las Vegas was behind him and concluded without mishap. Dinner the first night was friendly and comfortable, the conversation easy and full of laughter. There had been no mention of business until dessert and after-dinner drinks. Wyatt learned that Edward had similar taste in rock and roll, Cary was an avid hockey fan with season tickets for the San Jose Sharks and Sydney reminded him of Regan, extremely well educated and hungry for success. They all got along beautifully

Sloane had been a perfect dinner partner, laughing at the men's jokes, but not too loud, connecting with the wives about fashion and children, flirting with Sydney's husband but not too much. Wyatt noticed that despite the advances for women today, the two wives chose to stay home and raise families. Only Sydney had an equally successful husband, and of course, he and Sloane were both in demanding jobs.

Is it really still true that behind every great man there is a great woman? Sloane will not be happy with that arrangement after all her education and hard work. I wonder how we will figure that one out.

They transitioned to the business conversation seamlessly the next morning and discovered a common strategy and vision for Lyon Technical Solutions Software. Being familiar with the data before arriving allowed the VC team to make decisions quickly and by noon Wyatt had a commitment for ten million dollars. He would operate with that for a few years and then, if everything went as planned, go public.

"Let's celebrate." He twirled Sloane in the lobby "Cocktails? Gambling? Dancing? It's a bit early for dinner. Lunch? What is your pleasure?"

"Let's start with drinks and gambling then dress up and do some dancing."

Wyatt's mood was infectious. It was obvious to Sloane that he had just scored a great success. Sloane was a shrewd and calculating woman. She knew she was marrying a very wealthy, important man. He would still be a powerhouse from the Howe family, but now he would be a powerful CEO from Lyons Technical Software Solutions too. It was actually more than she had expected.

Wyatt knew she had targeted him years ago. She had been patient while he dated other women, been understanding and implacable. She never questioned him when he returned to her. She had just been there, waiting and available. Her parents had cultivated a tight relationship with the Howes. Sloane had been the perfect girlfriend, the perfect hostess and now she would be the perfect wife and mother.

Except that I don't love her.

She had brought up Keeli a few times since they had become engaged. She had been a little concerned about that redhead from the wrong side of the tracks. Sloane had complained about Keeli's wide-eyed innocence, her poor background, lack of polish and sophistication. She had conceded that perhaps Wyatt had needed to dabble with someone different from his usual women.

Sloane knew his weakness and she used it well. He was not the confident, cocky man he presented to the world. Tyler had once let slip that Wyatt believed no one loved him for himself, only for his wealth and for his name. Sloane never forgot about that. Wyatt had watched her use it strategically over the years to drive a wedge between him and anyone he was seeing, allowing her to worm her way back into his life. She accused Keeli of being a gold-digger so frequently that it was apparent to Wyatt that Sloane didn't believe it. It was also apparent that Keeli scared her. He could tell. Finally, thank God, she let it drop, but Wyatt suspected that Keeli had left a chink in Sloane's armor. She feared Keeli, as she had no woman before.

Tyler had solved that problem for Sloane. He let slip that Wyatt wanted to start his own company and that his father likely would not take the news well. Enter Sloane's equally high powered and manipulative father. Presenting Wyatt III with an opportunity to expand overseas, Mr. Huyler dragged the Howes into a potential nightmare with the Chinese government. If the news became public, it could destroy the credibility of Lyons Howe, and trust was everything in real estate.

Mr. Huyler had a simple solution. In exchange for a wedding between Wyatt IV and Sloane, he would release the Howes and LHRE from the contract for the amount they had spent to buy in. He promised to keep the deal secret as well.

That led to Wyatt's father presenting Wyatt with an ultimatum. He would marry Sloane and his father would welcome him and his new business back into the Howe fold with his ten million dollar blessing. No marriage, no deal. The ultimatum met everyone's needs, except Wyatt's of course.

Sloane knew he did not love her. He had been open throughout their relationship. He considered her a lovely and skilled hostess, a brilliant executive and a very dear friend. They had tried a serious relationship but it had fizzled pretty quickly on his side. Sloane had been working her wiles on him every since.

Now, as they entered the casino, moving through the crowds toward the high roller room, she slipped her arm through Wyatt's, favoring him with a dazzling smile and a light kiss on the cheek.

"What a great day, sweetheart. I am so proud of you."

It only took a moment for a good looking, well-dressed man with a slight French accent to encourage Sloane to share his blackjack table. Without a backward glance, Sloane disappeared with him to the opposite side of the room.

Wyatt pulled out his phone, starting to text Keeli. He wanted to share his good news with her, not Sloane. Mid-sentence he stopped and put the phone away. He had no right to text Keeli any more. Wyatt reluctantly went in search of Sloane. Somehow, his celebratory mood was gone. He longed for Keeli, knowing she was out of reach forever. Now he just wanted the sweet oblivion of a few cocktails and some privacy.

Sloane motioned to Wyatt and he grudgingly joined her. Sloane was looking to Wyatt to finance her gambling. Without a thought, he pulled five crisp 100-dollar bills from his wallet and laid them on the table for the dealer. Sloane settled onto the high-backed stool, smiled flirtatiously at the men sharing her table while Wyatt signaled for a drink and leaned wearily on the chair, content to watch rather than play.

More than an hour later, Sloane had amassed a large pile of chips, turning Wyatt's original 500 dollars into over $1,400. He encouraged her to quit while she was ahead. She cashed in her chips, returning her ante to Wyatt, keeping her winnings. When they retreated to their suite, Sloane was all smiles.

"Look, Wyatt, we both made money tonight. We are both triumphant." She was slurring her words from a combination of free cocktails and exhaustion, leaning heavily against him and placing small kisses along his jawbone.

"Yes, it has been a terrific day, Sloane, but I am tired and I think you could use some rest too. Let's head down to the pool and sleep in the shade."

Instead of going along with his idea, Sloane pouted. Wyatt suggested a nap, the spa or a walk but Sloane was sulking, complaining that she was bored. Wyatt moved away in irritation, longing for another woman in another elevator. In that moment, he decided he needed to break it off with Sloane and beg Keeli to take him back. He would just have to persuade his father. As the elevator door opened and Wyatt almost carried Sloane to their room, he prayed that when it came time to talk to his father his winning streak would continue.

CHAPTER THIRTY-THREE

Keeli and Missy were just finishing a lovely ladies lunch at the Neiman Marcus restaurant, arguing over the check in a friendly manner when a woman Keeli didn't know walked up to their table. Assuming it was a friend of Missy's and leaving the two to chat, Keeli reached behind her to get her wallet from the hobo bag slung on the back of the chair.

So Keeli was surprised to hear her name being spoken, only then realizing that the stylish woman had come to the table seeking her out.

"I'm sorry, I didn't realize you were speaking to me," she admitted with a ready blush.

"No problem. I did not mean to interrupt your lunch," the elegant woman extended a slim hand with long, slender fingers and a surprisingly strong handshake. "My name is Monica Marx. I am a buyer for Estime, just a few blocks away. You're Keeli Larsen, right?"

Keeli was shocked to be recognized but saw a contented smile moving across Missy's face. This was her doing.

"I am, but I don't believe I know you..." Keeli was not sure what to say next.

"I wouldn't normally just barge in like this but I recognized you from your Facebook picture. I have been following your page for a few weeks now. Recently two of our regular customers came

257

into our shop wearing your jewelry."

"Really? How wonderful." Missy was almost bouncing in her seat with excitement. "She is quite a talent isn't she? Hi," she extended her hand to the woman. Won't you join us?"

Monica said a friendly hello to Missy without needing an introduction, confirming Keeli's suspicions. She pulled over a chair from the next table, lowering her tall frame into it and leaning forward toward the table. She was probably in her forties, looked like she was in her thirties, hair and makeup perfect. She was dressed like she just stepped off a runway in a classic black dress that was draped to perfection. With it she wore simple, large diamond hoop earrings that were capturing the light.

"I am so sorry to bother you at lunch, but I couldn't pass up the opportunity to talk with you. I promise not to keep you long."

"Take all the time you like," Missy said graciously. Keeli wanted to be polite to this lovely woman, but she also wanted her to get to the point. Obviously, she and Missy were in on a secret yet to be revealed.

"My customers seem to be turning up in your designs lately. I thought perhaps it was time for us to join forces. Although you are a relatively new designer, I believe that there may be a place for you in our store. We could start with a small showing, perhaps 20 or 30-lux pieces and see how well they sell. What do you think?"

Missy grabbed Keeli's leg under the table. She was like a duck paddling furiously under the surface; she was giving Keeli strange hand and foot signals while her face remained calm. She was giving nothing away.

"I am not sure you are familiar with Estime, Keeli, being so new to the city. They are a very exclusive store. I think you would do well to align with them." Turning to Monica, Missy continued, "Keeli is from out of town, Monica, very new to the city."

"Oh, I didn't realize," Monica latched onto the explanation. "You are from out of town. I understand why I have not seen your work before now. You must come by the store, I think you will find us a good match."

Keeli went with the flow, waiting for her shock to wear off. Missy was making it sound like she was brand new to town. Keeli adored Missy, considered her one of her closest friends. She trusted her to look after her interests so if Missy said she had just arrived in Chicago, Keeli would swear she was still unpacking.

"I would be happy to come see your place, Monica, and review a possible arrangement."

Is that my voice sounding so cool and confident?

"Would later this week be convenient for you?"

Disappointment clear on her face, Monica said later in the week would be fine, "unless you could come today?" she finished anxiously.

"Today?" Keeli pretended to review her calendar, fidgeting with her phone. "Oh, I can make that work actually. At 3?" She feigned surprise at having an available time and Monica shook her hand enthusiastically, handed them both her business card and left in a flutter of black material and elusive perfume.

"OMG, did that just happen?" Keeli queried Missy once Monica was out of earshot.

"It sure as hell did. You, my dear, have arrived. You absolutely cannot do better than Estime. You know that, right? It is the most exclusive boutique in the city. They have an art gallery in house. It is unbelievable. I told her we would be here, but with Monica you can never be sure."

The two women were so excited, sitting with their heads together strategizing. Could Keeli complete 30 pieces? Would she need a new collection first? High end, she had said, that meant expensive materials. What should the store's cut be? What kind of marketing and advertising should Keeli demand?

"I feel like Alice through the Looking Glass," Keeli finally acknowledged, leaning back in her seat with a thud. "Lunch is definitely on me."

Missy gave her no argument, suggesting instead that they go find a dress for the wedding.

"I completely forgot that is why we are here. I better get my head back on straight by 3:00!"

"And maybe by then we can improve what you are wearing today, too." Missy looks at the worn jeans and the Keds on Keeli's feet.

Nodding agreement, Keeli linked arms with Missy, the perfect partner for her rare shopping spree.

"Missy, you are too good to me. I don't deserve it, really."

Missy responded cryptically, "You will, Keeli. I promise you will."

CHAPTER THIRTY-FOUR

Theo and Dylan's wedding day dawned clear and sunny, a perfect late summer day. The ceremony was at 4:00 in the judge's chambers at the courthouse across from City Hall. Only immediate family and friends were included for the intimate affair. The reception was another story entirely. They were expecting almost 200 people to fill "D's", Dylan's upscale restaurant.

Keeli was at the restaurant before noon, supervising the delivery of flowers and alcohol. Everything else was in the expert hands of the caterers and wait staff for "D's". The room was already set up with round tables under white tablecloths. Now the centerpieces had arrived and were in place, vases full of exotic blooms, greenery and strange branches providing extra height. They looked elegant and perfect in the space.

The place cards were set up on the table near the door and Keeli grabbed hers when she passed by. Checking to be sure the alcohol had been delivered, she stopped to take a quick peek at the cake before heading home to get dressed.

Lynn and Mark had offered their apartment so she would not fight the boys for the bathroom on their special day, so she headed straight up to their place. They had a few hours still, so they stretched out on the sofas and floor to catch up before donning their finery and heading downtown.

At two, Keeli jumped in the shower, styled her hair with the products Aaron had convinced her to buy and applied her makeup with a light hand. Lynn zipped her into the pale blue Elie Tahari dress she bought with Missy last month, instantly turning her eyes more blue than green. She grabbed a borrowed bag and a new pair of strappy sandals and waited for Lynn and Mark to finish getting dressed.

At 3:15, the three headed out. Keeli put her ear to the door downstairs, but all was quiet. The men must have already left. Luckily, there was light traffic. In a few hours people heading to the city for a Saturday night would clog every major road. But not now. They were pulling into the Lake Street lot right on schedule.

The courthouse was quiet. Closed in general, Theo had called in a favor for a Saturday wedding. The guards pointed the way and the three hurried along. Outside the judge's chamber, Keeli gave Theo and Dylan's parents quick hugs, along with the two best men, Dylan's older brothers. Theo's mother was hiding joyous tears, but Keeli noticed and handed her a tissue just as they were all ushered into chambers.

Theo looked so handsome in a black tuxedo with a gray vest and black tie. Dylan was elegant in a matching tuxedo, but with a silver waistcoat and white tie. They made a handsome couple, brimming with excitement and affection.

The ceremony was stately and solemn and despite the austere surroundings, it was infused with love. The men had written their own vows, bringing laughter and sweetness to the event. Theo's family was musical and sang "At Last" and Dylan's read "So Much Happiness," by Naomi Shihab Nye. The ceremony was incredibly personal, touching and abounding with happiness. Keeli wiped away a tear or two of joy. She was so happy for these two men she had watched fall deeply in love.

Then it was jumping back in cars for the quick ride to "D's". Guests had already started arriving, music was thumping from the stage of the large room and a real feeling of festivity abounded.

Keeli said hello to people she knew from the restaurant,

servers she worked with at the caterers and other family and friends. It was so great to see everyone. Great that was, until there was a small break in the crowd and Wyatt stood in front of her. Why hadn't the boys told her he was invited? She would have been better prepared.

Of course, there was Sloane slithering beside him, clinging for dear life. Could the woman never stand unassisted?

She watched him approaching with trepidation, trying to make her brain function. She would need something to say. Saved at the last minute, Theo's brother, Matthew, stepped between Keeli and Wyatt to wrap her in a big bear hug. He planted a big kiss on her cheek, grinning like a clown.

"Happy?"

"How can you tell?" He laughed in response, handing her a glass of champagne from a passing waiter. "Took these guys long enough, don't you think?"

Before Keeli could answer, Wyatt and Sloane joined them and she made quick introductions. Matthew recognized Wyatt instantly and the two began a spirited conversation about real estate law, effectively leaving Keeli alone with Sloane.

"Such a happy occasion," the slim brunette offered cordially. "I love weddings, don't you?" Did Keeli imagine the dig in that comment or was it really there? She couldn't be sure.

"I do, especially this one. They are perfect for each other. Are you planning your wedding? It must be coming up."

Good job sounding cool. Keep it up.

"Well, we want the Peninsula for the reception so we have to wait until April, but there is so much to do before then." Sloane was gushing like an 18 year old and although it would be a first marriage, it somehow seemed inappropriate behavior for a woman over 30. She went on and on about the details, the music, the flowers, her dress. Keeli was afraid she would be sick soon, but fortunately, at that moment she heard the men wrapping up their conversation.

"I will still have complete attorney-client privilege, right? Okay, I will call your partner tomorrow morning to set up an appointment." Wyatt shook hands with Matthew, Sloane claimed Wyatt and took him away.

Dodged that bullet, but do not let that woman near me again tonight.

From then on, the evening went by in a whirlwind of dancing, speeches, incredible food and time spent with good friends. Well after ten, Wyatt came to claim a dance, but Theo asked at the same time so Keeli danced with the groom.

"You can't avoid me all night, Keeli," she heard Wyatt growl as she walked away.

Sure enough, when the dance with Theo ended, Wyatt was standing there to claim her. He wrapped her in his arms for a slow dance and it felt like heaven. Keeli resisted the urge to stand closer, to rest her head on his shoulder, settling for just the warm strength of his hand holding hers.

"I miss you, Keeli. We really need time together. There is so much we need to discuss. It's important."

"I am sure you must be busy, Wyatt. I understand you launched your business recently. It is so exciting. I read all about you in Crain's Business. You are already doing so well. Congratulations." Keeli knew she was babbling, but could not stop. "You know I wish you only the best. But I can't imagine we have anything left to talk about. After all, that is an engagement ring on Sloane's finger, right? What is it? Five carats? Six? You have very good taste."

"Keeli, the ring means nothing. I swear."

"Really?" Keeli responded, her voice dripping venom. "That is a very expensive nothing, Wyatt."

"I am fixing things. Just give me a chance. A little time."

"Thank you for the dance," Keeli nodded her head, almost like a bow, let his hand drop and walked away.

Don't look back. Just let him go.

Wyatt headed straight for the bar when their dance ended, but Keeli walked around the outside of the room slowly, surveying the crowd. While Keeli had been dancing with Wyatt, trying to hide her heartache, Sloane had started a conversation with

Matthew. Keeli had known Theo's brother for quite a while now and knew that if Sloane were pumping him about his conversation with Wyatt, she would get nothing from the lawyer.

Still, Keeli was curious and maneuvered her way to where they were standing, staying behind them where she could not be seen.

Matthew's low voice was quiet and calm and Keeli had to strain to hear him over the noise. "So you don't want to marry him or you do? I am confused."

"Well, it's not like we love each other," Sloane was making no effort to keep her voice down. "But this is a very important business arrangement for our families. The Howe family has money, lots of it, and my family needs it to get back on our feet."

"But the family business you just described...?" Matthew queried, obviously confused.

"We need everyone to think things are fine, but in truth we are near bankruptcy. My father has totally mismanaged things the last few years and without our relationship with Lyons Howe, we would have gone under already. This marriage will fix all our problems."

The man mumbled some response, maybe words of sympathy? Keeli could not be sure but Sloane quickly continued, "Oh, he didn't propose exactly." Matthew must have asked if Wyatt knew about this when he proposed. "His father held his new company hostage. Want your company? You marry me. But that's okay; he will learn to love me. We are perfect for each other."

At that moment Wyatt came to claim Sloane and Matthew said his goodnights looking like he could not escape fast enough.

Keeli stood frozen in place, unable to move, unsure she had really just overheard what she thought she did.

"He doesn't love Sloane" kept repeating in her head. She could not think of anything else. Suddenly her brain kicked in over all the champagne she had consumed, reality hitting her like a ton of bricks.

He may not love her, but he was still going to marry her.

Nothing had changed.

CHAPTER THIRTY-FIVE

The wedding had been perfection and Keeli enjoyed herself more than she could have imagined. Her new dress and shoes along with her much-improved hair helped make her feel beautiful and she was delighted to pose for the photographer beside the happy couple. Never had she witnessed two people more in love. Still, while she could be thrilled for Theo and Dylan, she could not push through her own lingering loneliness. Perhaps a little too much champagne hadn't helped.

Now, just scant days later, she wandered lost and blue around the nearly empty apartment. Her roommates moved to their new house last weekend. It was a beautiful house with a big back yard. They promised to have her over as soon as they returned from their honeymoon in Spain but right now waiting two weeks to see them again felt like forever. She had become so accustomed to being with them daily.

Her footsteps echoed on the hardwoods as she moved from room to room. Her belongings were packed in boxes waiting for the movers scheduled to arrive early tomorrow. She had a rental car downstairs with a trunk packed to overflowing with the things she believed she would need for the next month or so. The rest would go into storage.

Keeli reflected again on all the changes coming at her with

warp speed. She needed a new collection, including more pieces than she had ever created at once, and pieces that were more expensive. She needed a new place to live. She had a completely new group of friends and a completely new set of demands on her.

She had moved from the world of designing all winter and selling all summer to selling year round and she was still struggling to figure out a schedule that worked in this new environment. She needed a new studio to accommodate the hot weather better and the larger output.

And she needed to get over Wyatt. The news she overheard at the wedding changed nothing. He would still marry Sloane and she would still be alone. All the work that kept her busy, all the pep talks she gave herself, they had not helped. Seeing him Sunday, stunning in his tuxedo, suave and sun-kissed, had confirmed her worst fears. She was nowhere close to getting over him. If anything, overhearing Sloane just made her love him more.

Overwhelmed by the amount of work, by the decisions, by the changes, Keeli came to a decision that surprised even her. She decided she would go home, back to Gilman, her family and the farm.

After listening to too many whining calls from her mother, she had finally decided to spend several weeks in Gilman. She would catch up on work and regroup without distractions. She missed her brothers and the quiet of the farm and she needed a roof over her head until she made new plans.

Going home allowed her to save on rent, savings she could apply to upgrading her metals and gems. She needed a luxurious collection, something new and innovative and she needed to produce a lot of inventory. Keeli had six trunk shows in November and her contract with Estime required that she have 25 pieces available to them at all times. They were aggressively marketing her designs and she needed to replenish their supply often. The work was grueling, more than she was accustomed to, but incredibly rewarding.

Keeli could not help but gloat. She was going home a success -

a major success. Chicago's elite had discovered her and so had the press. She no longer sold her work on Etsy. Instead she had her own website. She was selling at Estime, the two boutiques in Evanston and negotiating with four other posh boutiques in Chicago and its suburbs. She even had inquiries from New York and LA. She finally felt validated as an artist. She could believe in her talent at long last. The press called her an overnight sensation (ignoring seven years of paying dues).

Her head pounding from another night of drinking at an impromptu farewell dinner with Missy, Keeli carefully folded and packed the last of her clothes, sealing the box before dropping like lead to her mattress without washing her face or brushing her teeth, too tired to move.

It felt like an instant later when Keeli lifted her heavy lids to find the sun streaming through her window and blinding her. Covering her eyes, she found them crusty with mascara and sleep. Hitting the alarm on her phone with force, Keeli dragged herself to the shower, scrubbed her face hard to remove the last vestiges of her late night, then threw out the remaining shampoo and soap. She donned her comfortable jeans and t-shirt, boxed the sheets and pillows she had slept on and took one more turn about the apartment to assure herself she had everything.

The movers showed promptly at 7:00 a.m.. They had her meager belongings loaded in just 45 minutes and now she was following them to the rented storage facility. They unloaded even faster and she was on the road by 8:30. If it weren't Sunday she would be panicking about rush hour, but instead she looked forward to the leisurely, 90-minute drive. Stopping for hot tea and a scone, she had everything she needed for the ride. Soon she was merging onto the highway, long-haul trucks buffeting the rental car in their wake.

After almost an hour of moderate traffic, the number of trucks thinned out and she crossed the swollen Kankakee River. Houses gave way to fields of corn and soybeans and electric towers stretched as far as the eye could see like a chorus line of dancing metal women. Keeli felt her heart swell as towns became familiar, recognizing Clifton, then Pontiac, then the football field for rival Central High. It felt surprisingly good to be home.

No one knew she was coming and she was as excited as a kid on Christmas to see everyone. At the last minute, Keeli skirted the main road, turning off past the new library to come in from the West to surprise everyone. Now that she was actually close, Keeli suddenly worried that she should have called first. What if they did not want her, or they were too busy? Or what if her mother was her usual negative self? She could not afford to have her mother undercut her confidence now, when she had so much to accomplish.

Too late now.

Only Buster, their German Shepard, came to greet Keeli. She patted his warm body, breathing in his familiar smell and that of the fields. It smelled like home bringing a lump to Keeli's throat and making her so nostalgic. In that moment she could not imagine why she had stayed away so long. Keeli scratched Buster behind the ears for a few minutes and gave him a big hug before reaching into the rental and laying on the horn. Buster scampered away from the noise and retreated to curl around himself on the sagging front porch.

The farm was quiet. She could hear the far away sound of the wind whipping through the fields and the loud buzzing of mosquitoes and gnats. In the far distance she could hear the sound of machinery tilling under the last of the autumn corn.

The trees in the front were in full leaf - lush, green and shady. Keeli remembered climbing those trees, trying to keep up with her brothers until she fell and broke her arm, diminishing their allure. The buildings needed a coat of paint, that old barn needed to come down now that the new metal one was in place and the garden needed weeding. It all looked smaller than she remembered.

When no one came running, Keeli laid on the horn longer. This time it took only seconds for people to descend on the strange car. Keeli could see them trying to figure out who was making that racket on a Sunday. Realizing it was her, her older brother, Daniel, broke into a big grin and sped up his steps. Her brother James let out a whoop, came running and swung her around and around in his large arms.

Putting her down reluctantly, James gave her a loud kiss on the cheek, about to scold her for staying away so long when she cut him off by admonishing him for working in his church clothes. "Just running the tractor," he countered.

Then her mother stepped between them, quietly taking Keeli in an embrace. She hugged her for several moments before holding her at arm's length to check her out from head to toe. "Bout damn time you came home."

Questions came from everyone at once but Keeli was able to make them understand she had come to stay for a while. "Not for good though?" her mother asked in her gravely, chain-smoker's voice. Avoiding her mother's sour expression, Keeli pointed to the car and told her brothers that she had a lot of stuff for them to carry up to her old room.

"Will you work the farm, Keeli? It can be like old times," Daniel said, easily lifting heavy boxes from the trunk of the rental. "Or at least the county fair?" James chimed in. "Oh shoot, the tractor! I forgot all about it." James hollered over his shoulder heading back to the tractor he left running in the clearing.

"Well, I can see nothing's changed here," Keeli observed as Daniel abandoned her boxes next to the car and headed back to the fields, leaving her alone with her mother and an awkward silence.

"You look good," her mother acknowledged begrudgingly. "I like your hair like that."

"You look good too, Mama. I've missed you so much."

"Well, you could have called a bit more often, come home more."

Keeli was determined not to let her mother rile her so she pasted on a smile. She wrapped her arms around the woman's waist and responded, "Well, I am here now, and I plan to stay a spell."

"Are you out of money?" Her mother's tone was concerned

but Keeli had no trouble hearing the underlying satisfaction.

"No, Mama. I am just so busy that I needed a quiet place to work." After a moment too long she added, "and of course I missed everyone."

"Of course. Well come on in and help me get lunch on the table. The boys can get your luggage later."

Following her mother up the worn steps, Keeli noticed more gray hair on her mother's head, less weight on her body. She realized that her mother was aging and she made a promise to herself not to stay away so long next time. It was strange to compare her mother in her mid-fifties to the elegant women of the same age she knew in Chicago. The comparison was certainly not favorable to her mother.

"How you been feelin', Mama?"

"Same as always, I guess," came her mother's cryptic answer. She offered no additional information so Keeli changed subjects.

"Is my old room ok?"

When her mother nodded, Keeli took the stairs two at a time and dropped her tote bag and purse on a chair inside the door. The room looked exactly as it had in high school - single bed centered against one wall, a beat up dresser with a mirror above it that still had photo booth pictures with friends and ticket stubs tucked into the frame. She had painted that dresser and the desk against the other wall bright white back in college, trying to make it look new. Now she could see it was just old furniture badly painted. There were all her college textbooks neatly arranged on the lone bookcase. She walked over to run her fingers along the framed pictures from homecoming, graduation and an old faded picture of her dad. The curtains and bedspread were more faded, but otherwise unchanged.

Buster followed Keeli up the stairs and was about to curl himself on the rag rug when Keeli called to him over her shoulder, "Come on Buster, I'll give you a treat." The dog bounded ahead of her, almost knocking her down the stairs, and was sitting under the treat bowl when she arrived in the kitchen.

Her favorite room in the house, the kitchen still reminded

Keeli of growing up here. Nothing had changed and her nostalgia was heavy even as she recognized how desperately her mother needed new appliances.

"Mm. Smells yummy. Corn bread?"

"And a late season peach cobbler too. We will have to put some meat on those bones of yours," her mother said while handing her over mitts and directing her to get fried chicken from the oven.

I will have to do some serious exercise or I will go home fat as a pig.

The two women prepared lunch while conducting a strained conversation. Keeli told her mother of her growing success but her mother responded with enigmatic "oh's" or "mm hmm's" until Keeli's brothers came in smelling of the outdoors. Their presence instantly lightened the mood and their encouragement made Keeli feel much better.

In between grabbing food and filling plates, Keeli brought them up to date on the growth of her business. James was excited and supportive, anxious to check out her website. Daniel suggested he could buy something for his wife, "if I can afford any of your fancy stuff."

"And just where is Sarah today?" Keeli asked, a little embarrassed not to have asked sooner.

"She took the kids to church and Sunday school but they should be running through that door any minute."

"Shouldn't we wait for them before we eat?"

"The kids'll eat mac and cheese when they get here, and Sarah doesn't mind if we start." Almost on cue, Keeli heard the sound of car doors slamming and the high voices of her nephews.

"Whose car is that?" Sarah hollered from the hallway before joining them in the kitchen and grabbing Keeli in a fierce bear hug. "Oh my god, oh my god. Am I ever happy to see you," Sarah said, her voice muffled into Keeli's neck. "I have missed you so much."

Finally releasing Keeli, Sarah dropped a kiss on the top of her husband's head, starting the water boiling for mac and cheese and got her children's hands washed. Putting warm cornbread on each of their plates, they were quietly munching while conversation swirled around them.

"You have both grown so much," Keeli fussed over the little ones, now aged four and two. She had missed their entire toddler years she realized sadly.

"I'm four now. I'm all growed up," Joshua explained solemnly. Keeli nodded seriously and strived not to laugh.

"Yes you are, Josh. You are quite a man already. And so are you, Joe."

"He's still just a kid," Joshua quickly pointed out and the adults all started laughing.

"Oh Sarah, they are perfect," Keeli gushed, unable to hold her emotions in check.

"Did you know when you fixed me up with Daniel that we would have such perfect children?"

"Nope, I just knew my best friend was making goo-goo eyes at my big brother." Sarah rolled her eyes at the accusation, but didn't deny it.

They spent the rest of the meal helping Keeli catch up on town life - who was born, who got married, who died. She found out that James was dating a girl from the class behind hers at Iroquois West High School. She could see that the whole family was hoping he would settle down with her.

The farm was doing well they told her, giving her details on crop yields and plant rotations. Keeli felt a bit like she had stepped into an episode of "The Waltons." It was both strange and familiar at the same time.

"And what about you Keeli? You seeing anyone?"

Keeli had been dreading this question, but was prepared for it.

"I was seeing someone for a while, but it didn't work out and we went our separate ways. Now I am working too hard to date. I'll get back to it in a few months."

The too busy remark got her exactly the response she wanted as she was peppered with more questions about her business.

"Well, my business is finally growing," she explained

modestly. "I actually came home to get some work done. My roommates got married. They can do that now in Illinois," she gave her mother a snide look. "So they bought a house. I need a new place to live, a new studio and a new collection. It seemed like this was the place to figure all that out."

They asked a few desultory questions but were not very interested in the specifics of her work. At least they had congratulated her on making her business succeed.

"And you are too busy for a husband, Keeli?" her mother finally asked. "You are getting too old to put dating on hold, my girl. Time is passing more quickly than you know. Just look at Sarah."

"Leave me out of this," Sarah chimed in.

"John Remington just took over his father's place and he is still single you know. You own your own business now, Keeli. You can set up shop anywhere you please now that you use the Internet. No reason you can't just stay in Gilman now."

Keeli flashed her mother a look of frustration and began clearing the table without answering her mother.

"Did you hear me, girl?" her mother prodded. She would never drop this until she broke her, Keeli realized.

"I heard you Mama, but I am pretending I didn't cause I don't want a fight. I have been home less than two hours. Can we discuss this another day?"

"Keeli, that is not fair. It is a reasonable question," Daniel said firmly until Sarah put her hand on his arm gently to silence him.

"You're right, Daniel. I am not interested in John, Mama. I live in Chicago now. I am happy there. I am not dating anyone at the moment, but I was seeing someone wonderful and I am sure when the time is right I will meet a man to marry."

"You'll meet someone who will keep you in Chicago. Keep my grandchildren away from me. And just when will the time be right?" Her mother was relentless.

"I don't know, Mama. It won't be today though." Keeli threw down the dishtowel she was holding and with a mumbled 'excuse me' shoved open the back door and headed out for a calming walk in the fields before she said something she would regret.

Well, I made it through almost two whole hours before losing my cool. How the hell am I going to keep from killing her so I can get some work done? What on earth was I thinking when I came home?

Taking several deep breaths, Keeli got her emotions in check and strode down the road toward the barn and grain silo. Buster caught up and loped beside her as she got her temper under control.

"I better find a new place fast, Boy," she said to the dog. "Otherwise, I am not responsible if bodies pile up."

"I knew I would find you here," Sarah joined Keeli in a quiet corner of the large barn. "You always hid in the same place."

"Just cooling off before I head back."

"Yeah, good plan. She just needs to get it out of her system you know? Your mom wants to see you settled and taken care of. She doesn't realize that you can take care of yourself now."

"I can you know. I am really making it on my own."

"I can tell that you are Keeli, and I am so proud of you. You have worked hard for this success, and against some tough odds, you have made it."

"It was tough, and now I just want to be able to enjoy it. Is that too much to ask from my family?"

"Keeli, I am your oldest friend in the world. You might fool someone else but you can't fool me. It was not the work stuff that set you off, it was the guy you mentioned."

"That easy to tell?"

"Maybe not to everyone, but I could see you hurtin'. Want to talk about it?"

For the next thirty minutes, Keeli poured her heart out to Sarah. She told her how brilliant and funny Wyatt was, how sweet and caring, how incredibly good looking and sexy.

"So you slept with him?"

"Oh yeah," Keeli responded with a candor and expression that told the whole story.

"What the hell happened?"

Once the story of the star-crossed lovers had been relayed, Sarah sat in stunned silence while Keeli mopped her eyes. She had asked question after question, made suggestion after suggestion of how things might still resolve themselves.

"I give up," Sarah finally uttered. "I can't see a way out either. It is so sad. He will marry a woman he doesn't love and you will be heartbroken. It is so unfair."

They sat in companionable silence for several minutes.

"Keeli, maybe you should just go see John Remington. He is a good guy. And he inherited a very big farm, very profitable. He's pretty handsome too, you might recall. I would love to have you back home."

"Not you too. Traitor," Keeli teased, but it broke the mood and the two girls returned to the house arm-In-arm.

Sarah and Daniel took the kids and headed home, a lovely house built on the other end of the large Larsen property. Keeli returned to her room, unpacked her few personal possessions and laid out the studio materials her brothers had carried up from the car. Digging for her sketchpad, she started doodling anything that came to mind, drawing a profile of the dog, the branches of the reddening elm tree outside her window, the light fixture over her head. The sketches were to relax her more than anything else, but she was hoping for inspiration too. None came.

By dinner, the family had fallen into their usual pattern. Conversation ebbed and flowed through a hearty meatloaf dinner and then Keeli, James and their mother gathered in front of the television in silence. Soon James was texting furiously and announced he was heading to Boondocks for a beer and some live music. He suggested Keeli tag along.

"Come see all your old friends. It'll be a blast," he suggested. Keeli looked to her mother.

"Go on. It might be fun to see everyone."

Saying goodnight, the siblings headed to the local bar and meeting spot while James filled Keeli in on his new girlfriend. She had to admit it sounded serious.

"It's weird to think you might marry someone," she admitted

to James.

"No weirder than you getting married," he countered. "And Mama can't wait for that day."

"Don't you dare start that again, James, or you can just drop me off right here." Since they were on a long dark road in the middle of nowhere, Keeli knew that James would know it for the idle threat it was.

"If you want to avoid this conversation, Keeli, you better hightail your butt back to Chicago."

"I will start searching for an apartment tomorrow."

James was still laughing when he parked at the end of the street and they wandered into Boondocks, moving past the wooden booths and video slots to make their way to bar. Andy waved from behind the bar and welcomed Keeli with a draught beer. Soon all her old school friends surrounded her, laughing, hugging and catching up on old times. Her mother's dreams for her were put on hold, at least for tonight.

CHAPTER THIRTY-SIX

Regan had no idea what she was doing sitting in a strange lawyer's office, but Wyatt knew he could count on her to be there once he told her it was urgent. Still, she could be stubborn and so when he and Tyler strode in together, he was relieved to find her she has already arrived. In typical Regan fashion, she was sitting in the impressive waiting room, tapping one impatient foot. Wyatt could almost hear the wheels turning in her brain, making to do lists and cursing that she was wasting her time at some useless meeting.

But when he looked again, Wyatt realized that while her foot might be tapping, the look on Regan's face was not that of a woman consumed with work. Rather, she looked remarkably like a woman consumed with Tyler.

Even Wyatt could admit that Tyler looked like he had just walked off the pages of GQ. Not a hair on his head was out of place and with his impressive height and whipcord muscles, and in that Zegna suit, he looked compelling. But Regan had known him her whole life; they were like brother and sister.

Or maybe not.

Looking from one to the other it was obvious to Wyatt that they were not staring at each other the way siblings do. Regan's mouth had fallen open and a flush had risen becomingly to her cheeks. She was checking Tyler out from stem to stern, like a piece of meat, and she obviously liked what she saw.

Wyatt knew that things had changed for Tyler too. In the last year, Tyler spoke of Regan more frequently, and with increasing interest. He watched her with a soft expression or leered with blatant desire. Wyatt hoped it was just his imagination, but it felt like the man fairly smoldered around his sister.

Wyatt hoped the two could tame this unexpected lust long enough to participate for the next hour. This was a business meeting for heaven sake. He didn't want to have to deal with the repercussions of this discovery now, nor did he want his sister and best friend to embarrass either him or themselves.

Regan greeted both men with a dry kiss on the cheek and got straight to business. "What am I doing here, Wyatt? And what the hell is he doing here?" She tipped her head to indicate Tyler.

"I have a name you know," Tyler taunted back.

"Just sit tight, Regan, you will know soon enough and I would rather not say anything out here," Wyatt motioned to the receptionist sitting not far away. Wyatt recognized a game of flirtation when he saw one, but he was surprised that his sister had started it, not Tyler. This could get very interesting.

Wyatt pushed aside any more thoughts about the two of them. At some point he knew he would have to wrestle with how he felt about Tyler and Regan as a couple. While they were two of his favorite people in the world, he felt protective of his sister, and he knew every salacious detail of Tyler's previous dealings with women.

"Wyatt." A distinguished man of about 40, small in stature and obviously of Asian descent, walked toward them and shook hands with Wyatt. From that moment on, Wyatt was focused on the matter at hand.

"And you must be Regan," he said, taking her hand in a firm handshake as well.

"Tyler Winthrop."

"Jonathan Chen," the man introduced himself and motioned toward the conference room visible down the hallway. "Can I get anyone coffee or water?"

Beverages noted by the receptionist, the four settled around the polished glass table. Wyatt was relieved to see that Jonathan had everyone's attention. They were all back in their professional personas.

"So, Wyatt, I spoke with Matthew per your request, and now I have looked into things a bit myself as well. I believe we can help you."

"Really?" Wyatt asked hopefully.

"Help with what? Who are you?" Regan interrogated.

"Sorry, Regan, let me start at the beginning. Your brother met my partner Matthew at Theo and Dylan's wedding last week and they got to talking. He mentioned he was engaged, and then Matthew met his charming fiancé, Sloane, who called their engagement a business deal. You brother has asked our firm to help get him out of this 'business deal', and I believe we can do just that."

"Oh, that explains it," Regan interrupted, speaking over Tyler's "I knew you didn't love her."

"In his efforts to get released from the engagement, Wyatt came to me about some contracts your father entered into with Mr. Huyler. The two fathers are using this deal to force the marriage. I am an attorney specializing in international contracts. I focus on China, so I offered to review the contracts looking for a loophole."

Wyatt jumped in at this point to provide more detail. "When Father was sick, Sloane's father approached him about a large expansion into China. Father was asked to invest in the operation, which seemed completely legit. Father invested both personally and on behalf of LHRE. Since then, it has come to light that the Huylers are paying large, very-illegal kickbacks to the Chinese government and are likely guilty of patent infringement as well.

"I don't believe it," Regan sat stunned.

"Believe it, Regan. The proof is right here." Jonathan tapped a finger on the stack of papers in front of him.

"But, I cannot believe Father would make you marry Sloane."

"If your father tries to break the contracts, the Huylers are ruined. If the contracts become public, your father is ruined. Marrying the two families seemed like a good insurance policy," Tyler explained.

"Just what are you doing here, anyway?" Regan was getting testy. "Where is our lawyer, Wyatt?"

"I don't want the Lyons Howe lawyers to know we are trying to break these deals. Moreover, Tyler is here because he is about to become the new General Counsel for Lyons Technical Software Solutions. I want him to understand what we are up against. Father is both my biggest investor and my biggest customer. It will take down my new company if these deals get investigated."

"Wow, I had no idea," Regan admitted, deflated by the bad news. "We're ruined."

"No Regan, the good news is that you are not. I have reviewed each contract carefully – there are three – and they all share the same terms and conditions. One of the conditions states that Huyler Industries will not conduct any illegal activities. Another says that they will comply with all US and international laws. The have breached both of these terms allowing Lyons Howe to break the contracts without penalty."

"But what is to stop Huyler from going public and ruining LHRE anyway?" Tyler probed.

"The confidentiality clauses are airtight, Tyler. Mr. Howe could sue Huyler Industries for a fortune if they breach confidentiality."

"Oh my God," Wyatt sat stunned. "We are going to get out of this aren't we?" Regan watched as reality crossed his face. He was free of Sloane.

"I will draft the necessary papers and send them to your father for signature. We will need to engage the LHRE attorneys at that point too. Then we can send them over to Huyler. The whole thing should take about a month, Wyatt. Then you and your family are free."

"I cannot thank you enough," Wyatt surged forward to grab and pump Jonathan's hand enthusiastically.

"Oh sure you can, Wyatt. You'll get my exorbitant bill soon."

The group laughed and filed out of the room. Saying their goodbyes in reception, Wyatt suggested they head around the corner and grab lunch. Regan suggested a short drink instead, needing to get back to the office.

They were very excited, talking over each other as they entered the quiet bar at the JW Marriott. Sitting close to each other, hugging the corner of the large bar so they would not be overheard, they congratulated each other on their successful meeting and toasted.

"To a close call," Wyatt offered.

"In so many ways," Regan added.

"To Jonathan," Tyler chimed in and they saluted the lawyer who had just given them such good news.

"So, Tyler," Regan turned to catch him in her steely gaze, "you are jumping ship and joining my brother? I hope your father handled it better than mine did."

"I think your father is happy with how things turned out, Regan. He is a key investor in a new business that is showing incredible promise and he has a new president that is way more talented that the old one." Wyatt punched him playfully in the arm. "And way more beautiful."

Regan blushed five shades of red before smiling shyly at Tyler. They locked eyes and Wyatt had to interrupt to get them to look away from each other. He felt like a parent chaperoning a teen's date.

"I am free of Sloane. Hallelujah," Wyatt cheered, engaging them both in the conversation.

"You know, man, I owe you a big apology. I always thought she was right for you but since the engagement she has been a grasping bitch."

"I always knew she was a grasping bitch," Regan bragged. "But I thought you might care for her so I kept my mouth shut. Then you started talking about the artist and I realized you might really be in love. It was very confusing when suddenly you were engaged to Sloane instead."

"Well, I think now I have blown it completely with Keeli. She won't take me back, and honestly, guys, she was perfect for me. I didn't even care that she was poor. I could tell she wanted me, not my money. I offered her financial assistance to get her business off the ground, but she wouldn't accept my help. She insisted on doing it herself."

"You guys will help me get over her, though, right? You both should be very pleased that things didn't work out." Wyatt was bouncing his leg nervously against the barstool and shredding the cocktail napkin. Tyler recognized all the signs. "I know neither of you thought she was good enough."

"Do you want to get over her?" Regan was never one to mince words and Wyatt flinched visibly. "I guess if that is the case, if what we want is more important than what you want..."

"You should call her, Dude," Tyler offered finally, deciding to put Wyatt out of his misery. "You can be pretty irresistible when you want to be. And I promise to be nicer to her the next time. I was a dick."

"Yeah, you were. It doesn't matter. She is gone. Her home phone disappeared, she moved out of her place. Her neighbors won't tell me how to find her, and her roommates are on their honeymoon."

"Really? Now who is being a dick? You are going down without a fight?" Tyler challenged Wyatt just as he had since they were seven years old.

"I want to fight, damn it. I love her. Help me. I don't know what to do." Wyatt dropped the shredded napkin to run his hands through his hair, distraught.

"Did you ask Missy?" Regan queried in a small, innocent voice, knowing she was about to drop a bombshell.

"Why would I ask Missy?" Wyatt looked at her in complete confusion, but with a tiny ring of hope in his voice.

"They are, like, best friends now, Wyatt. You didn't know?" Regan was delighted to watch the shocked look move from Wyatt's face to be replaced by sheer joy.

"And no one told me?" Wyatt pretended to be incensed but could not hide his excitement. "This is fantastic. Missy will know where she is."

"You better wait until you break off the engagement, Wyatt," Tyler advised, laughing and slapping Wyatt on the back.

"Yeah, Ty is right. Oh and Wyatt," Regan broke into a satisfied grin, "don't expect to get that huge ring back."

"Small price to pay, baby sister, small price to pay."

CHAPTER THIRTY-SEVEN

"It will be broken by tonight, Father. She always considered it a business deal."

"Yes, well, it's for the best then. You'll forgive my high-handedness, I hope."

"Certainly, Father, we have moved past that already, correct?"

"Of course, Son, of course. You turned out to be right about Regan," he flashed her a contrite smile. "She is good at the helm of LHRE. And I can see that you are thriving at Lyon Tech. I j can only hope your mother forgives me when she finds out. She was craving another big society wedding. It has been too long since Melissa's. But your mother also wants you to be happy. She thought Sloane was a bit of a cold fish."

"Really?" Regan looked shocked.

"Of course she was a cold fish. We all thought so." This was surprising coming from his father.

"She had her moments of charm and grace," Wyatt admitted. "But she was very calculating. Even more than I imagined."

"Well, we would still love to see you settle down, Ivy. Your mother and I could use a few more grandchildren. From both of you." Wyatt III gave both of his children a gruff look.

"Well, Father. I happen to know a lovely woman. Perhaps she would like to help with that. And that reminds, me, I need to find Missy." Grinning broadly, Wyatt turned on his heel and headed for the backyard.

He had not seen Keeli in almost two months. He missed her every single day, thought of her every single day and now he could not wait to make up for lost time. He could already feel the softness of her skin under his fingertips and smell the combination of floral and fresh that was uniquely her. He could taste the sweetness of her kisses.

Finding Missy, he demanded without preamble that she give him a way to contact Keeli. She refused.

"Do you understand what I have been through for the last two months?" Wyatt queried, glum-faced.

"First I had to find a lawyer to get us out of those stupid contracts with the Huylers. Then I waited patiently while he took care of everything. Then two weeks ago, I was finally able to break off my engagement with Sloane without repercussions to our business or our family. Then I went round to her place in Logan Square and rang the bell. Then I rang all the bells. Some ogre finally released the door and I was heading in when the old man hollered to me.

"'Can I help you?' he asked in a chilling voice. He was clearly not amused.

"I told him I was looking for Keeli, told him she lives in 2C."

"'She lived in apartment 2C you mean? She moved out. Last to go. They are all gone now.' He was very curt with me, very rude.

"I told him I had no idea she moved and politely requested a forwarding address. Do you know what this guy said to me? 'Do I look like the post office?'"

Missy started laughing, covering her mouth in an effort to hide her mirth, but to no avail.

"Missy, this is not funny. Come on, help me out. I know you know where she is." Wyatt was pleading.

"If she didn't answer your text or calls, she doesn't want to see you, Wyatt. And if she doesn't want to see you, I cannot help you." Missy was firm even though she was sympathetic. Frankly, she could not understand why Keeli was not responding to Wyatt's pleas to see her, but she was not responding to Missy either, so as her friend, Missy did not dare get in the middle.

"Can you at least tell me if you know where she is? Is she okay? Did she move cause she couldn't pay her rent? I can help her with money. I don't care if she wants my money. I just want to be with her."

"Wow, did you just say that, Wyatt? Are you sure about that? You would be okay if Keeli needed you to support her? You wouldn't wonder if she is using you? Think about what you are saying here. This has been your issue your whole life."

"Let her use me, Missy. I love her."

"Well, in that case, yes, she is okay, or was the last time I talked to her."

"I am at my wit's end," Wyatt complained. "I don't want to tell her about Sloane and me in a text. I don't want her to think I ever stopped caring about her. It's so damn complicated. I need to see her and talk face-to-face."

"Well…there might be a way."

"Spill, Missy. I mean it. I am about ready to kill you."

"Have you Googled her lately?"

"Seriously, that is your idea?"

"Oh brother of mine, you are so clueless sometimes. I suggest you Google Keeli Larsen Designs," Wyatt could hear her laughing at him. "Then, brother dear, follow your instincts."

Did You Enjoy this Book? You can make a difference

Thank you for reading *Bedazzled*. I hope you enjoyed it. The second book in the Beguiling Bachelor Series, *Beholden* is now available. Read on for a preview.

Loyal readers and their honest reviews are the most my most powerful tool I have in helping new readers find my romances. As a self-published author, this is my way of competing with big publishing houses. Please consider leaving a short review here to help others romance readers find *Bedazzled*.

Want to know when a new release becomes available? Join my insider group and get advanced notice, exclusive content, deals and steals.

Or follow me on
Facebook at www.facebook.com/madisonmichaelromance
Pinterest at www.pinterest.com/madisonmichaelromance
Goodreads   https://www.goodreads.com/author/show/15221601

MORE BOOKS BY MADISON MICHAEL

The Beguiling Bachelor Series
Bedazzled – Book 1   Wyatt and Keely
Beholden – Book 2   Randall and Sloane
Bedeviled – Book 3   Alex and Charlotte
Besotted – coming soon – Tyler and Regan
Bewildered – A Beguiling Bachelors Prequel

Short Stories and Novellas
Studmuffin
Our Love is Here to Stay (2018)

Collections
Sultry Nights

HERE'S A PREVIEW OF BOOK 2 IN THE BEGUILING BACHELOR SERIES

BEHOLDEN IS AVAILABLE NOW

PROLOGUE – 18 Months Earlier

Sloane was floating on air. The evening had been a perfect success. She had been a perfect success.

Of course.

Everyone declared she was the most beautiful woman in the room, and even if she was the modest type - which she wasn't - she knew it was true. Oh, there were some pretty girls at the Howe Museum gala, some beautiful women, but none of them had her striking features – that alabaster skin, those lustrous sapphire eyes, the lush, kissable lips and that thick curtain of dark hair. She was just pulling the pins out of her hair now, shaking the heavy locks from a tight chignon that had been giving her a headache for the last two hours.

Wyatt Howe IV, her soon-to-be fiancé and chair of the evening's event, had been devastatingly handsome in his custom tuxedo. They had been a cover-model couple – a power couple – stunning, smart, successful, sought-after. They were leaders in that intimate club of Chicago's most elite, the movers and shakers who dictated everything that happened in Chicago society. Anyone who was anyone had stopped by to say hello, to be photographed or, at a minimum, to be seen with them.

Sloane slipped off her Jimmy Choos and reached her elegant arms behind her head to slide down the zipper of her Ellie Saab gown. The pale pink confection would have to go to the cleaners now. She kicked it off with frustration and left it piled on the floor like something she picked up last week at a garage sale, not the $8,000 designer showpiece she had ordered months ago. It would never be the same, she pouted. Not that she was planning to wear it again. Sloane Huyler wouldn't be caught dead in the same dress twice – it just wasn't done.

Still, that stupid waitress had dropped a salad right down the back of her dress. What an incompetent. Sloane had pretended to laugh it off in front of the guests, acted as if it was nothing. She knew better than to embarrass Wyatt by making a scene in public. Her public persona would never draw that kind of negative attention.

There was not a chance in hell she had been laughing. Once they were alone, Sloane had shown Wyatt the nasty temper for which she was famous, telling Wyatt to demand the catering company fire the incompetent, redheaded clutz immediately. The stupid cow was probably already looking for another job.

Boo hoo.

Now, after a few hours to reconsider, Sloane conceded that the server was probably quite capable. In fact, the service had been excellent before the salad disaster. Sloane suspected that the server wasn't paying attention. It was likely Wyatt distracted her. He had that effect on women. After all, he was considered Chicago's most eligible bachelor and he was undeniably scrumptious eye candy. Who was she kidding? The man was a serious hottie.

Then again, maybe she was staring at me. I looked damn good tonight. Either way, now she was out on her ass where she belonged. Even if it was a singular slipup, getting fired would teach her not to covet that which she could never have.

Although she demanded that he do it, Sloane was a bit disappointed when Wyatt went to speak to the caterers at the end of the night, abandoning her. She graciously rode home alone in the limousine and let him conclude the evening, but she knew she had just been played. Wyatt was up to something, had his eye on someone. Sloane was sure of it, although she couldn't put her finger on who the woman might be.

After years of on again, off again dating, she had learned to agree to Wyatt's every request. She was there when he wanted her, didn't whine when he wasn't available, asked for little, offered much and turned a blind eye when he sowed some wild oats. She made sure she was the perfect girlfriend so he would realize that she would be the perfect wife. After the years she had invested in catching him, Sloane made sure he had nothing to complain about. She wouldn't give him any excuse to walk away. Ever.

She had played hostess at his fundraising event perfectly, charming people into opening their wallets wider while helping him promote his real estate business and his philanthropic goals. If things had gone her way, she would have ended the night with him pumping with adrenaline, pumping hard into her to unleash the force of it or proposing marriage. She would have been happy either way.

Wyatt was a little unpredictable though, no matter how ready and willing she was. So here she was, alone again, when he should have been warming her bed. He did quite a good job of it, she had to admit, and so she was sincerely disappointed not to have him with her. She didn't actually miss Wyatt, but she did miss the sex. She wanted to seal the deal already and get the big ring.

Other that that, life was just about perfect.

Sloane had a job she loved as an executive in her father's consulting firm. She had parents she sincerely enjoyed spending time with who were still living in the gorgeous lakefront home in which she had grown up. Her weekends were filled with family visits, tennis games, and events at the country club hobnobbing with family friends.

Sloane had anything and everything that money could buy. In addition, she was well educated, well connected and well heeled. She had the right friends, lived in the right neighborhood, volunteered with the right organizations and committees, dined at the right restaurants, had the best seats at the right plays and concerts and any day now, she would be engaged to the right man.

Wyatt Lyons Howe IV was arguably Chicago's most sought after bachelor. He was CTO of a huge real estate conglomerate. His father owned it currently, but it would all be his someday soon. He was gorgeous and hunky. She liked him, she liked most of his friends and all of his family. He was brilliant, if a bit geeky, talented with a hockey stick and with his other stick as well. Sloane considered their sex life adequate. Wyatt could be a lot of fun in bed, but the passion just wasn't there. Both recognized that occasionally they were just going through the motions.

Still, he was witty and even better connected than she was, so she could overlook anything that wasn't perfect, including his slightly straying eye and unwillingness to commit – so far. He was old money, with all the cache and manners that construed. Their families were friends and everyone anticipated that soon they would marry. It was expected and although Wyatt had not yet presented her with the nine-carat ring she had been eyeing, he also didn't refute their future together when anyone alluded to it. She could wait. After all, being his wife would open the few remaining doors where she desired entrée.

At 29, Sloane knew that she would have to worry about tying him down in the next few years but she was in no hurry. He may be a catch, but he didn't make her heart race. She could look at him dispassionately and patiently. The prize was worth it. Sloane understood that she would be the envy of everyone once she married him, making her half of the most prominent couple in Chicago.

Scrubbing off her professionally applied makeup and running a brush through her lush mane of hair, Sloane slid into the short La Perla nightgown she had left out earlier. It was barely there, just a whisper of material, designed to arouse Wyatt. She thought about grabbing a tee shirt instead, but the nightgown felt so decadent against her skin that she wore it just to indulge herself.

Catching a glimpse of herself in the full-length mirror as she moved to slide between the sheets, Sloane knew she looked stunning and seductive enough to bring any man – even Wyatt – to his knees. She liked the image of him there before her, on his knees, making her feel incredible. She would go to bed slightly - not unbearably - dissatisfied. She was too tired to take care of things herself.

Wyatt should only see what he is missing. I would have him eating out of my hand, or better yet, eating out of my....

Sloane's last thoughts as she fell into an undisturbed slumber were how lucky she was. She would marry Wyatt sooner, rather than later, and then she would have attained her every heart's desire. She would have a handsome, sexy and dutiful husband, a challenging career, perfect children, influence, prestige and tons of money. She would go to the Alps and Aspen for the skiing, Saint Bart's for warmth in winter, Milan and Paris for the fashion shows.

Within a year, she prophesied, she would have everything she dreamed of – the perfect life she deserved.

CHAPTER ONE

"For our final piece of business," the president of the Children's Hospital board began quietly and seriously, "the board has determined that having Sloane Huyler head the benefit committee is no longer in the best interest of the hospital or the event. I am sorry, Sloane, but we are requesting that you step down and let Allyson chair the event going forward."

Her face burning with shame, Sloane made eye contact briefly with each board member present, some of whom returned the look, many of whom refused to meet her steely blue gaze. It didn't matter. She knew she was defeated. In fact, she had actually expected this humiliation to come at last month's meeting, or any of the prior meetings since August. She was surprised it hadn't happened months ago. She supposed, she had run out of any remaining goodwill with the headlines earlier this month.

"Of course, I want to do whatever is best for the hospital and the benefit," Sloane choked out reluctantly.

Sloane wondered if they were ousting her from the entire benefit committee or just the chair position, but she refused to give these blueblood wannabes the satisfaction of asking. She had busted her butt for this benefit already, so screw them if they didn't want anymore of her hard work.

"Sloane, of course we value your expertise and dedication, and appreciate the work you have already completed."

What? Did he read my mind?

"You are very welcome on the committee," the board president was quick to offer, "We welcome your continued help and input - just not as the gala chair."

"Please accept my resignation as chair of this year's benefit, effective immediately." Sloane spoke in a strong, sure voice, holding her back straight despite the proverbial knife they had just thrust in it. "While I am, of course, willing to help in any way I can, I find that I am no longer able to fulfill the responsibilities of chair. I will follow up with an email confirming this as well."

These people are not going to break me, damn it. I am Sloane Huyler. I used to eat people just like these for breakfast. How dare they turn their backs on me now? They are all just nasty hypocrites.

The motion to replace her was made, seconded and voted upon quickly. That last, unsavory piece of business completed, the meeting adjourned. The board members who would normally have stayed around chatting with Sloane, suggesting they go grab a drink or dinner, instead were slinking from the room avoiding contact with her at all costs.

Grabbing her Celine bag from the back of the chair, preparing to leave the room, Sloane was stopped by Allyson Riley, the new chair of "her" benefit.

"I expect you to send me all your notes, Sloane," she stated without emotion. "Also, I have already assigned you to work with the hotel on setup, catering and flowers. I will provide oversight and handle fundraising from now on."

"Sure, Al, I understand. Just send me your notes and we can swap roles. You will do well as Chair, I am sure."

As if that few sentences had not cost her dearly, Sloane offered a crisp nod to her replacement and exited the room. None of the anger and resentment simmering just below the surface showed on her flawless face.

One more minute with her and I might have put a fist through her perfect little nose job. What a toad!

Sloane had seen this coming but that didn't soften the blow. It was just the next disaster in the nightmare that her life had become. For six months now, she could not step out her door without another shoe dropping.

Really, is there anything left to go wrong? How on earth can it get any worse?

Sloane was tough. She always had been. For 30 years, she had lived a privileged life, assured that she deserved every minute of it. She was whiplash smart, cover-model beautiful, came from a wealthy family and she was about to marry into an even wealthier one. Her future was bright. Nothing could stop her from attaining her hearts desire. Then, suddenly, all that had changed and for the last six months, nothing had gone right.

And isn't that the understatement of the century?

First, her father was accused of doing a shady business transaction, stealing secrets from a client and selling them to the Chinese government. He needed to launder the payments so he tried to do it through the company of her soon-to-be-fiancé. When Wyatt discovered the scheme, Sloane's father planned to keep it hush-hush by blackmailing Wyatt's father, then sealing the deal by forcing the long overdue marriage of their children.

How did that all turn out? First, Wyatt called off the engagement but she was tough. Sloane survived that indignity by telling people that she did the jilting. Everyone knew she never loved him, so she pulled that one off pretty well.

The other problems were not so easily resolved. When the Feds arrested her father, Sloane thought he would be back home quickly, completely absolved of all wrongdoing. Instead, he was indicted, rapidly tried and just this month he pleaded guilty to theft, illegal transactions with a foreign government and money laundering. He was sentenced to eighteen years in federal prison.

Sloane was sure he would appeal but instead he cut a deal for a shorter sentence. Since then, like the fall of dominoes, Sloane had suffered a barrage of events from which she was unable to recover. Huyler Industries was bleeding clients and money. The business was failing and she was wracking her brains for a way to keep it afloat. The family fortune, such as it had been, was gone, used to pay taxes and penalties and the exorbitant fees of fancy lawyers. Now her parents' beautiful lakeside home would be sacrificed too.

She couldn't look for assistance from any of her influential and privileged friends and colleagues because they had all deserted her. She had lost her money, her reputation and her influence. With nothing to offer, she was a pariah. The city officials, the movers-and-shakers with whom she'd had great working and personal relationships were the first to desert her. Soon after, all her contacts at banks and investment firms wouldn't return her calls. Other business people, her fellow Northwestern graduates, the group that helped each other out, stopped helping. Finally, she lost her friends. That was the bitterest pill to swallow.

Until now.

She had just very publicly lost the chair of the benefit committee. She had been chairing the benefit for the last four years. With her name and connections, badly needed donations flooded into the Children's Hospital. She was able to charm everyone she knew into putting up items for the silent auction in addition to her accomplishments in gaining large, corporate sponsorship. She had a reputation for an enormous turnout, exciting and entertaining events and the ability to raise close to one million dollars year after year.

Even Sloane recognized that a pariah could not get the business leaders of Chicago to open their deep pockets. A pariah could not even get them to take her calls. The board was correct in assuming that her name on the top of the committee list was more problematic than useful. For Sloane, the benefit was the last star to which she hitched her wagon. Losing it was particularly painful.

Sloane had seen the faces around the room tonight, too. The board, her so-called friends and colleagues, were most likely gloating. She knew it. She wasn't surprised by it. She had too much before. People were spiteful and they took pleasure in watching the mighty fall. Like schadenfreude, those around her were experiencing the joy that came from watching her lose it all.

Besides, I was a bitch. Face it; they knew I was looking down my perfect nose at them, because I was. Well, they are enjoying the show now, Sloane. Each and every one of them is getting the last laugh.

It was a juicy story, after all, with all the elements of a good crime movie – Chicago-style. There was international crime, unethical practices and a perennial Chicago favorite – payola. Her father had expanded their business into China by engaging in illegal practices. And of course, there was the felling of the high and mighty.

The fancy lawyers had bargained eighteen years down to six, which her father had just started serving at the Federal Correctional Institution in Littleton, Colorado. Sloane's mother, Marianne, was left trying to make ends meet on a drastically smaller income and Sloane was left trying to hold together the company responsible for supplying that income. Not an easy task when her father had destroyed the reputation of Huyler Industries and with it any earning power.

It remained a hot gossip item for months, after all the news was ugly, but accurate. A get rich quick scheme by a man everyone believed to be worth millions. Why risk it? It turned out he was broke. Who knew? The Huyler name was dragged through the mud every night on the news, every day in the papers.

It didn't take long before Sloane was unable to show her face in public. Huyler Industries lost every client not bound by ironclad contract. Her mother checked herself into a 'facility' after three months of cameras and scrutiny, just to get away. It was a nice place too, on the beach in the south of France, with fabulous spa services and plastic surgeons. Her mother came home looking refreshed, rested and lovelier than ever just in time to stand behind her husband when he pleaded guilty.

That had left Sloane holding down the fort, trying to piece together what was left of the business and the family fortune. With her father in jail for another 6 years, everything sat squarely on Sloane's capable shoulders. At the moment, she was sinking under the weight. Publicly, she had been unable to separate her activities from those of her father. If he was guilty, she was guilty by association. No one trusted anyone named Huyler anymore. Sloane never understood why her father took the deal. Six years was a long time for an innocent man, hell one day was a long time, and a successful appeal would have cleared his name.

Sloane had braced herself for the loss of business, the bad press, and the painful process of discharging workers who had been with HI from its conception. She had withstood the bad news about the family finances and even faced the need to sell their beautiful lakefront home. She had done it all with her typical chilly demeanor. She had mastered the cool 'I don't give a damn' look when she met prying eyes. Sloane remained poised when she was slighted, when she saw people talking behind her back. However, it all took its toll.

After all, and despite what most people believed, Sloane was human.

When she failed to receive an invitation to the social event of the season, Wyatt's wedding, Sloane had chalked it up to her failed relationship with Wyatt Lyons Howe IV. After all, his new bride could hardly be expected to extend an invitation to Wyatt's ex-fiancé.

Still, the wedding had been splashed over every newspaper and magazine; even "Entertainment Tonight" and "Extra" had picked up the story. A Cinderella romance with a fairy tale ending for a poor artist and a real estate mogul did not happen every day. When the artist became a major success in the same year, it made the national news.

Over 750 people had attended the August wedding, according to the press. Sloane was not one of them. She had hoped to gain entrée as someone's 'plus one', but try as she might, she couldn't cajole anyone into inviting her when the charges against her father came to light the same month.

She had no expectation of attending the ceremony held in a converted Gilman, Illinois barn, knowing only close friends and family were invited. She had to admit though, when she saw the photos of the converted space covered in white flowers and twinkling lights, that she felt a small romantic pull and a bit of jealousy. Not that she would ever admit it.

However, when she was excluded from the big reception at the Howe Museum, she felt shunned. It should have been her wedding. Those thoughts consumed her in the days before and after the summer event. She was supposed to marry the handsome Wyatt. She had chased him relentlessly. She had waited patiently for her prize, only to have a little nobody swoop in and steal it. Such a thing just did not happen to Sloane Egan Huyler.

It became harder to maintain that cool façade when she had been unable to deny that they made a stunning couple, and Keeli made a beautiful bride. Sloane studied the photos of the wedding in every magazine and newspaper. The papers had zoomed in on the gorgeous tiara that Keeli designed to hold her veil. Orders for the now-famous tiara were flooding the workroom of Keeli Larsen Designs and other jewelers were rushing to copy it.

So here Sloane stood, on a cold, dark, February night, outside the meeting room of the hospital, the only person in society to have missed the wedding: jilted, broke, friendless, and the daughter of a notorious jailbird. Now, to add insult to injury, she wasn't even the chair for the Children's Hospital Benefit.

Hell, she could not even find a date for the benefit. Chill, you still have months to figure that one out.

Lifting the collar of her heavy coat and dropping her chin in case anyone from the meeting was still loitering in the building, Sloane took her signature long-legged stride toward the exit of the hospital, holding back the tears that were blurring her blue eyes, praying she could get to her car before they fell.

"Ooof, excuse me," a deep voice offered. Sloane lifted her eyes to see who she had just plowed into, whose large, warm hands were still wrapped around her upper-arms, steadying her as she wobbled in her Prada stilettos. "Steady there."

"Randall," Sloane was relieved when she looked up and recognized that the man she had tried to knock over was Randall Parker, III and not some stranger. "I wasn't looking where I was going."

"Sloane," Randall acknowledged Wyatt's ex with a nod of his head and a bit of a chill in his voice. "In a bit of a rush?"

"A bit." Sloane was clearly trying to make a getaway. She had bumped into him rather forcefully and he continued his hold of her arms. She just wanted him to let her go so she could make it out the door before she turned into a blubbering mess in the middle of the hospital lobby.

"Everything ok? Are you ok?" Randall's voice softened with concern. He still held her, but they both knew she was solidly on her feet. He was studying her face too closely and Sloane was squirming under the scrutiny. "Is everything alright?" he prodded gently, clearly seeing everything she was trying so hard to hide.

Without waiting for an answer, Randall removed his hand and

taking one of Sloane's, he led her to a wooden bench conveniently placed against the wall, encouraging her to sit down.

"I can see that you are upset. Is someone ill? What are you doing here?" He seemed genuinely concerned now but Sloane wasn't fooled by his soft voice and kind demeanor. All of Wyatt's friends had been giving her the cold shoulder since Wyatt dumped her and Randall was no exception.

Sloane knew him too well. Everything with Randall was about picking up a woman, about the conquest. She remembered, as she looked in his handsome face, that he – like his friends - was a player. This was probably just his strategy to segue into a hookup, despite his previous aversion to her. Randall was such a ladies' man that a few times during her engagement, he had hit on her after a few too many drinks. He chased anything in a skirt so she knew that his sweet ways now were nothing personal.

"Oh no, everyone is fine, Randall, and I really need to get going." The good news about running into Randall was that she just wanted to get away from him now and so she had forgotten that she felt like crying. "I was just here for a board meeting. Second Monday of the month," she offered as if that explained everything. She moved to get up again but his hand was holding hers in her lap and he was not letting her move.

"What about you? Are you visiting someone?" *She could at least be polite.*

"My cousin's son took a spill at a basketball game last month. I drove them over to see the doctor. His arm is broken, but he is a kid, so he's enjoying the attention. The cast comes off today."

"That was very nice of you." She was looking longingly toward the exit.

How much more of this chitchat is required before this oaf lets go of my hand?

"Sloane, what's going on? You look like you just lost your best friend. Where is that feisty woman I know?"

"C'mon Randall, you are not that naïve." Sloane's usual caustic impatience had returned and Randall smiled in spite of himself. "You know perfectly well what is going on, unless you have been out of Chicago for the last year. My world is falling apart and you know it. Everyone is blaming me for the accusations against my father. I did nothing wrong, but I am the one left to pick up the pieces."

"You did nothing wrong?" Sloane can hear the incredulity in Randall's tone. "You might get away with that with other people, but this is me, Sloane, and I am not falling for your usual crap. Go bat those baby blues at someone who will buy that garbage you are selling. You have never been completely innocent of anything and we both know it."

"Screw you, Randall." Sloane jerked her hand out of Randall's and rose to her feet. He was up like a shot, grabbing her arm. She fell hard against his chest. His arms wrapped around her automatically and he left them there.

It felt surprisingly good.

"Sloane, seriously, something happened tonight, didn't it, something to upset you all over again?" His expressive eyes were looking at her softly, but with concern, not pity.

I must really be a mess if Randall is being this nice to me. Stiff upper lip, girl.

"What do you care? Just let go of me Randall." She twisted as if to break from the embrace, but not forcefully.

"I know you Sloane. You can play tough girl all you want with these other people," using his head he nodded toward the few people still loitering in the large space, "but I think you are about to cry. And frankly, I am not sure I believed you were even capable of tears; so I thought I would stick around to watch."

"I got kicked off the benefit," she whined in a low voice. "Nothing worth crying over, so show's over. Let me go now."

"They kicked you off the benefit? But you are the chair. You have been working on this for months." Randall seemed shocked by Sloane's news. "Can they even do that?"

"They can and they have. They don't want my tainted name on the invitations, bad for business, I guess. I get to collaborate with the hotel caterers and that is it. Allyson Riley is in charge."

"Well, she is good," Randall acknowledged while Sloane flashed him a malevolent look. "But it was pretty unfair to you," he quickly backpedaled.

"Pretty unfair? Pretty unfair?" Sloane's voice rose in indignation. "It was unforgiveable."

"But Sloane, face facts. You have to understand that people around town might think twice before handing you money right now. You may not be the one charged with wrongdoing, but the suspicion is there."

"Thanks for reminding me, asshole."

"Just calling it like I see it," Randall had finally moved back from her, giving her breathing room that had been strangely lacking. "You can survive this Sloane. You can survive all of this. You are a tough broad. One of the toughest I know."

"Randall, no one calls a woman a 'broad' anymore. It's not PC," Sloane tossed back, starting to feel like herself again.

"Well, no one calls me an asshole either," Randall lobbed back at Sloane quickly. "Besides, I meant 'tough broad' as a compliment."

"Oh, well then, of course, my sincerest thanks," Sloane answered, her tone anything but sincere.

"You are hopeless, Sloane. It is time to stop feeling sorry for yourself and move on. It's been months since your father's arrest. It will be years before he gets out. In the meantime, you need to make a life for yourself. You are yesterday's news. Act like it. Show these snobs that you are made of tougher stuff."

"But what if I am not?" Sloane surprised herself and Randall with the insecure and hurt-laced question.

"Who is this mealy mouthed woman? Seriously, I have seen you cut a person to shreds with a look. Get your act together already and start walking on people again."

"Hey wait a minute. I do not walk on people." Sloane was indignant, but her voice had regained some strength and power at last.

"Do not bullshit a bullshitter, Sloane. You have made a career out of walking on people. You would have married my best friend for his name and his money. You tried to get his girlfriend fired. You are unscrupulous, but at least you are really good at it."

Damn Randall, he isn't wrong about any of this. I would have married Wyatt for his money, and when Keeli spilled salad on me, I tried to have her fired even though she seemed sincerely sorry. I would do it all over again too. She had no right to make me look foolish, damn her, or to steal my man.

"What the hell? Stop impugning my character," Sloane was standing taller, indignant at being so accurately sized up.

"Just calling it like I see it," Randall said again.

"Stop saying that!" Sloane said in irritation.

Randall was moving away from the bench and walking toward a woman and child coming from the elevators.

"Gotta go," he lobbed over his shoulder without a backward glance. Sloane stood there fuming.

Even if he was right about me, who the hell is he to talk? Just a stupid, womanizing oaf. On the other hand, no one ever had the nerve to say to my face what I know they say behind my back. Not even Wyatt.

Sloane started moving toward the exit, her tears completely

forgotten. She felt like her old self – imperious, elitist and entitled to anything she wanted. She tried not to think too hard about the fact that Randall had set her back on course, kept her from embarrassing herself. She tried not to think about the fact that she had been unable to decide whether to punch him or kiss him.

For an oaf, his hands felt incredibly good on me, strong and large and manly. Too bad he is so damn good looking. And smart. And successful. Yeah, and mouth-wateringly sexy.

Sloane realized with distress that if a woman could pin him down, Randall was a catch. In fact, he was the type of man she was looking for. He was highly accomplished and educated, strong willed and physically powerful. He had already taken over running his family's investment firm. He worked hard. He played hard. He traveled in the right circles, but he was no snob. And he was disarmingly attractive. Shaking off the idea of Randall as a catch, Sloane remembered that Randall was still a womanizer.

Oh, and he could be a drunk, too. Just walk away, Sloane. He parties too hard, likes his booze and his women way too much.

Sloane stood there for one more moment, remembering the feel of his arms around her, the way her hand had felt small with his big fingers wrapped around hers. She remembered the look in his eyes when he was concerned and the pleasure of bantering with him without having the upper hand. She had liked the time together, brief as it was. He had made her stand taller and prouder. He had made her heart beat a bit faster too.

Nope, not happening. I could never be sure of him and besides, Randall knows what a manipulator I can be. I would never get the upper hand.

Suddenly chilled by the cold wind blowing through her coat, Sloane moved quickly toward her car. She wasn't feeling sorry for herself anymore.

Beholden is available at your favorite booksellers or at:
www.madisonmichael.net/books

ABOUT THE AUTHOR

Madison Michael believes in sassy women, sexy men and happy endings. She lives in Evanston, IL with her feline editorial assistants and great views of Chicago's famous skyline. She is a member of Romance Writers of America.

Follow her blog at http://www.madisonmichael.net

Made in the USA
Middletown, DE
27 September 2023

39544959R10172